THE COLLECTOR OF BUTTERFLIES AND WOMEN

JEFFREY OBOMEGHIE

Elliott and Dylan
NEW YORK

Copyright © 2014 by Jeffrey Obomeghie

Published by Elliott and Dylan Books

info@elliottanddylan.com

First Edition

All rights reserved.

PUBLISHER'S NOTE

No part of this publication may be reproduced, stored in a retrieval system or transmitted in any form or by any means, electronic, mechanical, photocopying, recording, scanning or otherwise, except under the terms of the Copyright, Designs and Patents Act 1988 or under the terms of a license issued by the Copyright Licensing Agency Ltd.

Legal Disclaimer

The Publisher and the Authors make no representations or warranties with respect to the accuracy or completeness of the contents of this work and specifically disclaim all warranties, including without limitation warranties of fitness for a particular purpose. No warranty maybe created or extended by sales or promotional materials. The advice, instructions, and strategies contained herein may not be suitable for every situation.

Neither the publishers nor the authors shall be liable for damages arising herefrom. The fact that an author is quoted in this work does not mean that the author endorses this book or that the author of this book endorses the author quoted in the work.

ISBN-13: 978-0-991-3830-0-9

Stories

Hattie Mae 3

Drive 9

The package 19

The merriest widow in England 29

The woman in the dungeon 37

The hermaphrodite club of Osaka 45

My name is Aristotle 57

The man who beat his wives 76

The collector of butterflies and women 80

Coat hanger 85

The house of sin 88

Matthias the cannibal 94

My neighbor's wife 101

A beating, a burning, and an execution 109

If suicide is poetry 124

The lord of cockroaches 131

John Lennon. 137

The woman who drank her husband 142

Sam was found dead this morning 145

Zack and the prostitute 151

Fire 154

How to rob the dead 157

"Mess him up!". 162

I drop to the ground 170

The man who loves to drink raw eggs 176

Forbidden love 181

Can she be saved?. 185

Happiness 189

Meeting with Jesus 195

Angel 201

The city of chaos 207

Shogunle. 214

New year's eve 220

Is it rape?. 227

The man with the ugly hands 231

One day before the man with ugly hands 235

Two days before the man with ugly hands 239

Once more, the man with ugly hands 242

A woman is crying 244

The man who loved funerals 248

Don't jump in the well 254

Linda 262

My neighbor's wife is an adulteress 271

Death before dawn 274

With a friend like this 277

Shit 280

An endangered species 286

The missing ear 290

The prophet 303

He is dying 310

Who stole my penis? 317

Tragedy 325

Arrest 327

UNITED STATES
(Arcadia, Iowa)

Hattie Mae

Hattie Mae sits on her front porch eating the sun, drinking beer, and chatting with her husband, Earl.

Hattie Mae is on her fourth beer.

She is eighty-six years old.

Earl has been dead for twelve years, claimed by a heart attack that showed up like a surprise monsoon rain and left him clinging to a barn post, surrounded by horse manure. They found his fingernails clawed deep into the aged wood as he fell, found him with his face contused like a stubborn poet spitting out bitter poetry, like a sinner struggling with the stomach ache of sins not yet repented.

The year they buried Earl was the year Hattie Mae became pregnant. At least that is how she liked to think of this thing, this tumor that grew deep inside her stomach like a baby. They called it stomach cancer, told her she had six months to live before she would join Earl on the other side. She thought of it as dark root, no, as darkness itself, growing inside of her.

Six.

That number.

Dropped so effortlessly from the young doctor's soft lips.

THE COLLECTOR OF BUTTERFLIES AND WOMEN

It was after the diagnosis that Hattie started to eat the sun. She loved to sit on her front porch in the vibrant sunlight, letting the sun's rays enter her open mouth. She imagined that if enough sunshine entered her stomach, it would pierce through the darkness that was growing there, make it shrivel and then finally disappear.

But make no mistake. Hattie Mae was not afraid of death. What she was afraid of were the days that Earl did not talk back to her when she spoke to him, the days that she did not hear his soft voice, softer than saplings rustling in the evening breeze.

When they were young, they had lived in Lansing Michigan in a ramshackle clapboard house which whined and moaned whenever the wind came through. Earl worked in an assembly line in the local factory. Every morning, she packed him lunch in a pink plastic box she had found in a yard sale for which he suffered the insults and jeers of his co-workers. But Earl did not care. The man she married did not care about what the world thought, which is why she loves him so dearly. When Earl retired, they moved out here to Arcadia, Iowa a town of less than five hundred people. Moved to a house which overlooked the General Store on Main Street. Here, the wind was sharp and bitter and if you looked hard enough you could see the corn growing.

Six months.

That was what the doctor said, his pink freshly scrubbed face betraying no emotion. He delivered the news with that studied neutrality that was *de rigueur* for young residents. And then he asked her if she was going to be okay. Hattie nodded. "I'll be fine, Sir." When she walked out of the hospital that day and headed for the parking lot where her twenty year old Chevy waited (Earl only drove American cars) she walked faster than she usually walked, as if to rebuff morbidity, refute her own mortality.

Earl always said that Hattie Mae had the best laugh this side of the Mississippi. She was a woman who had been through drought and famine, through despair and disease, a woman who had forgotten how to quit, how to surrender. Even after they put Earl in the ground, Hattie did not forget how to laugh. She sat on her rocking chair and laughed at Earl's jokes until her ribs ached. She knew the neighbors thought she was odd, knew that the McCoys next door had long stopped eating the sugar cookies she baked for their kids every week because they were worried about her head. They thought that grief had driven Hattie Mae out of her mind, or that old age had robbed her of her marbles. But there was nothing wrong with her head. Of this, Hattie was sure. If only they knew how funny Earl was. If only they could hear his jokes. I bet they would be cracking up too.

Six months to live, Ma'am.

Earl loved to hunt. His pride was his Winchester rifle. Once a month, he went off into the woods and came back with game. She was a vegetarian herself, never touched meat her entire life, but she never criticized Earl, never complained even when the smell of deer stew choked her and made her want to throw up, filled her with existential guilt. After he died, she refused to give the gun away, although she had no use for it. There it was right now, over there, leaning against the peeling wall, right between the teakwood cabinet she bought from the Goodwill Store in Lansing and the crib that she had been trying to give away for forty years.

"Do you have any next of kin that you want us to talk to?"

She stares at the blond wisp of hair on the doctor's upper lip, his beautiful Roman nose, his intense blue eyes and she thinks of her two dead children, the miscarriages and she thinks how this doctor could have been her grandchild.

"Yes, my husband, Earl. He is my next of kin."

She relishes the look of confusion on his face, feels a sudden bolt of sympathy for him. No doubt he had read her file.

Hattie Mae picks up the bottle and takes another swig of her beer. It tastes comforting and rich, the smell of fermented liquid filling her nose.

THE COLLECTOR OF BUTTERFLIES AND WOMEN

No, Hattie is not afraid of death. Not Hattie Mae. What she is afraid of is being ignored by Earl. What she is afraid of is not being able to hear his voice anymore when he tells his jokes or sings her favorite songs.

Hattie gets up. She is not drunk although her walk is unsteady. If your legs were eighty-six years old, bet they would be unsteady too. Hattie Mae walks toward the cabinet and picks up the rifle. She caresses it for a moment, the memories flooding back, memories of Earl caressing the same gun.

"It's a beautiful thing, ain't it?" Earl says to her. Same thing he always says when he gazes at the rifle.

"Yes, it is" Hattie agrees.

"What're you about to do?"

"I am tired, Earl."

Hattie walks back to the rocking chair. She places the rifle down on the floor, near her right foot, the muzzle pointing at her.

"I love you, Earl. I miss you so much."

Earl does not answer, but she knows that he hears her. He has always been gauche when it comes to expressing his feelings.

Six months.

She is not about to wait for six months.

They came running.

It was exactly 6:23 p.m. on that Tuesday evening that the neighbors came running after they heard the gun shot.

RUSSIA
(Kaliningrad,
Kaliningradskaya Oblast)

Drive

He was thirty six when he started driving with his eyes closed. He couldn't explain exactly how it all started, how the idea took seed in his mind and germinated. He would roll down the windows, close his eyes, and drive for a few seconds before opening his eyes. After a while, Ivanov even started to take his hands off the wheel and let the car roll along for several yards.

He often braced himself for impact, for the crash and sound of bones breaking, but he always opened his eyes just in time, always put his hands back on the wheel. Often he heard the wailing and the screaming, cars honking, alarmed drivers yelling for someone to call the ambulance. There would be blood. Lots of it. Someone would yell, "That is Ivanov. The professor of languages. The one with the perfect elocution and manicured fingers." Perhaps one of his students. He knew how they made fun of him behind his back, spoiled pricks. He imagined the ambulance showing up too late, like most things in his life. Like his mother's love, revealed to him on her deathbed. Like his wife, Natalya showing up too late in his life, when there was nothing left but a husk. And his two children, the ones he had no real relationship with, born too late to a man who wanted no part of their life, wanted no part of his own life.

THE COLLECTOR OF BUTTERFLIES AND WOMEN

No, he wasn't suicidal. At least he didn't think he was. He was bored. But then isn't boredom a type of death? And if we all agree that boredom is a form of death, he had died a million times since he married Natalya Ivanishev, daughter of the pug faced Ilyich Sergeyevich Denisov. It was terrifying boredom that killed their marriage, trampled on it and left it dead in their small landlocked flat in Moscow's Tverskaya Ulitsa. Natalya fled the apartment eight years into their marriage, taking their two children with her. Ivanov had not had sex with her for the five years before the rupture. That is how he liked to think of it. The rupture. It sounded clean and antiseptic.

She accused him of being gay, of being an adulterer, of being selfish. All this in a fit of anger and frustration and then she laughed at herself, realizing how ridiculous she sounded. She knew he was neither gay nor adulterous. But he couldn't deny the charge of being selfish. Technically, he didn't think he was selfish. He simply had no use for people, no interest in their petty lives, like the rising price of milk the political issue with Chechnya how the women standing outside Moscow's Bolshoi's Theater dressed in skimpy outfits and the oligarchs were selling Russia to the West.

She thought it was the lack of sex and intimacy that killed their marriage. But Natalya as bright as she was, graduate of the prestigious Saint Petersburg State University, child of two doting parents, Natalya with the beautiful mismatched spaced apart almond eyes (one green, one turquoise?) was a child of hope, hopelessly hopeful. She believed in the impossible, believed in doomed rescue missions. She wanted to save him from himself. She was attracted to broken things like a moth to a flame. One boyfriend left her with a broken jaw.

She invited Ivanov to parties and he dutifully attended but he always left just before he stuck a butter knife in someone's eye. One can only suffer inanity for so long. Certainly everyone could understand that. As it became harder to drag him out of the apartment to the "socials," she started to plan the parties in their apartment. This was of course before the children showed up like locusts in the season of drought, harbingers of doom and pestilence. Ivanov would flee to the bathroom, sit on the toilet and pretend to heave and pant while she begged him to come out to socialize.

He had often wondered how it all started, this tempting of fate, this quotidian flirtation with death. He remembered reading Hegel's *Phenomenology* and being carried along on the wave of the philosopher's ideas. He subscribed to Hegel's position that a man could realize himself only after he had voluntarily risked dying.

Maybe it started way before Hegel.

Maybe it all started while he was young. School did not really interest him, although he was a great student. He flew through the texts, eager to move on to the next one. His teachers struggled to keep up with him, his fellow students loathed his fluency. He was morbidly unable to make friends, unable to keep the few friends who wanted to be around him.

At nine, he got tired of his adorable mutt and gave it away to a total stranger he met on a bus while riding back home from school. When he returned home, his mother was shocked. She screamed at him with that stentorian voice and cursed at him in her native Chenchen. His father could not even feign interest. Vadim sat in his tall wicker chair, smoking his beloved Belomorkanal cigarettes. Ah, his father.

Vadim was the reason he was making this journey to Kaliningrad. Flying from Moscow to Kaliningrad.

Ivanov had always been capable of incredible self-analysis, had always considered himself fatally self-aware. He looked for the heart of things, yearned to understand their essence. When he saw a clock, he wanted to take it apart. When he saw a car, he wanted to open the hood and peek at the engine. He differed from Natalya who wanted to fix things. Ivanov did not take things apart to fix them. He took them apart to understand them. At the grocery store, he picked up

THE COLLECTOR OF BUTTERFLIES AND WOMEN

apples and bananas and studied them with preternatural intensity before he put them in his shopping basket. He gazed for too long at people, which unnerved them and made feel awkward. When he spoke, he drew out his sentences, carefully enunciating each word, a habit which drove his ex-wife and students crazy. Ivanov was tall and thin, with long arms and a pianist's fingers. His hair was black and untamed, his eyebrows thick and generous.

As he drove now on Kaliningrad's streets, he wondered when Natalya realized that she had failed in her mission to fix him.

"You will go on Tuesday to see Dr. Kirichenko. I will make the appointment for 3 p.m." That was how Natalya was. A woman who did not understand preambles and prologues. A woman who would skip the thesis and go right into the paper. Like when they first met and she walked up to him in Anton's Book Market on Arbat Street while he was thumbing through an ill-used copy of Pushkin's *Boris Godunov*. "You are not a happy man."

Ivanov had stared at her. "You are going to ask to read my palm next. You are a psychic."

Natalya shook her head. "Your forehead is very wrinkled. Like an old man. And you have no laugh lines. You are too serious."

He wanted to shock her, deride her bourgeois assumptions, show her the scars on his back. Scars he had carried for over thirty years. He wanted to ask if she had ever gone to bed hungry…for three days. If she had ever been locked in a closet as punishment for wetting her bed. He wanted to read her the poetry of his life and watch her tremble as the stanzas pelted her. Instead what he did was stick out his hand and say, "I am Ivanov. You?"

He did visit Dr. Kirichenko. Saw him every week for two years. Cost him thirty percent of the salary he earned at the State University in Krasnogorsk, a city outside Moscow. On each of those visits, he sat on Dr. Kirichenko's drab couch and listened to the tall angular man with beady eyes and nicotine-stained fingers tell him about his life.

He listened while the therapist talked and smoked. He learned about Dr. Kirichenko's ambitious wife, about his three children and their Labrador and Dr. Kirichenko's struggle to get ahead professionally. For two years he visited the therapist.

But it didn't fix his sex life as Natalya hoped.

One day, Natalya woke up and finally realized that Ivanov was a hopeless case. Now, she was with a young talented artist often compared to a young Marc Chagall in Moscow's art circles. Ivanov imagined them now attacking each other frenziedly on the four poster bed that she took with her when she left, the one he bought on Karbysheva Street with his first paycheck from the college. Imagined her now in the throes of that perfect orgasm that he was never able to deliver. What woman wants a man who flees to the bathroom to brush his teeth right after oral sex? She must be happy now with her long-haired deliverer of perfect orgasms, her own Chagall.

The therapist could not fix the marriage.

And he could not fix Ivanov. Of course, Ivanov never told Dr. Kirichenko about how he indulged in risky behavior.

He continued to drive with his eyes closed.

Continued to take his hands off the wheel while he drove. Now, when he closed his eyes or took his eyes off the wheel, he counted, one, two, three, four…

"That is Ivanov, the English professor. Someone call the ambulance!"

He had caught a flight from Moscow into Khrabovo Airport. From Khrabovo, he hopped on a bus on the city bus line number 144 operated by Koenigtransauto which put him on Kaliningrad Main Bus Station. Alexander Nevskogo, the street where he was headed was one kilometer from the station. Ivanov had rented a car at the airport instead of catching a cab. He hated the distraction and commotion of public transportation. Hated the smells and smiles and the forced conversations.

THE COLLECTOR OF BUTTERFLIES AND WOMEN

This city had a bloody history. Kaliningradskaya Oblast was located in the northern part of what used to be East Prussia until 1945 and World War 1 when the Russians took it over. A majority of the German population was killed or fled to what would become West Germany. The others were expelled in the years after the war began. Kaliningrad was the largest city in the Oblast. Formerly known as Konigsberg, the city's economy was thriving. Kaliningrad Oblast located on the westernmost tip of Russia, was isolated geographically from the rest of the Russian federation, reachable from main Russia only by sea or air, surrounded by Poland in the south, Lithuania in the east and north and the Baltic Sea in the west.

Ivanov drove past roadside cafes and shops, noting how much Kaliningrad had changed since his last visit. This was a city that was in a hurry. It was all dressed up and impatient. There seemed to be billboards on every corner, blaring their products and offerings. There were massive televisions mounted on roadsides, running commercials, music videos and news announcements. Colorful brand new buses and late model cars whizzed by. Ivanov drove past the Cathedral of Christ the Savior, the largest cathedral in Kaliningrad Oblast, located in the central square known as Ploshchad Pobedy. It was an imposing white building, with gold domes and cross shaped spires clawing at the sky. Here now was the House of the Soviets, which Ivanov considered to be like a beautiful woman with no soul. The city authorities had planned to make this building, located where the famous Konigsberg Castle was once located, its central administration office. But that plan never got off the ground. After being constructed, the House of Soviets stood for years without windows, its interior unfinished. Before Vladimir Putin's visit of 2005, city officials had the ingenious idea of painting the building a vibrant light blue and installing windows. That they did. After Putin's visit, everyone promptly forgot about the building. Now, it stood ghostly and forlorn, reminding Kaliningrad about all that was wrong with the city.

But there were plenty of things that were right with Kaliningrad, the economy being one of them. One of every three televisions made in Russia was made in Kaliningrad. Ivanov thought of it as Television City. The people were an industrious lot. It takes a lot of resourcefulness to kill and chase off the natives so that one could take over the land. Ivanov smiled at the thought.

What brought his father, Vadim, to Kaliningrad? Why did Vadim move from his native Zheleznogorsk? Was it a woman, or a job? Was he escaping his past, or an enemy? Ivanov realized that he would never figure out the answers. Even if he had asked, Vadim would not have told him.

The streets were wide and well maintained. Young men and women milled on the sidewalk, students and workers. The aroma of coffee and food lingered in the air from roadside restaurants and coffee shops. An old man, bent over, with a long beard, dressed in a pink cotton shirt and incongruously large cufflinks stood under a street lamp, reading a newspaper, oblivious to the pedestrians shuffling past him. It was getting dark and the temperature was dropping. The weather forecasters were predicting 38 degrees tonight. Not that Ivanov believed the forecast or any weather forecaster.

As Ivanov drove now, he studied the street signs closely. He made a couple of wrong turns before he found Alexander Nevskogo. He turned into the street, drove to the very end and then parked. He would have to walk the rest of the way. He had come prepared. His shoes were comfortable. He stepped out of the car and began to walk. He walked into a wooded area, guided by memory. The night smelled like a wet hound, the wind licking his face with a moist tongue. The grass here was lush, tree trunks thick with age, mostly pine interspersed with the occasional maple, spruce, and birch. It smelled like pine and wet leaves after an early morning rain. Joseph Brodsky, the Russian writer, once wrote that the trees of East Prussia still whisper in German when the wind blows in from the Baltic. If the trees here still whispered, it was certainly no longer in German. The ground was soft under Ivanov's shoes.

He found the gravestone.

The name on it was Vadim Konstantin Mostovoi.

Ivanov stood now before his father's gravestone, the memories flooding his mind. A tear dropped down his cheek. He flicked it off furiously. This was the end of his journey. Every year he made this pilgrimage from Moscow to Kaliningrad just to carry out this ritual.

Ivanov walked closer to the grave, remembering his father's voice.

He saw the flowers on the gravestone next to his father's.

"Maybe I should have brought flowers." He thought to himself, and then he smiled wanly.

He unzipped his pants, took out his penis, pointed it straight at the gravestone and began to urinate on it.

When he was done pissing, he zipped his pants, walked to his car, got in and drove off. He did not look back.

Next year, on exactly the same day, he would be back.

MEXICO
(Nuevo Laredo, Mexico)

The package

Can death ever be beautiful?

It was a beautiful thing, the package. It arrived on a Sunday morning a few hours after Jose, his wife and three children returned from the Santo Christo church on Domingo Street in the bustling town of Nuevo Laredo. It was the first package that would arrive that week. Exactly seven days later, after all the crying and wailing was done and the neighbors had returned to their homes, a second delivery would arrive. The first package was a long cardboard box that seemly curiously light given its size. Jose Padilla's children jumped around for joy when they saw it.

"Christmas!" They cried. "Daddy, Christmas gift!"

But Jose was not convinced. It was October, still nearly three months before Christmas. On Christmas day of 2004, the locals of Nuevo Laredo woke up to find snow on the ground. Since then the children of Nuevo Laredo eagerly expected snow each year as Christmas drew near. Outside today, it was 103 degrees with the sun staring down angrily at the dusty border town. A moist wind blew in from the Chihuahuan desert and headed for the Sierra Madre Oriental Mountain to the south and west of the town. Jose was not expecting a gift, had not received a gift from anyone since the day Margarita delivered their last child, Marcos.

"Keep the noise down or you will wake the dead!" Margarita yelled at the children. They ran into the house, and continued their clamor inside.

What was inside the package?

Jose's wife, Margarita Alfonso, was a short, hard-bitten woman with gentle brown eyes and sunken cheeks. Twenty years earlier, she married Jose out of spite. Jose was the first man to propose to her, a man her tyrant of a father absolutely despised. She married Jose to give her father heartburn. Heartburn she hoped would turn into a heart attack so she and her mother could bury him deep in the ground like yuca root. But the bastard lived to be eighty eight years old and gave the two women hell for each year that they failed to kill him.

But that was not the only reason she married Jose.

Jose was a slight, wiry man with a pointed nose so sharp his wife said you could cut your hand on it. He sprouted hair everywhere, his back, neck, shoulders, face. Margarita had never met a man so hairy. *Ay dios mios!* When Margarita washed his clothes, she wrestled with clumps of hair that had found their way deep into the fabric. She joked that one day he would simply turn into a big ball of hair. Jose did not walk as much as spring. He seemed to walk on tip-toe, forever reaching for the new opportunity, the new task. He went about life with the zest of a whirlwind, quick to shrug off grief and misfortune. He was not a particularly good looking man, his mouth was too wide, his eyes spaced too far apart, but Margarita thought his face was wise. And he had character. That still counted for something in this sinful world, no?

This was another reason she married Jose.

Jose was a kind-hearted man, a man who would give you the shirt off his hairy back. The neighbors were taken with him, especially

Madam Inarritu, the widow next door. Jose often helped her mow her grass and fix the leaky roof on her crumbling house. Every so often, Jose would bring home candy for his neighbors' kids. *Caramelo, Tamarindo, Paleta* and *piñata* fillers. Some of the parents protested that he would make the children's teeth rot, but they never really pushed the issue. Some of them secretly indulged in the sweet treats. Jorge worked in a candy factory next to the Jose Reyes Meza Museum which was named after the muralist from Tamaulipas. When he came home at night, he brought with him the heady, sugary smell of candy. Margarita had never confessed this to him, but one night while he slept, she secretly licked him. Licked his neck to see if the sugar that he worked around all day had somehow seeped into his skin, his bones his very membranes.

Margarita Alfonso knew exactly how she would die.

She would die of too much happiness.

And Jose would be the cause.

Jose who loved to read was the one who shared a quote by the Russian writer, Anton Chekhov which soon became her personal favorite. "People don't notice whether it is winter or summer when they are happy." Margarita had not seen a winter since Jose came into her life.

Jose and Maria watched the two delivery men struggle with the box. It must weigh over 200 pounds, Jose thought. His employer, Javier Sotomayor, was a good man. Perhaps Sotomayor had decided to buy him the expensive stainless fridge that Jose had always dreamed of buying for Margarita. Jose did not think anything of the fact that the delivery men did not say a word as they dropped off the package by his feet. They stared at him briefly with a look that could have been amusement, consternation or boredom, and then they walked off. As they did, the smaller man stuck his hand in the back of his pants and scratched his butt, then spat noisily before he climbed into the white unmarked truck. As the truck drove off, its

THE COLLECTOR OF BUTTERFLIES AND WOMEN

rear view mirror caught the sun and momentarily blinded Jose. Later, a neighbor would report that he saw the same truck on the Juarez Lincoln International Bridge as it crossed the Rio Grande River.

"Let me get a knife." Jose walked through the front door, grabbed a knife from the kitchen and returned to the package. He felt an odd mixture of excitement and anxiety although he never would have admitted it to Margarita. He ripped open the paper wrapping on the box with one strong slash of the knife. What he saw was this.

A casket, burnished dark walnut, with matte wood lacquer finish. It was twenty-eight inches wide and eighty-one inches long. It was missing the standard adjustable bed and mattress, the kind that Jose had seen at the funeral of Pieto Ruiz, the police chief who was gunned down by the Los Zetas two months before. A beautiful poplar wood casket fitting for the rich and the narcos, the kind that one heard about in *narcocorridos*.

"My God!"

Margarita gasped and jumped back, crossed herself and burst into tears, this woman who never cried, even after she lost two babies to disease, even after Jose's mother called her *la bruja*. The sorceress.

Jose felt his heart tumble in his chest, his chest constricted. The world roared in his ears. The wind suddenly felt oppressive, congealed in his face. He smelled the shit from the chickens and goats that Margarita kept in the back of the house, heard the chatter of men and women going about their daily business. He smelled the grass, oak and mesquite of the land in which he was born, stamped his work boots on the hard-packed earth to steady himself. From the periphery of his vision, he saw his three children, Manuela, Joaquin and Marcos, come running out the door, alarmed by their mother's cry.

"Go back!" He yelled at them and they retreated, stung by his raised voice. They had never known their father to raise his voice. Jose saw one of the neighbors walking toward him in curiosity.

Jose stared at the small black jewel case taped securely to the bottom of the casket. He stared at it with horror, stared at it with the helplessness of a man chasing a rainbow and losing the race.

"Don't touch it, Jose. It's bad luck."

But Jose was not listening to his wife. He had been told that he was a stubborn man. Wilful, he thought but not stubborn.

A gift of jewelry inside a casket?

Beauty inside of death. Can death ever be beautiful?

Jose picked up the jewelry case, flipped it open.

A note.

A dire warning.

"You've got five days to move out. If you don't move, you can lay inside the casket and we will come put you in the ground."

So this is what it was all about, Jose thought. They had been sending him emissaries for the last two months. Apparently, they had finally run out of patience. Los Zetas wanted him to move his family out of the house because the house was located on a planned drug route. Word was that Los Zetas was constructing a major tunnel that would run all the way to Texas. Los Zetas had offered Jose money for his house, if he would just move. When he refused their initial offer, they doubled the offer. Jose still wouldn't budge. Now, they had resorted to threats.

For years, the Los Zetas had battled the Sinaloa Cartel for territory. As the battle raged on, both sides became ever more inventive in their attempts to display death at its most macabre. Heads were chopped off, torsos machine-gunned. Body parts were strewn on city streets like confetti at a wedding. People were left hanging from highway overpasses or gutted like farm animals and left to rot in the blazing Laredo heat. People were buried alive or burned to death. Entire families simply disappeared, never to be seen again. As the bodies rotted and the blood clotted on the sidewalks, El Diablo presided over the proceedings.

THE COLLECTOR OF BUTTERFLIES AND WOMEN

Miguel Trevino Morales, former head of Los Zetas was a native son of Nuevo Laredo. Morales took over the Los Zetas leadership after Heriberto Lazcano was killed in a gun battle with Mexican marines in Coahuila State. Even before Morales was recruited by Ossiel Cardenas Guillen, Jose had known the kid who would later become a stone cold killer. They had grown up together, played football on the dirty streets. Now on those same streets, if you looked hard enough you could see dried blood caked on the sidewalks, sudden like a Diego Rivera painting.

"What does the note say?"

Jose tried to give Margarita the note, but she wouldn't touch it. She recoiled as if the piece of paper itself were a curse. So he told her. Of course, he had no choice but to tell her, even though he knew that the news would destroy their world. But then their world was already destroyed. Destroyed since the day they moved into the house, and buried two children in San Fernando cemetery where the mesquite and yuca grew and the rats stared at you with no fear as you brought your dead. Some said the rats got to the bodies buried at the cemetery well before nature got to them.

"We must live, Jose. Tonight."

The fierce urgency in Margarita's voice shook him. He felt a hand on his shoulder. His neighbor next door, Macias. "Que Pasa?"

Jose did not answer. Macias simply took the note from his limp fingers. "Jose. Oh my God. I am sorry. What are you going to do?"

"We are leaving." Margarita answered for Jose, her voice hollow, distant. "We are leaving this cursed place."

But Jose would not leave.

Did not leave.

That night, he made love to Margarita's lifeless body even as she sobbed. Made love to her in frustration and anger. When he was done, he started to cry too, crying for something that they had lost, that he wasn't quite sure that they had ever shared. To tell the truth, he had never found happiness. This was a secret that he had never shared with the woman he loved dearly. He had read her Chekhov and shared the quote about happiness and summer and winter. What he had never told her was that he had never found happiness, even with her. "The happy man only feels at ease because the unhappy bear their burden in silence. Without this silence, happiness would be impossible." Another bit of wisdom from Chekhov that he had not shared with Margarita. He had carried the burden of his own unhappiness alone, dragged it around like a hunchback dragging his hump.

Of happiness, he thought himself incapable, being genetically programmed for melancholy. His own mother, the one who called Margarita a witch, had died of madness, literally lost her mind and walked into a busy thoroughfare where she was hit by one of those bright mass transit buses marked as *Transporte Urbano de Nuevo Laredo* on Hildago Street.

Despite all of Margarita's pleas, Jose refused to even consider moving. "If they want me dead, let them come for me. I am not afraid of them." He refused to be bullied or chased out of the home that he had built from his own sweat, years of cooking candy syrup in Sotomayor's factory. For the next several nights, Jose and Margarita's children heard their mother begging Jose to reconsider. With each passing day, her voice grew harsher, more urgent.

The neighbors who had heard about the note stopped by to talk to Jose but he was done talking. Nothing could breach the ramparts of his mind into which he had retreated. He wore the logic and conviction of his position like an armor, unswayable. One night when Margarita licked his neck, she thought he tasted bitter, as if the bitterness had entered his body and leaked into his skin.

And then Jose disappeared.

Not figuratively.

He did not come home from work.

THE COLLECTOR OF BUTTERFLIES AND WOMEN

Margarita panicked. She immediately feared the worst. The neighbors gathered in Jose's house to discuss the situation. A search party was sent to look for Jose. They did not find Jose. In Nuevo Laredo, disappearances were not uncommon. A part of Margarita feared that Jose had decided to abandon his family. He had given in to fear, had decided to surrender. The brave front that he put on every day was just that, a front. Her husband of twenty years had run off, giving his wife the justification to move out of the family's home so the Los Zetas could have their way. That night, when she lay on the bed all alone, unable to sleep, listening to the fierce thunderstorm outside, her head thrummed with frenzied thoughts.

The second package showed up seven days after Jose disappeared. The same two men who had delivered the first package showed up. This time, they did not come out of their truck. They simply tossed the package out of the back of the truck, got back in the truck and drove off. Margarita was in her little garden behind the house where she tended to her dahlia and cempasuchitl flowers, waiting, waiting to hear Jose's booming voice again and his full-throated laugh that she could never tire of.

"Take it away. Take it away! Don't open it here!" Margarita yelled at no one in particular. Macias the neighbor dragged the big box away from Margarita, then shooed the children away. Someone handed him a knife and he cut the bright paper wrapping on the box.

A casket.

A hush fell over the crowd. A woman started to cry.

Macias said a prayer, crossed himself, once and then twice for good measure before yanking the casket open.

They had returned Jose back to his family.

The Los Zetas had returned Jose.

They had returned Jose to Margarita, but without his body.

UNITED KINGDOM
(Shoreham-by-Sea, England)

The merriest widow in England

She could smell them.

The thousands of people milling around London's Victoria station from where she would catch the bus to go visit her mother. She could smell their furious perfumes, their explosive underarms, unwashed bodies in flux, the heady combustive smell of cheese and beer. She could tell with great acuity who had not taken a bath before jumping on the bus heading toward Kingsway Road. She could tell who had used body spray. Over there, the young bloke with hair hidden in a Kangol hat, the one with the ear pods stuck in his ear, listening to obscenity-laced songs, which he thought no one else could hear. He had not taken a shower this morning. He had eaten a garlic infused salad at some point the previous night. She could smell him now, the vinaigrette and garlic clogging her nostrils.

She thought that if she stood still long enough and if the wind was just right as it blew off the Thames River, she could smell failure and desperation. This mass of humanity trudging assuredly to its own extinction, caught in the grind of life's spinning wheel.

She could smell amatory body fluids from three meters, could tell who had had sex the previous night without taking a shower afterwards. She could sniff out hookers and women with particularly splendid sex lives. Unlike her. She had never been touched by a man and had no desire for men. Men revolted her. Frankly, the entire human species revolted her, biologically. Make no mistake, she did not hate people. She just preferred to deal with them from a distance. Preferred not to touch them or have them touch her. At fifteen, she learned a bitter lesson about the inelasticity of love. A boy she had a crush on dumped her because she wouldn't let him come close enough to give her a kiss. His response was quick and dismissive, viperine. For Angus Fairchild, there was no demarcation between love and lust, the two were conflated.

 It would be nice to say that Eleanor really loved kids and cute furry animals but she did not. She did not lack compassion. She did not disdain intimacy. What Eleanor hated was the physical sensation of being skin to skin with a living creature, of sharing space with people and animals. People and animals spitting, farting, coughing. All those germs. Children in particular, scared her, with their uncontrolled burping and pissing and shitting.

 When she saw a cat or dog, she wondered how many fleas and ticks were buried in the folds of their skin. For the past twenty years, she has cooked her own food, no longer willing to entrust her life to the sinister sandwich makers and homicidal bread bakers that they hired in the restaurants these days. She carried a bottle of water in her bag everywhere she went, rinsing the bottle out every night before she went to bed. Why take a chance with an ill-washed cup or glass? People thought she was strange when she showed up to buy groceries at Holmbush Shopping Center on Shoreham Road. She saw the look of surprise on the faces of the locals as she examined the tomatoes and oranges with her latex-gloved hands.

 Now as the bus drove down London's High Holborn Street with its cheerful shops, taverns and busy people, Eleanor got up from her seat and moved to a different seat two rows down. This time she sat next to a young well-dressed Pakistani chap who smelled like clean soap, a smell that surprisingly pleased her nostrils.

God, she hated London. The city made her itch. Made her hair stand on end. Hated big cities and their randomness. Cities rife with potential for noise and smells and unwanted human exchange.

"*L'enfer, c'est les autres.*"

"Hell is other people."

Jean Paul Satre.

So she had fled to the small town of Shoreham-by-Sea, a seaside town of just over 50,000 people. Here she lived a life of stunning boredom and anonymity. She didn't have to work. The trust left her by her late father, the late lamented Sir Vincent Barnaby, had seen to that. She lived in a small flat on Brighton Road. She went for walks daily, walking all the way to Brighton six miles in one direction or Worthing five miles in the other direction. In the mornings, the wind was often crisp and tangy, blowing in from the open valley of River Ardur or from Shoreham Beach. She could sit on her small balcony and watch the sun rise, its rays piercing the sleepy gloom of the quiet town. She could see the Church of St. Mary De Haura, sitting in sepulchral glory, reaching for heaven. She tried not to worry about the smell of manure wafting from the pastoral farms scattered on the edges of the town where local farmers raised livestock.

But the smell was only a part of Eleanor's problems. She was also cursed with acute hearing. She never graduated college. The slurping noises her roommate, Alicia, made while fellating Mike who came over every Friday drove Eleanor crazy. After she fled Imperial College in London, she moved to Shoreham-by-Sea, visiting London only once a month to see her mother who lived in a flat on High Holborn Street in West End.

Each time, Eleanor and her mother met, they struggled to recognize each other, Eleanor surprised by how much younger her mother looked since they last saw each other, Lucille surprised by

THE COLLECTOR OF BUTTERFLIES AND WOMEN

how much older Eleanor looked. They circled each other warily, each burdened by years of calcified memories. At nearly eighty, Lucille was not sick. Not unless you considered old age a sickness. Lucille did not have dementia, Alzheimer or any of the sophisticated diseases that beset people lucky enough to have lived long enough. There was nothing wrong with Lucille's mind or body. The relationship between mother and daughter was nursed like a bird with broken wings for forty eight years. When Eleanor looked in her mother's eyes, she saw disappointment refracted back to her, a daughter who never quite achieved her mother's lofty expectations. Pounding on the piano keys until she threw up from sheer exhaustion, recoiling from her mother's soft encouraging voice.

Stravinsky's *Petrushka* and Chopin's Prelude in E Minor.

She had long given up listening to music.

Eleanor loved her mother dearly, suffering this annual trip through the hordes of London, the madding crowds, the nameless horrors to see her. And yet here she stood now, in this room that smelled like cinnamon and vanilla, the Ziegler Mahal carpet, Tiffany lamps, the ostentatious mural on the walls, walls perfect for someone to bash their heads against, here she stood one meter away from Lucille, unable to give her a hug. Not because Eleanor did not want to but because she could not stand the terrible closeness. Lucille smiled at her. Eleanor could hear the tinkles and keys of what sounded like a concerto. And the thought struck her that the music was perfect for soothing mad people.

She was fifteen when Lucille made her go see a doctor. "Quite a hound, aren't you?" The doctor said with a levity that made Eleanor want to bludgeon him with one of the encyclopedias in his office.

She was diagnosed with hyperosmia and hyperacusis, They gave her antidepressants and prescribed therapy. She didn't get the connection. She was not depressed. There was nothing wrong with her head. But she dutifully accepted the pills and when she got home, she poured them in the toilet and flushed them down. Put vitamin pills in the pill bottle so Lucille would not know her secret.

And her condition remained the same.

She hadn't hugged her mother in eight years.

"How are you, Eleanor?"

Lucille was a tall woman with high cheekbones and bright eyes that burned a hole through diamonds and faithless men. Her hair was still full, although speckled with gray now. It came to her shoulders but she kept it imprisoned in a chignon. Even now, she was impeccably dressed, not a hair out of place, her fair skin smooth and flawless. She wore a simple black blouse with a turquoise pearl brooch. She was still pretty. Pretty in that offensive way that older people can be pretty because it provoked envy in young people. Lucille carried herself with immaculate grace. A woman with a high opinion of herself, she had worshipped at her own altar for most of her life. She had a knack for finding rich men willing and able to die of a heart attack or stroke just a few years after she married them. Serendipity, is what she once called it, delivering this comment while sipping on a glass of Vincent Dauvissat La Forest Chablis. She had been through three husbands, Eleanor's father being the first, the only one with whom she produced a child. Eleanor thought of her mother as the merriest widow in England.

"Terrific, Mum" She wondered if her mother picked up the artifice in her voice.

"Thanks for coming."

"Pleasure, Mum."

Eleanor sat down on the brown Belgravia leather corner sofa which had set Lucille back by a few thousand pounds. Lucille remained seated where she was, her customary perch near the window from where she could watch the hustle and bustle of London's West End below. Eleanor had always envied Lucille for her prodigious appetite for life. Lucille loved wine, good food, men and parties, although not necessarily in that order.

"So how is good old Shoreham?" Eleanor asked in her sophisticated voice with perfect elocution.

"Good."

They had never had much to say to each other. In fact, Eleanor thought that they had both exhausted their reservoir of conversation over the years. They both cared for each other, in the way that people yoked together must. Like two people who had survived a plane crash. Or a couple who had lost a child. They were the only ones left now. The survivors. They felt no need to clutter the silence with the perfunctory and the picayune.

For the next couple of hours, they sat in silence, comfortable silence. Lucille looked out the window, occasionally glancing at a book resting on her lap. Eleanor closed her eyes and dozed off.

When Eleanor woke up, she looked at her watch. It was time to make the hour and half journey back to Shoreham-by-Sea.

There were no declarations of love exchanged, no kisses or hugs. When it came to emotion, theirs had never been a relationship built on profusion or effusion. They both hated displays of any kind.

"I will see you next month."

"Looking forward."

"Bye"

"Cheers"

Eleanor walked out the front door, rode the elevator down to the lobby. She nodded at the young freckle-faced concierge and walked out the front door.

And once again, she was consumed by the noise and the smell and the bedlam of London.

INDIA
(Akbarpur, Uttar Pradesh)

The woman in the dungeon

There was a woman locked in the dungeon in his father's house. Growing up in the small town of Akbarpur in India's Uttar Pradesh State, Rama thought a lot about this nameless woman, wondered about her fate and how she came to be locked in his father's dungeon. He was nine when his father, Lohia, named after the great Indian warrior and freedom fighter, Manohar Lohia, finally answered his questions. And even then, Rama still did not understand.

Rama lived in a sprawling unpainted brick house with green doors. The house was located in a large compound circumscribed by an afterthought of a fence. The three foot brick fence was one of Lohia's unfinished projects, left uncompleted when Lohia ran out of discounted cement after he lost his job at the cement factory in which he lost his right eye. For Lohia, life itself was an uncompleted project. Goats and dogs roamed Lohia's compound, often taking refuge from the noonday sun under a copse of Ashoka and mango trees. The ground was dusty and hard-baked. When it rained, the ground turned a muddy, reddish brown. July and August was when it rained the hardest. Rama and his cousins played cricket in the mud, the noise of their shrieking blending with the howling of the woman in the dungeon.

THE COLLECTOR OF BUTTERFLIES AND WOMEN

If Rama took a deep breath and turned his nose to the gentle breeze, he could smell the sweet smell of turmeric and coriander and at times namkeen. Geetmala one of his aunts who had recently moved back to Akbarpur from the big city of Lucknow with her husband loved to cook. It was said that her cooking provoked murderous envy in many wives in Akbarpur whose husbands, enamored of Geetmala's cooking, visited Lohia's house too often.

Akbarpur is a small city of over one hundred thousand people located on the banks of the River Tons also known as River Tamasa. The River Tons divides the major city of Ambedkarnagar into two parts, one being Akbarpur and the other Shahzadpur. According to Ramayana, the great epic believed to have been written by Valmiki the Hindu sage, it was in Akbarpur that King Dashratha killed Shravan Kumar.

Lohia, was a slight man with bushy hair that curled up around his ears. He spoke very slowly as if he needed to elongate every conversation before he lost the facility for speech. He had lost his right eye while working at the cement manufacturing plant near Mihaura. Now, Lohia stared at the world like a Cyclops, one eye dripping tears whenever he was excited or angry, a rare occurrence indeed.

Lohia was a man who nursed silence like a monk, and his son was terrified of his pregnant silences, wished he could engage his father in a conversation that lasted longer than three or four syllables. They said that when Lohia lost his eye after the accident, after he came home from the hospital a bandage wrapped around his dead eye, he simply pointed at the bandage and told his family, "Eye gone."

"Who is the woman down there?" Rama was nine years old when he asked his father this question. Rama and his nephews and nieces were forbidden from ever going to the basement. But one day when there was no uncle or aunt in sight to stop him, Rama ventured down to the basement. What he saw shocked him. A tall, doe-eyed woman with wild looking hair, impossibly long black hair, eyebrows thick, teeth like jewels in her mouth, pretty eyes unfocused. She reminded him of his mother. Of course he had no memories of his mother. Lohia had told him how his mother died at childbirth, a fact that troubled Rama greatly, filled him with guilt and shame, the type of guilt he assumed that Germans must feel when someone mentioned the Holocaust.

"She is your aunt. Your mother's sister."

"Why is she there, Pita?" Pita was his term of endearment for his father on days that the two of them were able to sit side by side and talk.

"Babu, for her own good. She is there for her own good."

"But why?"

Even at nine, Rama understood that his father was a man given to ellipsis.

"Her head is sick. We have to protect our own. Can't let her run into the streets and have people hurt her or treat her like a dog."

"Does she have a husband, or children?"

Lohia shook his head. "We are all she has. Have to take care of her."

"What's her name?"

Lohia shook his head. "Doesn't matter. No longer matters."

Rama saw his father go down to the basement every day to visit his aunt, this aunt who had lost the dignity of a name after her mental illness corrupted her mind. No one else ever went to visit Mausi (Mausi meant "mother's sister") a fact which puzzled Rama. Lohia took trays of food down to Mausi, took her towels and water to cleanse herself. Every evening, Rama saw his father remove a bucket of waste from the basement. He knew there was no toilet down there. Rama marveled at his father's tenderness, his gentleness toward this woman who was his wife's sister.

Every so often, Rama would go down to the basement to stare at his aunt. The basement was a large space, with six concrete pillars positioned like centurions. The walls were dank and dirty. Food particles and grease spackled the walls like Rorschach blots. Like the tears of virgins. The smell of urine, sweat and madness lingered like a lover's embrace.

Most of the time Mausi stared back soullessly at Rama, her vacant eyes lost in space. He watched as she rocked herself back and forth back and forth inside the metal cage that Lohia, the beginner, but not the finisher of projects, had built for her. The cage was made out of steel bars buried deep in the cement, but the bars did not extend all the way to the wooden ceiling, not a surprise given the fact that it was Lohia who had done the construction himself. Which meant that if Mausi tried hard enough, she could climb the bars and leap to freedom. But Mausi would never escape from the dungeon. Something had shuttered her mind forever, the spark of intellect extinguished under the sediments of the strange trauma that had consumed her and turned her into a shell.

A chain was looped around the front bars of the cage, secured with a padlock. Rama had never seen the door open. When he stared at Mausi, what he noted was the strange fever in her eyes, not recognition or apprehension of her fate. Often, he watched her head bobbing back and forth, rhythmically with her body. He thought that he could hear her humming to herself, but he could not be sure, what with the noise of his cousins chasing each other around in the yard, screaming like dervishes.

He wondered what was going through her head. How her head had become sick. How she ended up locked up like an animal inside a dirty cage in his father's basement surrounded by her own tawdry existence and enervation. When did the family realize that Mausi was losing her mind? Whose decision was it to put her away, far from the prying eyes of the people of Akbarpur? How was the family able to get her into the basement? Did she wrestle and fight or beg for mercy and cry? Did she weep and yell and curse at her own family who had decided that she needed to be locked up for the rest of her life? Did Lohia and his brothers and sisters-in-law ever harbor doubts about Mausi's imprisonment and the rectitude of their decision? The questions filled Rama's mind, pushing against each other until he feared that he would himself grow sick in the head like Mausi.

At times, Mausi woke him up at night. He heard her baying like a wolf in the middle of the night or laughing like a hyena. For some reason, her laughter scared him more than her crying. Rama would wake up in the middle of the night, listening to her cries or laughter and the sounds always chilled him to the bone. Usually, she stopped after a few minutes, but one night she carried on for nearly an hour. Frustrated, Lohia picked up a towel and went down to the basement. A few seconds later, the noise stopped. That morning before his father woke up, Rama crept down the basement to look at Mausi. There she was, sitting on her chair, rocking back and forth, back and forth, her face full of unknowing, her mouth stuffed with the white towel, her eyes at blessed peace.

Rama did not feel terrible or sad or anything. He did not know what to feel. He knew that his father was a kind man. He would not have thought any less of his father if Lohia had decided to put Mausi out of her misery permanently. His father would have been just as blameless as Mausi would be if she were to decide to end her own life by *Prayopavesa*. *Prayopavesa* was the Hindu practice of starving oneself to death. People who had no responsibilities or ambition left were the only ones who could carry out this act without being condemned or punished in the afterlife.

So this was how Lohia and his family had buried their dirty secret. Buried it like afterbirth, never to be beheld again by curious eyes. Their secret was safe until the day Rama stumbled across his father's diary. Hidden under his father's pillow was the little book that would unravel Rama's world. When Rama flipped it open, a photograph fell out.

Mausi.

At twenty, twenty one or twenty two.

A stunning beauty at that age.

On the back of the photograph, *Reena, my beautiful wife.*

Rama recognized his father's handwriting. His breath caught in his throat.

My beautiful Reena is losing her mind and I don't know what to do about it. Since she had Rama, she hasn't been the same.

Rama did not need to read any further.

The woman in the dungeon was his mother.

JAPAN
(Osaka, Osaka Prefecture)

The hermaphrodite club of Osaka

Do you know how it feels like to be born with a penis and a vagina? Of course, you wouldn't know. Why do I even ask? You wouldn't know. Not unless you are one of us. Which you are not. Because if you were, you would probably be sitting next to me right now, in the back of Shiro's bar, in Shinsaibashi Suji in Osaka.

This is where we meet. Our sanctuary. Every Friday.

We are the freaks of nature. We work hard to remain anonymous. You wouldn't catch us talking about our condition in public or taking our clothes off at the beach. Well, except for Midori who works in a nightclub near Dotonbori Bridge where she entertains bored local businessmen and expatriates for one hundred dollars each night. There is a cure for dissolution, you know. As long as you are willing to spend a few hundred dollars. For that amount, Midori lets the men and women paw her private parts while she pretends not to be indifferent.

In this city of over two and half million people, remaining anonymous doesn't require any feat of ingenuity. You would have to jump from the Umeda Sky Building to catch anyone's attention. Talking of suicide, in Osaka, suicide doesn't quite have the same flair that it used to have when samurai sat cross-legged and disemboweled

THE COLLECTOR OF BUTTERFLIES AND WOMEN

themselves with great elegance. In 1837, a *yoriki* (low ranking samurai police inspector) named Oshio Heihachiro led a band of peasants in a rebellion against the *bakufu*-controlled Osaka to protest the city authority's refusal to help the poor. Nearly a quarter of Osaka was burned down before the rebellion was put down.

My nuts hurt when I sit for too long. I have told Shiro that his leather chairs are too hard, but he doesn't listen. He won't do anything about it, cheap bastard.

My parents left me in a garbage container after I was born. Who can blame them? They didn't know what to do with me, this squirming, squirrelly thing with an appendage and orifice between its legs. Tetsuya and his wife, Yumiko were afraid, so they left me in a garbage can near Akyobashi train station. But do not judge them too harshly for they did wrap me in blankets to make sure that I would be warm in the cold December weather of Osaka.

My parents taped a sign to my blanket with the two names that they had given me. Tsuyoshi, which means brave and strong and Keiko, which means happy child. The first was a male name and the second was a female name. Manabu and his wife found me. The couple would raise me as Tsuyoshi, their only male child. They never let anyone see me naked, dressing me like a boy, Manabu teaching me the ways of men, about the ancient warriors like Oda Nobunaga and Hasekura Tsunenaga. He taught me about the magic of the *kitana* sword and about honor. Our *ima* (living room) was a small space sectioned off by a *fusuma*, a sliding door fashioned from wood and paper. The floor was made from *tatami*, a mat fabricated from rice straws. The rooms always smelled like rice pudding, *okonomiyaki* (pan fried batter) and *udon*, a rich noodle dish. My adopted parents loved me and cared for me and I hated it because I was too selfish to love them back as much they loved me because I was still trying to find Tetsuya and his wife who dumped me like so much garbage twenty five years ago.

I eventually did find my birth parents and when I did, we had nothing to say to each other. Not even an apology. The meeting lasted for three eternities and when it was over, I fled from their house and never looked back. I tossed my parents into the compost heap of memory much like they had tossed me into a garbage can years ago. I wished them a happy death.

In Osaka, July and August are the cruelest months with heat baking the city and residents fleeing into air-conditioned shelters. The moist air blowing in from Osaka bay into Osaka and the other ten cities that make up Osaka Prefecture simply makes the humidity worse. Even during Tsuyu, the rainy season, the humidity never goes away. Osaka is big and noisy like a man who has had too much sake. The streets are clean, swept daily by city street sweepers. Street signs and company signs clutter the landscape. The Midosuji road divides Central Osaka into two halves; south and north. South is Kita while north is Minami. Osaka means "large hill." On city streets, business men, students, and street merchants jostle for space. The roads are well-maintained. Miles of shopping arcades and underground malls lure the unwary consumer. Tourists clutter the streets milling from Osaka Castle to the shopping district of Umeda in the north and Namba in the south, ending up in Rinku Town, located across the water from Kansai International Airport.

My favorite time of the year is April when the cherry blossoms set the world ablaze. It was at Kema Sakuranomiya Park that I met Shiro two years ago. I had gone there to watch the cherry blossoms. I was sitting on a park bench admiring the immaculate green lawns and cherry trees lining the banks of the Okawa River when Shiro came to sit beside me. Shiro is a lanky, sad-eyed creature with long muscular arms and the gait of an animated stick figure. He does not walk as much as hurtle forward, all energy and kinesis. He seems to travel on the balls of his feet, his unruly hair covering half of his face and falling to his shoulder. His laugh is harsher than the strongest *awamori* drink. He is twenty four. Or thirty four. Or forty four. Depending on the age of the woman he is trying to get into his bed on a particular day.

I ended up in Shiro's bed. He went to bed with Keiko and woke up with Tsuyoshi. I did not let him go too far before I confessed my deceit, my half deceit really, because I was only half lying. I am partly a woman after all. He forgave me. We became friends.

Once he even took me to Doyama, where Osaka's homosexuals hang out. Shiro was straight, but he enjoyed watching people who were different from him. At times, I wondered if I too was just a curio to him, a novelty, like a child taking apart a new toy to see what was inside. Once he was done with me, would he set me aside and find the latest toy to tinker with? We sat down at a bar and ate *takoyaki* watching people cavort with each other and I died of loneliness because I did not belong in the world of men or the world of women.

It was Shiro who suggested that I reach out to other hermaphrodites or *futanara*, as they call us in Osaka and the rest of Japan. My people have always been fascinated by *futanara* perhaps because of the ancient custom of worshiping Dosojin, a divine being in Shintoism often represented by carved male and female genitalia.

"Are you out of your mind, Shiro? Perhaps I should put an ad in the paper?"

I was being ironic of course, but Shiro did not notice or pretended not to notice. "Yes, that might be a good idea."

I thought he was crazy. I knew he was.

But Shiro went ahead anyway.

A week later, a small ad appeared in the Lifestyle section of Mainichi Daily News. "The Hermaphrodite Club of Osaka. Meeting next Wednesday at 7 p.m. Call the number below for an interview, if interested in membership". The ad then went on to mention that only people who were verified to be *futanara* would be eligible to join the free support group. It seemed like one of Shiro's wooly ideas, a group of *futanara* banding together to share their life stories, use each other for therapy, push each other back from the ledge.

Six months later, here we are.

At times we are six boys and three girls. At other times, we are five girls and four boys. You see, Midori and I like to switch bodies. Very easy to do with make-up and the proper clothing and hairstyle. Everyone else in the club appears to be a bit more comfortable with their gender. They call Midori and me shape-shifters, changelings.

Some of us have only male names, some like me use both male and female names. Today I am Keiko, the happy one. Last week, I was strong and brave Tsuyoshi.

Nine boys.

Or nine girls.

Five girls.

Four boys.

Me. Midori. Yumiko. Nanami. Kasumi.

Kazuki. Kyoshi. Akashi. Daichi.

Midori is nineteen, beautiful but she smokes too much. She never smiles because her teeth are rotting. She is saving money to get porcelain teeth. She needs to save eight hundred thousand yen. She was well on her way until her biggest benefactor and customer ran into a street lamp after filling himself with *shochu* liquor.

Yumiko is thirty eight, the oldest of us. She works in a *ryokan*, a small inn on Kappabashi Street. She is petite with the tiny feet of a geisha and long eyelashes. She rarely speaks and when she does, her voice is softer than fall leaves dropping on a graveyard.

At twenty eight, Nanami is driven by the desire to have a baby. A doctor at Osaka University Hospital where they perform 9,000 surgeries each year told her that she could have a baby. Her ovaries could be fixed he assured her. She was planning to do the last piece of the "restorative" surgery by having her male appendage removed.

THE COLLECTOR OF BUTTERFLIES AND WOMEN

Of course, I do not agree with Nanami that her surgery will be restorative. I tell her that it will be deformative. When I told her that, she pouted and didn't speak to me for six weeks. At times, I wonder what will happen once Nanami gets her elective surgery. Would she still have a right to sit with us *futanara*? After all, she will have her breasts and her voice and her redesigned female part with the protuberance that she hates so much removed. Tell me, what should we call an ex-hermaphrodite?

Enough on Nanami.

Now, Kasumi, she is an only child. A child woman really at seventeen. Like me, she was abandoned by her parents. They did not leave her in a garbage can. They simply walked out of the house and never came back. Kasumi, five years old, foraged through the house and managed to live on rice cakes waiting for her parents to come back. After three days, Nanami realized that they weren't coming back. Eventually, an aunt who had come to visit her parents found Nanami. This aunt would raise her.

Kazuki always dressed like a thug. He was rough and talked too loudly as if he was afraid that no one would take him seriously unless he did so. He was short and stocky with a paunch developed from drinking *Sapporo* every day. He shaved his head bald and made cruel jokes to the other *futanaras*. He mocked their self-pity, taunted them for being weak. "I am not like you people. I am strong." He wore baggy clothes and adopted the affect and speech of American rap musicians.

Kyoshi was a slight boy with curly black hair and a big smile who spoke with a lisp. He lived with his mother in Ashiharabashi. He worked part time at a school on Midosuji Boulevard where he taught Japanese to excitable American children. After work, Kyoshi would accompany his charges to the American Consulate near Osaka City Hall. There the grateful parents would ply him with candy and sundry treats which he brought to the *futanaras* every Friday. We gorged ourselves on Snickers and Tootsie Rolls, immersed ourselves in chocolate syrup. Except for Akashi and Daichi, the ones we called the twins, because they always stuck together as if congenitally conjoined. They both hated candy.

It was Shiro who introduced Akashi and Daichi to the other members of our club last year and the two friends haven't missed any of our meetings since. Akashi has big breasts which he is quite embarrassed about. He never shaves, his facial hair covers most of his face. He is training his voice box to make it deeper and even more masculine. This week, he is working on improving the bass range of his voice. Akashi has gone from using the *sarashi* to bind his breasts to using Ace bandages. When he showed me his body once, I was shocked by the scars that I saw, scars from the layers of bandages that he had wrapped tightly around his breasts. How can he breathe?

Daichi is the prettiest person in our club although he would fight you if you ever told him that. Daichi is the only beautiful person that I know of who wants to be ugly. He says that beautiful people get too much attention and that he really just wants the world to leave him alone. For someone born in Kumagaya, Saitama where the sun burned fierce and the summers melted the wax in your ears, Daichi's complexion is surprisingly pale. I reasoned that he might have some sort of skin disease. How else could one explain his color?

None of us will ever live to be sixty years old. Nature is cruel to us. I have never heard of a *futanara* living to be sixty years old. Have you? Death is a serpent coiled inside our wayward genes, waiting to strike when we least expect it.

Tonight, as usual, we sit and drink and share our stories. We learn about Mrs. Whitestone, the mother of one of Kyoshi's students, who has a terrible drinking problem.

"Who is the happiest one among us?" Nanami asks.

We all look at her. She likes to stir things up.

"I hate my landlord." Kazuki says.

"Why? He wants to sleep with you?"

Kazuki shakes his head. "He doesn't want to sleep with me. That is the problem."

"You owe him rent?"

Kazuki nods. "Three months."

There is silence for a moment and then Daichi asks Kazuki, "Do you need some money? I can loan you some."

Never one to accept charity, Kazuki shakes her head vigorously. "I will be okay. I have another week."

"A week to find the rent money?" Midori asks.

"No" Kazuki responds. "A week to get him to sleep with me."

At that, we all laugh.

Midori cracks open another pack of cigarettes.

"How about we all leave Osaka?" This was Kasumi, in her tinny pipsqueak voice. All ideas and childlike enthusiasm.

No one bothers to respond to her question. We all pretend that she is merely thinking aloud. But we all know one thing. None of us is going anywhere. What other city can provide the anonymity of Osaka? Who would be our support in Tokyo or Kanagawa? Where could we find another Shiro?

So what happens in my story? What happens to us *futanara*? How does our story end? I have learned a terrible thing about life, and that is the fact that life always ends with an anticlimax. We never live long enough and we never die soon enough. We never want what we get and we never get what we want. The movie is interminable, and it will play on in an eternal loop. There will be no fireworks and no clashing cymbals, no falling bodies and no rising ghosts. This is how our lives will play out in perfect and infinite tedium just like your life. We will eventually get sick like Nanami's mother, die, run over by a bus, like Kazuki's father, die, drink ourselves to death like Yumiko's boyfriend, die, crash into a street lamp while driving drunk from a nightclub like Midori's married boyfriend, die, live to a ripe old age like the parents who abandoned me and hopefully died of grief and guilt.

The noise in the restaurant bar is overpowering. The patrons seem to be trying to outshout each other, like people fleeing from a tsunami. My friends and I are forced to talk to each other in stage whispers, the smoke from a thousand cigarettes eating away at our lungs and throats. The smell of sweat and body spray coagulate into a dense fog. The music pounds away at one hundred plus decibels, some canned electro-pop song by Ayumi Hamasaki. There are forty odd tables in the restaurant, patrons dining at dimly lit tables, lights purposely set low to hide the cracks in the walls and the gashes in the carpet. When Shiro is mad at his cooks, he tosses plates at the wall like a mad Kitagawa.

I wave over to Shiro. He saunters over, a crooked pirate smile on his face, looking as dangerously handsome as ever.

"Another drink."

He nods, walks off and returns with my drink.

"Turn that shit off. Can't hear myself think."

He completely ignores me, gives me a "fuck off" gesture as he leaves.

I never did thank my birth parents for naming me Keiko, happy child. In Japanese culture, a name can be a gift or a curse. My name is a gift.

When my adopted parents found me, they said that I had a smile on my face even while lying in my own shit in the garbage container.

Somebody get me another drink.

Where is Shiro?

NIGERIA

My name is Aristotle

My name is Aristotle.
I was a thirteen year old boy when I helped my father beat a man to death. We caught him by surprise, this man. Caught him by surprise in the farm where he had gone to take a shit. It was a beautiful day with the sun grinning at the world like a half-drunk adulteress in smeared blue make-up. He was squatted on his haunches, flies buzzing around him when we sneaked up on him. He did not see us coming. Did not see his death coming. But then, what man ever sees his death coming?

My father was a hunter, a man who was familiar with the bush, who understood the spirits of the bush. He could track a deer for miles. He knew what herbs could cure a child's fever and what berries could kill you in minutes if you ate them.

I hit the man after my father handed me the stick. Hit him in the back of the head and watched the uprising of blood. He grabbed his head, screamed and fell back. It was not like what you see in the movies. Not like the Hollywood movies where people being attacked scream and scream and scream. He only screamed once and this fact surprised me. I kept hitting him after he fell. I heard the thwack-

thwack of wood against his skull. I kept hitting him until I broke his skull. Blood was everywhere and I could taste it on my lips. A furious metallic taste. The blood ran like a rodent on the sand, scattered like a Rorschach blot all over the wet green leaves.

But the man would not die.

Have you ever killed a man?

It is not easy to kill a man. You would know this if you have ever killed someone or tried to kill someone. But you probably have never tried.

The man would not die.

He kept wriggling on the grass, kept moaning and trying to get away. He was crying softly like a child, begging for mercy. I could see his lips moving but no words came out. He managed to get to his knees, stared at me with his destroyed face, one eye battered. He began to crawl, trying to get away. You want to know how I felt, what was going through my head? Let me stick to the details of what happened. I will tell you about my feelings later.

I hit him and hit him but Nduka would not die. He seemed to be shrinking, disappearing into a blur of blood and brain matter but still he wouldn't die.

"Give me the stick." My father said to me. I handed him the stick. With business-like efficiency, he began to hit Nduka with it. He hit him in the throat. Speared him with the wood, is more accurate. Speared him a few times and Nduka finally stopped moving. I will not go into any details about the excrement and the urine. I will only say that Nduka's body failed him at his moment of death.

Nduka was tall, dark, and intense, with big hooded eyes that women were said to find beautiful. He was a charmer, a fast talker. It was said that Nduka fathered more children in the village of Agbor than any other man. He slept with lonely wives when their husbands were at work. The women got pregnant and soon presented their husbands with beautiful babies who bore a suspicious resemblance to Nduka. Nduka was six feet tall. That is when he was alive. Dead, he was less than a foot tall. Have you noticed that no person is ever more than a foot tall when they are dead and lying on their back or stomach?

Later, I would find out that Nduka had a wife and four children. I would learn that he was a farmer. I would learn why my father had decided that he needed to die. I will tell you why later. For now, let me tell you how we disposed of his body.

"We need to bury him." My father said. "We can't leave him lying here like an animal. Can't let the animals feed on him."

My father began to dig a hole. He used a shovel that he had brought along with him. I used the small hoe that I had brought with me. We did not dig a six foot hole because we didn't have enough time. After three feet, we gave up.

"Every human being deserves a burial. It's the decent thing to do." My father said when we finished digging. He talked often about decency, about doing the right thing. I saw my father as a good man. A man who never raised his voice at his children, who never struck his wife.

We said a prayer for Nduka after we dragged him into the hole. My father wished him a safe journey in the land of the spirits. Next, we tossed Nduka's machete and the goatskin bag which contained his lunch and water into the hole. We did not take the yams that he had harvested and was preparing to take home to his family. My father was not a thief. He was the most honest man I had ever known.

All around us birds wept like abandoned babies. Insects buzzed around us. The ground was wet. It had rained the previous night. The smell of lush vegetation was everywhere. Wild flowers bloomed like fire. The rains had set the world ablaze. The leaves were damp with moisture. If you looked carefully, you could see the occasional small animal, scampering in the underbrush, darting through the bush as they foraged for food.

THE COLLECTOR OF BUTTERFLIES AND WOMEN

Before we walked into the bush that day to search for Nduka, my father did not tell me what the plan was. My father was not a man to talk much. I will tell you more about that later. It was only as we walked into Nduka's farm that my father told me in an inflectionless voice that Nduka needed to die. "Some men do not deserve to walk the earth, to breathe the air that righteous men breathe."

I did not question my father. My love for him was absolute. I did not question his judgment any more than I could have questioned the sun for waking up late in the morning. Before that day and after that day, my father and I never spoke about the man we killed.

Listen.

Listen.

Let me tell you right away that this is not really the beginning of my story. The beginning of every story is a path and this is a point along that path.

Now, about feelings. How did I feel about the murder? Maybe I should lie to you and tell you that I felt anguished about what we had done, or at the minimum, conflicted about it. But I will not. What I felt about the murder was…nothing. Perhaps, at thirteen years old, I had not yet learned how to feel. Perhaps the land of feelings is a country traversed only by adults. I will not try to be the heroic narrator as I tell you this story. I am not looking for your sympathy, or even understanding. You can judge me however you want. It doesn't really matter.

I do want you and me to become one. You will be me, Aristotle, son of Anozie, brother of Chima and five other siblings. That is the only way that you would truly understand my story.

I will take you on a tour of my head and let you meet my ghosts and my nightmares.

Lest I forget.

Lest I forget. I must confess this to you. Sometimes the language of the past and the language of the future run together in my head, like two distant waterways finding each other and merging, merging and then flowing in unison like a sudden chorus.

All autobiographers are liars. They present life in a well-ordered fashion, from a sequence of childhood to adulthood to old age. The baby in his cradle to the man in the winter of his life, every piece fitting together perfectly. But chronology is the last refuge of cowardly storytellers and to that temptation, I refuse to yield.

I will let you ask the question that you are probably dying to ask. The question that everyone always asks me. Why did my father name me Aristotle? I will answer your question later. Not now. As the preacher in my church once said, "there is a time for everything. Everything in life has its time and season."

I said that all autobiographers are liars. I should know. I know a lot about autobiographies and I know a lot about lies. I taught myself how to read at four and I haven't stopped reading since. My father said that I read more books at ten than all the people in the village of Agbor combined. I fear that he is right. I would borrow the books from the school library and stay up late into the night reading them until my mother made me go to bed or the wick on the lantern finally burned out.

You will need to follow my story very carefully. If I sometimes lie, forgive me, it is because my memory lies to me. But I do tell the truth most of the time. Trust me. Or trust me most of the time. No one should be trusted all of the time.

I ask that you forgive me if I do not always spend time describing the flora and fauna when I tell you some of my stories. You will agree with me that what took place is often more important than where it took place.

I will tell you not only about my life, but about the tragedy of life and the comedy of death. I want you to know that my story is not just about Nduka, the man that I killed, although in many ways it is all about him.

I am populated by many stories and these stories are captive spirits begging to be set free.

Did you hear me?

What would you do if a man raped your ten year old sister? Before you answer my question, think very carefully. Please spare me your platitudes about the power of forgiveness and vengeance is mine, saith the Lord, and all that. Seriously, what would you do?

My name is Aristotle. Did I tell you that already? I have a habit of repeating myself at times. Not because I like the sound of my voice but because I have found out that the world is hearing impaired and at times a man has to shout or repeat himself in order to be heard.

I haven't had a good night sleep in years.

After you read my story, you may not get a good night sleep for a while yourself.

My name is Aristotle.

They found his body

They found his body. They found the man we killed a few days after the murder.

Do you know what is so frustrating about dead people? It is the fact that they do not like to be ignored. They carry a bracing impatience. They want to be seen, want to be heard. They want to tell their stories. In this sense, I suppose they are no different from the living.

When Nduka did not return home from the farm, a search party was sent to look for him. The search party did not find him. They returned to the palace of the Igwe, the village chief to report that they had been unsuccessful.

Some people said that Nduka must have run off with one of his many lovers. His wife, Nonye, refused to believe the rumor. "Nduka loved me and my children. He would never do such a thing." Nonye was a thin high-strung woman with eyes of eternal sorrow. She presented a pitiable figure, this woman with sunken cheekbones and abused skin.

Nonye and my mother, Ugo, two women lashed together in a dance of destiny, could not have been more different. Nonye was fire and my mother was smoke. Nonye was all intensity and Ugo was all subtlety.

"Do you think Nduka ran away?" I ask my mother.

For nights, I have gone to bed, wondering if Nduka would soon be discovered. On one night, I dreamed that I saw Nduka climbing out of the shallow grave we had buried him in, shaking sand out of his eyes and hair, staring at me with those beautiful eyes, those ruined eyes.

This was a few days before Nduka's body was found.

We are sitting on small stools outside our house. We have just finished the evening meal. It is dusk. The sun has disappeared into the horizon, taking with it the long shadows of afternoon. It is humid. There is a restiveness in the air that seems to have infected the whole world. It is as if lightning has struck, leaving residual electricity in the air. The chickens and goats seem to move too quickly. People seem to talk too loudly. All around us, there are small mud and brick houses, baking in the heat. The houses are covered by dust. The dust billows in the wind like a drunk who has had too much to drink and is now determined to make a fool of himself.

My mother shakes her head. "Nduka is not the kind of man to abandon his family."

I wonder how well she knows Nduka. How she can vouch for him with such faith.

For some reason, I am discomfited by her words. I feel the need to comment. "Perhaps no one really knew him. You've said it yourself, that it is impossible to know what is really in a man's heart."

My mother turns to look at me, almost sadly. "I knew Nduka well. Your father thinks he was a rapist, but Nduka was no rapist."

A few days later, Nduka's body would be found. Some animal

must have dug up his body. A farmer found his corpse and alerted the villagers.

My father and I attended Nduka's funeral. My father was one of the elders chosen to speak about the man.

"He was a good man. A kind man. He would never hurt a fly. May the good spirits lead him on his journey to the land of our gods." This is how my father finished his eulogy about Nduka. I wondered how hard it was for my father to say those words. My father was not a liar, but on that day he lied.

My father took five baskets of yams to Nonye, Nduka's window. He also sent a male goat and bolts of *ankara* cloth. I was there when he presented Nonye with the gifts. The widow, face still smeared with tears, head wrapped in a black scarf, accepted the gifts and thanked my father.

When we returned home the night after Nduka's burial, my mother took me into her bedroom and closed the door.

"Aristotle, you have not been sleeping well."

I was surprised. I had been trying to hide my distress from her. I did not want to let my father down by appearing to be weak in any way.

"I know you have been thinking about Nduka. I know that you and your father killed him."

The breath caught in my throat. I felt my heart tumble in my chest. I was silent for what seemed to be an eternity and then I asked her, "Are you going to inform the police?'

She shook her head. "No family should ever give up its own."

My father's death

My father died nine months after we killed Nduka. A few weeks before he died, he had been complaining of stomachache. He was throwing up rivers of blood. The blood came in torrents, taking over the house like an untamable creature. The house smelled like death.

In the days before he died, I would walk into the room where he lay on a heavy mat on the floor and hear his heavy breathing, each breath a thunderclap. His eyes looked haunted, his brow shiny with sweat. In his eyes, I saw his death. In my eyes, he saw his death. But there was no fear in his eyes. He was ready to meet his maker.

I would hold his hand, stroke it tenderly. My father, a man who was not one to show emotion, did not flinch at my touch. He was too weak to do so. He smiled weakly at me, his eyes full of love. I had never loved him more than I did at that moment.

My mother, the great love of his life, the woman he had married when he was only nineteen, nursed him. She boiled *dogoyaro* leaves for his fever, rubbed *alabukun* ointment on his skin. His skin was beginning to flake. When she moved him on the mat to ease the pain from the bedsores which covered his body, he moaned weakly and thin crusts of skin flaked off his body, forming a rich down on the floor. His body was the sea and the pink sores which covered him were toxic vicious islands. These rebel islands spewed pus all over the dirty mat and my mother mopped up the pus, mopped it quickly, mopped it frantically, terrified of letting her husband's essence melt away into the dusty earth. There were two beds in the room but my father could not sleep on either one. He could not get comfortable. He needed enough space to roll around as the pain in his stomach gripped him, made him bite his lip in pain, refusing to cry.

My mother cooked my father *akamu*. The corn pap was the only food that his insides could handle. When he grew too weak to go to the outhouse, my mother made us leave the room while he relieved himself. She cleaned him up afterwards and took out the waste in a paper bag to be thrown far into the bush, this evidence of her husband's infirmity.

I never once saw her cry for him. My mother was not the crying kind. She was a strong woman who would hold her family together no matter what strangeness fate threw at her. I admired her strength.

It was not the sickness that killed my father. It was the blood. He coughed up blood, excreted blood. The blood took over him and

THE COLLECTOR OF BUTTERFLIES AND WOMEN

turned him into blood. My mother nursed him right until the day he died. But my father never once thanked her for nursing him. I would catch him staring at her with an inscrutable look, like a cartographer trying to unravel the mystery of a map that would take him to better climes. I noticed how my mother would always look away when he stared at her this way, as if she was uncomfortable.

At that time, I did not know what my father was thinking in his last days. But now, I know. Of course, I cannot be absolutely certain of it, I think I know what he was thinking. That knowledge makes me shiver. Stay with me, stay with me. You won't need me to tell you what Anozie must have been thinking, the same way I didn't need anyone to tell me what he must have been thinking. When you become me, Aristotle, you will also become my father, Anozie, and then you will understand what was going through Anozie's head as he lay dying with his wife stroking his hand and the smoky delirium of his life passing him by.

I remember the last thing that my father ever said to me. This was the day before he died, before the pain in his stomach stole his voice and left him writhing on the floor like a serpent.

"The world belongs to women, my son. Remember that always. Women always win. Even when a man thinks he is winning, the woman is really winning. Never, ever mistreat the person who prepares your food, and washes your clothes."

The day they buried my father, the heavy rains did not come. The birds did not fall down from the skies and beat their breasts in agony with angry wings. Market women went to the market as usual, farmers went to the farm at the crack of dawn as they usually did. The world refused to sleep, the goats did not weep for Anozie. I was surprised by this. This is not how it is supposed to be when a great man dies. A great man had died and the world had paid scant attention. It was a travesty.

I felt angry and betrayed.

I haven't told you why my father named me Aristotle. My father named me after Aristotle son of Nicomachus, the Greek philosopher whose name meant "the best purpose." Anozie believed that his son would grow up to be wise just like the philosopher he was named after.

A woman showed up at the funeral with her daughter who looked to be ten or eleven years old. No one seemed to know the woman. No one had seen her around before. I noticed how she moved gingerly among the crowd, like a creature in a strange land. I noticed how pretty her daughter was, her long hair knotted in thick braids that coiled around her neck. After the funeral was over, she asked to talk to my mother. I could see the two women as they stood a few yards away from me. I saw the woman point at her daughter, saw my mother study the child's face intently. Whatever the stranger said to my mother must have disturbed my mother. I saw a shadow cross her face. I would see the stranger again a year later. I will tell you more about that soon.

After they put my father in the ground, I left the cemetery as quickly as I could. I did not want to partake in the rich harvest of emotion that was in the air. I wanted to go home, to crawl into a hole and never come out. I did not want to hear about how much Anozie was loved by men who probably could not stand him. My father was not the most lovable man after all but I loved him more than life itself. I went into the bush behind our house where I usually relieved myself and cried. I did not want anyone to see me crying, especially not my sister Chima, or my other siblings.

My mother was in mourning for a full year. During that year, a smile did not cross her face. She drifted through the house like a ghost, dressed in black. She did not go to the market or the farm. Friends and family members came to visit, bringing their condolences and tears. Nduka's wife, Nonye, came to visit. She held my mother's hands, prayed with her and offered to help her cook. My mother thanked her but refused the offer. "You have plenty of work to do. No need to add mine to it."

THE COLLECTOR OF BUTTERFLIES AND WOMEN

My mother, tall and lithe, limbs of a gazelle. Her gaze is hypnotic, just as hypnotic as her hands which are long and thinly veined. For a woman who has delivered seven children, she walks with incredible grace, floating above the world around her like magic suddenly let loose. It was easy to see how she could have seduced my father with that easy laugh, that kind smile, the kind of smile that I imagine made berries fall from trees into her hands, begging to be taken home, a smile that made the goats come home at night when they heard her imploring voice.

What I will learn about Ugo, my mother, would nearly destroy my sanity.

My mother was a woman who had lived her whole life on the spear point of anticlimax; waiting in vain for her husband to come home on many a night when he stayed out late, waiting for him to reform and change his womanizing ways. Her whole life was a sentence, waiting for an exclamation mark. She was a drunken bridesmaid stumbling from one wedding to the next. A woman who had long lost the capacity for surprise, born prepared to receive bad news. Some whispered that she handled her husband's death well, too well, they said.

Our neighbor Nana came to visit as well, accompanied by his two wives. I ignored Nana but greeted his wives. I managed a smile for Rose, the younger wife, whom I liked.

A year after my father died, the strange woman whom I first met at his funeral would show up. I soon learn that the woman was one of my father's mistresses, one of the insects that the entomologist collected. The woman lived in the village of Umunede just a few miles from Agbor. Her daughter was now twelve years old, two years younger than I was. Her name was Ukachi. She was my half-sister.

My mother announced that Ukachi would be coming to live with us. The family elders had decided that she belonged in the house of the man who had fathered her out of wedlock. The decision was made for us and my mother could not question it, whether she liked it or not.

It is late in the evening. We are sitting at home. My mother has sent the other children out of the house so that we can have privacy. We have finished the evening meal, a heavy meal of pounded yam and bitter leaf soup. The aroma of bitter leaf soup hangs around like a drunk at a funeral who has overstayed his welcome. We are sitting on tired brown leather chairs picked up from some secondhand store.

The cries of children unleashed upon the world by their parents echo through the house. The noise is a constant hum, mixed with the occasional cries of a hen or a goat. Dusk sits upon the world like an elephant, choking it. The last spell of rain has covered the land with a heavy blanket of humidity. The room is humid and hot. My mother is wearing a green wrapper and a white blouse with long sleeves. As hot as it is, she will not let her arms be exposed. She is hiding the scars on her arms.

The week Ukachi moved in, my mother takes off her blouse and shows me her naked breasts. I stare at these breasts that I had suckled as a baby.

"Look." Her voice commands.

I do not want to look.

"Look, Aristotle. What do you see?"

My mother is naked from the waist up. I stare at her sagging breasts, her shrunken skin, her stomach distended from several childbirths.

I don't want to look but I understand that my mother is trying to tell me something. The urgency in her voice grips me. I stare at my mother's breasts and what I see are several bite marks. Marks from an adult's teeth. A man's teeth?

I am horrified.

"Who did this to you?" My voice is a choked whisper.

THE COLLECTOR OF BUTTERFLIES AND WOMEN

"Anozie. Your father did this to me. The man you once told me was not a violent man."

It can't be true, I think. Not my father. It can't be true. I had grown up believing that my father was not like the other men who beat their wives.

"It started a long time ago. The beatings started when he found out about my affair with Nduka. I apologized, told him it was all a mistake, would never happen again. But your father was not a man who believed in forgiveness. He did not want to divorce me because the world would mock him for not being able to keep his marriage together. He did not want to reveal his shame to the world, shame that I had brought upon him. He never wanted to be seen as weak. He started to beat me. He would beat me in the middle of the night while you and your siblings slept. He warned me about crying out. I learned to take the beatings silently, to welcome them because it was the only physical contact that I got from him. He would only touch me when he wanted my body or when he beat me. When he made love to me, he beat me and called me a whore. When he got really mad, he bit my breast. Bit it so hard, I bled, but he wouldn't let me go to the hospital. Instead he treated me with herbs and ointment."

I begin to cry.

My mother stands there, the breasts that nursed me as a child, dangling in front of me like an accusation, like a curse.

"Look, Aristotle. Look at my right arm."

I am afraid to look, but when I look, what I see are bite marks on her right arm, near her elbow. Smaller in circumference than the ones on her breasts, but bite marks, no less. I wondered why I had never noticed the bite marks and then realized that it was because my mother always wore blouses with long sleeves that hid her arms.

"He bit your arm too?"

"No. I bit my own arm. To stop from crying out when he beat me. There were times that I drew blood."

My mother was not done.

"I got tired of his beatings and his cheating. How many other children like Ukachi does he have out there?"

I am trembling. My mother's voice sounds distant, as if she and I are on opposite sides of the earth. Her voice is dull, without emotion.

"I poisoned him. Took me a year to do it. Just before he died, he asked me if I had put poison in his food, but I wouldn't respond. Asked me why I could not look him in the eye."

I thought of the last words my father said to me.

"Even when a man thinks he is winning, the woman is really winning. Never, ever mistreat the person who prepares your food, and washes your clothes."

That was when it hit me. My father must have known in his final hours that his wife was the one who killed him. But proud to the very end, he was determined to not expose his family to shame and ridicule. Determined to not appear weak, determined to spare his children the disgrace and scandal. The man who lived a life of the vigilante had died at the hands of a woman who had turned into a vigilante.

"Are you going to inform the police?" My mother asks.

I remember what she told me when we first discussed Nduka's murder. I use her words now, and I see a small tired smile cross her face. "No family should ever give up its own."

I give my mother a hug, as if to seal our blood pact.

"Aristotle, some secrets must never be dug up. Some things are best left buried under the ground."

The world would never know that I was the one who killed Nduka, that Nduka had raped my sister Chima and that my mother had once had an affair with Nduka.

As I looked at the woman that I loved so much, I noticed that she looked gaunt, much thinner than usual. Her cheeks were sunken, eyes unnaturally bright like the eyes of someone with fever. Her forehead was coated by a sheen of sweat. Was my mother crumbling under the heavy burden of secrets that she carried? Did she manage to get any sleep at night? If she did, were her dreams filled with strange moons that shed tears of blood like the ones that I dreamed of on the few nights that I managed to get some sleep? Did she dream of infants who came out of their mother's wombs with mouths full of teeth, and eyes blood red with hate?

My mother had never condemned me for killing Nduka. In turn, I had never condemned her for poisoning my father, the man that I loved so much. Without ever saying it aloud, we had reached a tacit agreement to let the dead stay buried. I did not love her any less because she had taken the life of the man that I worshipped. As hard as it was to accept, I knew that the terrible revenge she exacted on my father was justified.

You can condemn me if you like. I deserve your excoriation and your spite. Yes, I own up to being a coward and I will make no excuses. I will not ask you to put yourself in my shoes. I will not embark on any philosophical discourse about repentance and punishment. I refuse to be like Rodion Romanovich Raskolnikov in Fyodor Dostoevsky's *Crime and Punishment* who attempts to justify his evil act.

"What should we do?" I ask my mother. Like a coward, I was waiting for her to help me decide. Wait, that is not true. I was waiting for her to confirm a decision that I had already made. I knew deep in my bones that my mother would never suggest that I turn myself in. I was waiting now for her to tell me that I did not need to turn myself in. And she obliged.

"My son, we never had this conversation. Do you hear me?"

Her eyes are fierce, protective, shining like polished jewels.

I nod, throat tight. I cannot trust myself to speak.

"What is done cannot be undone. When you go to sleep tonight, think of that."

I dwell on her words. What is done cannot be undone.

"Did Nduka rape you when you were ten?"

One day I finally work up the nerve to ask my sister a question that I have carried in my head for years.

Chima does not look surprised. Now nineteen, three years my junior, she has grown into an attractive young woman. While I am tall, dark and skinny with big eyes and curly hair, Chima is of average height with fair velvety skin and small brown eyes. People say that we do not look like brother and sister. Chima is graceful like our mother but without our mother's eye-catching beauty.

"I have been waiting for that question for years."

There is a long pause. Silence rushes at us like a deluge. Outside, the indifferent world plods on.

I wait and I wait. When Chima finally answers, her voice is hushed, almost a whisper. "Nduka did not rape me."

I am stunned. Chima sees the look of disbelief on my face.

"So our father lied and mother told me the truth."

My heart clenches. Did I murder an innocent man? Did my father, the man that I loved, trick a child, a mere child of thirteen to do the unthinkable, the unpardonable?

Maybe Anozie did try to rape Chima. Maybe Chima's memory was failing her, after all she was only ten when the incident took place. Maybe my mother was wrong about Nduka. I am searching for hope amidst hopelessness, grasping for the quivering thread of logic.

"Chima, you were only ten. No one can be expected to remember all that happened to them at that age."

Chima shakes her head. "If the lie is easier to accept than the truth, then stick with the lie. But I am telling you this, Nduka did not rape me. He never tried to rape me. I never spent any time alone with him."

"So our father lied? And he told you to lie when mama questioned you?"

Chima does not speak for a while. When she does, her voice is even softer than before. "Our father was a man of strong will. His children would have done anything for him. All he had to do was ask."

The terrible truth of what she had just said struck me. My father had never asked me to hide the secret of Nduka's murder. He had not needed to, because he knew that I would never betray him. He knew well that my loyalty was like the strongest twine, woven from love, and that not even death could break it.

He made me help him kill an innocent man. And then he lied to my mother about the reason why the man had to die. .

Why?

My mother would not answer this question. She stared at me, eyes weary, suddenly looking a hundred years old.

"You are right. Nduka was not a rapist. So why did my father kill him?"

"Son, some things are best left alone."

"I need to know. I have to know."

Outside, a goat began to bleat. Wind lashes at the walls of the house and the zinc roof clatters. I hear the honking of cars and the sounds of excited children.

"Remember, I told you that I had an affair with Nduka? Anozie killed Nduka because of the affair. The affair took place the year before you were born. Anozie never forgave me. He hated me for it."

I am stunned.

"My father accused an innocent man of rape to justify killing him?"

"Yes. Your father was not a man to forgive."

"But why go that far? Why make up a lie, why have Chima repeat the lie?"

"He wanted me to believe the lie. Wanted me to hate Nduka. Wanted me to hate the very memory of the man."

But my mother was not done. "You are the product of my affair with Nduka. Anozie and I kept the secret from everyone. Anozie loved you like you were his own blood but Nduka was your biological father"

I am speechless.

"The man you helped Anozie kill was your father."

My legs turn to liquid. I realize that I am holding my breath. It dawns on me that my world would never be the same. I stare at my hands, the hands that helped beat a man to death. Not just any man. My real father.

My name is Aristotle. Did I tell you that already?

I haven't had a good night sleep in years.

The man who beat his wives

As a boy, I used to wonder why my father did not beat my mother. In the neighborhood where I grew up, love was a contact sport. Bloodletting was what men did after a hard day's work. They had dinner and then picked fights with their wives for perceived slights and unresolved transgressions. The family hearth was the Roman square and the man was the gladiator. Most men on the street where I lived beat their wives. Wives took their beatings in silence and then fixed breakfast the next morning with a swollen eye or busted lip. For most of these couples, marriage was like a dead animal. Once a living, breathing thing, now it had expired. They dragged its carcass between them for years, until exhausted they finally laid it down and let it rot.

I always wondered how these poor creatures stopped themselves from reaching for the rat poison and sprinkling a generous dose of it into their husband's meal before serving it Socratically. When I questioned my elders, I was told that any man who did not beat his wife was a weak man and that a woman needed to be kept in her place at all times. I was told that beating a woman was a way to let the woman know that you cared about her and that a woman would rather be smacked than ignored. This revelation made me think that perhaps my father did not love my mother enough.

Or perhaps my father was a weak man.

Our neighbor, Nana who lived next door did not consider himself a weak man by any means. Nana was a man fleeing from silence, stumbling along like an intoxicated sailor drunk on strange wine. He did not understand the world and the world did not understand him. And his anger…his anger was a many-tongued thing, sinewy and virulent. It was directed at his wives and children. He beat his wives with the fervor of a proselyte, with the passion of a man who had found his true calling in life. He beat them poetically. This flagellation could be heard all around the street, his wives screaming like wounded birds as the belt buckle descended. Nana did not spare the rod and he did not spoil the child. He took the biblical admonishment very seriously.

I heard of two women who got weary of being used as sparring partners by their husbands. One of them heated a pot of palm oil until it was scalding hot and waited for her husband to go to sleep. She then poured the hot grease over his face and ran when his skin began to hiss and froth. The second woman went even further. She took a knife, sliced off his penis and hurled it out the window.

Nana was as tall as a young bamboo tree. He was in his forties. Most of the time, he walked around without a shirt, upper body bare, hairy, pot belly daring the world. He walked around with the overweening confidence of a man who was gifted with an extra penis and who carried that appendage around in his pocket. He was as loud as a tin drum when he spoke, voice gravelly like tap shoes that had danced to too many songs. He moved with quick steps, like a man chasing spirits. Nana beat his wives when they refused to have sex with him. He beat them when the soup they fixed him for dinner was not to his liking. He beat them when they did not get pregnant. He beat them when they got pregnant.

THE COLLECTOR OF BUTTERFLIES AND WOMEN

When the urge took him, Nana tied one of his wives to the bedpost in their two room apartment and had sex with her while his children and the other wife slept in the next room. I remember lying awake, listening to her imprecations and cries and his grunts and harrumphing. While I felt sad for the poor woman, I also felt an odd fascination, frissons arcing through my body. I was horrified when I realized that I had an erection.

Nana had a face that scared newborn infants and alley cats. His face was as disturbing as incest, eyes taken with a strange fever, full of satyriasis. His brow was constantly furrowed in a perpetual puzzle, as if he was trying to unravel the mystery of the world. He looked like a man that you couldn't trust with your wife or your wallet. He had the eyes of a sinner and the hands of the sinned against.

One day, I got into a fight with Nana. I can't remember exactly what started the fight. I had always hated his guts for how he treated his family. On this day, he makes a comment which I find offensive. He comes at me with a piece of firewood, his eyes full of rage, arms flailing. I imagine that he is frothing at the mouth and that sparks are shooting from his eyes as he advances toward me, but I am only imagining. I run into our apartment and grab a machete and then emerge triumphant.

Nana's eyes widen in fear as he tries to assess this threat. Behind him, his two wives shriek in terror, afraid of the violence that is about to erupt. I can tell that Nana is afraid. Like any bully, he wilts when confronted by an opposing and potentially superior force. He is afraid but he refuses to show weakness in the presence of his wives.

I charge forward with the machete.

Nana takes a step back.

Nana's younger wife, Rose, who appears to be my age but in reality is in her early twenties, rushes forward. She is at least six months pregnant. A child woman. I had always liked her and had always wondered why she married her brute of a husband. She plants herself between Nana and me, big pretty eyes imploring.

"Please. Please don't." Her voice is dream soft, gauzy, leaves falling against a zinc roof in the midnight rain. Her voice holds optimism, faith in mankind, an elfin innocence. I drown myself in her magic, let her rain wash over me.

As if hypnotized, the two combatants step back and let their arms drop, lower their weapons. For a long moment, Nana stares at me, at his young wife, and then walks back into his house of misery.

A few months later, Nana's wife has her fifth child and names the child Blessing. The story was that she had had a difficult pregnancy and had almost died during childbirth. I do not understand why a pretty woman who had delivered four children before she turned thirty, who lived in a two room flea-ridden apartment would name her fifth child Blessing. There are many things that I do not understand.

I would come to accept the fact that wife beating was commonplace in the country of my birth. I would come to accept that Nana was an alchemist, just another magician who had discovered how to turn love into pain.

But I could not make the pain in my gut go away each time I heard Nana beat his wives. So I started to plan how to kill him.

A knife to the back.

A club to the head.

A rope around his neck.

Gasoline and a match in the dead of night.

My plans went nowhere. Maybe because Nana reminded me too much of my father, the collector of butterflies and women. If Nana was the curator of physical pain, my father was the custodian of emotional pain. Was Nana any worse than my father?

I never worked up the courage to kill Nana. And I never forgave myself for my cowardice.

The collector of butterflies and women

Are all women's vaginas exactly the same?
As a little boy, I thought about this question a lot. If all vaginas were designed exactly the same, what was the point of my father's infidelity? Why did he feel the need to sleep with different women?

I was five when my father started to collect butterflies.

He was gentle to these beautiful doomed creatures. He nursed them with a tenderness that gave my mother heartburn. She accused him of caring more for the butterflies than he cared for her and her children. He kept the butterflies in an old mosquito net rigged to four wooden stakes at the back of our house. Every morning before he went to work, he fed them flower nectar.

I was eleven when my father started to collect women.

The first time I saw my father romancing a woman who was not my mother, I was confused. Who was this woman? What was my father's attraction to her? Why was my father cheating on my mother? Did my mother have any inkling of what my father was up to? I never figured out the answers to these questions. What I would learn from my mother is that we often do not find the right answers simply because we do not ask the right questions. As children, what we believe to be reality is often just an assumption of reality. Reality is often an ugly bride hiding behind the gauzy veil of carefully nursed illusions.

Thankfully, my father never married any of his mistresses, although he could have. As a Muslim, he was certainly entitled to marry as many wives as he chose.

I am sure that my father's philandering did not begin with the woman that I like to think of as Butterfly. She was Butterfly simply because she was pretty and fragile. I think of her as adulteress number one. The preceding affairs, I must have been blissfully unaware of, as I was cocooned by age. As I grew older, I became used to the strange women who flitted through our homestead like moths buzzing toward my father's flame. If my father was Lothario, I was the entomologist who studied the insects in fascination, analyzed their etymology, and categorized them. To each adulteress, I gave an insect name. There was a short bad-tempered one who glared at me each time she visited. She was the wasp. There was a scrawny one with hollow cheeks, feverish eyes, and a whining voice. She was the mosquito. I noted who had big feet and misshapen toes. I catalogued who had wild rebellious hair like Medusa. I noted who had uneven, discolored teeth.

Butterfly first appears in our house one day after I return from primary school. Our living quarters consist of two rooms, a parlor and a bedroom. The bedroom has two beds, one for my parents and one for the children. When my parents want privacy, they simply pull a curtain which hangs from the bed poles as a screen. The children take turns to sleep on the bed and when we lose track of whose turn it is to sleep on the bed, we simply draw straws and whoever chooses the shortest straw has to sleep on the floor.

When I opened the door, there she was sitting on my father's lap on the sofa. Butterfly recoils when she sees me. I wonder why she is surprised. Did she not know that my father was married, with

THE COLLECTOR OF BUTTERFLIES AND WOMEN

children? Did she not fathom that one of her paramour's children might be showing up from school shortly?

Butterfly is attractive, her skin the color of a forbidden midnight. She is in her twenties and time has been kind to her. Her eyes are big and round and full of deception. Eyes that can make men mad. Eyes that can cure men of madness. Eyes that can first make men mad and then cure them of the madness. I like her and I am ashamed for this fact, this temptress who has come to seduce my father. I like her because she is pretty. And I hate her because she is sleeping with my father on my mother's bed.

My father does not show any visible reaction when I walk in the room and drop my school bag on the floor. He eyes me warily. I imagine that he rises, guilt-stricken, to give me a hug of reassurance. I imagine that he moves his hand away from Butterfly but I only imagine this. It is not material fact.

I had never had any doubt about whether my father loved me or not. He was the best father in the world but not the most expressive one. He kept his emotions sealed in a box and placed the box on a high shelf where his wife and children could not reach it. He was not the kind of father who held your hand or doled out hugs. I loved him but I did not understand him. How about your father? Did he dole out hugs and kisses to you as a child? We are fated to not understand those that we love. Perhaps if we understand them for what they really are, we might not love them. Perhaps this is nature's way of protecting us. Did my father love my mother? If he did, why was he able to cheat on her so willfully?

My mother, is tall and fair-skinned with a complexion that some call "Oyibo skin" – "white woman skin." When she walks, she moves with an easy grace as if she does not want to hurt small animals that live below the earth. She has a shy smile and a soft voice. When she is angry, which is not often, her big round eyes lose their delicious twinkle, her long pianist fingers curl.

My mother had always been in poor health. She had a history of stomach and heart problems and had visited a succession of herbalists, witchdoctors, and spiritualists. I had always worried about her dying, about her fragile body finally giving way under the weight of her sundry maladies. It was whenever she was away, seeking treatment in one of the nearby villages that my father brought his women home.

Butterfly would be one of the many women who passed through my father's life in Agbor.

My father had a "government job." He worked some sort of administrative position in the court system. On the totem pole, he was higher than the clerks, typists, court bailiffs, and court messengers but not as high as the lawyers and judges. I was never quite sure of exactly what his assignation or designation was, but it seemed to be a position of minor importance.

While my father's job did not make him rich, it imbued him with a certain amount of power. He could dispense favors like a potentate. He could provide access to judges and magistrates. He was in charge of auctioning off the properties of defaulters and delinquents on behalf of the local and state government. Dressed in his suits and shoes, he was like Nicomachus, the Greek scribe who headed the Athenian committee charged with publishing the laws of Draco and Solon.

Once I witnessed a man visit my father to plead with him to intercede on some court proceeding on his behalf. The man, dressed in flowing *Agbada* robes, prostrated himself as he chanted, "*Oga*, please help." *Oga* was pidgin speak for Boss. My father was incorruptible. He steadfastly refused to accept bribes. He was an ironist in a country of literalists. In Nigeria, graft and thievery by government officials is as commonplace as pregnant women screaming in a maternity ward.

I return home from school one day eager to tell my father about my adventures at school, but I cannot. My father, the entomologist, has captured another insect. He returns home with his conquest. As the cricket chirps and flaps around him, I make myself disappear and go seek out some of my friends.

As I grew older, I found myself hurting for my mother and for Nana's wives, women married to faithless men, women who bore the burden of marriage like a hunchback dragging his hump. My mother reminded me of Mrs. Alving from Ibsen's *Ghosts*, that long-suffering woman who stuck to her philandering husband, Captain Alving, until the very end. The poets say that love will light up a person's world. But I tell you that they lie. Love did not light up my mother's world. If love shed any light at all on her world, the light that it threw was crepuscular. It was a light that did not make my mother's heart soar or her tired body levitate. The effect that love had on my mother was carbuncular. It left her with sore knees and aching toes.

I thought of marital abuse as an elemental substance, imagined it to be something heavier than a piece of Uluru rock, something you could place on a scale to see how much it really weighed. I wondered if the weight of physical abuse was equivalent to or more than that of emotional abuse. Since my mother must have intuited that my father was not faithful to her, did she suffer as much as Nana's wives? Did she cry silently in the night while her children slept, while they dreamed of blazing sunsets?

Coat hanger

When they found her body, she had a coat hanger sticking out from between her legs.

She was thirteen.

Or fourteen.

Or fifteen.

Who knew exactly how old? What did it matter anyway? I thought she was probably younger than fifteen because she was in her third year in secondary school. I did not know her in person but I heard about her story after she died and it filled me with sadness. Sadness so heavy it was like trekking to the end of the world with an elephant strapped on your back. The fact that I did not know the girl made it even worse. I found myself thinking of her as the girl with the coat hanger. And each time I thought of her thus, I felt a sense of dejection as if I had defiled her memory.

I heard about her story from a classmate who was a neighbor of hers. Mercy lived with her father and stepmother near my classmate's house. A neighbor, an older man had set his eyes on her and began to buy her gifts. The girl who was from a poor family, succumbed to the man's advances, allowing her affection to be won with small gifts and small kindnesses. One day he lures the girl to his home while his wife is away and has sex with her.

When the girl becomes pregnant, she is terrified of having her parents find out what she has done. Being an unwed mother would bring shame on her family. She cannot face the wrath of her family. What she does next would spell doom for her. She finds a quack, a local man who promises a quick solution. The man performs the abortion on her using a coat hanger. She does not survive. When she begins to bleed heavily, he flees in panic. She manages to crawl from the small wooden shack where he had performed the procedure. She crawls into the street, dragging her life with her while her death mocks her from behind. When they find her, it is too late. She has hemorrhaged her life away, angry serpents of blood trailing through the timothy grass.

Each time I walked past the girl's house, I remembered her. This unknown child woman who died before the earth was ready to claim her. Her family compound became overgrown with weeds. Strange flowers bloomed and taunted the eyes like adulteresses. They said that laughter took flight from her parents' house the day that she died and never returned. People said that her parents, traumatized by their only child's death had lost interest in living. The man stopped going to his farm and the woman stopped going to the market. The couple survived on the yams and cassava that they planted in their garden next to their home. They said that the man and his wife retreated from the world that had wounded them so much.

But I never met Mercy. She who was so ill-named by her parents and so ill-treated by fate. I wonder if she foresaw her own death, if she realized that she would likely not survive the botched surgery. Was Mercy like Agamemnon who foresaw his own death at the hands of his wife, Clytemnestra? Since Mercy could not choose the course of her life, perhaps she had decided to choose the course of her death.

Although I knew about Mercy's death, I did not know much about her life. And what I knew of her life was shaped by other people's tongues, fragments around late night fires, hushed whispers in smoke-tinged midnights. In the village, the story told by the griot is often not as important as the magic of the griot. A good storyteller is the one who is able to weave magic and keep his audience enraptured. They shake when his voice shakes, they jump when he trembles with emotion. Stories are the diet on which people live. They provide food for the hungry, add color to the quotidian and texture to the banal. Thus village life is a constant interplay of construct and deconstruct, polemic and anecdote finely balanced on counterpoint, resonance and dissonance intricately melded at spear point.

On many a night when I go to sleep, I think of the girl with the coat hanger. Her story reminds me of just how cheap death is in Nigeria. In Nigeria, people do not usually die of sophisticated diseases, they die extraordinarily ordinary deaths. People die of gangrene and undiagnosed diabetes. They die of malnutrition and ulcers. They die of malaria and typhoid. They die of lack of knowledge. Death is a commodity that is always on the shelf, always being peddled at a steep discount, at 50 percent off of the marked price.

Growing up, death filled my nostrils and my eyes and my ears.

I went to sleep terrified of dying.

And I woke up terrified of living.

The house of sin

For just twenty-five cents, you could sleep with a prostitute for half an hour. Twenty five naira was the equivalent of twenty five cents. It didn't matter that you were only twelve years old. Nor did it matter that the prostitute or *ashawo* as they were commonly known was three or four times your age. The house of sin was on Hill Street in Agbor, a short walk from Lagos Benin Road where I caught the bus to school, on days when I had bus fare.

I am fascinated as I walk past the brothel. It is a large compound with three houses. There is a syphilitic white wall that shields the buildings from prying eyes. The wall is full of graffiti scrawled with chalk or scratched with pebbles. The graffiti is lubricious, the product of the fevered imaginations of oversexed adolescents. Scrawled on the wall are phrases like *"toto is good for boys and girls," "ashawo kobo kobo" "Toto"'* is pidgin speak for vagina and *ashawo kobo kobo* simply means "cheap prostitute." The front entrance is an open doorway without a door and this is the entry to damnation, the path to iniquity.

The road in front of the brothel is always wet and muddy. This is because the women routinely toss out buckets of water used for washing themselves after servicing each customer. Not all of them do this, of course. The less pretentious ones chose to forego these ablutions and carry around amatory fluids and odors.

The prostitutes do not like to stay confined in their compound because is easier to peddle their wares outside of the compound. It is easier to snare new customers who are passing by. So they emerge like tragediennes in short skirts, wrappers and maquillage, lips blood red, eyes full of spite and sin. They stand arms akimbo, daring any virile man to pass by without staring, challenging any man who cursed at them to come in to prove his manhood. They sit on tall wooden stools, legs spread apart, vaginas on display like fruit at Boji Boji market.

At times when school boys walk by, they call the women names. The women chase the boys around with pails of dirty water that they have used for washing their private parts, hurling the water at the boys who run and yelp in excitement.

One of their oft-repeated lines is, *"ashawo* no be work, na management." This is pidgin speak for, "prostitution is not a career, it's just a hustle."

Men buzz around the house like fruit flies, drawn by the smell of sex which is as thick as a soldier's boot. They argue, they curse, they laugh, they smoke. I am amazed at their boldness. Didn't they worry about their wives finding them here? Every now and then, a patron allows himself to be cajoled into the house and he disappears through the doorway, to emerge later.

Whenever I caught a bus back home from school, I made it a point to pass by the house of sin. My friends and I were curious to see the goings-on inside the house. Having done enough studies of the human anatomy at school, we were eager to put our knowledge to use. We had no desire to become masters of the universe, we simply wanted to be masters of fornication. We discuss this subject one day on our way back from school.

THE COLLECTOR OF BUTTERFLIES AND WOMEN

"You think they will let us do it?" George, a classmate asks me.

I stare at him wondering if he has lost his mind. "Of course, they won't. Who wants to sleep with a kid?"

George, a skinny boy with sallow skin and a pockmarked face was not lacking in confidence. "I think they will. I've heard that they do children, as long you have money."

I shake my head, unconvinced.

"Want to bet?"

"No."

Weeks later, George would work up enough courage to enter the brothel, after saving enough of his pocket money. He recounts the story of his sexual encounter to me the day after.

George walks boldly into the brothel dressed in his Sunday best, wearing his father's tie and hat. "The tie and hat made me look older, you know."

I stare at him in wonderment.

"Small boy, what're you doing here? Looking for your mama?" One of the hookers demands upon sighting George.

"I can pay."

"Pay for what?"

"*Toto*"

The hookers erupt in laughter when they hear this. They gather around George, fascinated by this twelve year old boy who is bold enough to walk into a brothel looking for sex. George takes out his crumpled, greasy *Naira* bills. He clenches them in his palm. He does not look at the floor. He does not look straight ahead. He does not look at the wall. George stares the prostitutes in the eye, women his mother's age, his grandmother's age, he stares them in the eye one after the other.

One of the women steps forward and offers to take George up on his offer. George is concerned, worried that the woman might take his money and then send him off with a slap on his face. These hard-bitten women are a tough lot for whom violence comes as naturally as twitching a muscle.

The woman takes George into a dimly lit room. Behind the mismatched couple, the women cackle with laughter. The woman tells George to undress. As if in a soporific haze (he describes this as 'slow motion.') George undresses. The prostitute yanks down her short skirt, sits on the edge of the tiny bed and urges George to come on.

George mounts the woman, his penis at half-mast, unable to penetrate. She scolds him for this.

"*Oya*, don't waste my time." *Oya* means, 'come on'

Embarrassed and perturbed, George watches his penis droop even lower.

George is about to call the whole thing off but the woman decides to help him out. She grabs his penis between her callused hands, strokes it vigorously until he feels like the skin is about to peel off like a snake molting like corn being shucked until he becomes hard partly out of terror and shame and partly out of excitement. The way George tells it, he takes over at this juncture and proceeds to pound the woman mercilessly for an hour before departing.

"You should have seen her walk when I left." He crowed. "She was walking funny. I put the hurt on her."

I believed George's story until the part about screwing the prostitute for an hour. Especially since George had told me earlier that the money he had was good for just half an hour. I suspect that George, swollen like a fruit with lust, exploded into the woman as soon as he climbed on top of her. I suspect that the mating took one minute and not one hour. But I was not looking to hurt George's feelings, so I held my peace.

Another friend of ours, Ibe, who heard George's story, would decide to also visit the house of sin. His experience was different from George's. Ibe recited how the experience of carnality turned out to be less than what he had expected.

THE COLLECTOR OF BUTTERFLIES AND WOMEN

"She smelled bad." He wrinkled his nose in disgust. Ibe told me that the prostitute he picked had not cleaned herself after her last customer. I asked why he chose her and he gave me an answer that was positively Freudian. "She looks just like Miss Rosemarie."

Miss Rosemarie was our English teacher in secondary school. She of the elongated vowels, the ellipses, the syllogisms and the neologisms. She who wore sandals with her tiny strangled ankles peeking out from below wide trousers. She who visited the feverish dreams of her pupils many a night and left them panting in unrequited desire.

It turns out that the prostitute Ibe named Miss Rosemarie was reading a newspaper all the while he was on top of her, sweating and heaving like a consumptive whale.

"Can you believe it?" He looked disgusted.

I listened politely. I had become the curator of sexual maladies.

A few months later, a panicked Ibe summons me to the bush behind his parents' house. He has something to show me. He drops his pants and whips out his penis. I am horrified. Right there, in the middle of his penis is a sore. A pullulating, suppurating sore. Ibe has caught a disease. An exotic disease. Syphilis, Chlamydia, herpes? We had no idea. Although Ibe was later forced to tell his parents about his condition, he never told them about the source of the disease.

Ibe's parents decided that a witch, likely a neighbor, had put a spell on Ibe. Instead of taking him to the hospital, they took him to a medicine man. The medicine man bathed Ibe in a cleansing ritual and pronounced him healed.

If Ibe is not dead yet, he is likely still walking around with syphilis, Chlamydia or an even more sophisticated disease.

I remember many other incidents that occurred at the house of sin.

A woman caught her husband, a local pastor, at the brothel. Unbeknownst to him, she had followed him to the compound one night. She found him *flagrante delicto* as he humped away. She launched a fusillade of punches on him and dragged him out of the house of sin with his trousers around his ankles. She was said to be a big-boned woman with a quick temper.

One year, a strange thing happened at the house of sin. A woman from Ghana moved into the compound and profits went up soon after. Madam Ghana, as she was known, had a unique attribute that made her a big draw and the main attraction at the house of sin. She had a full beard which she refused to shave off. Despite her facial hair, the rest of her body was loudly feminine, big breasts, wide hips, and big buttocks.

Men were attracted to her because they wanted to confirm that she was really a woman. The word on the street was that she did not disappoint. It was said that when Madam Ghana had sex with a man she drove him to the edge of madness and quite often he never returned. He literally lost his mind. She was like a year old palm wine, full of yeast and madness. They said that her screams as she made love could be heard within a mile radius by the wretched wives whose husbands she had seduced.

I always wondered what it would be like to have sex with one of the women at the house of sin but I could never work up the nerve. There was a part of me that objected to communal or pecuniary sex. At twelve, my vision of sex was chaste, unsoiled. My ideals about sex were rooted in aestheticism rather than exoticism. But time would soon rob me of such illusions.

My innocence, whatever was left of it, was soon to be lost.

Matthias the cannibal

Nightfall belongs to the rats.
They wake us up in the middle of the night, squealing and screeching like crazed bats. I chase after them with a big stick, banging on walls and furniture, spraying rat blood everywhere. My sisters, all four of them, shriek. Terrified, they jump on top of beds, chairs, anything they can find, trying to levitate, trying to get out of the rats' way. I am the man in the house. The only man in the house. It is my duty to kill the vermin.

We are alone in the house. My father is in Mecca on pilgrimage to the Holy Land. My mother is in the village. We are expecting her to arrive in a few days. Until she arrives, I will have to fend for my siblings.

When my sister, Saffy, develops a tapeworm infection, it is my responsibility to calm her nerves. She is ten years old, soft-spoken, with my mother's olive complexion.

For a child in Nigeria, a tapeworm infection can be the most terrifying thing to happen in one's life. As she squats on the ground, I watch the tape worms coming out of her anus. She is screaming in horror. She leaps up from her position and begins to run, with a long tapeworm dangling out of her backside like undigested spaghetti.

"Stop running!" I yell at her. "Just stay still and let it come out."

But Saffy doesn't stop running. Even though she cannot outrun the intruders that have laid siege to her intestines. I chase after her, catch her and make her seat down.

"Close your eyes."

She does.

"Now, let them out."

Eyes firmly shut, Saffy strains to let the worms out of her. The creatures are the color of uncooked pasta, slimy and sickly. They wriggle as they emerge and land on the sand. I am filled with horror and anger. I stamp on them and crush them, splay them open, watch the whitish discharge spread on the sand, watch them try to escape, crawl, crawl, but there is no escape for these invaders, no escape as I grind them into the earth, my stomach turning, my sister again howling, my feet smelling like shit,

smelling like shit

smelling like shit.

I knew exactly how Saffy became host to the slimy creatures.

If you ate food or drank water that contained tapeworm larva, the larva developed into adult tapeworms inside your body. The fully formed tapeworms then settled in the intestines. An adult tapeworm has a head, neck, and a segmented body, that is like a chain. The segments of each chain are called proglottids. When you have an intestinal infection, the tapeworm's head clamps on to the wall of your intestine and the proglottids grow and produce eggs. An adult tapeworm can survive for nearly twenty years inside your body.

We live in a village called Urhonigbe, less than an hour from Benin City, the capital of Bendel State. Nights in Urhonigbe are long, the longest in the whole world. Darkness strikes like the claw of a hammer. It comes swiftly, sneaking up on us like the second arrival of the son of Joseph. At dawn, it leaves like a covetous lover, slowly, lingeringly. The village is dotted with mud and brick houses. At night,

THE COLLECTOR OF BUTTERFLIES AND WOMEN

when it is pitch dark, the houses look abandoned like the corpses of an army that has tasted defeat. At night you can hear the sad hoots of owls carrying longing in their breasts. Chickens squawk and goats bleat outside mud houses, seeking admittance into the family hearth. The town fills me with a primordial horror at night.

There is a main road which runs through the town from one end to the other. The road cuts through the busy market where traders sell yams, cassava, palm oil and assorted goods. Next to the market is the village shrine. It is an ochre red building baked out of mud and the toil of acolytes. The main feature of the shrine is a giant iroko tree with hump-backed roots that rise from the earth like malignant tumors. Every day, worshippers attired in flowing red and white gowns congregate to serve *Ogun*, the god of iron and war. They bring goats, yards of cloth, cowrie shells, palm oil and the strange fever of the possessed.

They whirl and twirl, these dervishes, these mendicants at the feet of a pot-bellied deity. Their supplications rise with the tendrils of smoke from an open fire that is always burning at the shrine. They dance on bare feet, moving the earth, these dancers. They dance this dance of incoherence and mellifluousness, stopping the world with the flywhisk, only to restart it with the maracas.

My father was the registrar at the magistrate court in town. I had not yet figured out exactly what a court registrar did. I imagined that he was a man of high station, a man of letters whose job was the recordation of things essential. But I didn't know this for a fact. My father leaves home dressed in a suit and tie every day. He looks very important. Although his shoes are polished, the leather is as wrinkled as the face of an aging Hollywood actress, before the miracle of the surgeon's knife. He walks with a lofty air, my father, the keeper of secrets forbidden to the uninitiated, available only to the cognoscenti.

Matthias is one of my father's friends. He first met my father at the courthouse when he was involved in some civil dispute. The two men soon become good friends. Matthias comes to visit often. He is a kind-hearted man who always brings us gifts, especially our favorite candy. He is generous to a fault.

He is a short jovial man with the stiff military bearing of a general. He has a bushy mustache that looks as if a tarantula crawled on his upper lip and died there. He is a great raconteur. Like the best storytellers, he is a man who enjoys his own jokes. He would hold his sides after telling what he believes to be a great joke and laugh until you thought he would fall over and drop dead. He has a laugh that is a cross between a bark and a choke. When Matthias got that laugh going, you didn't know if to hand him Kleenex or if to do the Heimlich maneuver.

Matthias is a cannibal.

He told us this himself. It happened during the Nigeria Biafran civil war when Nigeria convulsed with internecine violence. During the war, Matthias who fought on the side of the Biafran rebels, found himself trapped in a village, hiding out from the Nigerian soldiers who were conducting a painstaking search to root out rebels. After a week in their hide-out, the rebels had exhausted their meager food supplies but they couldn't dare to leave their hide-out to search for food. They faced a tough choice. They could stay put and die or they could eat some of the rotting bodies that were nearby.

"It wasn't a very difficult choice for us." Matthias told us in blithe tones. "The tough part was depersonalizing the corpses. Not thinking of them as sons, fathers, mothers, or children. Just meat."

I am horrified as I listen to him.

My father tries to change the subject, but Matthias, will not let go. He is a dog that has found a bone, a leper scratching a sore. He is not a man given to the elliptic or cryptic. He is a man of declamations and explications.

"The meat is a little tough." He tells us. "Well, not all the way. Depends on the piece that you eat and how long you roast it for. The leg is tough, the mid-section and thighs are softer. The breasts were the best part in women."

In spite of my revulsion, I find myself asking, "You cooked a woman?"

Matthias smiles at me benevolently. "Many women. And men. There were corpses near our hide-out. We ate several of the corpses. The tough part was taking off the boots. You have to understand that these corpses had been in the sun for days. Swollen like ripe fruit, some burst open when you touched them. We cut the clothes off, but the boots took a while to get off. Some we had to cut the feet off with the boots still in them. The women were prostitutes who followed the soldiers around to the war front. Such women made a lot of money in those days.

"You know the funny thing? We all said the grace before we ate the meat. Many of us were devout Catholics. Went to mass. Took communion. A lot of the bodies were useless, already rotted. Couldn't do anything with them. Even the fire couldn't burn off the smell and the maggots. The freshly dead ones were better. Some of the men refused to eat young children. But me, I harbored no such reluctance. Maybe because I had no children of my own back then. Maybe because I was just bloody hungry. I ate a boy no older than twelve."

Matthias stares at me pointedly when he says this. He seems to enjoy my discomfort.

"You going to ask me how he tasted?"

My mouth is dry. I do not utter a word.

"Just like pork. A little tougher. More like monkey meat."

The room is so still I can hear myself breath. It is as if the world itself is holding its breath as we listen to Matthias' ghoulish tale. I wait for him to clap his hands and announce with false contrition that he has merely been joking. But I know that the tale which he tells is true. I have heard snippets of it before, told one night while we sat outside watching the stars chase each other around in the firmament.

"If it's any consolation, we did not eat any of our fellow rebel soldiers. We only ate the federals. Hunger can make a man do strange things."

A few weeks before my father departed for Mecca, Matthias showed up at our house in the middle of the night. We had just finished dinner when we heard the pounding at the door. The man at the door does not wait for anyone to answer before he screams, "It's Matthias! Please open the door!"

My father opens the door. My mother emerges from the kitchen where she has been putting away the remnants of dinner. Curious, my sisters and I enter the living room. When the door swings open, what I see is a shadow of the storyteller that I have known for nearly a year. His eyes look haunted, his face harried. He has undergone a transformation that is complete, turned into a creature utterly shrunken with fear.

Matthias collapses into a threadbare sofa. "Water. Please. I need water."

I go into the kitchen to get him a glass of water.

And once again, I find myself captivated by Matthias's tale.

"I didn't see him." He shook his head ruefully. I swear, I didn't"

My father urges him to calm down. "What happened?"

Matthias had been involved in a car accident. Matthias was driving home that night in his yellow Volkswagen beetle when he ran into a young street hawker. The hawker had sprinted across the road at the last minute as the headlights bore down on him. Like an indecisive roebuck, he stopped in the middle of the road for one moment too long. The impact damaged the front of the car.

"Is the kid dead?' My father asks.

"I don't know. I had to run. They were going to lynch me."

In Nigeria, it is not uncommon for a man involved in a fatal car crash to be beaten to death or near death by an angry mob. The survivor of such a crash is always at fault, as if the mere fact of his survival is an indictment, the evidence of his culpability. This in itself presents no surprise since the society is one that is founded on superstition and the unseen hand. People do not die by natural causes. There is always a sinister force at work, a dark-hearted malefactor. An evil witch. A jealous relative. A vindictive enemy. It made sense then that a society used to pointing the finger of blame would blame the driver who could not swerve fast enough to miss the unlucky hawker.

Matthias had stopped to check on the injured youth when a crowd began to form around him. As the crowd grew in numbers, so did its intensity and its malady. The rabid crowd yelled at Matthias, called him names and glowered at him. Knowing what fate awaited him if he stuck around, Matthias, jumped in his car and ran for his life.

My father urged him to turn himself in at the police station the next day. I don't know if the young boy Matthias hit with his car survived or died. I don't know if Matthias ever turned himself in, or if he chose to let the ghost of the boy haunt him for the rest of his life like all the other ghosts that he kept locked in the rusted cabinetry in his head.

My neighbor's wife

The second time I saw a woman's vagina, I was twelve years old. The woman was a neighbor's wife, a corpulent, cheerful woman who looked like she had just stepped out of the imagination of Peter Paul Rubens, the Flemish painter. Her husband worked for the local utility company and every morning at the same time, she liked to take baths.

The trick was to time her correctly.

I had always been curious about sex and the human anatomy. I was ten or eleven years old when I first read DH Lawrence's *Lady Chatterly's Lover* and Gustave Flaubert's *Madame Bovary*. I waded through the dense prose, entranced by forbidden sex, immorality and debauchery. The smell of sex burned through the pages and lit up my young imagination.

So I waited for Angelina to take her shower. Next to the house where we lived, there were two makeshift structures. The first one was made of brick and it contained two stalls; the men's shower and the female shower. It had an open doorway. Before taking a bath, you simply draped a piece of cloth across this doorway. There was a length of wood provided for just this purpose that was mounted at

THE COLLECTOR OF BUTTERFLIES AND WOMEN

the top of the doorway. The cloth provided privacy from prying eyes. When you were done with your bath, you retrieved your cloth and the next person who came along had to bring their own cloth.

Fights broke out on several occasions when impatient tenants got tired of waiting for their turn to use the bathroom. The bath room itself is a dreadful affair. You place a bucket of water in front of you, with a small pail inside for scooping water onto your body. You lift yourself up on a brick whose sole purpose is to prevent the muddy water and grass on the ground from touching your ankles. The water you are about to use comes from a well or rain water and is full of mosquito larvae and tadpoles. If you are lucky, you have had time to heat up the water in a firewood stove in order to get a warm bath. If you are in a hurry and are unlucky, you bathe with cold water. The water hits your skin with a purgatorial vengeance. You wince in pain and soldier on bravely.

I knew of some kids in my school who had decided to permanently forego cold showers. They showed up at school with a stench that hit like a fist to the gut, a smell that threatened to knock you off your feet.

Angelina takes her bucket of water and walks to the bathroom with a towel draped around her neck. As she waddles, her ample buttocks jiggle. Her hair is tightly imprisoned in a nylon scarf but strands of obstinate hair poke out cheerily. I watch her through the window of our two room apartment as I get dressed for school. She walks into the bathroom, puts down her bucket. Takes the towel from her neck and hangs it over the entrance of the bathroom. She steps back and undresses.

But I do not see her. She is standing in a corner of the bathroom, out of my covetous view.

I am frustrated, excited, holding my breath, and when I expel air at last, I am taking fish breaths, quick breaths, eyes wide open like a surprised mackerel.

She hangs the length of cloth known locally as a *'wrapper'* over the doorway and removes the towel. She hangs the towel as well.

Angelina begins to bathe.

I measure out a lifetime in each scoop of water that she takes. It takes several lifetimes but finally she is done. I step closer, put my head on the metal grate on the window. I can barely breathe.

She lifts the curtain…I mean, the cloth and my breath catches in my throat. I forget how to breathe. Her skin is like a copper penny, as smooth as the trickster's tongue. I stare at her big stomach. She is not pregnant. I stare at her breasts. They are the size of cassava yams after a fruitful harvest. The nipples are elongated, surrounded by dark areolas that are like stray islands in a restless sea. And then my eyes drift down to her thighs and the valley between. I wonder how anyone can have so much hair between their legs. Surely, it could not be possible? Angelina had not yielded herself to the ministrations of the scissors.

Angelina, pilferer of my overwrought, adolescent, soul.

The second structure adjacent to the house is the toilet. This structure is made out of zinc on all four sides. There are two stalls, one for females and the other for males. The floor is constructed from pieces of timber lashed together with a square gap left in the middle. This gap is what you squatted over and defecated into. As you defecate, you can hear the lumps of shit hitting the thousands of other shits below, forming one giant shit mountain rumbling below the earth. Quite often, someone missed the hole and sprayed or "cannon-balled" shit on the wall like the impressionist painters Edourad Manet or Claude Monet. I thought of it as expressionist shit art or "shat.

The smell from the open hole is worse than Lucifer's breath. As you shit, flies buzz around you, producing a symphony that rivals Mahler's Symphony No 9. At times, pale maggots crawl up triumphantly, apocalyptically from the fetid dump and slither across the wood floor. Every once in a while, the landlord would schedule a contractor to dump acid or some sulfurous chemical down the hole. This only aggravated the stench. I thought of this as setting shit, literally, on fire.

Some of our neighbors had it even worse. Instead of shitting into a deep hole in the ground like we did, they used a shit bucket. A shit bucket is a very large aluminum bucket that is placed below ground. Once a week, when it was full, a shit carrier known as an *agbekpo,* stopped by to pick up the shit bucket. He replaces the bucket with an empty bucket and takes away the old one that is full of shit. As the *agbekpo* hauls away the communal filth, an unappeasable smell trails him like napalm. The smell scorches the nostrils, sets the lungs on fire, roils the insides.

As the *agbekpo* departs, he is often mocked by a gaggle of kids. We chase after him and cuss at him for his stink. We throw pebbles at him. He curses back, wishing sudden death on us and our parents. Shit carriers usually scheduled their visits for late at night or early in the morning. It was of no avail. The kids could always tell when the *agbekpo* was around. The smell chased us out of beds or our morning chores and we went running down the street, chasing the poor wretch and his burden.

The *Agbekpo* had the lowest job on earth. His lot was worse than the gravediggers and the water fetchers and the wood hewers and the beggars and the men who washed women's clothes for a living and the prostitutes on Hill Street who stared at you with blank eyes measuring the size of your dick and the size of your wallet at the same time. He was simply a beast of burden. His existence was cheap, a two dollar hand job in a massage parlor, a wasted metaphor tossed by a drunk scribbler. He was a man created too late, created by God on Saturday night when God was getting tired and ready to rest. The merchant of doo doo was nothing but God's doodle.

Like the bathrooms, fights often erupt over the right to use the toilet. The building houses five families all boxed into two room apartments. Baba Ajayi lives next door with his wife and uncountable children. Mama Esther lives in the apartment across from us. Her daughter, Esther, is in her late twenties, unmarried, a sad-eyed woman recently jilted by the man to whom she was affianced. Two other families occupy the remaining two apartments, but their stay is transitory. For a reason unknown to me, the tenants in these last two apartments never stayed for more than a year or two before moving out. Someone said that there was an evil spirit roaming the two apartments.

We live like rabbits in a nest, practically on top of each other. We hear when the neighbors fuck or fight and when our parents and guardians fuck or fight. We hear babies being delivered and victories being celebrated. We are present at the moments of anguish, of which there are many and the moments of triumph, of which there are few.

One day, Baba Ajayi, who is reputed to be a powerful medicine man threatens to use *magun* on one of the neighbors because the said neighbor was taking too long to take a shit. *Magun* is an evil spell that supposedly leads to death or perdition for the victim on whom the spell is cast.

Baba Ajayi is a tall, craggy man with a face as uninteresting as safe sex. If he was a building, he would be a cathedral, all hollows and crevices, full of secrets. Today he is pressed. He stands at the entrance of the toilet while the neighbor is in his most private moment, yelling at him, and wishing death and impotence upon his family. All this time, Baba Ajayi is switching his weight from foot to foot, doing a jig that would rival Chuck Berry.

He pounds on the zinc door.

"Come out, you son of a dog!"

After a while, the man inside the latrine emerges. The two men grapple with each other briefly, but Baba Ajayi is in no mood for a

THE COLLECTOR OF BUTTERFLIES AND WOMEN

fight. He is pregnant with a biological storm that is about to erupt. He disengages and heads for the latrine, still cursing at the neighbor.

Whenever I used the latrine, I was in mortal fear of falling into the pit. I imagined the hole below as an organism, a fevered hungry creature with a gaping maw. I imagined the wood underneath my feet giving way and my body tumbling through the maw into a Nietzschean abyss and centuries of putridity.

I had heard stories about young girls who delivered their babies into these pit latrines. These wretches had hidden their pregnancies from their families, terrified of the consequences. A girl who delivered a baby out of wedlock had committed an abomination and faced stiff punishment. Punishment ranged from a brutal beating administered generously by family members to ostracism and disownment.

I heard the story of a young girl whose baby survived. A suspicious neighbor heard the young mother screaming in pain as the baby was being born. The neighbor summoned help. The villagers who showed up could hear the baby's faint cries from below. Wielding axes, they quickly broke through the wood floor and fished out the baby using a bucket tied with a length of rope. When they rescued the innocent, her body, mouth and nose were completely covered in feces and maggots. They crawled over her like jellyfish. Like napalm, the feces had burned her skin. It was a miracle that she survived. It took months for the child to recover from her ordeal.

On the floor of our pit latrine is a metal bucket that is designed for collecting newspapers, cloth and leaves. Even in the abject filth of the toilet stall, there is a certain social order at work, a stratification along class lines. The bucket tells it all. The message is this; although we are all poor, some are poorer than others. Even among the poor, there are classes; the upper class poor, the middle class poor, and the lower class poor.

The upper class poor used toilet paper to wipe their behinds, the middle class poor used newspapers, and the lower class poor used leaves or stray rags of cloth. The idea was to not clog up the latrine's hole by dumping in objects that would quickly fill it up. Papa Iyabo, the landlord was very firm on this point. He inspected the shit bucket regularly with the fastidious eye of an empiricist, nodding his approval or clucking disappointment if the bucket was not used as often as it should.

Papa Iyabo was a squat man with a bulbous nose and the twinkling eyes of a lecher. He was kind to young children, especially to young girls. He had impregnated three underage girls and married each one of them after presenting the bride's family with a hefty dowry. The joke was that if a potential renter had young daughters, they stood a good chance that the landlord would rent them an apartment. Lacking the gift of discernment, many young daughters found themselves being pawed by the landlord while their parents were away at work. Papa Iyabo was a jolly old Santa Claus but you had to keep your eyes on his hands at all times, if you were a sensible parent.

Some sick bastard had decided to poke holes in the zinc wall separating the men's latrine from the women's latrine. The lecher's hope was to gaze through these peepholes at women while they were conducting their daily rites. I was quite intrigued by the ingenuity of this character, whoever they might be. While I acknowledged that the person was obviously debased, I wholeheartedly applauded their inventiveness. Often, I found myself teetering on my toes, butt sticking in the air, while I peeped through that hole.

But I never saw any flesh.

Nothing worth seeing anyway.

I never saw any of Baba Ajayi's nubile daughters or Esther or Angelina. What I usually saw was this: a hunched shoulder, a lowered head, a leg covered by cloth. It occurred to me that the peephole needed to be bigger but the lecher who created it in the first place had apparently abandoned the task. I lacked the courage, will, or moral turpitude to attempt to expand on his work. It takes a lot of work to be a pervert.

"Are you day-dreaming again? You're going to be late for school." This was the voice of Mama Dede, my guardian.

I snap out of my daydream, grab my school bag and rush out the door to make the four mile trek to school.

That night, while her husband is asleep, Angelina sneaks into my room and I hold her in my arms for the first time. I rub her soft skin against mine and let her warm breath fan my face. I squeeze her big breasts against my chest. Move my hand along the flatlands of her back all the way down to the twin peaks of her buttocks. She moans like a surprised animal, wraps her legs tight around my thighs. Without warning, her husband appears in the room. His face is rigid with anger as he lights a match and hurls it at us. The room erupts into smoke.

I wake up in a panic, sweat pouring from my body, looking for smoke. But there is none. A few months later, I would be nearly burned to death, in a real fire.

I will tell you how it happened. Be patient.

A beating, a burning, and an execution

The year I turned fourteen, I witness three singular incidents that would be stitched in my memory for the rest of that year. The first was a beating, the second was a burning and the third was an execution. The first incident involved a woman, the second involved a man and the third involved a group of men. All three incidents involved a death or a near death. I was hawking fish when the first incident took place.

Although I was hawking fish on this particular day, I did not always sell fish. I occasionally hawked old newspapers to traders at Boji Boji market. They used the newspapers to wrap fish, bean curd, known as *akara*, vegetables and various other food items. I appropriated the old newspapers that my father or neighbors discarded. I salvaged newspapers from dumpsters, stacked them on a tray and sold them for pennies. With my proceeds, I would buy myself second hand clothes, known as *okirika*.

Boji Boji market was a strange place, a locus of the dead and the living. It was said that restless, rootless spirits roamed the market, seeking to do commerce with the living. They said that men who were gifted with the 'third eye,' who could communicate with the dead, had the ability to see these ghostly beings as they flitted mournfully among the living.

Like most markets in Nigeria, Boji Boji market was an open air market. Market women attired in colorful wrappers, known as *lappas* sit on backless stools plying their wares. Yams, tomatoes, *garri*, meat and spices are laid out on tables or on the ground. Haggling is conducted vigorously, at times with a curse, at times with a laugh. Each trader lays claim to a small section which is blocked off by a wooden fence. These fences all interconnect, as if they are children holding hands dancing. Often fights break out between two traders involved in a turf battle. When this happens, people surround the combatants, cheering them on or coaxing them to stop. Carefree children laugh and play in the mud that runs through the market like a fever while careworn parents try to corral them.

Rain is cruel to Boji Boji market and the traders. When it rains, puddles of water collect in the maws of the earth as if the earth were gargling, showing its broken teeth. Since each trader's stall is uncovered and unprotected from the elements, the wind snatches the traders' wares as it blows by, howling and mocking their cries of anguish.

The smell of rotten meat mixes with the smell of desperate unwashed bodies and raw meat. The smell is heady, acidic, strangely excitatory yet repulsive.

In Boji Boji market, you can buy death or life for the right price. You can buy a blessing or a curse, herbs that can cure you or ones that can kill you. If your child is sick, you can buy herbs to cure their sickness. If you buy from the right trader, the herb will cure your child's ailment. If you buy the wrong herb from the wrong trader, the herb can kill your child. The year before, a woman bought some wild mushrooms from the market to prepare soup for her family. What she did not know was that this particular mushroom was the poisonous kind. After they ate the soup, the woman and her husband along with her four children never woke up from sleep.

The beating

When I see the woman, she is howling in pain, dishabille. What drew me toward the small crowd gathered around her was her screaming and her pleas. It had been a successful day for me. I had sold most of the fish that I went to the market to sell. I was getting ready to leave for the day when I happened upon the scene.

She is in her early twenties, a tall, slender woman, a palm frond, swaying gently against the bloodthirsty crowd that has gathered around her. She is pretty with big almond eyes and a surprised expression. She is flinging her arms in the air, waving away the hands that are trying to grab her, to rip her clothing to shreds.

"Thief!"

"Beat her! Beat the thief!"

I realize then what the crowd is accusing the woman of. I realize just how much trouble the woman is in. My first instinct is to help her, to save the woman, guilty or not. Having seen mob beatings before, I knew that it didn't matter if you were guilty or not. What mattered was what the crowd believed. If the crowd believed that you were guilty, you could get beaten to an inch of your life, or simply killed.

I wonder what the woman was accused of stealing. I wonder who her original accuser was.

The woman's blouse has been ripped to pieces. Her breasts are exposed. Her breasts are the breasts of a young woman, a woman who hasn't nursed a child. The nipples point in the air, black areolas spread on her light skin like stains. Despite myself, I am aroused. And then I am immediately disgusted at myself for the carnality of my response, the corporeality of it.

"I am not a thief. I didn't take anything!" the woman protests. Her voice is hollow, strangled, vocal chords shriveled by panic. The mob, full of froth and froideur, is not impressed. The ringleaders press forward, grab the woman and begin to undress her.

The air is toxic and intoxicating all at once. It is as if it has congealed, formed a gelatinous blob around the mob which is itself caught in a time warp, preparing to mete out punishment as a formless, bodiless mass.

I hear the exhalation of the crowd. The crowd is breathing in unison, waiting for the kill. I think of a pack of hyenas circling a fallen prey, cackling in maniacal laughter, teeth bared. Sharks chasing the scent of spilled blood. Saint Telemachus stoned to death by an angry mob for trying to stop gladiators from fighting each other in the Roman amphitheater.

I imagine myself saving the woman.

I step forward. I put up a hand and yell at the crowd to stop. The woman stares at me with eyes full of relief. The crowd stares at me with hostility. "Get away from here, little boy!" A man barks at me. I ignore him. I grab the woman by the arm and lead her past the crowd. Past its madness that is raging like tuberculosis, past its sinister anticipation that is running like diarrhea.

But I lie.

I do no such thing.

I do not have the courage.

Instead, I stand silently, my insides turning to mush as the woman is being savaged, as the crowd whips itself into a frenzy, as the divertissement continues.

A stocky man with a bull neck and broken teeth steps forward. He grabs the woman by the neck and slaps her hard.

The crowd squeals in delight.

"Beat her! Beat her"

The woman's head drops. She screams in pain and fear. The man slaps her again. Harder. "You thief! You know what we do to thieves in this town?"

The woman cannot answer. She is wriggling, twisting, trying to be free of his iron grip, but her effort is futile. She stands there in concussive fear, mouth wide open as if puzzled by this sudden turn of events, surprised that her life is about to end here on this sodden day in this muddy piece of earth in this accursed market haunted by ghosts in this place, this most miserable place on earth. She looks fragile like a broken bird, denuded, a bird without wings, standing half naked in the rheumy sun, covered only by a tattered wrapper that is in danger of being ripped off of her body.

The brute grabs a fistful of her breast and squeezes it. The woman gasps in pain. Some of the women in the crowd retreat in horror, unable to witness this desecration of the body, this illumination of the bestial. Many of the men moan in near religious ecstasy.

Blood welts under the woman's skin and then breaks through. A drop runs down her cheek to her exposed neck. The brute is all worked up now. His face is strangely contused, his eyes bulged with excitement, body rigid, possessed with an incurable fever. He reaches down, and yanks the woman's wrapper off, with one swift movement. The wrapper drops to the mud and someone snatches it and then crows in victory, waving it around like a scalp taken in battle.

The woman begins to beg. "Please. Please. Don't do this. Let me go."

Tears begin to fall from her eyes. She is overtaken by sheer terror. Totally humiliated now, she knows that the crowd's bloodlust will not be satiated until more gruesome terrors have been inflicted on her. The beast of madness has been unleashed from its cage and its hunger must be fed before it will be contained again. Why are we so enthralled by violence? Perhaps it is because we have become so dissolute, so jaded, that we can now respond only to unspeakable horrors, to dead babies, biblical floods and conflagration. Perhaps our lives lack spontaneity and invention and we have become like old people having sex with the lights off and eyes tightly closed.

I imagine that the woman's tears are planets, falling into a universe of mud. I imagine that each planet holds a history, a mystery too deep for any soothsayer to decipher. I realize that I am trying to shut down the spectacle in front of me.

THE COLLECTOR OF BUTTERFLIES AND WOMEN

The woman's hands are covering her groin, her arms forming an X as she tries to shield her privates from the world. She is wearing black panties with a little red rose stitched in front. The rose looks incongruous like a Christmas tree lit in a graveyard. The brute's hand's grab the edge of the panties and rip. The piece of cloth falls off and the woman's nakedness is fully revealed. In spite of my shame and disgust, I find myself staring at the thatch of bushy black hair between her legs. I am revolted. And fascinated.

The brute punches the woman in the stomach. The sound of a closed fist against her pliant flesh is sickening. I want to retch. She crumples to the ground, balls into a fetal position, begins to shake. She is going into shock.

But the brute is not done. He bends over her, yanks her feet apart, bends over like a man picking up a dropped coin. He shoves the fingers of his right hand into her vagina and begins to rape her. Some of the women in the crowd scream and run off in horror while the remaining women curse at the man for going so far. One woman throws a pebble at the man. It strikes him on the shoulder. He looks up from his act, offended, but not troubled enough to stop.

I think of what I am witnessing as crowd rape, collective rape. The crowd is accessory to the act. I am an accessory to the act because I have not done anything to stop it.

A piece of wood sails through the air and lands squarely on the brute's head. It opens a gash. He gets up, enraged, cursing, eyes searching through the crowd to find who had attacked him thus.

"Who throw de stone?" he demands, but the woman who threw it had wisely disappeared into the body of the crowd. I mutter a blessing for her brave soul. She has shown more courage than I have. I am filled with self-loathing and shame.

Another man leaps into the small muddy circle where the woman is prostrate with the brute towering over her. He is a slender handsome man with long pianist fingers. I notice his fingers because of what he is holding. A bamboo stick. He wants to combat the brute. He wants to save the hapless woman. I fear for him, worry that the brute will knock him flat on his back with a punch.

But I am wrong.

The skinny man raises the stick and delivers a blow to the naked woman's head. The blow wakes the woman up. She gets up and runs but she doesn't get far. The brute and the skinny man pursue her. Before her, the crowd parts like the sea before Moses as she runs. She falls, rolls around in the mud, tries to get up. The brute kicks her in the head.

I cannot take it anymore. I drop my tray, two tilapia fish sail to the ground. I take a few steps back to get behind the crowd. I look around, find two pieces of rock and pick them up. I hurl the first one and then the second one. Both stones find their marks on the two men assaulting the woman. They rear back. The brute, I hit in the forehead, the skinny man in the teeth. I see blood. Both men stop. The woman gets up, begins to stagger blindly in an attempt to run.

The skinny man does not resume the pursuit. He is too busy spitting out a chipped tooth. But the brute is made of sterner stuff. He is not about to let his prey go that easily. As he lunges after the naked woman, a man emerges from the crowd. He tackles the brute to the ground and delivers an array of punches to the man's face.

"What is your problem? You animal! You want to kill the woman?"

The savior punches the brute some more until the brute begins to moan for mercy. His nose and teeth are smashed, eyes covered with blood. The sight is enough to stop the crowd in its tracks and bring it to its senses. The skinny man, sensing that he might be getting a beating as well, disappears into the crowd.

A woman tosses a spare wrapper at the naked woman. The savior picks it up and reaches for the woman. She is still stumbling around like a somnambulist, completely disorientated. Her eyes are closed, she is a sculpture etched out of fear, covered by blood and mud, a specter that would haunt my dreams for the rest of that year.

THE COLLECTOR OF BUTTERFLIES AND WOMEN

The woman rears back in panic, afraid that one of her attackers is about to resume the attack. "It's okay. It's over." The man tells her reassuringly. He wraps the piece of cloth around her body. His humanity and his strength make me tremble, fill me with gratitude. He takes the woman's hands and leads her away from the market, toward the road. The crowd begins to disperse. I follow as the savior hails a cab and tells the cab driver to take them to the hospital.

This was the beating.

Next would come the burning.

The burning

The burning took place on a field near the Lagos Agbor Road not far from Boji Boji market. We were on holiday from school. I happened upon the scene when I saw a crowd gathering. In Nigeria, whenever a crowd gathers, laughter or fear are sure to also be in attendance. If you were seeking excitement, you learned how to follow the crowd. The gathering of a crowd is like the gathering of clouds. It is always a portent of something that is about to happen, something pleasing like an impromptu performance by a one legged dwarf or street musician, or a portent of something ominous like a man about to be beaten to death or a fight about to break out.

The man is dressed in a white singlet and dirty ratty denims with wide hems. He looks like a man who stumbled upon a consignment of clothes hidden in a nuclear bunker dug in the seventies. He is a young man in his twenties with a bushy afro that is all crinkled and knotty. He looks scared. Very scared. And he has good reason to be.

Death is ripe like grapefruit blooming in the cool morning air.

I tap a man on the shoulder. A fat man with a generous stomach overflowing under his *agbada*. He has wide tribal marks on his face.

"What did he do?" I inquire.

When the man responds, his breath is harsh and rank. "*Gbomo gbomo.* They say he tried to steal a child."

Gbomo gbomo referred to ritual kidnappers. They kidnapped children and adults off the streets and spirited them off to be used for ritual purposes. The poor victims were often found with eyes and tongues missing or sans genitalia. At times headless bodies were found abandoned in mangrove swamps or in heavy bush. The kidnappers either worked for themselves or for rich men who were looking to acquire more wealth. *Gbomo gbomo* believed that they could gain favor from the gods by offering human sacrifice. It was not uncommon to find corpses dumped on the roadways, exploding in the hot sun like so much overripe fruit. I once saw a young girl with head missing dumped on a bush path. As a fascinated twelve year old, my friends and I went back to the corpse, staring at it in mute fascination, watching the mottled flesh swelling in the sun.

"I am innocent. I was only playing with the child." The man protests.

The crowd jeers at him, curses him.

From what I gather, the man had lured the eight year old child with candy and tried to put her on his *okada*. *Okada* is a bike, often used as commercial transport. The child became afraid and cried for help. A woman who knew the child's mother heard the child's cries and raised an alarm. On-lookers soon approached and grabbed the would-be kidnapper before he could make his escape.

"Why did you put her on your bike?"

"Are you her father?"

"Are you her uncle?"

The crowd peppers the man with a staccato of questions, not letting him respond. His eyes look doomed. He looks around, seeking escape, but the men holding him are not about to let go.

And then he says something which seals his fate, dooms him.

"I have money. I can share it with everybody. Please let me go."

One of the man's captors turns to the crowd, like a matador seeking the gallery's consent before impaling the bull. "You see? The man is definitely *gbomo gbomo*. He has been making money from killing our babies. Now he wants to give us some of his blood money. Do we want his blood money?"

"No!" The crowd roars.

"Burn him! Burn him!"

The sound of the crowd rises to a crescendo, builds into a fortissimo.

"Give him the necklace!"

From somewhere, someone finds a tire. The tire is draped around the man's neck like a necklace and then tied with twine around his upper body.

The man fights, tries to pull off the tire, but a fist crashes into his head. He is held in place. In the distance, I see rain clouds beginning to gather. The air smells fetid, brackish, pregnant with danger, tinged with foreboding. I wonder how long it takes for rain to put out fire, how long it takes for a man to burn to death. I think of a blood map, a death graph, the arc where extinguishment intersects conflagration.

The sound of the crowd becomes a diminuendo.

Above us, indifferent clouds scuttle across the skies like dirty socks on the feet of little children. The skies are reddish brown like a clown's dirty face, about to bleed make-up, about to cry rain.

The kidnapper seems to have accepted his fate. He knows now that there is no escape, that darkness will claim his soul this night. He stops fighting, begins to mutter a prayer to whatever god he worships. His eyes grow big, his chest heaving with dread. The *mise en scene* is oddly cabalistic. I watch, unable to turn away, watch enthralled like a worshipper at the altar of a depraved god.

Someone finds a book of matches. And a rag soaked in gasoline.

"Move back!' the self-anointed executioner tells the crowd. We all move back a few steps.

The executioner stuffs the rag inside the tire, lights a match and tosses it at the tire. He takes a dainty step back, a step worthy of Mikhail Baryshnikov.

Fire blooms.

The wretch with the tire is caught by surprise. The flames are quick, pitiless. They surround him. His head is on fire his face is on fire his neck is on fire. The fire is spreading. The man with the necklace runs and his necklace follows. He tries in vain to pull the tire off of his neck but the tire will not give because it is strung across his body. He howls and as he howls he burns. The acrid smell of singed flesh sears the air fills my lungs. The man's afro disappears and his skull is exposed for one minute before it too begins to burn, turning black. The man falls face down, writhing in the sand like a millipede caught by salt.

The crowd's cries fall to a perdendo.

We watch the man burn as if his cremation will cleanse the world of sin. As if he is the last body snatcher that will roam the streets of Nigeria. It does not take long for the man to turn to bones and ash. Someone kicks his skull with a booted foot. The head rolls obscenely into a divot in the grass.

We left the field of death but the smell of death followed us around like a mangy dog. Like a spurned lover with jealous eyes, it would not leave us. Even when we no longer wanted death's embrace, death wanted to embrace us. The rain clouds came later but they did not wash away our sins.

The execution.

The execution took place in a public field in Agbor. The field was where local sports competitions took place. It was where the town hosted visited dignitaries. It was a place of festivity and laughter, of pageantry and pomp. Today, it would be a place of death.

The three men are tied to wooden stakes driven into the soil. Strong rope coils serpentine across their chests, crisscrossing their waists and their legs. They stare at the sun, at the crowd gathered around them, foreheads shining with sweat.

THE COLLECTOR OF BUTTERFLIES AND WOMEN

Women and children are hawking bread and bananas. Sellers of smoked fish mingle with sellers of *akara* and *agidi*. Cold water, popularly known as 'ice water' is sold in transparent plastic balloons. The thirsty purchase water and drink to cool themselves off. Women walk around with babies strapped to their backs. Some nurse their babies as they walk, the children's lips fastened tight around leaky nipples. People are camped out on the grass picnic style. A few have brought blankets to sit on while others sit on adjustable camp chairs.

The chatter of the crowd is dense, a many tongued thing. The voices carry in the air without wind, like the citizens of Babel building a towel that will poke God's feet. Arguments and brags, threats and pleas, catcalls and summonses blend with inhalations and exhalations and the constant shuffle of feet. Policemen armed with batons and cowhide whips known as *kobokos* keep the surging crowd in check, beating anyone who tries to breach the perimeter drawn in the grass by white paint.

It is unbearably hot. The air is a stubby finger poking at the skin. There is no sanctuary from the sun. The crowd has formed an L on the field. I am sitting on the grass in the vertical arm of the L. The horizontal section of the L is where the town officials and dignitaries sit. This section is protected from the sun by a canopy. The floor is elevated and there are sturdy wooden chairs, some with cushions. The Divisional Police Officer, known as the DPO sits there. The local ruler and town chiefs are there as well. They are surrounded by assistants, friends and family members. This is where the gentry sit as opposed to the section where I sit which is strictly proletarian. Like everything in Nigeria, seating in any public area is assigned by position and status. It is a stratified society where the rich devour the poor and the poor devour what is left of themselves.

If you drew an arrow through the point where the vertical and horizontal axis of the L intersected and then followed that arrow out in a parabola, it would lead you to the spot where the three men were tied to the stake. The spot that I thought of as the sand of death. Sitting in any position of the L, you were afforded a panoptic view of sand, of death.

The men who are about to die are dressed in striped prison garb. They are young, none of them older than thirty. They seem to be in remarkably good shape, as if they subscribed to some rigorous exercise regimen. The look on their faces is that of resignation. They have known that this day was coming. They have had enough time to curse God and the day of their birth. They have had enough time to beg God for forgiveness or to ask the devil to claim their souls. Their stare now is blank, devoid of emotion. They show no fear, show no pain. They say nothing. They wait for death. And death in turn waits for them.

I wonder what dire circumstances had driven them to prey on others, to become armed robbers. A man who chooses to become an armed robber in Nigeria is a man who has crossed the Rubicon. A man who has decided to gamble with his life. The punishment, for anyone who is caught, is usually death. Most robbers are executed summarily by the police when caught. I had grown used to seeing the corpses of men believed to be armed robbers paraded on TV by the police. Watching the local news one evening, I saw a police officer being interviewed by an over-anxious reporter. She questioned him about the successful police raid that had led to the death of three armed robbers. Men whose carcasses lay on the dusty ground outside the police station. Stepping gingerly around the corpses, while she trailed him, the policeman narrated his derring-do like a bard reciting his new poem. As he talked, he kicked at a corpse. "This one is the gang leader, the one I shot first."

A lucky few armed robbers end up in prison and are tried for their crimes. Once convicted, the punishment is execution by firing squad. To serve as a deterrent to others, the executions are carried out in a public place where anyone who is interested can watch. An

THE COLLECTOR OF BUTTERFLIES AND WOMEN

execution thus becomes a place to do commerce, to ply one's wares and make new connections. Even the prostitutes on Hill Street have come out in their Sunday finest, in their full plumage. I recognize two of them today, eyes like jackals, trolling for customers.

A loud megaphone goes off.

I know what the signal means. The soldiers are coming.

The soldiers emerge. Six of them. They are in full battle dress, shoes glinting in the sun. They carry their weapons lowered as they march forward. They walk into the center of the field like gladiators about to engage. They head straight toward the sand of death. When they get to within twenty feet, they stop.

The crowd erupts in a cheer and I do the same.

This is the moment that we have all been waiting for.

A man emerges from nowhere. A tall angular man with an austere face as expressionless as the gingerbread man. He is dressed in a black suit with a priest's collar. Carrying a bible. He is about to administer the last rites to the three men. It seems to take him forever to pray for each man. The crowd begins to grow restless and I wonder how long the soldiers can remain in their cramping position.

When the priest gets to the last man, he moves close. I do not hear him but I imagine that he is asking the man to pray with him. The last robber pumps his cheeks and hurls a big ball of spit in the priest's face. The priest rears back and retreats, surprised by this coup de main, this rejection of the sacramental. He swats the saliva away from his cheek, completes his prayer from three feet away and then departs.

The soldiers lifts their rifles, listening for the voice of the man with the megaphone, the man that I imagine is their drill sergeant.

"On your marks!

The soldiers take positions, drop to one knee, rifles still lowered.

"Set!"

Rifles go up. Point straight at the three men on the stakes.

"Go!"

The volley of shots, when it comes, is ear shattering. The men on the stakes do not dance like puppeteers on a string. They do not moan in their death throes. They do not twist or do any of the things that I see in testosterone-fueled Hollywood movies. They simply stop moving. Simply die. Blood geysers from bullet holes in their bodies. Their heads, missing chunks of flesh, drop to their chins.

I am surprised by how quickly it all takes place. I am filled with guilt and disgust, troubled by the violence that has stained my childhood like a Rorschach inkblot. I tell myself that wickedness, Faustian and Conradian, is native not only to the land of my birth and that many nations have convulsed with the perversity of violence. But this reasoning proves to be no consolation. My argument rings hollow to me.

This would not be the last time that I would watch someone die.

If suicide is poetry

Esther is trying to kill herself again.

We lived on Catholic Street in Agbor. Esther and her mother, whom everyone called Mama Esther, lived across from our apartment. Mama Esther had five children, four of whom died in infancy. People said that Mama Esther was a witch. Many people were afraid of her. They said that the real reason most of her children died so mysteriously was because she ate their souls. And that it was only a matter of time before the empty shells of these consumed children followed in death.

But Esther is not trying to kill herself because people call her mother a witch. She is not trying to kill herself because she has lost four brothers and sisters who all died before age twenty.

Esther is trying to kill herself because her boyfriend has broken up with her.

Esther is a tragic heroine, unlucky in love. Each time, a boyfriend breaks up with Esther it is too much for her fragile constitution to handle. It sends her into a depression that makes her wonder why birds do not fall from the sky dead why rain does not destroy the earth with a flood worse than Noah's why the earth does not close its immortal eye and go to sleep for eternity. Unable to find symmetry in love, Esther finds poetry in suicide. But if suicide is poetry, then Esther is a failed poet.

On this day, the neighbors are woken up by the piteous cries of Mama Esther.

"Esther, why? Why do you keep doing this?"

Mama Esther was a rail thin woman with big sunken eyes. Her gaze was unblinking, disturbing. When you looked at her, it was like staring at the sun in noonday heat. She was as prickly as a porcupine, with the temperament of volcanic ash. People stayed away from her. When she was upset, she threw pots and knives, and even hurled herself at people. Small wonder that people thought she was possessed and not of this world.

When Mama Esther walks in her apartment, she sees her daughter dangling from the ceiling, feet scraping the floor, a rope knotted around her neck. Esther is not dead but she is drifting in and out of consciousness. Mama Esther screams for help. She needs someone to help her cut her daughter down but her hoarse screams draw no helpers.

The neighbors are all gathered near Mama Esther's open door, but no one is going in. We have been witnesses at Esther's near deaths before. We have heard her mother's anguished cries in the past. Her cries evoke pity for Esther, that lost, hurt soul, but no one is willing to walk through the 'witch's' door to help.

So Mama Esther climbs on a stool and cuts down her daughter herself. She is cursing babbling weeping praying as she splashes cold water over Esther's face from an earthen pot. She pounds on Esther's chest as if to restart her heart, although Esther heart is working fine, well, yes, her physical heart is working fine but her emotional heart is the problem.

This is the third installment of Esther's suicide attempts. Each attempt has been made using a length of cloth which she wraps around a wooden beam in the ceiling. She always manages to get the cloth around her neck and climb on a stool. It is when she kicks the stool from under her feet that her plan invariably goes awry. You see, Esther is a tall girl, a giantess, some might say. She is over six feet tall, all arms and legs, all planes and angles like a carpenter's workbench. Some say that her suitors all eventually leave her because they cannot stand the idea of a wife that is taller than them. Somehow, Esther's feet always manage to find purchase on the floor, aborting another suicide attempt.

Unlike Esther, I was lucky in love. At least that year I was. I fell in love for the first time. It was a strange feeling that quickened my heart, a feeling of fullness like a man who attends a festival and takes a bite of every food that is on display.

Bea was my first love. I was fourteen. She was sixteen. Bea was a neighbor who lived in the house next door with her parents and siblings. Her mother was a kind-hearted hard-working woman who tended over her brood of nine children with a hawkish protectiveness. Bea was the oldest child. Her younger brothers were my friends. It was through them that I gained entrée into their home.

Bea was the kind of girl for whom clichés were made, the kind of girl that inspired Byronesque poetry. She was the mystery that I wanted to solve and the mystery that I wanted to become. Although she was only a couple of inches taller than I was, she looked ten feet tall to me. Her eyes were round or almond or heart-shaped, depending on what path I let my imagination roam on the particular day of my imagining. And when it came to Bea, my imagination lied to me. When we love someone, we make gods out of them. We recreate them like threads through a yarn maker, like clay through a kiln. We remake them to be what we want them to be, we airbrush them so that we see only the things that we want to see.

At times her breasts were perky and small like unripe pears dangling from a loose-limbed vine. At other times, they were heavy and rotund like watermelons in harvest season before they are bruised by callused hands. She had wide flaring hips and a flat stomach. In my mind's eye, Bea was a changeling, a shape-shifter, a mercurial spirit with demiurgic abilities. She was my religion and I worshipped at her altar with the pliable devotion of a Sadduccee. When she was listening intently, she had a way of cocking her head, askance, staring at you with those wide innocent eyes that will drink up the whole world, drink you right up with it. Holding Bea was like stepping on quicksand, a slow disappearing of the self, a rapturous tingling that sets the senses afire.

Our love was peppery, fierce like a spiteful sun, like a liquid sun. It burned us consumed us devoured our waking and sleeping hours. It thinned my blood and left me breathless, heart fluttering like a Ulysses butterfly floating in spring breeze.

Bea's father was a short wrinkled man who nursed silence like a relapsed alcoholic nursing a drink. I thought of him as the gardener of silence. The gardener of silence who nursed his tree, watered it and watched it bear fruit, watched its wrinkled prunes drop to earth. He was in his fifties but to a boy like me, he was a hundred years old and would live forever. When he spoke, which was rarely, his tone was stentorian, pregnant with menace and assorted bodily harms. Like many fathers that I knew, Mazi whole-heartedly embraced the whip as an enforcer of discipline. He was quick to lash out with his whip or belt at any child of his who fell out of line. As Bea grew older, she learned to stay out of his way, to avoid his baleful eye, his venomous strike. This rattlesnake that never hibernated. But he was a good provider.

I tried to win Mazi over by helping his sons with their homework. If he was impressed with my efforts, he did not show it. Bea assured me that he did not dislike me. That was as much as anyone could

THE COLLECTOR OF BUTTERFLIES AND WOMEN

expect from Mazi. He was a man who either disliked you or did not dislike you. To expect him to like you was asking for too much. He was a small man with sinewy arms and the suspicious eyes of a stray cat. He had developed a supple muscularity from years of farming. Hands that could swiftly uproot a cassava tuber from the ground with one pull could also smack you in the back of the head and send you tumbling down.

I never saw him beat Bea. When I asked her about it, she dismissed my questions. She did not want to talk about it. Mazi ran a tight ship. The children were expected to help out at the farm several times a week. Household chores were assigned and carried out with military precision and Spartan discipline. Although the family was not rich, there was always food in the house.

I remember the first time that I saw Bea naked. I had courted her for many months, bringing small gifts, stealing kisses whenever we were alone in the room. In a house full of people, this was no small feat to achieve. On occasions when Bea was left at home to watch the younger children, I quickly I learned how to bribe the youngest children with candy to get them out of the room. In the few furtive moments that followed, Bea and I would paw at each other greedily, fumbling with body parts, reaching for newly discovered and as yet unexamined appendages.

On this occasion, Mazi had gone to the farm and left Bea at home to watch her younger siblings. Her mother had gone to the local market. When I showed up, Bea was fixing lunch.

I watch her walk to the wood stove outside and my breath catches in my throat.

When she returns, I wrap my hands around her in an embrace. She gently pushes me away, eyes alarmed as she looks out the door for an intruder.

"Don't do that. You will get me in trouble."

I retreat but I do not surrender. I reach into my pocket and pull out several lollipops. I raise them up victoriously, a look of mischief on my face.

Bea shakes her head ruefully but I can tell that she is not displeased.

I find her three younger siblings and dole out the lollipops like the Pied Piper. They screech in delight and disappear to their own devices. Which leaves Bea and me to our own devices.

We do not close the door because there is no door to close. Instead, we move to a corner of the scantily furnished room. Pots and pans line the floor like sentries bracing for an ambush. The walls are unfinished, rough-hewn. A mattress is propped up against the wall. The smell of food mixes inextricably with the smell of excitement. I imagine pheromones floating like gauzy butterflies in the air, hormones coiling and uncoiling in our bloodstreams like moths set afire.

I hold Bea, kiss her, suck the life out of her. She begins to moan like an animal caught in the trapper's riddle. We grind against each other for an eternity. We are both terrified. Terrified of being discovered by her snot-nosed brothers. Terrified of her iron-handed father showing up prematurely from the farm. I shudder as I think of what the consequences would be.

But we can't stop.

I push her against the wall, jam myself against her, pull out my penis. I make the wall move to my motion or imagine that I do. I reach under her dress and touch her wetness. The smell of her fills me with madness.

"No. We should stop." She says, but she doesn't stop me, doesn't stop herself.

I do not speak. Cannot trust myself to speak.

I pull down her underwear to mid-thigh. Lift her dress, grab her buttocks.

I penetrate her.

She howls like a wolf cursing the moon, shudders against me. I try to silence her by covering her mouth but it is too late. I hear tiny feet pattering against the concrete. Her siblings are coming out to investigate the disturbance.

In one fluid motion, I stuff my penis back in my underwear, pull away from her and dash into the next room. She barely has time to pull up her panties before the two urchins stumble into the room, still sucking on their lollipops.

That was the first time that I had sex. I think of that encounter as coitus interruptus.

Premature extrication.

With time, I learn that sex is full of comic potential. There is nothing funnier than bad sex and nothing more terrifying than great sex. Bad sex is unfulfilled expectations. It demands a corrective performance. Great sex is heightened expectations. It demands a repeat performance that is just as great, thus putting pressure on the performer. Sex is like alcohol. The first time you try it is always the worst. After that, it gets better, if only by sheer repetition. There is no worse sex than sex between two teenagers. Like jackrabbits, we huff and puff, slant and cant, seeking symmetry in an asymmetrical world. We sweat and strain against each other and then collapse on one another exhausted like fish on a pebble-ridden shore.

The lord of cockroaches

I am the lord of cockroaches.
 I was the fifth among ten children. I never felt displaced or unheard. I never begrudged my older siblings the accident of faith that had expelled them from my mother's womb before me. I never chafed at the tyranny of time.

Growing up, our family was neither particularly happy nor particularly unhappy. Instead, we occupied a median point between both of these Tolstoyan extremes. We dwelled in the interstice between these parallel suns. Even now, I realize just how little I know my siblings. I never lived with any of them long enough to know them. We lived under different roofs most of the time. We were like animals in a glass cage. Every now and then we saw each other and recognized the fact that we existed. We could see the world around us and recognized the fact that the world existed. But we could not interact with each other. We pawed greedily at the cold glass but found no escape. Tragic.

My father sent some of my siblings to live with aunts while some stayed with my mother in Auchi. Most of the time, only my older sister Mary and I lived with my father, as he moved from town to town, frequently forced to relocate for his government job. Often times, I have wondered if he wanted the children out of the way because they were a burden to him. These children that he shed as easily as a snake molting.

Okpekpe, where my mother was born, is a small village, about an hour's drive away from Auchi, the town where my father was born. Auchi is the seat of government. The local government itself is named Etsako Local Government. Auchi's claim to fame is the fact that it houses Auchi Polytechnic, a collegiate institution which attracts students from all parts of the country.

My childhood was a protean one. My father, a civil servant who worked for the courts, did not seem to mine being moved from one job to another. With his Dickensian travels, I came to learn the world "transferred" and its odious connotations very well. As a child, I learned that to be "transferred" meant imminent dislocation. I dreaded the day that my father would return from work and utter the dreaded phrase, "I have been transferred." Being transferred meant leaving all of the friends that I had made at school. It signaled a departure from the comfort of the familiar, a return to angst. What I craved was stasis. What I got was flux.

We moved from town to town and village to village, roamed the world like cursed spirits blinded by their curses. Like Aristotle traversing the Lyceum of ancient Athens.

I learned not to make friends too quickly, not to expect loyalty from the people that I met. Okpella was where we went fishing in the small stream that ran behind our house, where we caught tiny fish the size of a pinkie finger and tiny helpless crabs. Igarra was where I stuck my foot on a nail and was taken to the local hospital while my parents worried about tetanus infections and sudden death. Igarra, a picturesque town with the brooding Somorika Hills, was where we spent idyllic days climbing rocks. Agbor was where I went to secondary school, where I would fall in love for the first time.

Auchi, the town where I was born, I do not remember much of. At seven or eight, my cousins and I went to the local market seeking work. We are offloading cases of beer from a truck and moving them into a shop in the market. The shop owner is to pay us a small fee for our efforts. On what would be our final trip, my cousins deliver their cases to the shop owner. As I approach the shop, I trip and lose my balance. The case of Guinness Stout tumbles from my head and smashes. I stare at my cousins in horror, as the shop owner comes running out of the store. He stares at me with volcanic eyes, enraged.

As if on cue, my cousins take off running. I follow.

Onene was a madman who lived on a hill in the outskirts of town. He ran around naked, traveling in a cloud of flies and dust. We called him Long Scrotum because he had a distended scrotal sac which drooped all the way to his knees. We found him to be an object of endless fascination. We stared at him in amazement, this man whose genitals possessed the ability to induce shock.

He was a tall angular man with hollow cheeks and eyes so fierce they could break brittle bones. His hair ran like a wayward river down his shoulders in knotty kinks. He walked around naked, mumbling prayers and curses to the birds and the rocks. He foamed at the mouth like an unspent river. If you caught him in a good mood, which was rare, he stared at you with those eyes of *brillantine*, those eyes of adamantine, and walked away with a half moon of a smile on his face.

When you caught Onene in a bad mood, which was not infrequent, he glared at you, swore at you and threatened to kill you. Every weekend, we paid our daily pilgrimage to Onene's hide-out. As we walked up the hill, we quivered in fear, knowing that we were daring a hornet's nest. We stood a safe distance away and called out, "Onene!" "Come out, you s-s-s-s-son of a whore!"

Onene emerges like an apparition from the bush. He doesn't walk as much as run. He emerges with urgency like a man who needs to relieve himself or a man who has stepped on an anthill teeming with red ants. He begins to walk toward us, one arm outstretched, cursing, foaming at the mouth.

"I…will…kkkkkkill you, little fuckers I will…kill you."

But we have come prepared. Before Onene can come any closer, my cousins and I reach in our pockets. Onene realizes what is about to happen but it is too late. As he attempts to retreat, we begin to pelt him with the stones that we have hidden in our pockets. We howl with glee as Onene runs. He squeals in pain. We chase him. We are pitiless. We are cruel. Pathos is a stranger that we are yet to meet.

Auchi is a ragged cough of a town, with pale consumptive houses scattered on brown dusty sand like sputum. The streets are sad and broken like women newly widowed, wrinkled by floods and pockmarked by a thousand rude feet. Men dressed in cotton kaftans brave the noonday heat as they walk to the mosque or to the village square. Women walk the streets with babies strapped on their backs and food baskets on their heads. Bikes and buses fight for space on the narrow streets with goats and chickens. Children squeal in the sand outside their houses, building mud castles, playing hide and seek. Many are dressed in dirty underwear, some in shorts or in secondhand dresses. Boys kick soccer balls, using wood stakes as makeshift goal posts. The smell of firewood from open fires clenches the chest, mauls the nostrils. The smoke disappears quickly like unrequited love, like aborted dreams.

We lived on Polytechnic Road in Auchi in a huge rambling compound with four conjoining houses facing each other. There was a sea of uncles and aunts, cousins and nephew and nieces. Many of my uncles had multiple wives and several children. Polygamy was woven through the tapestry of our families. Children were like rotten fruit. They were everywhere. If you weren't careful, you could step on them. We went to sleep with the yelling of children and woke up to the yelping of goats. Silence was an infant strangled in its crib.

The streets were dirty and misbegotten, the village itself full of bastards, these unclaimed children abandoned like luggage at some dying airport, whose fathers snuck into their mothers bed at night and then disappeared before their evil was revealed nine months later.

Nights on Polytechnic Road were always raucous and often times ribald. Our families were locked in eternal warfare and bloodless vendettas. We shared love and discord in equal measure. Revenge was a dish served well done while anger was served rare. Happiness came in seasons like the Harmattan trade winds that blew dust into our eyes and made us cower like cowards. I learned that happiness was like a full stomach, something that one could not expect to have all of the time. Often, when happiness came, it was soon followed by travail. It was as if God had decided that we could not be trusted with too much happiness. These were the years that I started to wonder about God's sense of humor and I began to think of the Deity as a divine jokester, who floated gauzily above mankind and chuckled in superior amusement at man's foibles and fecklessness. I learned to build magnificent palaces of air and festooned empires of water that dissolved when touched by reality. Reality often intruded in the form of a parent walking into a room where I was day-dreaming, or a sibling calling out my name.

It was in Auchi that I became the lord of cockroaches. The brown six-legged creatures were everywhere. They scuttled around the rooms where we lived, hiding behind food baskets, among piles of laundry. They hid in the pages of dusty books, sought refuge in wooden cabinets. My cousins chased them, screeching in glee as they caught the little critters. They stamped on them with bare feet and the awful metallic smell of their insides filled the room.

I begged my cousins to stop, begged them to spare the cockroaches. I was fascinated by these foul-smelling creatures that no one loved. I collected them in a glass container and studied them daily. I fed them bits of food, watched them claw at each other as they fought for food. Soon, detached legs and arms filled the bottom of

THE COLLECTOR OF BUTTERFLIES AND WOMEN

the glass jar as the poor creatures ripped each other apart. I marveled at this, marveled at how much they reminded me of humans in their desperation, in their prosaic struggle. I watched their hairy arms and legs scratch the glass, watched their futile and furtive exertions. I felt bad for them. How did it feel to be completely unloved, to be hated by the rest of the world? There were days that I felt like a cockroach, totally unloved, totally isolated from the rest of the world.

Scorpions on the other hand, I hated.

I was ten when I was stung by a scorpion at moonlight.

I am sitting on an upturned mortar, the kind used for pounding yams into a hard paste to form the local delicacy known as 'pounded yam.' I am leaning on the wall of the small structure that functions as a kitchen. We are telling stories at moonlight. When the pain comes, it does not register as a sting initially. I think that it is a mosquito or some other pesky insect. I reach behind my back to swat away the insect and find my fingers wrapped around a scorpion. In my terror, I yank the scorpion from my back but leave the stinger.

One of my uncles comes to my rescue. He applies some kind of unguent to my back. The sting of the ointment is almost as bad as the scorpion's sting. I am screaming in pain, cursing the universe.

I had heard stories of people paralyzed from scorpion bites.

Would I be paralyzed?

I was not paralyzed. Fortune smiled on me and I soon made a full recovery. It dawned on me then that life is nothing but a series of encounters with death. When we are seriously sick or injured, we encounter death. When we nearly get run over by a bus or dodge a bullet, we encounter death. Each time we survive a close encounter, we have cheated death. But death cannot lose forever. The deck is stacked against us. Being mere mortals, we are doomed to taste defeat someday. A few months later, filled with the strange bravado of men who have once cheated death, I would tempt fate. And this time, death would nearly get the last laugh.

John Lennon

The village in which I discovered John Lennon was the same village in which I lost a piece of my left ear.

The day of the accident, the day that I nearly died, started out just like any other day.

I am seven years old and about to confront death.

It is dusk, with storm clouds gathering in the skies. I had returned home from school and was bored. Seeking an adventure, I went to visit my friend and classmate, Ado, who lived in a house just across the street from mine. His house was directly next to the village elementary school in Okpella.

When I get to Ado's house, I find him finishing up his evening meal with his parents and sister. I feel awkward as I walk up, wishing that my timing was better. The heavy smell of bitter-leaf soup curdles the air and makes my stomach turn. Ado and his sisters are sitting on the bare earth around a big bowl of soup and a mound of *eba*, a local delicacy. Ado's parents are sitting on small wooden stools. His mother, a willow thin woman with pale skin like overripe lemons, gives me a kindly smile. His father, a dwarfish man with powerful shoulders, acknowledges me with a nod.

"How are you, boy?"

"I am fine, Sir. Good evening, Sir."

"Join us for dinner." He stares at my eyes as I start to mumble that I have already had dinner. "No, no…a man can never have too much food. Need all the energy you can get." He beckons me to sit down.

Although I had eaten less than an hour before, the smell of the food wafting in the air makes me hungry. I need no further persuasion.

After the meal is done, Ado and I decide to head over to the elementary school yard to play. We start by climbing the cashew trees dotting the yard. The goal is to see who can climb the most trees in the shortest period of time. Although Ado is shorter than I am, he can climb much faster and is soon ahead. He has conquered four trees while I am still struggling to get to the top of my third tree. At school, we call him the cat. He is often eager to display his prowess at climbing, making short work of the teacher's desk when the teacher is absent, leaping from one desk to another like a trapeze dancer executing a piece of classicism. "I won." He crows. "C'mon, sissy."

I ignore his taunt and keep climbing.

"I bet I can climb that roof over there." I follow the direction of Ado's pointed hand. The new challenge is a small brick house near the elementary school with a zinc roof. My eyes widen. "Sure you want to climb that? Could be dangerous."

Ado's eyes glitter mischievously. Danger is a word that he loves. With his short squat body that is always as taut as a hunter's bow, he is itching to grapple with danger.

We make our way to the brick house surreptitiously. Walking quietly, we listen for any sounds that might emanate from the house but hear none.

I am like a spooked cat, all jumpy.

"Are you afraid?" Ado asks.

I smirk. "Are *you*?

Of course, I am afraid. But I would have rather died than admit it, heart leaping in my chest like Cerberus, the hellhound, straining against Heracles. I am gripped by fear and hope, fear that things might go terribly wrong and hope, hope that things would ultimately work out. Hope is the disease of the young; they have too much of it. Hope is also the disease of the old; they have too little of it. Fear is the disease of the young; they have too little of it. They do not know enough of the world to be afraid. Fear is also the disease of the old; they have too much of it. They have seen too much of the world not to be afraid.

"They are probably at the market." Ado whispers. We know that the young couple who inhabit the house, is often at the village market, selling yams and cassava harvested from the farm. Still, I can't shake the nagging feeling that the house might not be empty. I am filled with a cold dread. But I can't back out. If I do, I would totally earn the epithet that my friend so gleefully hurled at me earlier.

To ascend to the roof, we have to first climb an avocado pear tree that leans dangerously close to the house. From one of the branches of the tree, we can drop onto the zinc roof of the brick house.

"Want to go first?" Ado asks.

"Go ahead."

"I knew you were too chicken to go first."

I move past Ado and bound up on the tree. As we climb the tree, I think I hear what sounds like a baby crying. As I pause to listen, Ado pushes past me. We climb the tree branch that dangles over the zinc roof of the house and then gingerly lower ourselves on to the roof. Cackling in glee like hyenas in rut, we walk on the roof like trapeze artists, amazed at our own daring, our athleticism. We have conquered the world and are eternal.

We gaze at the expanse of mud and brick homes, at evening fires lit as families cook dinner. Night is a spider crawling in through the cracks of the evening. From afar, the squawking of flirtatious chickens mixes with the mournful bleats of world-weary goats. In the evening, Okpella seems to blur at the edges and coagulate like the half-remembered dream of a village idiot.

The breeze is a lecher with bruised fingers, undressing the sand, sending cotton clouds of dust into the air like the parasol of an anxious bride.

And then we
F
A
L
L...

It happens so fast we don't know what is happening. The zinc roof which must have been weak and defective in places simply gives way. I feel myself hurtling through eons of time for what seems an eternity, what is an eternity. As I drop through the roof, my mouth opens in a yell of terror.

I land hard on concrete and for a minute cannot move. I am paralyzed with sheer terror. My eyes had closed as I hurtled to the ground. Now, I open them and look around me. I see that I am in a room. Next to me is an infant in a makeshift crib. The baby's eyes are closed in blissful repose. I can't tell if it is a boy or girl, but the infant must be less than a month old. There is a small lantern burning in a corner. There are pots and pans and a bucket. There is a small flat mattress near the baby's crib. The room smells like soap, like boiled meat, like baby shit, like baby, like fear.

As my senses reawaken and I am sheared from my dream state,

I suddenly realize that there is a woman screaming. It is the child's mother. And then I feel a hand pulling at me. It is Ado. He is already on his feet.

"Let's go!"

He yanks me to my feet. As we run out the door, a woman collides into us and the three of us land in an untidy heap on the floor. The woman yelps and calls out for help, presumably from her husband.

Lightning fast, Ado and I are back on our feet, before the woman can get up. We sprint out the front door of the house and race down the street.

High on adrenaline, driven by panic, we run, lungs on fire.

I did not realize that a piece of my ear was missing until I got home.

It was then also that I noticed the gaping slash on my right thigh.

Each time I hear Eleanor Rigby, my favorite Beatles song, I remember how I got my scars, scars that I will carry for the rest of my life like Hester Prynne in Nathaniel Hawthorne's *Scarlet Letter*

The woman who drank her husband

It was through our neighbor, Baba Ajayi, that I met the woman who was forced to drink her husband. The widow had lost her husband just a few days before she was brought to Baba Ajayi, the witchdoctor. Her in-laws were accusing of poisoning her husband with a spell. Funmi's husband of many years had died after an agonizing battle with some mysterious stomach disease.

Funmi declares her innocence but the family is not persuaded. Ignoring her pleas, they drag her over to Baba Ajayi's shrine. Baba Ajayi who had earlier supervised the last rites on the dead man, washes the corpse with water. The water from the washing is saved in a container. Funmi will be forced to drink this water to prove her innocence. If she refuses to drink it, it will be proof that she is guilty and that her hands are bloody. If she drinks the water and dies, it will prove that Funmi is guilty and that her husband had exacted his revenge from the grave. If she drinks the water and does not die, she will be declared innocent.

The day the widow's in-laws brought her to Baba Ajayi, my brothers and I ran out of the house to see what was going on. It was quite a racket outside. Funmi is weeping, protesting what she knows is about to come. Her in-laws shove her around and rain curses on her.

"You are a witch! You killed our son!"

"You will die, Funmi! You will die for what you did!"'

"I am innocent. I swear, I didn't do anything to Ayo." Funmi pleads.

Funmi is a tiny woman with big eyes, an islet surrounded by an ocean of bile. The in-laws, men and women, shove and kick her, push her forward.

Baba Ajayi presides over the proceedings. The door to his two room apartment which also functions as his shrine and office is open. I watch as the contingent crams into the room, a dozen men and women full of bad intent. One of the men makes a half-hearted attempt to shoo away the onlookers.

"Go away! Mind your own business."

We ignore him. Minding other people's business was our business.

The woman is made to kneel before the shrine. The shrine itself is a macabre sight. Statues and sculptures splattered with blood. Bits of white and red cloth. Cowrie shells, the shell of a turtle, calabash, bottles of whisky, fragments of what we all believe to be a human skull, animal bones, divining beads. A mirror. I can see my own fascinated eyes in the mirror.

Baba Ajayi, stands over the broken woman, whose eyes are full of horror. His face is stern as he hands her the calabash containing her husband's effluvium.

The woman is in shock but she takes the small calabash, puts it to her lips and drinks. She drinks for what seems an eternity and then she hands back the calabash, eyes full of defiance, eyes hardened by resolve. She refuses to cry any longer, she stares at her tormentors, shaming them with her courage. They wait for her to wilt but she does not die. They wait for her to drop dead but she does not. Instead, Funmi rises majestically to her feet, unbidden. She walks to the door and without looking back, she walks out of Baba Ajayi's shrine and out of our compound.

I never saw her again, that petite brave woman so badly maligned and abused by her husband's family. But I did hear that she was alive and doing well. She had taken her two children and left Agbor to move back to her family in Igarra.

Sam was found dead this morning

At sixteen, I was a skinny lad, all arms and legs, full of questions about the cosmological, the theological, and the illogical. I went to bed with Bertrand Russell, stimulated myself with Immanuel Kant and woke up with Nietzsche. I devoted myself to all things philological, immersed myself in the Hegellian dialectic and Schopenhauer's aesthetics. I was trying to find the meaning of life.

Did I find it, you wonder? No, but I learned plenty about the nature of evil and the cruelty of man.

I was sixteen when I befriended a policeman named Johnbull. JB, as he was known by his friends, worked at the same courthouse in Iguobazuwa where my father worked. One day, JB came over to our house, which was located next to the courthouse and we became friends. JB was short with stocky arms and a muscular build. For someone so physically intimidating, he was surprisingly soft-spoken. He was a man who spoke in semicolon; always elaborating, always clarifying as if the world might not catch what he truly meant unless he explained just a little bit more.

I am not sure why he took an interest in a young boy who was half his age but I liked to think that it was my intellect, my 'maturity.'

THE COLLECTOR OF BUTTERFLIES AND WOMEN

JB told me that I read too many books and that all those books were bound to mess up my mind and drive me insane. I replied that insanity was a luxury that I could not afford.

I was suspicious of JB's motives at first. I knew how men who wanted to get in your sister's skirts would befriend you first and then use you to gain access to the quarry. But I soon realized that I was wrong and that JB was not after one of my sisters.

I liked to think that JB was attracted by my intellectual curiosity and my 'maturity.' He told me that I read too many books and that all those books were bound to mess up my mind and drive me insane. I replied that insanity was a luxury that I could not afford.

JB lived in a one room apartment near the main market. He was a deeply thoughtful man who nursed the ambition of going to college. His dream of a college education was dashed when his father died. He found himself stuck with the burden of taking care of his siblings and mother. He became a policeman not because of a passion for social order and moral stasis, but because he needed a steady pay check.

In Nigeria, people have a love/hate relationship with the police. Policemen are either elevated to apotheosis or scorned like apostates. A policeman is like God, looked at with dread and a certain queasiness. They have power over life and death. They can extinguish your life with an 'accidental discharge' of their antiquated rifles. If they decide to be really creative, they can shoot you and tag you as an 'armed robber' who was caught in the act. Murder by hired cop is not uncommon. Policemen have been known to loan their weapons to armed robbers in exchange for a share of the loot. Given the choice between an armed robber and a policeman, any Nigerian would understand that their chances of survival are fifty-fifty.

What is the cause of this corruptibility, this wanton disregard for human life? Policemen in Nigeria are poorly paid. At times, they go for months without receiving a salary. The country teeters bewilderingly from an oligarchy to an autocracy, from a plutocracy to a faux-democracy, locked in the iron grip of kleptocrats and megalomaniacs. It is a dangerous thing to put weapons in the hands of the hungry.

But not all policemen are criminal minded.

JB was a good example.

I hung out on many occasions with JB. He was the first adult friend that I ever had. We played music in his constrained apartment and talked. He talked about his desire to return to school and to earn a college degree. He surmised, correctly, that his prospects in Nigeria were bleak.

"If you ever get a chance to go overseas, please take it." He urged. "There is no future here in this country."

For someone who was always cheerful, I was surprised to hear the despair in his voice. He is a man sunken into despondency, completely drained.

I did not know the cause of his melancholy until I asked him what was wrong.

"You won't understand. You are too young to understand."

I wasn't buying it.

"Cop out. You always say that when you don't want to talk about something." There was a heady challenge in my voice and JB responded to it.

"Okay, I will tell you what it is. When you have nightmares later tonight, you can thank me for it."

Stretched out catlike on the bed in the sparsely furnished room, JB told me the story. I listened intently, enraptured and revolted. In the far distance, a cock crowed in the late afternoon. A strange omen, since a cock was not supposed to crow that late. Through the open window, I could see dusk gather as the sun retreated behind a blanket of clouds and wrapped itself up. Outside, children played hide and seek while mothers prepared the evening meal at open fires.

THE COLLECTOR OF BUTTERFLIES AND WOMEN

"Sam was found dead this morning. They cut his penis off."

Sam was a policeman, a colleague of JB. Although they were not exactly friends, the two men knew each other well. While JB was assigned to the court house by the police department, Sam was assigned to guard the residence of a magistrate who presided over the local court. Sam was on night duty at the home of this magistrate when he was attacked and murdered the night before. No one knew exactly how it happened.

The magistrate and his family did not hear any disturbance in the night. Or so they said. They woke up in the morning and found Sam dead at his post in front of the house.

Sam's genitals, penis and testicles, had been neatly removed. The job was done with surgical precision. The policeman must have been caught by surprise as there was no evidence of a struggle. His gun was on the ground beside him, with not a single shot fired from it.

Of course, there were speculations about the identity of the assailant or assailants.

Some people suspected a murder for hire plot. But who would want to kill an impoverished policeman in the middle of the night? Some whispered that the magistrate had some questions to answer. Perhaps the policeman had found out some damning information and had been silenced because of it. But why would the man's genitals be removed? Who would defile his body in such fashion?

JB thought he knew the answer and so did everyone else who speculated on the case. Sam was killed for ritual purposes. There were superstitious people in Nigeria who believed that the gods of prosperity or adversity could only be appeased by ritual sacrifices. So a man who sought quick wealth would go to a 'native doctor' or 'spiritualist' for help. A woman who was unable to conceive a child might do the same. So would a man who wanted a promotion at work for himself or a demotion for his enemy.

At times a chicken was all it took to gain or regain favor with a deity. At times, it took a goat, or a lamb, or a cow...or a human being.

As a child, I was terrified of these 'body snatchers' these 'man hunters' who stalked men women and children and sold them to ritualists. We called them *'gbomo gbomo'* People disappeared from farms and were never seen again. Children went to school and never returned, baited by strangers and then abducted. Corpses were found sans body parts. Eyes, tongues, teeth, and genitals, were said to command the most price. Hair, fingers, and toes, were said to rank next in price.

JB and I both grasped the reality of what had happened to Sam. Sam had been used as a human sacrifice to the devil.

I am consumed by a sense of loss, a sense that I have lost something that can never be regained. But I do not know what it is and this not-knowing fills me with unease.

Like Sadducees, my country is impressed and overcome by its own religiosity. We are overwhelmed by our own piety. Every Sunday we go to mass or to one of those strange Pentecostal churches where we beat our brow and pound our chests in simulated charismatic anguish. On Fridays, we go to the mosques and bow facing the east. We are building churches and mosques in every corner. See, my minaret will be taller than your minaret. My steeple will be taller than your steeple. We are getting ourselves dressed in our Sunday best, our Friday *Agbada*. We are taking out the bible and the Koran. We are taking out the crucifix and the prayer bead. Watch the smoke drift from our fiery prayers. We are taking out the knife and the ax. Watch your head.

God took an extended vacation from Nigeria and Nigerians are still waiting for Him to come back. Until He comes back, we will continue to do what we excel at:

killing

raping

maiming

THE COLLECTOR OF BUTTERFLIES AND WOMEN

robbing
destroying each other
and praying
to God
or
gods.

Zack and the prostitute

My guardian, Zack, has brought a prostitute over to the house. She is one of the girls at the brothel on Hill Street. Zack is the man that I lived with for over a year before moving in with my father's friend, Papa Dede.

Zack was a sanguine man in his thirties. A handsome man who wore an afro that was always neatly combed. He was jovial, good-natured, gentle. A bricklayer, who worked in a construction company. He was a hard worker. He usually left home at dawn and did not return until the late evening. I am not sure how my father struck up a friendship with him. Not sure how my father decided that he would make a good guardian for me. The choice was made for me.

When my father was transferred to Urhonigbe, he decided that he wanted me to finish my secondary school education at Agbor. At this time, I was attending Ika Grammar School. I ended up with Zack and his wife and found myself next door to Nana and his wives.

Zack's wife, Ramat, was a short timid woman who kept her opinions to herself. If she knew of her husband's infidelities, she did

THE COLLECTOR OF BUTTERFLIES AND WOMEN

not discuss it with him or with anyone else. They had one daughter, a cherub faced girl who was five years old. Zack was a caring husband, a loving father, a good guardian.

Most marriages are balloons, suspended in time, full of air, perfectly shaped, until the pin prick comes, and then they deflate. Zack and Ramat's marriage then was like most marriages. The couple slept together, ate together, played together and argued only when it was absolutely necessary. Zack told his wife his lies and she pretended dutifully, like a good wife, to believe them. He kept his string of mistresses and she pretended not to know of it. The key to a long marriage is to ignore your eyes and your ears, to accept that what you do not know will not kill you.

Whenever Zack got restless, he sent his family on vacation. Ramat took their daughter and went to Auchi, the village of our birth, to visit her parents or his parents. She stayed for a week or two and while she was gone, Zack immersed himself in a Dionysian orgy of wine and women.

Zack and the prostitute arrive at midnight when all the neighbors are asleep. Zack usually waited until the midnight hour for his trysts. I am not sure why. I don't think that any of the neighbors really cared. And if they had confided in Ramat about her husband's indiscretions, she would not have done anything about it.

They show up and I pretend to be asleep on the sofa in the parlor.

I can smell the woman. She brings a smell to the room that my nostrils identify with some specificity. A strange effusion of Johnson & Johnson baby lotion, the smell of rubber, like a condom peeled open, and sweat. These various smells assault my nose. When they walk past me into the bedroom, I peek out of an eyelid at her. I notice her wide hips and big buttocks. Definitely Zack's type.

The door to the bedroom is slammed shut.

For the next hour, I am subjected to the animal noises of Zack and his paramour having steamy sex. They go at it hard and long.

I am aroused. Not content to be merely a witness, I want to participate.

I sit up on the sofa, unzip my shorts.

For the next half hour, we have a ménage a trois. Except that the couple in the next room does not know that I have invited myself to their party. I rock myself back and forth to the rhythm of their movements.

I steal their sex.

And when I am done, I am filled with self-loathing.

Fire

The year that I discovered the beauty of prostitutes was the same year that I was nearly burned to death.

When I wake up, I am on fire.

A few weeks earlier, my mother had departed our constipated apartment on Ojeifo Street in Agbor and returned to Auchi, the village where I was born. The fire started in the middle of the night. The building where we lived had lost electricity that evening. Our usual practice on such occasions was to use kerosene powered wick lanterns, but on this day, we discovered that there was no kerosene available. So we lit candles and placed them strategically around the apartment like centurions standing guard. My father fell asleep in his bed and my sister and I soon fell asleep as well.

I wake up in the middle of the night and scream. The sheets on the bed are burning.

I push my sister who is sleeping beside me and leap off the bed. My sister screams and jumps off the bed. The room is filled with smoke. My father, who is asthmatic, is sleeping on the next bed. When my father slept, he was Poseidon, god of the sea, horses and earthquakes. He was all movement. There was a certain spatiality and boundlessness to his sleep. The air vibrated with his snoring, the bed rumbled with each inhalation and exhalation. His sleep was a multi-dimensional thing; something that you could see, hear and feel. His sleep was a constipated locomotive wheezing on rusty train tracks, Elijah's chariot of fire clattering on pebbled ground.

"Papa!"

My yell rouses my father from slumber. He is naked from the waist up, clad in a pair of boxers. His eyes go wide as he sees the conflagration around him. Thoroughly panicked, my sister and I want to flee the room but are unsure of what to do. We look to my father for guidance as the room gets hotter and tendrils of flame lick all around us. It takes an eternity for my father to move. Like Dante Alighieri, we have all descended into Hell and time has become a butterfly trapped in an hourglass.

"Water!" My father yells, "Get water."

Like a man possessed, he dashes to the big plastic container in the room which holds our supply of drinking water. He finds a bowl, scoops water and hurls it all around the room, muttering to himself in some strange vernacular that I cannot comprehend. My sister and I find some bowls, rush over to the water container, and begin to throw water all over the room. Since the room is covered by smoke, we have no idea how much damage the fire has already done to our humble abode. Indeed, I do not understand how I am still alive, why we are still alive.

Perhaps all three of us were dead and just not aware of it. Perhaps we had left the Middleworld and joined the netherworld and its legions.

It was later that I realized that the fire was confined to the bed.

It was later that I realized how the fire started.

We had lit candles to give us light. But the flames that gave us light wanted our bodies in exchange. The candle flames were hungry and needed to be fed. Tongues of flame from a candle had licked

THE COLLECTOR OF BUTTERFLIES AND WOMEN

greedily at the drapes hanging around the bed and the flames had spread quickly around the bed. It was a sheer miracle that we were not burned to death on that day.

Much later, I realized that the hair on my arms and face was burned off. I was as hairless as a lizard, the spiny tailed lizard that I had learned in school was known as the *uromastyx geyri*.

I had a fascination for lizards. I think it is because we shared a common trait; we both distrusted people. While other kids hated the reptiles and threw rocks at them, I fed them and loved to watch them scurry around. The best place to watch the lizards at play was at the local cemetery. At the cemetery, fat lizards lounged on tree branches and sunbathed like rich Florida housewives. Let me tell you about my visit to the cemetery when I went to rob the dead.

How to rob the dead

We fill the bag with human fingers, toes and bone fragments
We are here to steal the bones of dead men.

We are walking through the cemetery in the late evening. The sun is a yellow orb in the sky, an old man's jaundiced eye.

I am with the man who is my current guardian, Papa Dede. Mama Dede and Papa Dede took me in when my father was redeployed to Urhonigbe, a town an hour away from Agbor. Papa Dede's oldest child was named Dede, which is why everyone calls my guardian Papa Dede.

Papa Dede is blind in one eye. He is a taciturn man with a severe face that abhors laughter, a man who rarely raises his voice, rarely cracks a smile. He has lived a hardscrabble life, a life of privation and deprivation. So like a crab, he has become hardened, has developed a carapace that will remain intact all of his life. He does not find much to laugh about in life, and he does not bother to look for mirth. When neighbors greet Papa Dede with warmth and cheer, he responds with a grunt, and resumes whatever task he was engaged in before the interruption. Some people said that he was unfriendly, perhaps even hostile, but I did not agree. To me, Papa Dede was simply a man who cherished the music of silence.

THE COLLECTOR OF BUTTERFLIES AND WOMEN

On this day, our mission is to find as many bones as we can collect. Papa Dede has a goatskin bag slung around his left shoulder and carries a machete in his right hand. He carries thunder and lightning in this bag. It is full of power. The bag contains cowrie shells, small calabash containers, and some potions. He is a medicine man who can cure many diseases and ward off evil curses. At least that is what I believe. He is a big man in his late fifties and his health is failing. I never learned how he lost his eye. I don't think his children know either. Papa Dede uses the bones that he collects from the graveyard for making some of his rituals and potions. It is commonly believed that human bones can be used to make very potent medicine. Some witchdoctors in Nigeria have been rumored to kill people, especially children and women for ritual sacrifices.

Although I am bothered by what we are about to do, I tell myself that the dead do not feel any pain anyway and that we are not really harming anyone. The bones that we are looking to collect are small bones, bones from the fingers and toes of corpses. We are looking for old bones, not the newly buried. We will take a skull if we come across one, but we won't dig the earth with a shovel or hoe. We plan to take only what we can scavenge with our hands and feet. You see, even in grave robbing, there are rules to abide by.

As we walk grimly through the city of the dead, I shiver. I am frightened, but not frightened enough to want to run or scream. A cool wind blows across my face and I imagine that I hear the hushed whispers of the dead, querying our presence in their sanctuary. The voices are somber, leaden, dry like firewood. In the distance, an owl begins to hoot, its mournful cry sending a chill down my spine. Owls are said to be able to smell and see the angel of death before it descends.

Papa Dede has been here before, has dug for treasure in this patch of earth before. His stride is purposeful. He knows exactly where to go. I follow him, occasionally sneaking glances behind me to make sure that we are not being followed. I have an unsettling feeling that we are being followed. Perhaps the ghosts of the dead are following us, watching to see what we plan to do. The grass is wet, its long tongues licking at our feet. As we walk, we hear the incessant humming of insects. Trees sway coquettishly in the wind like festival dancers. A green snake slithers across our path.

Ahead of us are two fruit trees and they stick out in the bush. One is a mango tree and the other is a cashew tree. My favorite fruits. My throat aches with a sudden yearning. I stare at the ripe fruit on both trees. The fruits are heavy and ready for the picking. As I stare at them, I am suddenly overcome by nausea. The fruits look garish and unreal, sickly and troubling. My mind flashes to a book that I had read about a Nazi camp guard who planted the bodies of dead men in his garden and then planted vegetables and fruits on this fertilized soil. I immediately lose my appetite for the fruits.

Papa Dede must have seen the queasy look on my face. He asks me, "Are you okay?" He seems unsure about me. He has previously taken his two older boys out on a visit to the graveyard and now it is my turn. I do not want to appear like a coward. I do not want to be here. I want to be in the comfort of home, reading one of the two authors whose books I had recently stolen from the public library. Bertrand Russell and Frederic Nietszche.

"I am fine."

Papa Dede finds a spot that he likes. It is an inclined part of the land. Erosion from rain has washed away the top soil, creating the effect of a valley on either side of the piece of land where we are now standing. Papa Dede drops his bag on the grass, drops to his knees and begins to claw at the ground. I follow his lead. I pull out grass from the ground, dig into the soft earth.

We do not have to dig far. We literally hit pay dirt. The bleached bones of the dead are right there at the surface of the ground. These must be the poor people whose families could not afford a coffin. These poor wretches had simply been wrapped in cloth or some makeshift coffin and buried in shallow graves. Over the years, erosion and landmass movement had gradually pushed the bodies to the surface.

I realize that our coming to this spot was not blind chance. Papa Dede knew exactly where to dig.

We fill the bag with human fingers, toes and bone fragments. While Papa Dede goes for the big pieces, I focus on finding bone fragments. It is easier to rationalize this act if I do not see the human form shaped in our harvest. So I think of fine china and clay and pottery. I make believe that we are merely playing with the earth, fashioning men out of clay like Prometheus.

For what seems like an eternity, we dig. The hooting of the owl grows louder, more urgent, as if the creature is issuing a warning, asking us to desist and to depart. Finally, Papa Dede rises to his feet, and waves at me. "Let's go."

We trudge out of the graveyard. By now, the drowsy sun has closed its eye and gone to bed like a child after a heavy meal of *fufu*. It is the final hour before it becomes completely dark.

This was the first time that I went treasure hunting with Papa Dede and also the last time. I was thankful that he never asked me to accompany him on future visits. Perhaps he sensed my unease. Perhaps I had passed the test, survived what he considered a rite of passage for the males in his family.

I would see people from the town visit Papa Dede to purchase his services. He delivered his potions and charms to those who could afford to pay. Women who were desperate to have babies visited him. Men who suffered from impotence. Girls whose boyfriends strayed because the girls didn't give them enough sex. Men who wanted their girlfriends to give them more sex. Husbands who wanted to keep their wives in check, wives who wanted to keep their husbands in check.

In the superstitious world that we lived in, God was everywhere but nowhere to be found. People searched for Him and His son Jesus and when he didn't come to their rescue quick enough, they ventured out to intercessors, men like Papa Dede who claimed to be able to talk to spirits.

Poverty, fear and illiteracy drove people to worship at the altars of strange gods. In a society overrun by Philistines, the rich and the poor turned to 'drive-through' demigods who promised to deliver salvation and solution for a price. Even the so called elite and educated people often displayed this reliance on superstition, this atavism, this totemism.

And today, my guardian and I refused to let the dead rest in peace.

"Mess him up!"

The teacher raises the whip and I brace for the pain…
This is how my memory of high school begins. The school was Ika Grammar School. An all-boys school. As a teenager, I thought that it was the largest school in the world. But that is the nature of a teenager's worldview. As teenagers, we believe that we are immortals and that the earth revolves around us and not the sun. Out of clay, we fashion our own gods and worship them. We walk through the fire of the world, hoping to emerge unscathed.

The school was located on the outskirts of Agbor, near the Lagos Agbor road, on the road leading to the village of Umunede. The school had a main building which housed the principal's office and the administrative offices. The building was flanked by smaller hump-backed buildings cowering like abused children. One of them was a dormitory for boys.

Every inch of land appeared to be taken over by grass. Every day, students were assigned tracts of grass to cut. Indeed, a portion of the school day was dedicated to cutting grass. The taskmasters who assigned the work were the teachers and school prefects. School prefects were students appointed by teachers to supervise other students and institute discipline when required. Inflated by their authority and position, these demigods strutted through the school, meting out pain and punishment as they deemed fit. We regarded them with a robust contempt fit for traitors and child molesters.

We come to school armed with machetes and hack away at the stubborn grass daily. But the grass always wins. It always grows back. It is our nemesis.

Two of the teachers in the school have a reputation for being bad-tempered. The Agricultural Sciences teacher and the Assistant Principal. The Agricultural Sciences teacher is nicknamed 'Agric' by his students. The Assistant Principal is nicknamed 'Agoro Pepper.' The nickname originated from Agoro Pepper's habit of threatening to punish the students. "I am going to show you pepper." To show someone pepper meant to inflict pain on them.

Agric did not like my guts. He thought that I was stubborn and cocky and he wanted to break me, to trim me down to size. One day during class, he singles me out for punishment for some perceived misbehavior.

"You!" He points a stubby finger at me. "Step forward."

Agric was a furious expletive of a man. A dwarfish man with skin the color of trodden mangoes. He carried lightning in his eyes and storm clouds in his wake. We never saw him crack a smile. It was as if everything that transpired around him was a trifle and he did not have time to waste on trifles. He walked with short, purposeful steps, arms dangling beside him like a matador preparing to challenge a bull. He was always colorfully dressed and many of us were convinced that he was color blind. Ergo his other nickname, 'Color blind.' Agric wore his purples with his pinks and his reds with his blues. He was a man who listened to his interior voices and often those voices told him to dance while the rest of the world was merely walking. He moved too quickly for a man in his late fifties, as if fleeing from the reality of his age, a reality that was bound to overtake him no matter how fast he ran.

THE COLLECTOR OF BUTTERFLIES AND WOMEN

I step out in front of the class. I hear titters and giggles behind me. I keep my eyes aimed at the black board, refusing to look Agric in the eye.

The classroom holds forty or fifty students. We sit at small wooden desks and chairs, roughly hewn out of unpolished wood. The seats are hard on the buttocks, like pew chairs, hard on the constitution like organized religion. The floor is cement, bark-rough. The class lacks any adornment. There are no flowers, no ornaments, no photos of happy faces, no maps of foreign places. The walls are stark and unsympathetic. A large chalkboard takes up a section of the wall near the teacher's desk. On the wall, Agric has scribbled what I think of as hieroglyphs and starfish and stickmen. His handwriting is barely legible. It looks like the maunderings of a demented man. I happen to think that he *is* demented.

"Tough guy. Right?"

I do not respond to his taunt. I know what is coming. It is inevitable like rain clouds gathering, like cobras molting, like chickens coming home to roost.

"Face the wall."

I obey his bidding.

"I will teach you a lesson. You will learn not to joke around in my class."

Agric retrieves his whip from the floor.

He raises the whip and lashes at my buttocks. The pain is searing, bracing. I do not cry. I think of the Son of Mary Magdalene being led down the *Via Dolorosa*, the way of Suffering and Sorrow. I think of the Roman centurion raising his whip, the whip tipped with bone and lead, contoured with the fevers of a hundred wounded men.

Agric is the devil's spawn. I grab him and hand him over to the devil. The devil drags him down into the pit of hell. As Agric burns in lower hell, in flames that are eternal, he is taunted by wild eyed beasts with jowls dripping blood.

But this is just my imagination seeking escape.

There will be no escaping Agric's whip.

Agric raises the whip and lashes me again. I flinch but refuse to cry. Agric whips himself into a frenzy as he whips me mercilessly his mouth working wordlessly eyes bulging with a strange inflammation.

My buttocks are sore. The back of my thighs are on fire.

Agric is spent. He stops whipping me. He stares at me in bewilderment. Stares at me with revulsion as if I am a creature stricken with an unnamable plague.

"Get back to your seat."

I give him a long look, eyes full of defiance and triumph.

I walk back to my desk on unsteady legs.

Agric decides that he has had enough of his class for one day. He dismisses the class and like Pontius Pilate, he runs off to wash his hands. Or so I imagine.

That was the last time that Agric ever flogged me.

Agoro, the Assistant Principal, inspired terror in all the students. He was a light-skinned man with a stare that could wither the fruits on a tree and turn plums into prunes. That was when he was angry. When he was not angry, he had the smile of a cherub. He was genuinely interested in helping his students better themselves. What terrified students about Agoro was how quickly he could go from being the smiling jocular man to a volcano spewing hot ash.

Agoro rode his rickety bike at high speed around the school's campus, seeking out malfeasance and misdemeanor. He chased down wrong-doers on his bike like an angel of retribution. When he yelled, his voice competed with thunder. When he caught an unlucky bastard, he upbraided them in his loud voice. Agoro spoke perfect English with a colonial accent. No one liked to be cursed out in perfect English.

In school, being bullied by older boys was very commonplace. I had to fight off my fair share of bullies. I was not a big kid. I was skinny and not exactly an intimidating sight physically but I was sociable and made friends easily. I was not picked on as much as some other kids. My reputation grew when I represented the school in the regional debating competition. Although, I finished second, I became something of a celebrity in school. Not long after, I also won a writing competition and received a certificate. The certificate was proudly displayed by the principal in his office. I was on top of the world.

An older student nicknamed Correspond decided to pick on me. Correspond was one of the high school toughs whom many kids avoided. He was squat and muscular with the clean shaven face of a castrati and the disarming smile of a child molester. Behind that smile was a viciousness that some unlucky students had witnessed. Correspond had been known to punch an opponent until they were bloody, break someone's fingers and kick a fellow student so hard in the stomach that the student bent over and vomited balls of *fufu* on the grass. I had heard that he broke bottles of beer on his head when enraged. When he did this before a fight, it usually scared off any opponents. On one occasion, he was said to have chewed at the shards of glass and swallowed them.

I am not sure exactly how or why Correspond added me to his enemies list. One day, I observed him glaring at me while I was talking to some friends of mine. He pointed a warning finger at me and spat in the sand.

"Mr. Know It All."

"Fuck off." I responded.

"Really? I will teach you a lesson after school."

Later that day, after school is over, Correspond and I meet outside the school compound to settle our scores. We meet in a field half a mile from the school. The grass is almost knee high. He is waiting for me when I show up. A gauntlet of students circles him like buzzards readying for dinner, waiting on a corpse. A couple of my friends are around me. We are all dressed in blue shorts and white shirts. We are standing on soggy ground, feet and sandals wet.

I drop my school bag, my breath coming fast. My senses go into overdrive. All of a sudden, I become aware of the smell of the lush vegetation. I hear the wind moaning like a lecher as it caresses the limbs of coquettish trees. Birds trill and coo in the afternoon. The air is damp. Insects buzz cheerfully around us. The skies are as cloudy as the eyes of an old man slowly going blind.

I am no match for correspond and I know it. My friends know it. Correspond knows it. His friends know it. But I am stubborn and too foolish to acknowledge defeat. I know that I am going to get beat up. But I won't make it easy for my opponent.

Correspond grins like a cat about to devour a bowl of milk.

"Ready to get your butt whipped, pussy?"

I am too terrified to speak although I do not show it. My senses are heightened, blood rushes to my brain, my mind becomes rapier sharp. I am thinking hard, trying to figure a way out of this. There appear to be two options; neither good. I was going to get beat up or I was going to get beat up badly.

Correspond lunges at me wildly. I step aside and dodge his thumping jab. Just barely. Correspond is thrown off balance but quickly recovers. He comes at me again with an Armageddon swing, ready to knock my lights out, to end my world. I duck again, but I am not as lucky this time. The blow catches the side of my head, although I escape the full impact of his tomahawk shot. It is only a glancing blow but I stagger and lose my balance.

Correspond leaps on me as I try to get up.

Bad mistake.

I stick my foot out and kick him in the groin.

Hard.

He howls in rage and pain, like a hungry man who has found a worm in his soup. He drops to the ground and grabs his testicles.

THE COLLECTOR OF BUTTERFLIES AND WOMEN

I sense my opportunity and move in for the kill as the big bully lays in a fetal position. I jump up and slap him in the face. He lets go of his nuts to protect his face. I grab his testicles with both hands and squeeze. He lets out a blood-curdling yell, a hyena caught in a hunter's trap. His eyes go wide with pain, fill with tears. All of a sudden, he looks like a little boy.

He tries to push me off, to loosen my grip but I squeeze harder with each attempt that he makes. He tries to move closer, to head-butt me, but it is of no use. I move my head back and squeeze harder.

"Please. Please stop. Let go."

I become aware of the roars of the small crowd that has gathered around us. Correspond's friends are baffled and shamed by this spectacle. My friends are cheering loudly. "GET HIM!" "MESS HIM UP!" "MESS HIM UP!"

I am tempted to do him permanent damage, to satisfy the bloodlust of the crowd. In Nigeria, when your enemy is down, you never walk away. You kick and stomp on them until blood runs on the ground like blood on the shrine of a bulimic god, until the saltiness of blood fills the air like the smell of seawater and seaweed. You hit them until they cannot move anymore. Hit them until they cannot do you harm anymore.

"If you ever come after me again, I will kill you."

Correspond does not reply, eyes bulging with pain and fear.

"You hear me?" My voice is hoarse, exultant, demonic. I feel insuperable, eternal.

Correspond nods.

"You may be bigger and stronger than me but I will get you. I promise."

"Let him go." One of Correspond's friends urges. "You've won. Let the man go."

"Stay out of it!" I yell at the speaker, still holding on to Correspond's balls.

"Unless you are prepared to kill me, don't ever come after me again. If you don't kill me, I will kill you."

Correspond nods piteously.

I give his balls one last squeeze before I let go. He is bent over in pain when my friends and I walk off.

Correspond left me alone after that.

That year, our school principal, a man that I liked very much was knifed to death in a fight. The students never found out what the fight was about. But they did learn one thing.

The man who did him in was his own brother.

Growing up, violence was in the very air that we breathed and the water that we drank. Perhaps a strain of it must have somehow got into our mothers' breast milk and doomed us from the very first day we were born. I was destined to encounter more violence as I grew older, destined to ponder the nature of violence on many more occasions.

I drop to the ground

I can see the blood pouring out of my ankle. I am fascinated by it. The blood eddies out of my foot like a geyser, like a fountain. I think I am dying. Or I am already dead. Why else don't I feel any pain? I think of gored bulls, of men decapitated at war, of guillotines and gallows, of fetid corpses blackened with tumescence. I think of whitewashed blameless souls being admitted into the Elysian Fields.

"Somebody help him!"

I hear a gaggle of panicked voices, children, students milling around like roaches blinded by smoke.

I drop to the ground.

The place where I sustained the injury was at school. Ika Grammar School. Several days each week, students were assigned by teachers to cut the grass that grew like Medusa's hair all over the school. The grass was stubborn and perversely verdant. At the back of the school where the grass was tallest, tongues of grass licked your face when you walked. Inside the school field where we played, fingers of grass stroked your feet when you walked. You cut the bloody thing by Monday and by Tuesday, it seemed it had grown back overnight.

The teachers marched the students out to the grass as if to an execution. The teachers spread their feet apart and marked out a section of grass for each student to cut. They strode through the tall grass, these taskmasters, these purveyors of pain and suffering and apportioned lots to each student. When the teachers were too busy, they simply delegated the task to some of the senior students. The seniors, cherishing their roles as prefects, ruled their fiefdoms with an iron hand, taunting and prodding, shoving and browbeating.

Arm was a tall strapping kid who had recently arrived in Nigeria from America. He was now living with a relative in Agbor. I remembered when he showed up for school with his funny American accent. The entire class trooped out to talk to him, this big kid with the serious face who chewed and then swallowed his words, speaking too fast for anyone to understand him. It took a while for us to get used to his furious diction, his lolling cadences, his mellifluous inflections. I yearned to bridge the spatiality between the world that he had left and the world that he was now in.

I was fascinated by him. In truth, not really by him, but by where he was from. I had many questions for him about America, the land I had heard so much about. I wanted to hear about George Washington, Abraham Lincoln and Jesse James. I knew a lot about America from the books that I had read. I knew about American history, art, music, politics, crime and literature. The local library opened up the world to me. I went to bed with J D Salinger and Hemingway at twelve, dined with Sylvia Plath and Flannery O'Connor at thirteen and masturbated to Anne Sexton at fifteen. I immersed myself in Americana seeking escape from my putrid surroundings.

Some of the kids picked on Arm. They regarded him as a curio, as something to be explored. They were like a man who had woken up to find a six foot tall naked plastic doll on his front lawn. Who could blame the man for wanting to take it inside his house to examine it, to understand the thing of the matter?

THE COLLECTOR OF BUTTERFLIES AND WOMEN

"Hey, American boy. Whazzamatter wid you?" This was some jester's idea of the American idiom one day in class. The class erupts in laughter. The comedian struts around the class, pleased with himself.

'Dynamite, baby!" Another one says, mimicking Jay Jay, the Jimmy Walker character on the *Good Times* TV show.

Arm looks uncomfortable and rather pained, but he puts up with all of these inanities and shenanigans in stiff-lipped silence. Which only emboldens his tormentors. One day, I step in to defend Arm. I was tired of seeing him being picked on, tired of the invidious comments.

"Guys, why don't you cut it out? Get a life."

The two ringleaders stared at me with hostility but did not respond. It appeared that word had got around about my fight with Correspond, the bottle eater.

From that day on, Arm and I became friends. I peppered him with questions about America and he indulged me. When a boy tried to con Arm out of his lunch money by laying some hard-luck story on Arm, I told Arm not to give in. Arm was a generous kid, always willing to share with others. That was how he became a mark in the first place. Growing up, showing kindness and gentleness was often taken as a sign of weakness. Those who were brutal and violent were feared and avoided. Those who were kind and gentle were conned and exploited. These were hard-won lessons that Arm had to learn. He was a quick learner. We stuck to each other and became very close friends.

That was how I found myself assigned a lot of grass to cut right next to Arm.

From the moment Arm showed up on the grass field with the machete, I had an uneasy feeling. He wasn't holding the machete properly. He dangled it on the tips of his fingers instead of holding it in the palm of his hands. I could tell right away that he had never used a machete before.

"Here, let me show you how to use that."

I show Arm how to hold the machete. The machete is a long slender curved knife about three feet long. It is wickedly sharp. The handle is made of two bits of wood, nailed together in a hurry as if the blacksmith was hurrying home to dinner or to his wife's warm embrace.

"Sure you know how to use this?" I ask.

Arm has a dubious look on his face. "I think so." I hear the lack of confidence in his voice.

I beckon to Arm to move back. He is standing too close to me. I grab the machete.

"Watch me."

With short, vigorous strokes, I begin to hack at the grass. I cut a swath through the grass, leaving dust, insects and grass in my wake.

I was impressing Arm but not the teacher who was assigning the work this particular morning. He called my name and I paused.

The teacher measured out my portion of the grass, did the same for Arm and then moved on to the next student.

We set to work in earnest.

Arm has the portion of grass on my right side while another kid has the portion on my left. I am focused on the task at hand which is why I do not see the blow coming. I do not really feel it. What I feel is a sudden numbness that seizes my right foot. It grabs me like a retiring pro football player holding on to a pre-nup and would not let go.

It takes me a split second to realize that my best friend, Arm, has just cut my foot, nearly severed it off at the ankle. Cut a vein.

Time stands still. I think that it does. Arm's mouth is wide open in shock. He is mouthing, "Ohmygodohmygodohmygod."

That is when a student shouts, "Somebody help him!"

But no one helps me.

I think of one of those corpses that turn up every so often on the

THE COLLECTOR OF BUTTERFLIES AND WOMEN

streets of Agbor, a man run over by a car, a woman found face up in a puddle, feet poking invidiously at the sky, a goat with its entrails spilled open like hot lava. The commonality of these images is that people usually walk by, and no one stops to cover up the dead.

I am dying.

Arm picks me up and hoists me on his shoulder, my right foot dangling uselessly.

A teacher emerges and directs us to the principal's office.

We head to the main building where the principal's office is located. I am losing blood, leaving a blood spoor on the grass and sand. I feel a sense of peace, an extraordinary lucidity. The world has come alive, sharpened at the edges. The wind slaps my face and my ears fill with the excitation of alarmed students. I hear Arm's harsh breath as he takes each step, trying to save the life of the boy yoked to his back. His breath is as loud as a thunderclap, as loud as the ominous sounds of an invading army pressing an attack.

When we arrive at the principal's office, the big man emerges and immediately takes charge.

"We need to get him to the hospital. Right away!" The principal is a tall man with a booming voice. He quickly arranges to have me taken to the hospital in a car. Before we depart for the hospital, my foot is bandaged to stanch the flow of blood.

We arrive at the local hospital after successfully battling traffic and demented bus drivers. We walk past the maternity ward where women litter the room like withered rose petals at yesterday's picnic, like pot-bellied flies trapped in pain's unyielding web. They curse their husbands for impregnating them and curse themselves for yielding to their husband's propositions. Their keening fills my ears as we move down the hallway looking for the doctor who will stitch my wound.

I am not sure how we ended up in the Dispensary, a small building behind the maternity ward. It appears that a doctor is not on hand to perform the required medical procedure so a nurse will be sewing me up. He is a busy man who barely glances at me as I moan and grunt in pain before him. I think of him as the curator of pain, a man who has seen pain in its various incarnations and refinements, in its various permutations and contours. I resent his briskness, his business like efficiency, his self-assured air.

He does not have any anesthetic on hand. If he does, he is saving it for some more serious procedure, perhaps a cesarean section or heart surgery or an amputation.

I am terrified of having my foot amputated. I had heard horrible stories of botched surgeries committed (I mean, performed) by unqualified hospital personnel. I had heard of surgical implements forgotten in the bowels of patients while the patient was stitched up. Surgeries performed without morphine by intoxicated surgeons still tacking Friday night's hangover.

I wonder if the man in front of me is even a nurse. Perhaps he is the hospital janitor working for some extra cash. Or the groundskeeper picking up some overtime. I wrestle with my paranoia and my fear.

I lose.

And so it begins.

My surgery without anesthetic.

The tool the nurse uses to stitch my foot looks like a fish hook. It is a metal ring with surgical thread looped through a hole at one end of it. Somebody holds me down while the nurse goes to work. He begins to stitch up my injury.

I try to be brave. Give up after one second. Howl. Like a hound from the innermost pit of hell. Try to pass out. But I do not pass out.

The Romans used the gibbet for impaling the condemned. They crucified enemies of the state, slaves and lawbreakers.

I felt like I was being nailed to every kind of gibbet possible.

Long before I was thirteen, I had learned that self-pity was a waste of time in a world that had no pity.

I howl.

The man who loves to drink raw eggs

The man who loves to drink raw eggs is in the next room having sex with his wife.

I am curled up on the sofa listening to the steady thump thump as he goes airborne and then crashes down, up, down, up down.

There is a monotony to his movement that is almost melodious, oddly comforting. His wife emits soft strangled moans, the keening of a child who has happened upon a spider on its bed.

I am aroused as I listen to a man attempting to make a baby with his wife. This then is how procreation works, I think, a mechanical grinding, a tedious friction of two bodies, flesh on flesh, lip on lip, appendage to appendage. A wheeze and a groan, rumbling and fumbling toward an eternal sigh.

At least three times a week, I listen to Yaku, a man in his fifties, chase immortality. In Africa, a man's sons are the transport through which he attains immortality. A man with a son or several sons is assured that his lineage will last forever and that his blood will pump in the veins of many generations to come. A man without a male heir is a man who is dreaming silent dreams, worshipping strange moons. Yaku, my guardian, badly wanted a male child.

Yaku's wife, Sube, is a pretty woman with high cheekbones and deep set dimples. She has a twinkly smile and guarded eyes. Her teeth are whiter than clouds on a sunless day. I think that they are the most beautiful teeth that God ever made. The woman is kind to me. Her husband thinks that she is too kind.

"You need to help Sube around the house. You don't do enough." He tells me.

I fetch water from the nearby river. One day, I nearly drown because I am foolish enough to accept a challenge to go into deeper waters and I am not a good swimmer. I remember choking, lungs filling with water, eyes bulging as I screamed but did not scream because I could not scream and asked for help but no one came and I thought this is what it feels like to die before you are a man before you have solved the riddle of life.

I wash clothes. I wash them in an aluminum bucket using *Omo* soap, wring them out to dry and hang them on clotheslines outside where the wind twirls them like an old man lifting up a young girl's dress.

I clean dishes and pots. Scour them with passion as if seeking the philosopher's stone. Scour them like a groom searching for his lost ring on his wedding day.

I cook. Using a mortar and a pestle, I pound yam into the local delicacy known as 'Pounded Yam. I am Shango, hurling down thunderbolts as I bring down the pestle to make the evening meal for the man who loves to drink raw eggs.

But it is not enough.

Not for Yaku, the man who is trying to find immortality.

He hates my guts.

Justifiable perhaps. I was unwanted baggage, after all, detritus blown in by a fitful wind.

I was pawned off on Yaku after I moved out of Zack's house. After my father was transferred by his employer to yet another town,

THE COLLECTOR OF BUTTERFLIES AND WOMEN

my father sent me to live with Zack and his wife. Although I liked Zack and derived vicarious thrills from the many nights he brought home hookers from Hill Street, I sensed that his wife was tiring of me. When I told my father that I no longer wanted to live with Zack and his wife, my father decided to send me to his friend, Yaku who lived in another part of Agbor. I was not happy about this decision but I had no choice. Yaku's house was the interval between Zack's house and Mama Dede's house.

Yaku, his wife, daughter and I lived in a two room apartment. The apartment was located in a large compound that contained three ugly buildings. Each building was divided into multiple apartments, each separated by a narrow grimy corridor. The three buildings – I thought of them as the Gorgon sisters – Medusa, Stheno and Euryale, crouched in a semicircle, wearing ochre make-up and zinc headgear.

A communal kitchen faced the buildings with several small rooms, one door for each renter. If you opened one of the doors and peered into one of the rooms in the kitchen, what you would see would be walls blacker than a tobacco chewer's spit, a wood or kerosene stove, and pots and pans.

On any given day, the smell of fish frying in palm oil or goat meat boiling mingles with the smell of assorted spices and condiments. If you listen, you can hear the sounds of pestles beating the mortar, of pepper and tomatoes being blended in a grindstone, of firewood crackling and lizards scuttling around.

You can hear a husband and wife arguing. The young married couple. The man does not trust his wife. He has seen the landlord ogling her. Why does she walk so jauntily whenever the landlord is watching her, why does she add that extra bounce to her step? The wife protests her innocence, but jealousy is insidious, this disease of the soul. And it often leads to raised voices and raised hands.

You can hear children playing *boju-boju*. Hide and seek. It was during *Boju Boju* that a girl first showed me her budding breasts, made me touch them and then challenged me to show her my penis. Quid pro quo. Craven child that I was, I ran off, while she jeered at me and warned me not to tell anyone.

If you listen, you can hear dinner time conversations, tall tales told by moonlight or lamplight, voices hushed so as not to disturb sleepy ghosts. You can hear the roar of time fill your ears like a tide and feel the tautness of the world as it stretches out on its toes like a ballerina.

They said that Yaku had waited too long to discover marriage. They said that his children ought to be his grandchildren. They said that he was a man trying to roast yams when the fire had already become embers, when the fire now merely smoldered. Yaku was determined to prove them wrong. He was determined to engage this fight with biology, to challenge destiny to this dance. So far, he had won the first round. He had produced one daughter already. With the help of egg yolk, he expected to win the second round, hopefully, with a male child this time.

Yaku was a tall balding man with the icy eyes of a reptile. His walk was slow and ponderous, as if he carried on his shoulder a heavy load of unforgiven sins. He was a man of abbreviated sentences, a man of elongated silences. When you told him something, he first chewed on your words and swallowed them before forming his reply. I found the silences in his conversations operatic and maddening. A conversation with Yaku took a lifetime. Given a choice, I would have preferred to be subjected to the Chinese water torture invented by the Bolognese lawyer, Hippolytus de Marsiliis. Yaku was an old man dreaming a young man's dreams. I on the other hand, was a young man dreaming an old man's dreams.

I did not live for long with Yaku.

His resentment for me continued to grow. At first a blister, his resentment soon grew into a sore that would begin to ooze pus. When it reached suppuration, it became clear that he wanted me out of his house.

THE COLLECTOR OF BUTTERFLIES AND WOMEN

One cloudy evening, when rain droplets as large as elephants dropped from the skies, I packed my bag and left Yaku's house. As I walked off, heading for Mama Dede's house, I began to cry silently. I cried because of my nomadic life, my unstable family. I missed my parents and my siblings badly. I wondered why my life had to be one of constant motion, of dislocation, of impermanence and erasure. I wondered why my father could not find another job that would be more stable and would not require frequent relocation. I wondered if there was honor in a man leaving his family behind while he sought to earn a living for them.

Isn't the greatest bravery of all the bravery of those who stay behind? The men and women who do not go to war but have to keep the villages and towns running? Men and women whose callused hands hold the bricks and the scaffolding, men and women who sing canticles and hold conventicles.

Perhaps it is a form of escape on my father's part, that he has chosen this path. The warrior says to his wife and children, I must go to war, for the greater good. Isn't the warrior's decision really a form of abdication, rather than the abnegation that it masquerades as? Isn't it much easier to save the whole world than to save your own household?

I had not seen some of my sisters in a couple of years. I had not seen my mother and father in months.

The rain came to me in my moment of weakness and self-pity. It washed away my tears as I plodded on, through muddy thirsty streets, past cheerful little houses with winking kerosene lanterns, inside which men loved their wives or beat their wives, past the wreckage of unfulfilled lives and the tumescence of yet unrealized ambitions, past the spirits of yesterday and the ghosts of the future. I carried fear in my left breast and hope in my right breast.

Forbidden love

I was fifteen when I fell in love with Tee. She was fourteen.
I was enchanted by her eyes that were as hurtful as sea anemones and just as beautiful, by her smile that turned young boys to pillars of salt. She was light skinned with big eyes that could mock you one minute and laugh with you the next. For a fourteen year old, she was already well developed. I do not care to go into details about her bodily endowments and attributes. I lusted for her with biblical passion, my soul full of corruption.

I was enthralled by Tee and she knew it. I considered Tee my sister although we were not related by blood. Her parents had taken me in when my father was forced to relocate to another town for a new job.

Tee always teased me that I was too serious, that I needed to loosen up, needed to laugh. Poverty had made me sad, and stolen my laughter. I lost my capacity for mirth long before I was fourteen. In family photographs taken in my teenage years, I see a skinny kid with a stern expression and adamantine eyes. I had seen the world bloody and the world depraved and I had decided that I didn't like the world very much. I was like Heraclitus, the weeping philosopher.

THE COLLECTOR OF BUTTERFLIES AND WOMEN

On this day, Tee and I are sitting in our tiny apartment. Our other siblings are away. Mama Dede and Papa Dede are also away. It is just the two of us, listening to the rain.

The water is hitting the zinc roof like a thousand precious jewels scattered from the fist of a drunken god. There are no gutters in Agbor, no drainage system. When it rains in Agbor, land becomes water and water becomes land, an enemy that can steal children or buckets and pans left outside. Mothers corral their young children when the heavy rains come, lest they get carried away in the deluge. You walk the streets during the rainy season and find yourself ankle deep in red mud. The muddy water is a serpent and a hallucination, carrying dirty rags and broken dreams, carrying leaves and food wrappers.

We place plastic buckets and metal drums outside to catch the water. If it rains hard enough, we will have enough water to last a few days and not have to go to the public taps. We thank the rain gods. If it rains too hard, the water invades our houses, knocks flimsy roofs from the top of buildings. We curse the rain gods.

We are sitting in the tiny humid room watching the small TV mounted on a dresser. The TV is snowy, the sound full of static.

I hold her hand, rub it gently. She looks up at me, somewhat surprised. I cannot tell if she has ever sensed my feelings toward her. I am ashamed of these feelings. Inappropriate feelings that a boy should not be feeling for his sister. I have struggled with them for months. It has made our communication awkward, difficult. I had often tried to avoid being alone with Tee, not trusting what I might say.

But on this day, lust gets the better of me.

Tee had always been rather inscrutable. For a fourteen year old, she was remarkably perceptive. Although, she was very smart, she knew how to make you feel that you were smarter. If she was aware of my tortured feelings, she never acknowledged it.

She pulls her hand back. I recoil as if wounded. As if sensing that my feelings might be hurt, she takes my hand in hers.

For months, I have practiced exactly what I would say to her. I would woo her with my poetry delivered with aplomb and Shakespearean heft.

I would recite her Elizabeth Browning.

As strange as it seems, my lust for Tee has always been more sensuous than sexual, more romantic than rabid. I close my eyes and make believe that I am Lord Byron and that Tee is Augusta Leigh, the half-sister with whom Lord Byron was said to have had an incestuous relationship.

Both of us were aware of the danger of taking the relationship further. We both knew that we could never consummate this forbidden relationship. We had both heard stories of young girls who were subjected to nameless horrors for daring to get pregnant. I had heard of mothers who slashed their teen daughters with razor blades and then rubbed pepper on their skin. Some parents ground red hot pepper and rubbed it in the offending vagina. Some parents slashed off their daughter's clitoris and portions of their labia to punish them for their act of shame.

I always thought that the punishment meted out to these young girls was unfair and that there was a double standard. How come no boy ever got punished for sleeping with a girl or getting her pregnant? Why did the girl always have to bear the brunt end of the stick, to carry the scarlet letter of shame?

I saw a neighbor's daughter subjected to the pepper treatment. Uche's sin was not that she got herself pregnant, but that she almost got herself pregnant. She was caught having sex with a boy. The boy ran off but Uche had no place to run. Her mother grabbed her and beat her with her fists, kicked her, and shoved her to the ground. As Uche begged for Mercy, Mama Uche told her, "I will teach you pepper. You think you can become a harlot in my house?"

THE COLLECTOR OF BUTTERFLIES AND WOMEN

I could hear Uche begging for mercy, praying to God to save her soul, but on this night, Jehovah was taking a nap. He did not respond to her cries.

Mama Uche found a bottle of ground *atarodo* pepper, commonly called Yellow Lantern Chilli pepper or capsicum chinense. Her thirteen year old daughter would be her guinea pig in her experiment to test the frontiers of pain. How much pain could the body handle before it broke like a bough before monsoon winds?

And Uche screamed.

I heard Uche scream and I found her cries comical.

Humor comes easy when tragedy visits someone else's doorstep. An old lady slips on a banana peel and it inspires a deep belly laugh. A rich man catches his wife in bed with the houseboy. Empathy is not a virtue that comes easy to a child of fourteen. Most of the time, I was a sociopath, cruel and selfish in the cheerful way that only children can be.

My efforts at romance were gauche. I offered Tee cashew nuts and bubble gum known to all kids as Bazooka Joe. I offered goody-goody candy. I offered purple prose and convulsive poetry that came in fits like the exertions of an epileptic.

Tee and I would never consummate our relationship.

It took one year for our folie a deux, our non-relationship, to die a slow tortured death. After it died, I buried it deep below the floorboards, this red-veined wound, this bastard child, and I let the arterial blood run until there was nothing left.

Can she be saved?

My mother is sick and I am afraid that she might die. As a child, I died many deaths.

If my childhood is considered as one act, one life lived, this then is the epitaph of my childhood.

My mother was always sick and each time she took ill, I was the one that died. One year, my mother takes ill while visiting us in Agbor. I return from school to find her curled up in bed, brow shiny with perspiration. She hacks softly, eyes rimmed with pain and a strange fever. A snake crawls up my insides and takes up residence.

I do not know what is wrong with my mother. I have grown used to her undiagnosed diseases, to medicine men who promise to cure her maladies, medicine men with efficient eyes that peer into the dark recesses of people's souls, men who consort with the devil and restive spirits. I have seen healers come and go, toting bags full of cowrie shells, divination beads, animal claws, potions, bright feathers, mirrors, and assorted objects. My mother believes in magic and in men who can intercede with the gods.

Can the men of magic cure her this time? Can she be saved?

THE COLLECTOR OF BUTTERFLIES AND WOMEN

When it came to matters involving God, there was a divergence in my parents' beliefs. While my father firmly believed that there was only one God, Allah, my mother was far less certain about this. So she took an approach that was decidedly Pascallian; she would hedge her bets, play it safe. She settled on polytheism. On the few occasions that she went to the mosque, she was an imposter, a Christian in the mosque, an apple among oranges. When she went to church, which was often, she was an imposter, a pagan in the house of Jesus. My mother Magdalena was as comfortable offering chicken blood to the god of the sea as she was singing halleluyahs to the son of Man. She is the woman of many religions, the woman who collects gods like a polyandrist collects husbands. She has learned to become a shape-shifter, a woman of amorphous identity. Having spent all of her life trying to be what her husband and children wanted her to be, my mother was still trying to decide who she truly was.

My mother acknowledges me with a nod, eyes full of love and compassion. The room is dark and smells like fever. My mother is swaddled in blankets although the room is hot. The windows are shut. I notice the smell of an astringent ointment that has been rubbed on my mother's body. The smell grinds against my stomach like the feet of oxen plowing the earth.

My father is sitting on a threadbare sofa in what passes for the living room. A small Binatone black and white TV purchased secondhand weeks ago sits on an arthritic stool. The pictures on the screen are not clear, merely spiders crawling through a chiaroscuro. The walls are stained with dust, smoke and last year's dinners. A few bright posters of western rock stars hang incongruously on the wall, as out of place as confetti at a funeral.

I greet my father and he smiles tightly at me. A man who has lived on a steady diet of optimism all of his life, he has consigned his life to Allah for safekeeping. He has put his wife's fate in God's hands. His oft-repeated lines are, "God will take care of it." "It's all in God's hands."

My father was a man doing battle with life and I often wondered if what I saw on his face was resignation, the resignation of defeat, or rapture, the rapture of victory. Was his calmness the quiescence of Crypto-Jews marching boldly to the stake during the Spanish Inquisition or the resignation of moribund 'witches' condemned at Salem? His favorite prayer was the Serenity prayer. Can a man hypnotize or drug himself with the Serenity prayer?

Some days, my father shone as bright as the sun, on other days he was as cloudy as a thunderstorm. I regarded him like I would an actor who was playing various roles, at times Euripidean, at times Aristophanic. Regarded him like a boy watching a magician, wondering what new rabbit he would pull out of his capacious hat.

I wondered how he reconciled his adulterous behavior with his piety, how a man who prayed five times a day could cheat on his wife. Even as a child, I saw the contradictions in my father's life. He was a devoted husband who loved his wife yet cheated on her. A staunch Muslim married to a woman who believed in spirits and magic. A loving father who would hand over three of his oldest children to family and friends to raise. My father was not a man in the midst of a crowd; he was a crowd by himself. A man of multiple personalities and many lives, brimming with many truths and many realities.

That evening, the medicine man shows up to see my mother. He is a small man with quick steps. He has the ostentatious manner of a general who has won several bloody wars, the hauteur of a man who communes with spirits. His eyes are blood-red, his hair has taken flight from his skull, leaving recalcitrant patches. He brings with him a smell that assaults the nostrils. The smell of rot, the smell of birds afflicted by filicollosis and schools of poisoned fish rotting on a pebble-strewn shore. When he speaks, his voice rumbles like a disturbed volcano roused from sleep. He waves me away. Children were obviously forbidden to hear his Sibylline words.

THE COLLECTOR OF BUTTERFLIES AND WOMEN

I exit the room into the corridor that leads outside. Instead of heading outside, however, I sneak back into our living quarters through the second door, the door that leads out from the bedroom.

As I eavesdrop on the conversation, I catch snatches of things that the medicine man wants my parents to do. They include sacrificing a chicken, drinking some potion, taking a bath in the bush in the middle of the night.

I died again that night.

Went to sleep that night terrified, wondering if my mother would die.

My mother did not die.

Fate, I come to realize, has a way of sparing us from one horror in order to save us for the next.

A week later, she would leave Agbor fully recovered and return to Auchi where my younger siblings were anxiously waiting for her. Life and normalcy, as we knew it would resume for my sister, Mary and me in Agbor.

But life turned out to be a trickster and a court jester, always full of surprises and jokes. And as we would find out, the joke was always on us.

Happiness

There is something very dangerous about normal people. Normal people who plant gardenias in Spring and water their lawns every week, who go to the hairdresser or the barber once a week, pick up a bottle of Merlot from the corner store on their way from church where they have gone to sing hosannas to the Son of Man and dry-cleaned their souls so thoroughly that their souls are squeaky clean and they are ready now for another round of sinning, sex, murder and theft.

Even more dangerous are happy people. As a child, I hated happy people because I found them suspicious. What were they so damned happy about? The way I saw it, a man or woman who walks around with a smile on their face is someone who has something to hide. Coming across a happy man or woman first thing in the morning was like seeing a black cat. It was an ill omen which filled me with dread.

Mama Dede was one of the happiest people that I knew. One of few such people that I liked and was not terrified of. Despite the fact that she was raising seven children in grinding poverty, she did not bemoan her fate, did not let the smile slip from her face. She treated

THE COLLECTOR OF BUTTERFLIES AND WOMEN

me just like her own children. The family adopted me as one of their own.

Mama Dede worked hard to take care of her family. She went to the local market to buy cassava tubers. She peeled them for hours on end and then took them to the local mill to grind them into a paste. She allowed this paste to dry into a powder and she baked the powder to make *garri*. *Garri* is a staple in the diet of many. When added to hot water and stirred, it hardens to a paste known as *eba*. Mama Dede sold garri to the neighbors and earned a small income from this. She also sold *eko*. *Eko* is made from corn paste. The paste is wrapped in banana leaves and then steamed over fire. Many a time, all we had to eat was *eba* and *eko*. So we ate this everyday for a week or two, until something else came along.

The apartment where we live is a two room affair on Catholic Street in Agbor. One room is the parlor and the second room is the bedroom. In the parlor, there is a small bunk bed and two chairs, an oversize cabinet mounted with a small black and white TV. The floor is bare. A couple of rolled raffia mats are tucked in a corner. These are used for sleeping at night. Every day, we toss a coin to decide who will sleep on the bed. Lucky, Mama Dede's second son is usually the winner, living up to his name. But whoever is lucky enough to sleep on the bed with Lucky soon finds out to their chagrin that they are really unlucky. You see, Lucky is a kicker. He plays soccer in his sleep. The football that he kicks around is the person lying next to him. Lucky talks in his sleep too. He chats and kicks his way through each night and you wake up sore and bruised.

The bedroom is a tiny room dominated by a large king sized bed and a second bed. The king sized bed is where my guardians, Papa Dede and Mama Dede sleep. The bed is curtained off with a piece of cloth, to provide privacy. The second bed is where my adopted sister and two of my adopted brothers, the younger boys, sleep. Once a week, like clockwork, I wake up to the sounds of two middle aged people having furtive sex. Mortified, I ask God to make me deaf on the spot. But God, used to ignoring me, does not respond to my prayer.

There is a small window with cross bars that looks out to a plot of land with thorny bushes. A few houses, dressed in unadorned brick, wearing silly zinc hats, peek through the vegetation. Outside of our house, the ground is either baked to a hard cake by the sun or soggy from the rains that never seem to stop. I peer through the window like an animal in a cage and wonder if the lives of the people across the street are as perfectly miserable as mine. Pots, pans and plates are scattered all over the floor. A large pot-bellied plastic container sits on the floor. This contains our drinking water. When you lift the lid of the container, there is a film at the top of the water. The water is not clean. Whenever I take a cup to dip in the water to drink, I realize just how dirty the water is. My mind flashes to my studies in hygiene and sanitation. I think of germs, salmonella, bacteria cultures, typhoid, cholera, the black plague, typhoid. I think of death, slow painful death but I drink nonetheless.

People do not seem to worry too much about sanitation and good hygiene. I suppose that when you already live daily with the disease of poverty, poverty so palpable that you can touch it, feel it, inhale it, it is difficult to worry about unseen diseases. In the compound where we live, young urchins sit on rubbish heaps and take dumps then rub their backsides vigorously on sand and let the backsides air dry afterward. Some indolent parents simply dig a hole in the ground and let the child shit in the hole, then cover it with sand. That way, they don't have to bother to scoop up the waste. Ayeni, one of our neighbors, takes it even further. After his young children take a shit, he simply calls out his two dogs to eat the shit as their dinner.

I am terrified of the two brown mangy dogs, their eyes fierce with unnamable fury, jowls dripping shit. I keep away from them, knowing that a bite from them could mean rabies. The two hounds

THE COLLECTOR OF BUTTERFLIES AND WOMEN

from hell are always in a vile mood, barking at even babies, keeping the neighbors up late at night. They get no mercy from their master, Ayeni. He beats them with a cane, a shoe, hurling anything in his path at them whenever he is angry. The dogs are terrified of their master and we are terrified of the dogs.

Children walk around with the stench of shit haunting them like vengeful ghosts. Meals are cooked in an open fire stoked by fire wood right next to the dumpster where children shit. The rubbish heap is malodorous, piled high with forgotten lives, articles of clothing, cans and containers, old newspapers, feces, chicken bones and regrets.

On any day, if the wind is right, you can catch the smell of feces and pepper stew at the same time. It is a troubling combination, repulsing and inviting at the same time. The smell of feces drifts in from the pit latrine while the smell of cooking wafts from the open kitchen area near the dumpster.

We rarely wash our hands when we use the toilet. There just isn't enough water to waste on such frivolities, such whimsies. Water is just too hard to come by and we never seem to have enough. My brothers and I wake up early in the morning before school to fetch water. We walk a half mile to a nearby house to buy water. The home owner has a big well known as a 'borehole' in his compound.

We wait in line with our jerry cans, large plastic containers designed just for the purpose of holding water. On days when the queue is too long, we walk another half mile to another house. In some other villages and towns where I grew up, we used to go to the river. But river water is not safe to drink unless you boiled it first or fetched it from a high spot on the river where people did not swim. Unfortunately, Agbor did not have a river that was close enough for us to walk to, so we had to buy water.

A few years later, some landlords would install taps in their compounds, taps that actually delivered running water. Hearing that tap water was better than 'borehole' water, we switched. Epic fights took place daily at the taps. Boys and girls brawled shamelessly. I once witnessed a fight where a boy had several teeth knocked out of his mouth by a head butt. The spectators never attempt to break up the combatants, as long as they were fairly evenly matched. Fists flew, hair was pulled, punches were thrown but tears never dropped. Crying after a fight was simply not acceptable. It was considered weakness. If you were the loser, you took your punishment and walked away to fight another day. As boys, we lived for the moments when girls ripped their blouses to shreds and we caught an exposed breast before the loser ran off, seeking cover.

Rats and mice are common in the compound where we live. The rats, fattened from a steady diet of excrement, are bigger than small cats. They scurry around the compound in slow motion while children chase them around excitedly. When we catch the rats, we bash their brains out with a rock and leave their entrails splayed on the ground. We are angry because we cannot eat the loathsome animals. We did not eat house rats, but we did eat bush rats. Frankly, bush rats did not look much different from the house rats, except that they were bigger. The reason we didn't eat house rats was simple. Rats ate human waste. I had another reason for hating the critters. They chewed at my toes at night while I slept.

When I was nine or twelve, I was woken up by a rat which had crawled into my pocket. It was after a piece of *akara* ball that I had stashed there during the day. While I had forgotten about the food in my pocket, the rat had smelled it and waited until I fell asleep to strike. I remember screaming in anger as the rat fled with the piece of food.

All around, mosquitoes breed on puddles of water. Day and night, they attack in formation like Quintus Sertorius's army. They attack with military precision, with vengeance, leaving welts and bruises in their wake. At night, before we go to sleep, we splash kerosene on the floor to kill the little bastards. The next morning when we wake up, we find a rich harvest of dead mosquitoes. The floor is the battlefield, the mosquitoes are dead soldiers who have lost the war and we are the victors. But at times, our victory proves pyrrhic, and the vectors overcome the victors, when we succumb to malaria fever.

In a country where the life expectancy rate is at fifty, it is a mystery that people even make it to forty.

Flies spread typhoid fever.

Mosquitoes spread malaria.

We spread tuberculosis.

We catch meningitis.

We spread them to each other.

The insects kill us

We kill each other.

The great comedian in the sky gave us the gift of life. We in turn give each other the gift of death.

Meeting with Jesus

I am running a fever.

Dying of an unknown disease. Meningitis or malaria fever. Cholera or typhoid fever. I don't know which. The particulars of one's morbidity become rather unimportant when one is dying. The biological facts become quotidian, banal. All that sticks in the mind is the realization of one's own mortality, the acknowledgment of ephemerality.

I am about to die.

I am lying on a bed that is all rusted springs. It is more like a cot really, elevated three feet above the concrete floor. The walls are unpainted brick, dank and dreary, an overture to pain. There are dirty pots and dishes on the floor, which is wet in places. A waste bucket sits in a corner to be used for urination and defecation. I use it often since I am wracked by dysentery and can hardly walk. The poverty here refuses to be voiceless. It speaks with fury and urgency. It begs to be acknowledged.

I am reminded of Dostoyevsky telling his brother about the Katorga prison camp in Omsk.

THE COLLECTOR OF BUTTERFLIES AND WOMEN

In summer, intolerable closeness; in winter, unendurable cold. All the floors were rotten. Filth on the floors an inch thick; one could slip and fall... We were packed like herrings in a barrel... There was no room to turn around. From dusk to dawn it was impossible not to behave like pigs... Fleas, lice, and black beetles by the bushel.

I can hear birds chanting a dirge outside. I think that they have come to sing at my funeral, to prepare me for internment.

Why am I here? Where am I?

For a moment, I struggle to regain my bearings, to find my internal compass. I am inside the home of a prophet, a man who is said to cure all diseases. A man who banishes demons and wayward spirits with the bible and a torrent of prayer.

The man who might cure me is Baba Udo. His house is a small brick and mud structure consisting of four bedrooms and a living room. The living room doubles as his church. Every evening, his congregation gathers in his living room, seated on small stools and worship. I did not know what the prophet's real name is. Everyone calls him, "Baba Udo" which means father of Udo. Udo is a small village located about an hour from Benin City, the capital of Bendel State.

Udo was founded by Prince Aruaran, a royal prince of the Bini empire. He was said to be a giant of a man who stood nearly seven feet tall. Although Aruaran was extremely strong, he was also simple minded. His younger brother, Prince Esigie, was able to exploit his intellectual weakness and push him aside for the throne of the Bini Kingdom. Realizing that he had been cheated out of his birthright, Aruaran left Bini in frustration and set up his own kingdom which he called Udo.

This is where I met Jesus.

Baba Udo's flock is small but passionate. Charged with religious ecstasy, men and women gyrate, somnambulate and perambulate in the church, howling, weeping, laughing, eyes wild, arms waving. The prophet casts out devils and when the devils are released, the bedeviled scream in anguish as if pained, as if the exorcism itself is childbirth. They mutter gibberish in strange tongues, twitching, twisting, and giving testimony to the power of Jesus. Men babble and women wobble, children not wanting to be left out, stomp their feet and wave their hands. Men speak in tongues and women see visions, goats and chickens hearing the fracas bleat and squawk. If Jesus came to earth on any Sunday and saw these worshippers in utter delirium, they would scare Him right back to heaven.

I am not sure how my mother became acquainted with Baba Udo. I imagine that my mother heard about Baba Udo's spiritual powers from some friend or neighbor. One day, my mother gathered the family and announced that we were going to church. I was a little surprised, especially since my father was a staunch Muslim. But my father didn't seem to mind. While he stayed home, we all head to Baba Udo's church for the first time.

I am not sure what I expected to see as we drew near the church. Maybe I expected a huge cathedral like the ones that I had seen in books. A cathedral with gables and arches and cavernous insides crowned by bronze colored steeples that grope the clouds like the fingers of a drunk lying on his back. Maybe I expected a place of gothic whimsy mixed with Venetian stoicism, a 'City of God" blazing on the hill, beckoning to the lost and to the forsaken, blazing with glory.

What I saw instead was a small building baked out of mud and brick, with rough walls and a rusty zinc roof that winked obscenely at the sun. What I discovered was that this was a house that doubled as a church, or a church that doubled as a house. The house was a walnut cleft in two halves by a corridor. Baba Udo and his family used one section of the house as their living quarters while the church took up two rooms in the other section.

THE COLLECTOR OF BUTTERFLIES AND WOMEN

We walk into the church and are immediately transported into a landscape that is simply otherworldly. It is as if we have fallen into a surrealist painting by the Catalan painter, Joan Miro i Ferra. Baba Udo's church is like no other church that I have seen before. There is no vestibule, no pews, and no podium. There are a few hard-backed chairs, not enough for the twenty or so people gathered in the room.

A few children are sprawled on the floor, bony legs and dirty toes on display. There is an almanac of an anorexic Jesus on the wall. He looks famished as if he has missed too many meals. Sad eyed and thin-lipped with a severe aspect to his face. The painter, striving for serenity and sublimity had missed the mark widely and ended up at ferocity and rapacity instead. The Messiah looks decidedly feral and churlish.

The atmosphere in the church is always rich, fraught with self-denial and surrender. So we chant along with the other worshippers, thumping our feet on the floor, the air full of the kind of beatitude that only dipsomania and saturnalia and religion can induce. We chant and we get caught up in the whole orgiastic enterprise.

That was our first time in the church.

We returned after that time and kept coming back. When my mother became sick and we couldn't figure out what was wrong with her, she went to Baba Udo. When my sisters became sick, they were taken to Baba Udo. The prophet's healing rituals involved a strange alchemy of herbs, fetish traditions and biblical exhortations. People who needed healing were variously asked to fast, pray, and then bathe in the middle of the night at the crossroads or sacred bush. They had their bodies rubbed with some secret ointment.

Baba Udo seemed to be a pleasant enough man, if rather taciturn. A short man with a bald head and an urgent smile, his eyes were the only part of his face that I found disturbing. And I could never figure out why. I thought perhaps it was because they seemed to pierce into my very soul.

I secretly wondered why many of his healing rituals involved women being bathed in the middle of the night and why he always had to be present at these events. He seemed to be a fairly harmless man and I never witnessed any inappropriate behavior from him, but still my mind puzzled over what I saw.

I was the one who held the lamp one night while we took my younger sister to the bush for a cleansing bath after she had fasted for several days. My sister followed behind me, while Baba Udo brought up the rear.

The night coiled around us like a serpent. Birds cooed and crickets chirped. Toads ruling empires of mud croaked. Darkness was a curtain draped over the village. As we walked, we could hear the sounds of men and women snoring through mud walls. Sand trembled below our feet as we walked, walking on a grassy path that led out of the village into the bush.

When we arrived at the spot that Baba Udo had chosen, he told us to stop.

"Take off your wrapper."

Me, the lamp bearer, continues to hold the lamp while my sister strips naked. The prophet mutters some words of prayer, commanding whatever spirit of evil or bad luck hovering around my sister to vamoose.

"I bind you in the name of Jesus" he declares. "Leave this child alone! Leave her alone!" Baba Udo motions to my sister to begin her bath.

My sister scoops water with a pail from the bucket that she is holding. She shivers when the cold water hits her skin. The water is full of leaves and candle wax. The earth spins around the sun once, twice and several more times before she is done.

"Put your wrapper back on."

My sister picks up her wrapper, wraps it around her chest and we make our way back to the church.

THE COLLECTOR OF BUTTERFLIES AND WOMEN

We visit Baba Udo's church on many other occasions. I become quite familiar with Jesus hanging on his perch on the wall. At times, I think that he is looking at me with a mischievous smile reading my soul like stone tablets. At other times, I think that he is mad at me, glaring at me with eyes as furious as the sun.

Now as I lay on the bed with the iron springs racked with fever, I think of the son of Mary. I wonder why he is not answering my prayers, why he is not healing me, getting rid of the unknown disease that has rendered me immobile. Maybe Jesus is taking a break from answering prayers. Maybe I just haven't prayed hard enough.

I certainly hadn't lived a blameless life. All the nights of frenzied masturbation, days of fantasizing about people's wives, times that I stole things that did not belong to me. Maybe Jehovah, great and terrible Jehovah had not forgiven me. Maybe I did not deserve a place at the top of his priority list.

Angel

It is midnight and we are inside a car near Maryland Road in Lagos. The car is parked outside a church that has a statue of Jesus Christ on its façade. The church grounds are lit with fluorescent lighting. The parking lot outside the church is empty and there is no sign of life.

I am in the car with my friend, Amos. We are taking turns on the prostitute. Since this midnight escapade is Amos's idea, and the car is his, he got to go first. I sit in the front seat and listen to the mechanical sounds of Amos pounding on the prostitute. He seems to go for what seems like an eternity but is probably no more than a few minutes since we are paying by the minute. When he finishes, it is my turn to take over. We trade places. Amos squeezes into the front seat to act as look-out while I move to the back seat.

Amos will look out for any passers-by who get too close and for policemen. If we are caught by any of the roving bands of policemen who patrol the night, it will cost us a stiff bribe. The policemen will likely take most of the money that we have and do the same to the prostitute.

"Take it easy." The woman tells me. "Don't ride me like an animal." I pause between my fevered thrusts and then resume. Amos laughs, a deep trombone of a laugh. His laugh fills the night and seems to rattle the small car.

As I grind against the woman, my eye catches the statue of the Messiah. I imagine that he is staring at me balefully.

The woman tells us tonelessly and without irony that her name is Angel. She is a tall dark skinned woman with the long-suffering face of a saint. Her features are delicate and her voice is soft. I find this to be quite surprising. This is the first prostitute that I have ever slept with. I had always imagined that prostitutes were raspy voiced termagants who belched cigarette smoke, whose fingernails were shaped like claws, who like the Siren Sisters, lured men to instant damnation.

Her hands. They caress my memory. Rough like yesterday's bread set aside to ferment into cheap wine. Like gravel before it is poured by bricklayers to build a road. I think of her as the woman of infinite sorrows, a woman condemned to roam the world in sackcloth and ashes like a wayward spirit. Not once did she smile as we committed intercourse with her. Her face was taut, like someone about to swallow something bitter, someone bracing for a cruel revelation, a piece of bad news.

We picked her up at the corner of Opebi Street in Ikeja. She was standing in a gauntlet of women under a bright streetlight when we drove up in the Toyota. We crawled to a stop, and studied the women standing on the corner.

There were prostitutes no older than fifteen wearing frightful make-up and wigs, trying to look older than their age. There were prostitutes no younger than fifty wearing frightful make-up and wigs, trying to look younger than their age. Women in the prime of their lives, gambling with destiny and already losing the bet. They walked around with shell-shocked eyes, as if they were returnees from a war that everybody had forgotten. The night was humid, moody and obstreperous. We were in Lagos, the craziest and most fascinating city in the world.

All around us, cars screeched by on snaky roads with pot-holes deeper than craters on the moon. Taxi cab drivers battled with private car owners, battled to the death for supremacy on the road. Pedestrians and hawkers fought for space on the side of the road. People jostled and jockeyed, howled and yelled, cursed and laughed. The city of Lagos was a madman who woke up at dawn yet refused to go to sleep until just before another dawn. The night was full of promise and perversion.

The hookers studied the car, studied Amos and me, trying to gauge our seriousness and assess our potential.

Like birds, they adjusted their plumage, pushed their chests out a little higher, presented their backsides. Put their figurative best foot forward. They were dressed in mini-skirts the size of postage stamps and shorts so terrified of the ground that they stopped in mid-thigh. High heeled shoes that turned the very act of walking into a trapeze act, where the performer might fall on their face any minute.

il faut souffrir pour être belle.
Beauty does not come without suffering.
Many of these women suffered mightily and still did not attain beauty.
"Oga, check me out." One called.
"Na fine *toto* dey here."
"I go satisfy you. Try me."
The coquettes spoke in pidgin English, tried to impress, to approximate seduction and what it should look like. Despite my ardor this evening, I was strangely unmoved.

Until I saw Angel.

Although she stood with the small crowd of prostitutes, she seemed far away from the crowd, as if she floated above it all, as if she was above it all. She did not react to our presence, did not call out to us or attempt to peddle her fleshly wares in front of us. She simply stared at Amos and I, and I found myself staring back, trapped in her gaze, drowning in the liquid depths of her eyes.

THE COLLECTOR OF BUTTERFLIES AND WOMEN

"How about that one?" I asked Amos. "The one with the red bag."

Amos, a round man with an orotund voice, followed my gaze. "She looks expensive."

"Would you rather have one that looks cheap and well-worn?"

"Suits me just fine."

I didn't know if Amos was serious or not, but I thought to myself that he was probably right. Expensive sex was really no different from cheap sex. Indeed, the only difference between the two kinds of sex was whatever difference the beneficiary of either assigned them.

"You want to negotiate?" Amos asked. "Knowing you, you will do it in the Queen's English. Might get us a discount." Amos exploded into laughter.

Like everything in Nigeria, sex between the sexes is negotiated with delicate parries and thrusts, with studied feints and bobs. A man who wants sex with a woman dances around the subject with verbal agility. He compliments the woman, buys her gifts, befriends her family and friends and waits for his lucky break. A man negotiating sex with a hooker does much of the same. He pretends to be angry when he is not, feigns ire when it is only pretence, walks away until he is asked to come back. He wears righteous indignation like a cattleman wearing a hat. The entire country of Nigeria is one big bazaar, with a never ending negotiation of goods and services, bribes and transactions, betrayals and avowals, loyalties and treacheries.

I let Amos do the negotiation.

"You." He pointed at the woman with the red bag.

Angel walked over with a dainty walk. More like a stroll. She was not in a hurry and she wanted us to know it. She walked like the whole world was waiting on her.

The negotiation did not take as long as I expected. But then, what did I know? This was my first transaction with a prostitute after all.

"What is your name?"

That was when Angel told us her name.

She was sitting in the back seat of the cramped car. Amos was driving. I was in the passenger seat. Angel was not one for chit-chat. She responded with monosyllables to my feeble attempts at conversation.

"Got a hotel room?" She asked.

"No." Amos responded.

"I know a spot. Near Maryland Road. It's quiet."

Angel did not mention that the spot she was guiding us to was directly in front of a church. She did not mention that there was a statue of the Messiah right in front of it. She was probably not a religious woman and the symbolism held no significance for her. Perhaps, she was a lapsed Catholic, driven to self-abasement or apostasy by the suffering she had been through.

That is how we ended up outside the church at midnight.

The car smells like stale sex, condom wrappers, and fried rice. I try to shut out the smell as I insert myself in Angel. The sex is hard and fast and unsatisfying. Angel seems rather uninterested, immune to my self-absorbed jack-hammering. Ego bruised, I begin to pound even harder, grabbing her by the shoulders, sticking a finger deep in her anus.

That is when she tells me not to ride her like an animal. And Amos begins to laugh.

I stop as suddenly as I began. Like a man getting off a rocket. All of a sudden, I feel drained and dirty. Rotten to my very core. I stare at the face of the woman who has stoically withstood my spastic gyrations and I feel sad. I wonder what has led her to this prurient life in this godforsaken city where human worth is measured out in dollars and cents. Where poverty and privation has swept away the best and the brightest that the country has to offer, washed them to the shores of other lands.

Because Angel's English and diction is impeccable, I find myself asking her if she went to college. She nods wanly.

"I spent four years at Lagos State University. Earned a degree in English Lit."

THE COLLECTOR OF BUTTERFLIES AND WOMEN

"So why are you…"

She cuts me off before I finish the question, reading my mind, "Why am I doing this?"

I nod.

"Because I can't find a job. Like eighty percent of the college graduates in this country. Studying Wordsworth and the Bronte sisters hasn't done me much good." Her tone is matter of fact, her lack of bitterness or self-pity cuts at my core.

"Don't feel sorry for me. I am not the hooker with the heart of gold you have read about. Just a girl trying to make a living. I can always move back to the village and become a farmer's wife."

She spreads her thighs, wipes the wetness off with a handkerchief she takes out from her hand bag. The smell in the car is ammoniac, scorches the nostrils.

"Here you go." Amos reaches over from the back seat, hands some Naira notes to Angel. She flicks through them and stuffs them in her hand bag.

"You should give my friend a small refund. You know, he couldn't ejaculate."

Ever the joker, Amos erupts into another round of laughter. I want to tell him to shut up. His levity fills me with irritation.

Angel steps out of the car with that same delicate bounce, this woman who is beaten but not bowed, she steps out like a princess about to claim her rightful throne.

"Are you going to be okay? Do you need a ride back?" I am suddenly filled with dread for her, one of the faceless millions struggling to make a way in an anonymous city where the old eat their children and the rich bury the poor even before they die.

"I'll be fine."

Angel closes the door, walks into the jaws of the night and the night swallows her.

The city of chaos

I went to Lagos to pursue fame and fortune. Prostitution and promiscuity were just two of the things that happened along the way. A man who goes to the toilet to take a shit does not set about to explore his own excrement, but what man wouldn't pause to study his own shit were he to find blood in it?

During my high school days, I made three friends who would end up becoming my partners in a music group based in Lagos. The way it started was fairly inauspicious. When I finished secondary school, I took the WAEC exam – the West African Examinations Council exam which every secondary school student is required to take before graduation. I did well in the exam. Next, I took the JAMB exam – the Joint Admissions and Matriculation Board exam, which every student seeking admission into college has to take. I also did well in this exam.

My father, his own aspirations of becoming a lawyer, dashed on the sandstone of poverty, has my career path mapped out neatly for me. He wants me to be a lawyer. The prospect seems intriguing, but not intriguing enough for me to want to get into college right away. I decide to put college on hold. I want to be a reggae musician.

THE COLLECTOR OF BUTTERFLIES AND WOMEN

I form a music group with three of my friends, Simeon, Jude, and Chukky. We adopt the Jamaican patois and let our hair grow crinkly and twisty in an attempt to develop dreadlocks. Bob Marley, the voice of the oppressed and downtrodden becomes our idol. We spend nights practicing in Agbor until we decide that we are ready to make a demo tape for a potential sponsor or record label.

We travelled to Oguta to meet with the music producer, Charly Boy. Charly Boy's real name was Charles Oputa. He was the flamboyant maverick son of a respected Supreme Court Judge. We were in awe of the man when we arrived at his studio in Oguta. He was a big, hulking man with a soft voice. He was known for his outrageous outfits and controversial comments. He was a man who knew how to get people riled up, who relished being the *agent provocateur*.

For the next couple of days, we work with Charly Boy to produce a demo tape. We travel to Benin City to visit Akpola Records, a local record company. We quickly meet with disappointment. The record company does not know what to make of our music. Steeped in highlife and traditional music, the company has no interest in reggae music. Despite this temporary setback, we are far from ready to give up. Our next plan is to visit Lagos, a city of nearly ten million people, to stake out our fortunes.

We spend a few months, preparing to make the journey. One day, when we have all saved enough money, I bid my parents goodbye and we catch a bus bound for Lagos.

As the bus entered the city limits of Lagos, I was filled with exultation and exaltation. The city is big and boisterous like a drunk. Death and danger loom in every corner along with beauty and celebration. The subterranean and the transcendent co-exist in perfect stasis. The roads are choked with traffic and people, rickety buses and taxi cabs fighting with sleek luxurious cars for space on pot-holed roads. The smell of car exhaust mixes with the smell of food and unwashed bodies, the smell of urine and perfumed bodies mixes with the smell of stagnant water and roadside debris.

And the noise…the noise is infinite. Volcanic. A jarring cacophony of car horns, raised voices, admonitions and ululations, vituperations and explications, anger and joy. Men, women and children, some as young as ten, peddle clothes, bottled water, plantain chips, faux-Rolex watches, and heaven to passengers in cars and buses. A man is selling black Victoria Secret panties with a cheerful red rose stitched in the crotch section. "Buy it for your wife, and you will get action tonight, I promise you." Another man offers cell phones which he tells everyone are the best that the white man has to offer, "straight from America." Not to be outdone, a wiry man with yellowing rebellious teeth the size of Casino chips, offers an aphrodisiac that he calls, "Man power" "It will make your penis happy again."

The street vendors offer blessings to anyone who will spare an ear, and curse anyone who chooses to ignore them. Women with children strapped to their backs ply their wares on the side of the road. Men holding bibles (King James, Gold Leaf Edition) sell salvation for a discount. The beggars and the insane, the great unwashed, walk around vacantly, seeking alms, sweating in the mirthless sun.

The entire city is tactile. Like tear gas, it soaks into the skin, itches the eyes, burns the throat. Lagos is an insatiable lover, a city that demands that you feel it in your head in your skin in your very bones. Like an importunate child, it will not be silenced. The city of dreams is also the city of chaos. A city where tragedy and comedy are inextricably wed as bride and groom.

The city is carnivalesque and Rabelaisian. A city ripe for satire, a canvas on which the human condition is illumined in stark relief. Fela Kuti, the great musician once wrote about the 'suffering and smiling' masses. Lagosians can be divided into two broad categories; those who suffer and those who smile. The haves and the have-nots.

Lagos reminds me of the characters in two of my favorite books, Samuel Beckett's play, *Waiting for Godot*, and Jean Paul Satre's *No Exit*. In Beckett's play, two characters, Estragon and Vladimir, waste their

THE COLLECTOR OF BUTTERFLIES AND WOMEN

days, waiting for an unknown and unknowable man named Godot. Lagos, I believe, would have been a perfect setting for the play. In *No Exit*, Jean Paul Satre writes that "hell is other people." *"l'enfer, c'est les autres.* He introduces us to a group of people trapped in a room and forced to endure each other's life story, miseries and confessions.

In Lagos, hell is definitely other people.

Lagos is the city where phantoms chase phantom dreams through phantasmagoria, where men and women fight daily to carve out a piece of heaven from hell. They claw you with their kindness and clobber you with their wickedness. They bludgeon you with their odor and smother you with their ardor. Their symptoms make you sympathize, their traumas make you traumatized. But even in its ugliness, Lagos is a place of desperate beauty, where hope is a tender rose sprouting in a wasteland.

There is a church or a mosque in every corner. At times, on some of these corners, you can find a corpse abandoned, blooming like an evil plant in the hot afternoon. God's children walk by as they head for Sunday service or Friday prayers. They hold their nose and say a prayer for the dead, or simply say, *"Tufiakwa!"* or *"Oma se-o!"* or *"Allah ya sauwake!"*

My friends and I find meager accommodations in an area of Lagos known as Ketu. We are living with IG, a young man from the Ishan part of Edo State who has a room inside a hotel known as Papa's. He works as a Disc Jockey in the hotel and in return is provided with room and board. IG allows us to sleep in his room at night while he is working. Since all four of us cannot fit in his tiny bed, we take turns sleeping on the bed. When Chuks and I sleep on the bed, Simeon and Jude have to stay up. They have to hang out in the hotel until morning.

It is IG who introduces us to Mr B, the owner of the hotel. Mr B is a gregarious man in his thirties. He is tall, slightly bow-legged. His father had made some money in the hotel business and had passed on the family business to his son.

When we walk into his office on the second floor of the hotel, I am impressed by how big and organized it is. There is a huge desk surrounded by chairs. A music player rests on a cabinet. Posters of Michael Jackson, Prince and Billy Idol adorn the wall. Although Mr. B is in his late thirties, he is a man who seeks to capture time in a bottle. He is clearly a big fan of music.

"I hear you guys write music."

We nod collectively. I look around the room. Jude is short and light-skinned with thin angular features. He has been my best friend since secondary school. He is handsome. A lady killer who always attracts a swarm of women. Not the most romantic of sorts, but that didn't seem to stop the women. Simeon has the face of a cherub. He is mild-mannered and soft-spoken. Chukky is tall and dark and intense. He didn't always get along with the rest of us, perhaps because he was the last entrant to the group. Perhaps because he was a few years older than the rest of us. Driven by our shared aspiration of music stardom, we get along well enough.

"Let's hear it."

I reach into my pocket, pull out an envelope containing a cassette tape. I hand it to Mr. B. Without getting up, he inserts it into the music player. The sounds of reggae music fill the room, my bass, Chukky's falsetto, Simeon's tenor and Jude's alto. Mr. B appears to be impressed.

"Who produced the tape?"

"Charly Boy."

Mr. B nods sagely. "It sounds good."

And that is how our journey into the Nigerian music scene begins. Mr. B gives us our own room in the hotel, right next to IG's room.

In Papa's, we soon discover a whole new world. The world of prostitutes. At night, the place is like Sodom and Gomorrah. Hookers, fat or famished, overrun the grounds of the hotel like an invading army of locusts. They grab your penis as you walk by, stick their breasts violently in your face, and threaten you with sex. While IG spins the records, men and women dance, flirt, and haggle over the proper market price of flesh. I soon learn how the simple laws of supply and demand, the laws of economics affect sex. I learn that the price of flesh can vary depending on demand, depending on the day of the week. Sex was more expensive on Mondays and Tuesdays when most of the call girls were not available, presumably working other hotels or street corners. Fridays and Saturdays were the days that sex was cheapest. The law of supply and demand. Most of the girls were around on those days. On those days, the ratio of women to men was easily four to one. At the end of the month, when most government workers were paid their salary, there was a market correction and the ratio of women to men changed sharply. Prices spiked.

Fridays and Saturdays was when the most fights occurred amongst the sex workers. The reason for this was simple math. Those two days was when there was the most number of people around. The more people there were, the greater the likelihood that a fight would break out. Drunk on fermented liquor and Guinness, Bacchanalia often gave way to brutality. Wigs were ripped off to expose patchy scalps. Blouses were shredded to expose shrunken or nubile breasts. Long fingernails and shoes were used as weapons. The winner was led away like a conquering prizefighter while the loser stood in the corner, trying to re-gather the cobwebs of their self-esteem.

I was witness to several fights among the prostitutes.

Fights broke out from the slightest provocation. Someone stole someone else's pack of cigarettes, or customer. Someone said a cross word. Accused a girl of having given a John gonorrhea. Refused to pay back a debt.

Fists flew. The combatants were always given enough time to get it out of their system before being stopped. It was a cruel spectacle and I recoiled at it, yet I could not walk away. And for this, I was ashamed.

I was a teenager surrounded by dissolution and depravation, and it was not difficult for me to become seduced. I was soon consumed by this riptide of sex, spending my nights in dangerous liaisons, washed ashore in the morning like a crippled seagull. On most occasions, I used condoms during my sexual encounters. On a few drunken nights, I did not.

I wake up disgusted with myself. The room smells of stale sex and cheap liquor. I make up my mind that this would be the last time that I would ever sleep with a stranger.

I did not go to Lagos to become a whore, but Lagos turned me into one.

Shogunle

When the gods wish to punish us, they answer our prayers. I lived with my friends in a two-room apartment in Shogunle, Lagos. We had come to Lagos seeking fame and fortune but our dreams turned out to be ethereal and febrile, our spaceship crashing to earth with a thud.

Shogunle is a solidly working class neighborhood located between Oshodi and Ikeja. If Ikeja is the commercial nerve center of downtown Lagos and the head of the beast, Oshodi is the beast's wounded extremity while Shogunle is its anus. Shogunle is a crowded, filthy maelstrom of humanity. The houses hug each other like cheating spouses, seeking comfort in each other's arms. They hug each other so close that a man and woman having sex are sure to be heard by the neighbors next door. The streets are dusty, pebbled, strewn with garbage and the residue of unresolved existence. Laundry hangs on twine clotheslines in front of buildings or over balconies. It waves in the breeze like a man about to jump off a bridge. There are no goats or chickens here. Hardly a dog or cat in sight. People are too busy struggling to manage the business of living to have time for pets.

The house where we live is a dilapidated building painted baby shit green. The paint is flaking in places as if it was applied by a painter with the shakes. There is no drainage system. What there is, is a man-made gutter that overflows when it rains. The water washes into our yard and rushes through the corridor like a man late for an appointment. It rushes into our rooms and drenches anything that is not elevated. But we are usually prepared. At the first sign of rain, we lift pots and pans off the floor, move valuables to higher ground. When it stops raining, we mop the water and put the items back.

It is easy to get rid of the water. What is not so easy to get rid of is the smell. The smell of dirty water. It is an urgent smell that infects the concrete wall, the floor and our nostrils. Often, I wondered what tumors, what traumas were carried in the water that ended up in our living quarters. Cancer was just beginning to come into style in this part of the world, the news imported from American and England. I wondered about the toxicity of the dirty water, the effect of the smell on our lungs.

Our neighbors are a motley lot.

Sonny F was a slight drink of a man, with a bald patch. He wore cowboy boots and tight jeans. A chain smoker, he smoked cigarettes as if his life depended on them, and it probably did. He had the superior manner of a man who had walked through fire, and had solved the riddle of life. His face was a mask of ennui, big eyes hidden behind dark sunglasses. He had lived in France for several years. He never looked at you directly when he spoke, eyes focused on the middle distance. He spoke in a weird amalgam of English and French, erupting into his native Yoruba occasionally.

There is Segun the witchdoctor who lives with his wife and children in a small shack attached to the side of our building. A small hard-bitten man with a snake charmer's eyes hidden in a gullied face. Some neighbors claimed that he possessed the ability to see into the future. I thought that the only ability he possessed was making

THE COLLECTOR OF BUTTERFLIES AND WOMEN

babies. His snot-nosed offspring roam the compound, laughing, playing hide and seek, blissfully oblivious to the poverty fermenting around them.

When Segun performs his incantations and divinations, we can hear him, mumbling, chanting, invoking spirits. He chews tobacco. After he chews, he spits out generous wads of tobacco and they land splat! on our window.

When Segun makes love to his wife, Taiye, a sweet-natured fat woman who walks around barefoot, he howls like a constipated wolf. When he makes love to his wife, the tectonic plates holding the earth together shift. Mexico crashes into Mali and Tijuana crashes into Timbuktu. We hear him in the middle of the night and we laugh. If he hears us, he is not deterred. He pounds away. In the middle of the night, Segun's wife often gets up to take a shit. Instead of using the communal toilet, she places a container, known as a *'po'* outside our window and she defecates. Often, we wake up to the smell of feces wafting through the open louvers of our window. Closing the window is never an option since it is always oppressively hot. Despite these daily olfactory assaults, I liked the woman. She was a generous soul.

There is Paulo the sailor. Paulo, a hulking man with big eyes, full of joviality. He tells us stories about his journeys to foreign countries with names that sound like an old lady's curse; Costa Rica, Puerto Rico, Trinidad and Tobago. We listen with rapt attention as he tells us of the women he has bedded and the foods that he has tasted. When he returns from some of the trips, he occasionally brings us small gifts.

I do not know how many of the fabulist's tales are true, but I enjoy his telling of the stories. When you are surrounded by abject poverty, suspension of disbelief comes easy. Small wonder then that magic realism is a continent mapped by the dispossessed and the deprived. Nigeria is a country gripped by the supernatural. Magicians, makers of myth and performers of miracles are the spiritual elite, planted firmly on a pedestal. Upon them the rabble gazes in adoration.

There is a family of seven crammed into a two room apartment. We call them the Maharajis. They are followers of Guru Maharaji, a spiritual leader who is drawing quite a following in the country. I never found out what the family's real name was. The Maharajis isolate themselves from the other tenants in the house. They do not communicate. When spoken to, they do not respond. Like ghosts, they flit through the compound, sharing the communal bathroom, kitchen and toilet. The children in the compound find them fascinating, especially on days when they dress up in their red robes and head out to prayer.

The Ibrahim family is right next door to us. Ibrahim is a retired military man. He goes out every morning in starched shirts and polished shoes and returns late at night smelling of liquor and female perfume. He is a man who womanizes with military precision. His wife never says much. She is the most submissive woman on earth.

Ibrahim reminds me of Arnolphe, a middle aged roué who is the protagonist in Moliere's comedy *L'École des Femmes (The School for Wives)*. Arnolphe is convinced that submission is the most important character trait required in a wife. He sets out to develop the perfect wife. The woman he has his eye on is Agnes. He has her brought up in a convent in complete isolation. Alas, his plans will be derailed when Agnes falls in love with another man and abandons Arnolphe. But if Ibrahim is Arnolphe, his wife is not Agnes. Mama Ibrahim washes and irons her husband's clothes, cooks him dinner, keeps her mouth firmly closed when he returns home in a sour mood.

I find her docility terrifying.

They have the perfect marriage.

In Shogunle, the rats would chase the cats if there were cats. But there are no cats. I hear the rats doing battle in the middle of the night, screeching, biting each other, as they forage for food. I hear

THE COLLECTOR OF BUTTERFLIES AND WOMEN

them running into buckets and dirty pots leftout in the yard. I find the rats to be allegorical. The rats are the poor of Lagos who claw, bite and devour each other inside their godforsaken shithole. The rich are the cats who invariably find the rats and invariably devour them. At times, we wake up and find a dead rat, clawed to death by one of its own in the yard.

It is the white rats that I dread the most. One night, I see a couple of them chasing each other around in our little apartment. They are as white as polar bears, bleached by lack of sun, these creatures that live in the gutters of night and avoid the light.

I howl with rage as the two rats scuttle behind the pot of soup that we have fixed for dinner. I hurl a shoe at them and miss, remembering a similar battle fought years before in Urhonigbe. I won that particular battle. Now, the rats have returned for revenge. On this day, both rats would escape, disappearing into the humid night.

The rats have a favorite spot. The communal toilet at the back of the house. There are two stalls. In theory, one stall is supposed to be for females and the second for males. In reality, no one pays attention to this gender demarcation. The walls of the toilet are splashed with fresh and dried feces like a canvas of Salvador Dali when he was experimenting with cubism. The toilet bowl itself often overflows. Whenever I go into one of the stalls, I make sure that I have on shoes with a quarter inch heel in order to avoid the puddle of urine and shit that is always on the floor. Renters were supposed to take turns to clean the toilets, but no one seems to stick to the schedule.

My friends and I were a long way from achieving the wealth that we dreamed of. Instead, we were stuck in purgatory in Shogunle. A bare apartment with a mattress mounted on bricks. A rug purchased in Mecca that I had liberated from my father, after he returned from the Holy Land. Pots and pans. Shoes and clothes scattered in an untidy pile. The totality of my success, or lack of it, in Lagos.

Jeffrey Obomeghie

I wondered how much longer we could hold on before things totally fall apart.
I was a man clinging to a tenuous raft.
And the hurricane tide was approaching.

New year's eve

New Year's Eve is not a good night to die.

This is the thought crashing through my head as I stare at the barrel of the rifle pointed at me and my two friends, Jude and Simeon.

It is 2 a.m. in the morning. The night is blacker than the inside of a crone's gums. Night birds coo and warble. A cockerel crows in the distance, crows four hours before dawn. At this inopportune hour, the sound is strange, disconcerting, and somewhat tragic, like stumbling on a mother nursing a dead baby. A child coughs in the distance, whimpers in its sleep and coughs some more. A lone lantern shines through a glass window. It is technically already morning but dawn seems to be far away. The streets are dark.

This is not how we planned to end the night.

This is not how we planned for our lives to end.

We were in Shogunle, just a stone throw away from our apartment. We were on our way back from a nightclub in Ikeja. We had caught a cab to take us home. Along the way, the cab driver arbitrarily decided to increase his fare. Since the laws that govern commerce in Lagos are often fluid and often non-existent, the driver did not see his behavior as improper. We argued with the driver. He called us sons of he-goats and whores, wished pox on our households. We cursed him generously, told him his wife was riddled with fleas and deformity. He stopped his cab and told us to get out. We got out of the cab and decided to walk the remaining two miles to our apartment.

Bad mistake number one.

We soon run into one of the neighborhood security patrols, known as vigilantes or 'shoot first, question later.' Plagued by home invaders, armed robbers and cat burglars, many neighborhoods had decided to form their own security patrols. Lagosians understood that relying on the police to protect them was a waste of time. Faced with an emergency, you couldn't connect to the police department by phone if you called.

People called the police while being attacked only to have the police show up hours later, after the smoke had cleared. At times, the police refused to come out to confront robbers because they were out-gunned. While the policemen toted rusty Mark IV rifles, the criminals were armed with sophisticated automatic weapons. At times, the robbers bribe the police beforehand so that the police would not interrupt their operations. The police were complicit in many crimes and were at times proxy for the criminals. While not all policemen were corrupt, a goodly number of them were.

The concept of neighbors banding together to protect their streets appears to be noble and prudent on the face of it. The trouble was that many of the so called security patrol teams were really vigilantes who were every bit as dangerous as the criminals that they were supposed to guard against. If you wanted to settle a score with a man who slept with your wife, you could simply hire a vigilante group to solve the problem. If the man ventured out at night, they would wait for him and beat him to a pulp or shoot him, under the pretext that he was an armed robber that they had caught.

So here we were facing one of the bands of vigilantes roaming

THE COLLECTOR OF BUTTERFLIES AND WOMEN

the streets of Lagos. We had walked into a *trou de loupe*. We were in deep trouble.

There are six men in the vigilante group. One look at their bloodshot eyes and shell-shocked faces and I knew that they were high on some mind-bending drug. The leader is a short fellow, with stout muscular arms. He has a fleshy pugnacious face that has been corroded by time and misery. His stare is that of an untamed animal, dull and pitiless. He is bare-chested, a pot belly sagging over his dirty shorts. He has a dagger strapped to his waist on a belt. He is the alpha wolf. The one who will decide our fate. The rest of the men are an assorted bunch. Old men eager to shed their age and recapture their youth. Young men eager to prove their manhood. Dressed in shorts, some in tattered jeans, one in what looks suspiciously like boxers.

"Where are you guys going to?"

The leader's tone is flat, inflectionless, bored.

"Home." I respond. My voice is a mere squeak. I feel like a pipsqueak.

"Really? Where do you live?"

Jude responds. He gives our street address.

"Liar. You guys are robbers."

I am stunned by the accusation.

"We are musicians." I blurt. "We play reggae music."

The leader is not impressed. Nor are any of his men. "Magicians?"

I stare at the man. "Not magicians. Musicians."

For a moment, hilarity almost overtakes me. What did music have to do with magic?

"Sir, we are not armed robbers. Search us if you like. We are musicians. We are returning from a night club. Let us go."

The leader is unmoved. I am not sure if he truly does not believe us or if he is merely pretending not to believe us. Either way, I am getting upset.

"Can you let us go? Why are you harassing us?" I demand.

Bad mistake number two.

The leader shakes his head. "Harassing you?" He laughs, as if this is the funniest thing he has heard in his life. "You haven't seen harassment yet. We will show you harassment. Get down! Now!"

We freeze in place.

He kicks me. "Face down! Now!"

As if on cue, the men with the two rifles jab them at us. I am terrified. I think of the gun going off. This is how it ends.

We hit the ground. My heart clutches in my chest.

We are going to be killed, shot in the back by wild-eyed men with iron hands who dream bloody dreams, men who have outlawed their own consciences, given themselves over to the angel of darkness, mutinous men who travel like a plague in the night, punishing the innocent and the guilty.

I begin to say a prayer.

"Let's shoot them all." One man says.

'Wait!" The leader says.

"Please don't shoot." I beg. My friends join in. *"ejo-o."* Please.

"We are children. Just like your children."

My mouth is moving fast now as I babble, my lips trying to keep up with my mind as it spins, toboggans down a slope of fear.

A thought flashes across my mind. Maybe I can offer these men money.

"We have some money. You can take it all."

"You think we are thieves?" the leader bellows.

"No, no." I respond hastily. "You work really hard to protect our community. You don't even get paid."

The leader seems to ponder this for a minute. He likes the absolution that I am offering. He will accept my peace offering.

"Get up."

We all rise shakily to our feet. I reach in my pocket, take out the cash in my pocket, crumpled *Naira* notes that smell like a dog's arse.

THE COLLECTOR OF BUTTERFLIES AND WOMEN

Jude and Simeon reach in their pockets as well, fish out whatever cash they are carrying. We hand the money to the leader of the vigilantes. He accepts it. The covenant is sealed.

"You can leave now." He tells us. "Be careful the next time."

We thank the men, dust ourselves off and walk away. As we walk away, it dawns on me that we have just been robbed by men who were supposed to protect us. Men who knew that we were not criminals. What armed robbers went out to rob wearing bright red matching leather outfits?

No one speaks as we walk home. We all realize that we have just narrowly escaped death. The vigilantes who kill with impunity could have murdered all three of us and tossed our corpses in one of the fetid gutters that run through Shogunle. Our families would never have found us. We would have been part of the rich harvest of dead bodies that litter the streets of Lagos like rotting leaves in dry season, the great mass of the unknown dead, men, women, and children, that will never be identified, swallowed up in the wolverine maw of the city. Death is a prankster that stalks the city of chaos, pushing children into open sewers when it rains, forcing pregnant women to have babies before their due dates, grabbing passengers in *molue* buses and taxicabs in its deadly embrace. Death episodic and death operatic chases criminals and innocents through the city of chaos.

The next day is New Year's Day. We decide to celebrate life, celebrate our escape from the vigilantes.

Jude has bought some bottles of whisky. The cheapest brand that is on the shelf. We also have Guinness stout as well as Gulder and Star beer. There isn't much food in the house but who cares? We have invited some girls over. Being modest pop stars, we always have women around. They follow us around like flies chasing an urchin's backside. Jude's girlfriend, Ono is here. So is my girlfriend, Linda, as well as Simeon's girlfriend, Tinu. The air is festive, electric. Even the terrible smell from Segun's shack next door is manageable today.

Music is playing loudly in the background but we are not worried about disturbing the neighbors. Everybody plays their music loud in Lagos. Parties are often held outside and they last all night. Music blares through our collective nights. Like Macbeth, it kills sleep. Everyone seems to be used to the cacophony, the constant vibration of the world in which we live. It is as if we cannot trust ourselves with silence. As if silence is too painful, that it need be eroded by the beating of the talking drums, the shaking of the maracas, and the wailing of velvety singers. Not even the ghosts in Lagos are quiet. Listen. Listen. If you listen, you can hear them rattle the rafters, push against the door, moan in the breeze. Demanding to be heard and acknowledged.

Our little apartment offered no real privacy during our sexual encounters. We took turns on who would use the bedroom which also doubled as our kitchen. The lucky fellow could close the door between the two rooms to achieve a measure of privacy. But it wasn't much. We become used to hearing each other's feverish exhalations, smelling each other's bodily emanations. One night, I am woken up by a female's urgent voice screaming, "Don't release-o! Don't release-o!" She was the girlfriend of one of my friends, and she was begging him not to ejaculate. I could hear my friend grunting like a speared bear, fighting to hold himself in check. I find the whole scene entirely comical and I laugh heartily.

Linda, my girlfriend, was a tall dark-skinned girl with the build of a gazelle. She was a dangerous creature, Linda. Slow to smile, quick to anger. She had been in many fights, most of which she emerged from as victor. She was from the Edo tribe, the same tribe that I was from. I handled Linda the way a snake charmer handled a rattlesnake, gently, carefully, constantly aware of the lethal potential of the thing.

The sexual attraction between Linda and I is strong. When we make love, it is not a sensuous thing of two bodies fused and flowing in rhythm. Instead, it is a grinding, pushing, clawing struggle for dominance, a battle of wills, a death match. Linda was a stubborn creature, and so was I. We buck against each other until we both collapse in sheer exhaustion.

Sex with Linda was tyrannical, imperialistic. She was tireless. Although I was not much of a drinker, the only times that I could keep pace during our sexual marathons was when I was intoxicated. Linda on the other hand, needed no such stimulant.

On this day, New Year's Day, I consume half a bottle of Black Whisky. The world slows down, speeds up, whirring, whirling and I am caught in the blur. Colors as if spun by a kaleidoscope, dance in front of me.

"Are you okay?"

Linda's voice comes to me from an infinite distance, disembodied, faint. I cannot answer, although I try to. I am fading. She starts to shake me. I moan wearily.

I hear Linda calling out to my friends, voicing her worries. I hear them respond, telling her not to worry, that I will be okay.

Just let him sleep, Linda.

Leave him alone.

He will be okay.

I try to open my eyes but cannot. My eyelids are glued shut. I feel like throwing up. Like not throwing up. I want to die. Do not want to die. Somebody save me kill me let me alone heal me please PLEASE!

I black out.

Is it rape?

She was sixteen and I was eighteen when we had sex. I am not sure that I can truthfully say that *we* had sex. I had sex with her, is probably more accurate.

Was it rape?

I don't think so.

Yet I struggle with the question.

It is easy as adults to look back at our youth and wonder what the big deal was about sex. In my adolescence, I consumed and I was consumed by sex.

Angela was a secondary school senior, who lived a few streets away from our apartment in Shogunle. We met one day when she walked up to me and introduced herself. I thought that she was rather bold and confident. I liked that in a girl. I liked her immediately. She was an easy girl to like. Pretty in an abstract way, but not absurdly beautiful like some women are. More like a work of pottery than a beautiful painting. More Monet than Salvador Dali. What Angela lacked in piquancy, she made up for with her vibrancy. Wide apart eyes. A mouth full of perfect white teeth stuck like pearls to her gums.

THE COLLECTOR OF BUTTERFLIES AND WOMEN

"I would like to see you again, Angie."

"Don't call me that. I hate it."

"Okay, Angela. When can I see you again?"

"Soon. Don't worry." She had an impish smile on her face when she said this, eyes twinkling.

"When?"

"Soon."

I knew that she lived in one of the houses on the street, but she refused to tell me which one. Instead, she told me that she knew where I lived and that she would pay me a visit.

She shows up at our little apartment one afternoon after school.

I had not told my friends about her, not knowing if she would actually show up or not. They look at her, look at me, and do not act surprised. But they know what to do. Angela is a new catch. For a new catch, the rule of the house is to give the catcher space. They exchange quick hellos with Angela and then clear out of the apartment.

We have the place to ourselves.

I offer Angela a drink but she declines. She tells me she does not drink.

"Such a chicken." I tease her.

"I just don't like the after-effect. Makes me feel lousy. Gives me a headache."

We are sitting on the sofa. I lean over and touch her. Angela pulls away.

"Are you okay?"

She nods.

I wonder if to give up, let her be. I had dealt with girls like Angela before. Cock teases. They bait a man, reel him in but when the man becomes hot and intoxicated by lust, they wriggle away and leave the man to cool his ardor. The inamorata enjoys being chased, enjoys the game of cat and mouse.

I decide to let her be.

Once I back off, Angela gives me a look that is a cross between amusement and curiosity. She reaches out and touches my hand, strokes it gently. She embraces me, buries her face in my shoulder. Her skin is soft, rain on a hot night, tapping on the skin. She smells like talcum powder. Like bath soap.

Lust overtakes me. I yield myself to the inferno and I am consumed. I grab her and kiss her. I reach under her blouse, encounter filmy, flimsy resistance. Her nipples are as taut as bowstrings. I yank the blouse open, snap a button. But I don't stop.

Angela is moaning, soft anguished sounds emit from deep within her being. Her eyes are wide, breathing tortured. The air vibrates with tension as if from a glockenspiel. My hands travel down her flat stomach. I reach for the moist space between her legs. I hold it in the palm of my hands and caress gently.

She moans as my fingers move faster. Her eyes are now closed. We are both flat on the sofa. The sofa is uncomfortable, like a small bony creature rubbing against our bodies for warmth.

"Stop!"

Her voice is a knife cutting through me.

Stop?

But I am too far gone to stop.

I push up her dress, pull down my underwear, and yank clumsily at her panties. The cotton peels off.

"No! Don't." She begs.

She is afraid of going too far, I think. Perhaps she is a virgin.

Caught in the fever of desire, it is too late to turn back. I no longer have control of myself. I do not own myself. I am merely a serf in lust's fiefdom.

I pierce her. She screams. Fingers rake against my back. Fingers form fists, beat against the back of my head. She lashes her feet around my waist. We tumble to the floor in a clumsy heap. Wounded birds falling from the sky. She wraps her hands tight around my shoulders as I move back and forth. Words race across my mind.

Oscillation.

Amalgamation.

Transmutation.

Liquefaction.

Angela and me.

Two stars in space, space that is forever a changeling. Two stars streaking across time, time that is infinite. Two stars orbiting the universe for eternity.

And then we explode. Grip each other hard in a sweaty embrace, like two gladiators dying from each other's knife wounds. Afterwards, I asked her if she liked it. She tells me that she did. This is not the first time she has had sex.

Is it rape?

Angela and I see each other a few more times after that, but the relationship is not the same. The affair is now a balloon without air, drooping like an old man's penis in his winter years, drooping toward the earth. Angela seems embarrassed whenever we see each other. Her gestures are furtive, her hands move too quickly, eyes dart around the room. We carry the awkwardness of a couple wrestling with the sin of infidelity. We bear the silence of a man and a woman who have lost a child and do not know now how to blame each other. Our love is a small furry animal that has crawled into a hole and died an untimely death.

Is it rape?

The man with the ugly hands

The man who is about to cut open my stomach has ugly hands. He is a tall, mournful looking man with eyes that are a thousand years old and shoulders that carry the weight of a hundred lives. His eyes are what hold my attention; they are sharp, beady, feral. He is not dressed in a surgeon's scrubs. He does not have a stethoscope around his neck. He does not have the soothing bedside manner of Dr. Kildare. When I stare at his crinkled slacks and scuffed black shoes, I imagine that I see a bulge in his pants, a bulge from the wad of cash handed to him just a few hours earlier.

The room smells like cheap sex like yesterday's liquor like tomorrow's dreams. I look around at the whitewashed sterile walls and realize that the walls have freshly being painted. The room I am in is small, with walls the color of a nun's guimpe. The ceiling is pockmarked just like the walls. Despite the generous effort of the painter, the effect is that of a prostitute's make-up, applied a bit too generously, a bit too hastily.

The flat is in a fly-infested, filth-ridden part of Warri, located in a nondescript duplex. As I lie on the makeshift gurney, I remember the journey to the house over uneven water-logged streets. We make the journey in a rusty cab driven by a man with misshapen teeth. His jaw

THE COLLECTOR OF BUTTERFLIES AND WOMEN

looks like he picked up some pebbles and stuffed them in his mouth. His manner is aloof and grumpy. With each lurch of the cab over potholes and muddy terrain, my insides hurtle. I am writhing in pain, dying slowly. We drive past street hawkers peddling newspapers, fruit and sodas known as "minerals." Past street urchins who detonate at warp speed out of ramshackle houses, running around half naked on bare feet with dirty faces and eternal smiles. Past women cooking meals over firewood stoves. Goats and chickens scatter in our wake, their cries mixing with the general cacophony of the street.

My father has accompanied me on the journey to the duplex where Dr. Oghene lives. He hands the cab driver several bills of the local currency, known as Naira. The driver counts the money, licking his finger as he counts. Satisfied that he has been paid the correct amount agreed upon, he nods his head at my father. My father steps out of the cab, leans over to help me out of the cab. I push myself into his arms, wincing in pain at the effort. A thousand fire ants march across the right side of my lower abdomen in formation like soldiers onto a killing field.

My father picks me up and hoists me on his shoulder. My father is a tall quiet man with a serious manner. An educated man who speaks in measured tones. He moves forward, headed for the small duplex which doubles as residence and operating room for Dr. Oghene. For a minute, a traitorous thought crosses my mind. Could Dr. Oghene be an imposter? Perhaps he is not really a surgeon, just a quack who defrauds poor people out of their hard-earned savings and carries out deadly surgeries.

Now as I lay on my back, on two school tables that have been converted into an operating table, staring at the dusty ceiling fan, I am grimly reminded of my mortality. I think of the transitory nature of life itself, and I feel the cold fingers of death crawling up my spine like a black beetle running from winter. I am acutely aware that I might be dead in the next few hours. Even if I survive the surgery that is about to be performed on me, I might not survive an infection that could potentially result from it.

The door creaks open. In walks a short, balding man with skin the color of overripe blackberries and lips that seem to run from cheekbone to cheekbone. He smiles broadly at me, eyes as twinkly as a child on Halloween night. Dr. Oghene acknowledges him with a tight-lipped smile. There is an easy familiarity between the two men. It is clear that they have worked together several times before. This is Dr. Oghene's assistant.

The assistant takes his place beside Dr. Oghene at a small sink that has been rigged up in a corner of the room. I notice that Dr. Oghene now has on surgical gloves. He is moving various surgical instruments from the top of the sink into the sink bowl. The assistant squirts some soap from a plastic bottle into his palms, rubs it vigorously on his hands, and turns on the water. When he is done, he lets the hot water splash over the surgical instruments in the sink. Lets it run for a while.

On a small stool near the sink are bottles of chemicals, syringes, surgical gauze, bandages, and other items.

"Doc, you ready?" The assistant asks, smiling like a pupil about to be presented with a diploma.

Dr. Oghene nods. "I'm ready."

"Bet you can't count how many of these you have done."

"Let's say, a few."

Dr. Oghene turns to me. "This is my assistant. He will take care of the anesthesia. You are in good hands.'"

The assistant nods at me unctuously. "You will be okay. Nothing to worry about. Won't even feel a thing. Right, Doc?"

Dr. Oghene nods. "Right. Won't feel a thing."

"Want to say a prayer before we start?" The assistant asks me.

I shake my head. "No.

The assistant looks surprised. His brow furrows, mouth opens to ask a question, that he never asks. He is used to men and women who cry and ask God for mercy while lying on the operating table. He has come to expect this deluge of anguished emotion, this confession of private sins under hushed breaths.

Having successful surgery in Nigeria my country of birth is a fifty-fifty proposition. You are half as likely to survive as you are to die. People go in for tonsillectomies and appendectomies and never wake up. People have surgeries and discover much later that a scalpel or a wad of gauze has been left in their insides. People are diagnosed with migraines when in fact they have deadly tumors that will soon explode in their brains.

I refuse to pray now because I am not on speaking terms with God today. I had said all that I had to say to Him and got no answer in response. It didn't matter to me anymore if I lived or died.

In what could have been the final moment of my life, what is going through my head, curiously, is a poem. One of my favorites. Phillip Larkin's *Aubade* in which the poet meditates on death.

Till then, I see what's really always there
Unresting death, a whole day nearer now
Making all thought impossible but how
And where and when I shall myself die.

In the last stanza, Larkin goes on further to write:

Courage is no good: It means not scaring others. Being brave
Lets no one off the grave.
Death is no different whined at than withstood.

The assistant reaches for one of the syringes, inserts it into one of the small bottles with chemicals and draws some liquid. He turns toward me, his sickly rictus of a smile still in place.

The man with ugly hands reaches for a scalpel and moves toward me.

One day before the man with ugly hands

"How am I going to get this money?" My father asks. His eyes look haunted. He is a general whose army has been besieged at dawn.

Tears are falling down my face in rivulets. Outside, fat rain drops tattoo a beat on the zinc rooftop. We are sitting in my parents' bedroom. My father is hunched over, staring at the floor, defeat mapped on his face. My mother, soft-spoken, given to a few words, sits beside him.

The subject of discussion is my surgery, specifically, how to pay for it. A few days ago, I was diagnosed with peritonitis, an infection resulting from a swollen appendix. This appendage had apparently become infected and like an alien mutation, needed to be removed. I had spent nights howling in pain like a wounded wolf, unable to sleep. That pain had dragged me back, like a prodigal son, to my parents' humble abode in Warri, Nigeria. When we visited Warri General Hospital, we learned that I needed to have surgery. The doctor who is supposed to perform the surgery is Dr. Oghene, the man with ugly hands.

He walks up to my father as we seat expectantly. In his hand is a clipboard with notes. He studies it for a while like Pythia divining the

THE COLLECTOR OF BUTTERFLIES AND WOMEN

future at the Delphic Oracle. When the sage finally looks up, he says to my father, "this is serious. He could die at any moment."

Panic stitches itself across my father's care-worn features. Hell hounds ride a chariot across my mind, hooves clattering.

My father does not speak, does not trust himself to speak.

"He has peritonitis. His appendix is inflamed, about to rupture." Dr. Oghene says. When he utters the last word, his ugly scarred fingers make a shearing motion, a movement of paper ripped asunder, a corn cob split in two, a clothes hanger twisted to breaking point.

My father still does not speak.

Dr. Oghene turns to me, "How long have you been in pain?"

I take a deep breath, exhale hard. I want to tell him the truth, that I have been in pain all of my life, that I have been like a wounded animal since I was expelled from my mother's womb. I want to tell him that I was born howling and that I have never stopped howling. I want to tell him this truth. But this is not the truth he is asking for. Dr. Oghene is not the type of man on whom to waste a metaphor. His whole carriage and demeanor is brisk, business like, like a fruit seller at a bazaar. He looks like a man who washes his hands before every meal, a man who rinses with mouthwash after every meal. A man focused on inner vitality in a society teetering at the edge of outer decay.

"Weeks." I answer. "I've been in pain for weeks." My voice comes out coarse, rough like the hands of an *Ikenga* drummer.

The doctor turns to my father.

"He needs surgery right away. It will be expensive." He pauses to study my father's face for a reaction, but finds none. My father's face seems strangely slack, immobile and robotic, as if he is holding his breath.

"I can help you."

My father looks up hopefully. Dr. Oghene makes a theatrical

pause, and then like a benevolent deity bestowing blessings, he announces, "I can do the surgery at my private clinic for half the price the hospital will charge you."

I glance around me and see another young doctor talking to an elderly woman with tribal marks on her face who is rocking silently on her heels. I wonder if the young doctor is similarly trying to strike a deal to perform some surgical procedure on her at his "private clinic." I wonder how many of such covert transactions take place every day.

It is a well known fact in Nigeria that doctors, some of the best and brightest that the country has to offer, are often underpaid, if paid at all. Doctors' strikes are not uncommon. When doctors go on strike, entire hospitals shut down and sick and dying people litter hospital hallways like bubble gum wrappers, hallways that smell of antiseptic and tomato stew. In Nigeria, when a family member is hospitalized, you have to deliver food to them at the hospital on a daily basis. On several visits to hospitals, I have always found this odd conflation of Dettol antiseptic and tomato stew to be quite an assault on the nose.

It does not take much to convince my father that Dr. Oghene's proposition makes sense. The fact that my family is hard-up for money narrows our options.

My father is a civil servant, an honest, God fearing man who has worked for the government all of his life. Every day, he goes to work wearing a suit, his tie knotted in a big camel hump on his throat. He looks respectable, speaks with the rarefied diction of a man who has attended college and has read all the classics. The fact that he is generally as poor as "a church rat," does not make him stoop or walk less tall. His shoes, of which he owns only a couple, are worn, scuffed and in mortal need of shoe polish. He carries himself with dignity, as if behind him is a pedigree of broad-shouldered blue-blooded forebears, as if ahead of him is a bright shining future that holds

THE COLLECTOR OF BUTTERFLIES AND WOMEN

endless promises. In Nigeria, civil servants are at the very bottom of the totem pole. They are the proletariat, the Sudras, the drones.

So the deal is struck. The surgery will be performed at Dr. Oghene's "private clinic" the next day as long as my father is able to rustle up the doctor's fee.

Now here we are, a day before the surgery is to take place and my father is at his wit's end trying to figure out how to raise money.

The room is silent for what seems an eternity. I close my eyes for a minute and imagine that I hear a dirge, see a funeral procession marching across a muddy landscape.

My death.

I see black birds falling from the sky, swooping on a bloated carcass abandoned by the roadside.

My body.

Azrael, the angel of death, hovers over me, eyes piercing like polished jewels.

My mother, a tough woman, who rarely cries, begins to whimper. The cry comes from deep inside of her, stoked by pain, but her eyes remain stubbornly dry as she refuses to yield to the tears. I can see that she is hurting and choking back her tears in order to stay strong for me.

My mind flashes to TS Elliott's The Hollow Men.

This is the way the world ends
This is the way the world ends
This is the way the world ends
Not with a bang but a whimper.

This is the way my world ends.

Two days before the man with ugly hands

"How can I escape from here?" I ask my friends, Jude and Kenneth, who have accompanied me to the hospital in Shogunle, Lagos. "I need to get out of here."

The reason I am trying to escape from the hospital is quite simple. I cannot afford to pay the bills. In the few days, that I have been here, the bills have continued to mount. If I cannot afford to pay them, I will not be discharged. I will be detained at the hospital and prevented from leaving. Although, I am far from well, I need to leave.

Today.

I am lying on a tiny bed, head elevated by a pillow. My right arm is attached to an intravenous drip containing a clear liquid that is dripping into my veins. I suspect that the liquid is probably just water and I think that the water is entering straight into my soul, diluting the essence of my being.

The hospital room smells like fear and pain and religion. A young man lies on the bed next to me, tossing in a chemical induced sleep, muttering imprecations or supplications, or both. A woman who looks like his mother is dressed in traditional Yoruba attire, in a *buba* and wrapper. Her lips move as she mutters a quiet prayer. When

THE COLLECTOR OF BUTTERFLIES AND WOMEN

I tune in and listen, I can hear the words, *Jehovah Jireh*. God, my provider.

My nurse, a short impatient woman with deep tribal marks, left the room a few minutes before my two friends arrived. Now, I need to figure out how to escape from the hospital before she returns.

My friends glance around the room and flash each other a conspiratorial look. "We can get you out." Jude says.

"Let's do it." I reply.

The plan devised by my friends is remarkably simple yet audacious. Under the ruse of helping me make it to the bathroom, they would sneak me out the back door and into a waiting cab. Jude leaves to hail a cab while Kenneth stays with me.

When Jude returns half an hour later, we are ready to set our plan in motion. Jude goes to look for the woman that I like to think of as Nurse Ratched. Nurse Ratched from the movie, *One Flew Over the Cuckoo's Nest* because of her humorlessness. Although, I have known her for only two days, I can tell that she has never met a joke that she liked. She treats the world with weary suspicion, always on guard, like a hyena marking its territory with urine, standing on its hind legs ready to attack.

Jude asks Nurse Ratched if she can unhook the intravenous drip attached to my body so that I can use the restroom. Without a word, she walks over and not so gently disconnects the plastic tubing attached to my body. I wince in pain and mutter a curse under my breath, wishing a pox on her and her house.

As soon as Nurse Ratched leaves the room, my friends spring into action. Holding me by each arm and half lifting me off the floor, we make our way to the exit. The restroom is located by the hallway outside the hospital room.

We have no intention of going to the restroom.

Once we make it out of the hospital room, we proceed down a dingy staircase directly next to the restroom. Pain racks my body with each step. I grit my teeth and try not to cry out.

When we get to the first floor level, there is a cab waiting outside for us. My friends hustle me into the cab. We make a brief stop at the apartment in Shogunle which I share with my friends, Jude and Simeon. They help me pack a bag. We get back in the waiting cab and head for Yaba bus station.

I had just fled a hospital because I couldn't afford to pay the bill.

Now, I was on my way to Warri, a city located in the southern part of Nigeria where my parents lived.

I still did not know what was wrong with me and why my lower abdomen hurt so much. The doctor at the hospital I had just escaped from had ostensibly run a series of tests and still could not figure out the problem. It is common knowledge in Nigeria that doctors often administer more diagnostic tests than required on patients. Patients often find themselves caught in a labyrinthine maze of blood work, X-rays, and ultrasound scans. Procedures that are often unnecessary. Procedures designed to separate patients from their hard-earned money.

As I made the journey to Warri, I wondered just how dire my situation was.

I began to think of all kinds of sophisticated diseases. I thought of ravaging cancers that swelled up like volcanic peaks and discharged tendrils of fatal ash all over my insides. I thought of suppurating tumors that grew to the size of the Hindenburg, sickly green and pulsating with fetid organisms and malignant ectoplasms.

Was I going to die?

Once more, the man with ugly hands

I did survive my surgery.
Barely.

The surgeon must have been running out of anesthesia. I am awake throughout the procedure but I cannot move. I can hear the ribald jokes about horse size penises and vaginas so wide you could fit a man's head through, the sloshing of water, the ragged breathing of the men working on my body.

I hear what I think is the scalpel cutting into my flesh. There is nothing more disturbing than the sound of a knife slicing into your own flesh.

My eyes are too heavy to move.

I cannot move.

Like Edgar Poe's Fortunato condemned to die in Montresor's catacombs, my spirit begs to escape from my trapped body.

Death is water, breaking its dams, rushing into every orifice of my body into every pore, filling me up, consuming me whole like a serpent. Death is succubus with icy hands eyes like rubies vagina like an eternal tunnel.

Jeffrey Obomeghie

On my right abdomen, I still carry the scars where the man with ugly hands cut me. There are two cuts. The first one, I think, is the practice cut. The second is where he made the actual incision once he had steadied his scalpel.

Death comes cheap in the land of my birth. It hangs in the air like halitosis and every breath takes us closer to its final embrace.

A woman is crying

It is 5 a.m. in Lagos. A woman is crying.

Night is a wounded beast, stabbed by daybreak. Dawn bleeds out of the entrails of the beast, staining the trees and ground with drops of light. The cry that woke me up from sleep is coming from the room next door. The room is in our apartment. Since the door between both rooms is open, I can hear the sounds of a palm slapping flesh, the sounds of a fist hitting skin.

"You animal! Go on and hit me." The woman screams.

The hands take her up on the challenge and deliver another punch. She whimpers, begins to beg.

The man who is administering the beating is my best friend. The woman that is being beaten is his girlfriend. I do not know the reason for the fight. Frankly, in Lagos, the screaming of a woman being beaten in the middle of the night by her husband or boyfriend would not rouse anyone out of sleep. They summon no pique.

Here, no one calls the police because a neighbor is beating his wife. No one rushes to help the poor woman that is being abused. Many women are taught that being beaten by their husband is a sign of love. They are taught that a man has to love you hard enough in order to hit you. They are told that being beaten is far better than being ignored, and that indifference is the worst slight of all.

For a lucky minority of women, love is flowers and gifts and sunsets so tender they make you want to cry. For the unlucky majority, love is a fist in the gut that makes you bend over and a slap on the face and teeth so sore that it hurts when you cry. These are women who have not known love. They have heard rumors of love, seen it from afar like smoke rising from an abandoned smokestack, but they have not known love. Love is a hooded stranger that they have passed on the street, but with whom they have exchanged no eye contact. This then is the shame of our mothers and sisters, beaten in the dark, crying softly so as not to wake the children, trying not to crush innocence in its crib. The shame of our fathers and brothers, men who succumb to their anger, men who hit just because they can. Men like Nana.

They say that what a man does to his wife in the privacy of their bedroom is nobody's business. The very term 'bride price' with its suggestion of the pecuniary and its reductionism, finds eager usage among philistines. For these poor women, life is depreciated while pain is amortized.

But Ono is not Jude's wife. He has not paid her bride price. I know that I shouldn't interfere but I feel that I must. I get up from the floor where I am sleeping on a mattress. Light spills through the louvered window. Segun's wife who usually takes a shit every morning outside our window is not up yet. I hear birds chirp outside, hear the sound of snoring from one of the apartments down the hall. The morning is full of promise.

But not for Ono.

I tap on the door that separates the two rooms.

"Jude, what's going on in there?"

Ono is still moaning.

For what seems like an eternity, there is no answer. When Jude

THE COLLECTOR OF BUTTERFLIES AND WOMEN

finally answers, his voice is hoarse and tired-sounding. Like a town-crier who has been making his rounds all night, waking up the villagers, alerting them to some imminent misery.

"She is acting out. You know how she is."

Jude is an easy-going guy who happens to have a hair-trigger temper. He believes that Ono has a special talent for provoking him. Ono is a girl of accidental beauty, a girl who seemed to have stumbled on beauty while picking fruits in the bush. She carries herself with the exuberant indifference with which such women carry themselves, completely unaware of the devastating effect that they have on men. No more than eighteen or nineteen, she is ambitious and driven, face full of gentle laugh lines, eyes full of wicked humor.

I am not quite sure of what Ono does for a living but I know that she has her own apartment and seems to always have money. On many occasions, she has helped Jude out with money. I sense that on a certain level, he resents the hand-outs. He resents the fact that their roles are reversed. He wants to be the provider but he cannot provide. I have heard him shouting at her for belittling him, talking down to him, just because she has "a little money"

Things have apparently come to a head today.

I enter the room. Ono is lying on the bed naked. Her black night dress is ripped to shreds. Her breasts, big and pale, rest on her thighs as she hunches over to avoid the blows. Jude is sitting on the bed, chest bare, glaring at her. The bedspread is on the uncarpeted floor. The room smells like unfinished sex and bitterness. Like leather in the second stage of being cured. In spite of my altruistic motives, the physical reaction that I experience is purely animalistic. I push down the animal of lust, grab it by the neck and choke it to death.

Ono does not try to cover her nakedness, nor does Jude. They sit there as I walk in, as if it is perfectly natural for two people, one naked, the other half-naked to sit on a bed at 5 a.m. in the morning while a man walks in on them.

"Put on your clothes, Ono"

Jude gives me a questioning look but doesn't say anything. We have known each other since high school and we trust each other. We are more like brothers than friends. If anyone can walk Jude back from the cliff of his anger, it is me.

Since Ono's night dress is shredded, she wraps a towel around her body. I lead her into what passes for our living room, the room where I was sleeping. Our other friend, Simeon, is still asleep.

"Want to lay down?" I offer my position on the mattress, beside Simeon.

Ono shakes her head. "I'm tired." She says, and then she begins to weep. Slow agonizing sobs rack her body. I look at her and I wonder why beautiful women are attracted to damaged men, why they must carry the mark of the beast. Moths sucked into the flame's breath. Lemmings running blindly into the sea.

Some men and women are just not good for each other. When they rub against each other, what they generate is not passion but friction, the by-product is not excitement, but incitement. When they rub against each other, the sparks they throw off are sparks of fire and not sparks of light. Love becomes nothing but tinder, nothing but kindle, a device for self-immolation. Love becomes a fire that consumes and consumes entirely, leaving nothing but ashes and cold regrets. Love is not a drug that should be prescribed for everybody. Its side effects do not agree with everyone's constitution.

That morning, Ono fixes us breakfast. It is a hearty meal. Bread and tea, fried eggs and plantains. When we finish eating, she clears the plates and then announces cheerfully that she would like to get married to Jude.

The man who loved funerals

I am mourning a man that I do not know.

The man who died was not my friend or family member. Prior to showing up at his funeral, I did not know his name, his age or the particulars of his existence or even how he met with his demise, and whether that demise was timely, untimely, or ill-timed.

I was in search of a good meal. And there is no better place to get a free meal than at a funeral. In Nigeria, no one needs an invitation to a funeral or a wedding or a christening. Such celebrations are open to anyone who wants to attend. There is never a guest list. All that is required is that the uninvited show up dressed in their best finery and that they wear the proper expression for the ceremony. If it is a funeral, one must come armed with a sad face. If it is a funeral, one must come prepared with a troubled brow and be ready to beat one's chest in grief.

So there I was eating rice and stew with generous chunks of goat meat. All around me, colorfully attired men and women huddle, parley, drink, and grieve. There are open and unopened cartons of Gulder and Guinness stacked high. I am seated under a huge canopy amongst strangers. The smell of rice, pounded yam and stew is intoxicating. *Juju* music plays in the background. The music is a steady rumbling beat. A few people are dancing, wearing bright *buba* and wrappers, *agbadas* and *Kaftans*. The air is dense with gaiety and spontaneity, condensed with sweat and cheap cologne. The skies are cloudy, pregnant with surprise and mischief like a sorceress.

Not far from where I sit, the family of the dead man gathers in a semi-circle. One man, presumably the head of the family, is leading the conversation. He is making rapid gestures, talking fast. His listeners follow his movements and speech respectfully. When the wind blows toward me, I catch snatches of his monologue.

It is late afternoon and it is hot. The heat seems to attract flies. They buzz and circle the crowd of on-lookers. Those who are armed with fly-whisks swat them away. Others slash at the air with their hands, attempting to ward off the pesky creatures. The flies are drawn to the smell of food and beer. I remembered the story of a man who was drinking beer when a fly dropped into his drink. Angry, but undeterred, the man reached into his glass and pulled out the obstinate insect. He put the fly in his mouth and sucked out the beer from the fly and then cast it away, declaring, "Go and buy your own beer. This is mine."

This was the fifth funeral that I was attending in less than a month. I had learned to keep myself informed by reading the local newspapers which publish lavish information about the recently deceased. Family members often take out full page ads, extolling the dead, listing all of his or her accomplishments, their offspring, college degrees, and God knows what else. Witness then the mundane and the abstruse, the esoteric and the picayune.

A man seated next to me is shoveling spoonfuls of rice down his throat. He chews noisily like a small rodent. He is a short unremarkable man with a high forehead and small porcine eyes. He looks like a man to whom life has been unkind. He eats with the quiet desperation of the prodigal son, of a man long exiled from

THE COLLECTOR OF BUTTERFLIES AND WOMEN

celebration. I watch him chew and I try to make up my mind if to detest him or not. But I find that I cannot detest him. He catches me staring at him. He chews one last morsel, sticks his dirty fingernail in his teeth and pulls out a piece of stray meat which he regards thoughtfully, almost wistfully I think, and then he sticks it back in his mouth and it disappears into the abyss.

"He was a good man."

"Who?" I ask, then quickly realize my faux pas.

"Alhaji Oludare Deji."

I nod in agreement.

I wonder if the man seated near me knew Deji. Was he like me, a stray cat hunting for food who had wondered into a feast? Curious, I ask, "You knew him well, then?"

The stranger pauses, broods on this for a moment. "Yes, I knew him. Long before he became wealthy. Knew him when he was a washer man who did people's laundry for a living. But he never changed."

I am about to ask another question when a loud scream interrupts my thoughts. It is a heart-rending shriek, a wail of utter despair, from some forlorn, abandoned soul. I look around to see the source of the disturbance. It is a young woman in her mid thirties. She is tall and brashly pretty, legs longer than an eternity by two inches. I wonder who she is.

"Deji's daughter. The eldest."

I nod. She is a strange sight, Deji's oldest daughter. She looks incongruous, like a nun in a nightclub, Santa Claus in a graveyard. Sorrow looks out of place on a face this beautiful. Some faces are just not made for tears, I think. When they cry, tears deform them. Instead of pathos, what their tears and contorted faces elicit is surprise and aversion. I want to turn away from this graceful woman with ungraceful tears, tears streaming down her face, her empire of make-up crumbling before the lachrymose assault. Yet I feel sad for her. I wonder how close she was to her father. Perhaps she is only doing a daughter's duty; this public dissolution, this unloading of emotional baggage.

As if on cue, the crowd begins to rise. It is time to bury the dead. My stomach is full. I have drunk a couple of beers. I really do not want to witness the burial, yet I cannot get myself to walk away. Guilt seizes my innards like an unwelcome lover. If I must eat and drink the dead man's beer, don't I at least owe him attendance at his funeral?

So I shuffle along with the crowd. Shuffle along as we walk into Alhaji Deji's compound. The daughter leads the way. I follow her screaming. The crowd follows her screaming. She is surrounded now by a gauntlet of men and women. Comforters. They whisper to her, try to calm her, but she continues to scream, braided hair waving this way and that, slender neck imperiled.

Deji's compound is large. There are three houses on the grounds, surrounded by trees. The houses are as big, standing tall like bullies in a school yard. Considering that the street outside Deji's palazzo is unpaved, the street that is currently closed off for his funeral, I find the dead man's residence meretricious. Several luxury vehicles, mostly American and Japanese are parked all around. Plenty of terrazzo or marble everywhere. The grass is manicured. The landscaping is impressive. When a great person dies in Nigeria, the occasion of their death invites platitudes and polemics. I prepare myself for the platitudes. The polemics will follow when the children of the deceased man, of which I suspect there are many, begin to divide his wealth.

In the middle of Deji's compound, a big hole has been dug. Fresh earth is strewn all around. It is reddish, dry. I wonder how long it takes for two men to dig six feet into the earth. I wonder if out of frustration, they curse the man that will be going in the hole, curse him for dying, for bringing upon them such hard labor. Or perhaps they thank him, thank the man for dying, for allowing the gravedigger to earn a living thus. An odd thought, thanking a man who is dead for dying.

THE COLLECTOR OF BUTTERFLIES AND WOMEN

Deji's body is inside the casket. The casket is already inside the grave.

Some people ask to be buried in their compounds when they die. I suppose this is their way of holding on to the world that they are leaving behind. Staying close to their worldly possessions and family. In the Benin culture, householders are often buried in their living room or bedroom. The ghost of the dead is left to wander at will, roaming over his earthly kingdom, fixing a disapproving eye on the maunderings and meanderings of the survivors.

The crowd gathers around the grave, careful to leave a path for the casket bearers. A man emerges from somewhere, the man who will preside over the ceremonies. He is a rusty faced man with thin lips and a hooked nose. His manner is intent, saturnine. He has the demeanor of a man used to unpleasant tasks. The face of a circumciser or a garbage collector. The face of an executioner or a jailer.

"We have gathered here today to mourn a special man." The man begins. "A man who changed the lives of many people."

That is as far as he gets before a group of twelve mourners interrupt. The mourners are all dressed in black. Middle aged women well past their prime. They begin to cry loudly. They beat their chests, pull the black scarves from their heads. They lament, berate death for his effrontery, curse this day for its betrayal.

Everything comes to a standstill. Everyone is hushed as they watch this scene play out, this scene that is equal to any that Sophocles, Aeschylus and Euripedes combined could have conjured. The women howl and collapse to the ground. They roll in the dirt like fat earthworms recoiling from salt, they howl and they howl. Their cries fill me with an existential despair.

I watch one of the mourners rip the wig off her head. She must be the lead mourner, I think. The one crying the loudest, the one with the most theatrics. Her tears flow easily, her face used to contortion, twists into odd shapes. I watch her crumple to the ground, her black wrapper quickly gathering dust. She begins to roll. Like an orange, she rolls, closer and closer to Deji's grave. I watch fascinated, watch horrified. When the mourner gets within a foot of the grave, a hand reaches out and grabs her, pulls her to her feet. But she will not go quietly. She struggles against her rescuer.

"Let me go! Let me go with Alhaji! Let me go with him!"

She tries to break free, asks to be set free so that she can jump into Deji's grave. When the man holding her loosens his grip, she breaks free and sprints toward the grave. She pauses at the edge of the pit. Pauses as if summoning courage. Stretches out her hands like a bird about to take flight. Takes a deep breath and...

The man who rescued her the first time steps forward with the quickness of a cat. He grabs her once more and lifts her off the ground, hoists her on his shoulder. She is kicking and screaming, arms and feet flailing as she wails. "Let me die with him. *Olorun mi-o!*"

The mourners continue their weeping for a while. And then as if on cue, they stop and walk toward the main residence. Their job has been done. A worthy performance. The dead has been honored. The world has been duly informed about the weightiness of the lost life. The world knows now that Alhaji Deji was an important man, a man who will be missed. Most people in Lagos were not rich enough to have a dozen professional mourners show up at their funerals. Like thespians on Broadway, these mourners did not come cheap.

"They came all the way from Yaba" A woman standing next to me tells me. "The very best you can find."

"Expensive, huh?"

The woman nods. "At least ten thousand naira for each one."

I shake my head in wonderment.

If I died, how many paid mourners could my family afford to hire to cry at my funeral?

Don't jump in the well

Mina ignores my plea. She is moving closer to the deep well in front of the house where we live in Shogunle.

The well is cavernous, easily thirty feet deep, fungi and weeds sprouting from its walls. The weeds are obnoxiously green, nauseating. The water is brackish, stale. Insects buzz above the opening. This was where we fetched the water that we used for bathing and cooking. Before we drank the water, we were always careful to boil it first. To fetch the water, we used a bucket with a twine rope attached to its handle. Every now and then a tenant would fish out a dead rat, its body half decayed in the water. At other times, a cat or dog would emerge from the watery depths, stiff, dead for a day or two before rising to the surface.

It was a little after midnight. The would-be suicide was my girlfriend. One of my many girlfriends, to be specific. The very reason Mina wanted to kill herself. She wanted to be my only girlfriend, and not one of many.

Mina was nineteen years old. A dark-skinned girl of medium height. Life had showed her the ultimate cruelty that it could inflict on any young girl - it had made her ordinary. Her eyes did not inspire poetry, her voice did not transform melancholia to euphoria. She was neither pretty nor unpretty, neither charismatic nor phlegmatic. If she were a dress in a shop, she would not be the canary yellow one with iridescent pearls and shimmering cotton, not the Cerulean one with the frills and high hems, floating in the soft breeze like a frigate on an immaculate sea. No, Mina would be the one over there, the battle-gray dress draped on a rack near the glass window all by itself, sitting by the window, all by itself by the window, the dress that all the beautiful men and beautiful women walk by without honoring with even a glance.

I could tell you that I was attracted to Mina for her intellect or character but that would be a lie. I wasn't attracted to Mina. Sex with Mina was like drinking stale coffee, insipid, tepid, and oddly unsatisfying. Its aftertaste was more memorable than the original taste itself. Why was I with her then?

I don't know why I stayed with Mina. Perhaps it was because I felt sorry for her, because I was the custodian of her shameful secrets. Perhaps I saw in her a kindred spirit, a fellow keeper of secrets. What are these secrets, you wonder.

Mina still wet her bed at nineteen.

I found this out the first time we slept together. When I woke up in the middle of the night, my underclothes were wet. When I touched the girl beside me, I realized that she was wet too. It took me a few seconds to realize that the sharp smell of ammonia that burned my nostrils was from urine. Mina had wet herself as we slept. When I woke her up and asked her about it, she cried bitterly and confessed her secrets. She begged me not to ever tell anyone and not to leave her.

I said that I did not know why I stayed with Mina, but I lie. It was guilt that bound me to her like a muslin fabric and it was pity that wrapped that fabric tight around me. It was her cobweb of secrets that prevented me from being able to look past her. You see, when

THE COLLECTOR OF BUTTERFLIES AND WOMEN

Mina was 12 years old, when she was just a child herself, she delivered a baby. This baby died even before the midwife cut the umbilical cord and buried the placenta. This baby was conceived after Mina was raped by a neighbor. Her young body struggled to carry the child for nine months, her bladder stressed to the point of incontinence. Mina had lost control of her bladder. Now, when she laughed, she tried not to laugh too hard because if she did, she wet herself. She took several showers every day, stayed up on some nights so that she wouldn't endure the excoriating shame of wetting herself while she slept.

I had tried to end the relationship several times in the past but Mina was not a girl that you could rinse out of your mouth with mouthwash. Oh, no. Not the type of girl who sneaked in at night and then stole away in the morning. Mina was the type who wanted to cook you dinner and also breakfast, who wanted to wash your clothes and also make babies. I found the prospect of marital bliss and domestication terrifying. The reason was simple. Mina was just the kind of girl that I could fall in love with, unless I was really careful. She was homely and loyal, self-assured and stable. Kind-hearted and righteous and I did not deserve her. Like Abelard who considered himself unworthy of Heloise's love, I was unworthy of Mina's love. She was everything that a faithless philanderer like me did not want and everything that a faithless philanderer like me needed.

I did not want to be attracted to Mina. Did not want to be weighted down by her common sense, did not want to be tamed by her sincerity. So I set about to destroy her faith and her love for me. By so doing, I felt that I could save her from me and save myself from her. My life as a musician was unstable, my income was meager, my prospects opaque.

I had sent a letter to Bea, my first love, who still lived in Agbor. This *billex doux* was written in soaring lyrical prose. My goal was to win back the heart of the girl that I had fallen in love with when I was just fourteen. I hadn't visited Agbor in a couple of years, but I had heard that she was still unmarried. She would be twenty two now. The object of the letter was to rekindle our relationship. Bea received my letter and responded. She informed me that she would take up my invitation to visit Lagos in the next couple of weeks.

Sure enough, on the day that Mina would try to kill herself, Bea arrives. Her arrival would be the final straw for Mina. I was alone in the room with Bea when Mina knocked on the door. I open the door and there she is. Mina looks past my shoulder at the unknown girl sitting on the sofa behind me. Her eyes ask, who is she, or more correctly, who the hell is she? I ignore her unasked question. She pushes past me into the room.

"How are you?" I ask?

She doesn't answer. Her face is grim.

Bea looks surprised and uncomfortable. The air hangs heavy, curdles, liquefies, drips to my feet like acid rain. I am suddenly hot. There is going to be trouble.

"Who is she?"

My sister. My cousin. My neighbor. But none of those lies come through my lips. Instead, I say, "My friend."

"Another one of your harlots? You've been fucking her, haven't you?"

Mina's face is a mask, eyes darkened with injury. She is breathing hard. Bea, sensing imminent trouble, gets up from the sofa, not wanting to be attacked while in a defenseless position. I feel sorry for Bea and I feel sorry for Mina. None of them deserves this, I think. I feel vile and reprehensible. What right did I have to put these girls in this position?

"Let's not make a scene." I begin. I stand between both girls. Bea looks bewildered. Mina looks bellicose.

"Is this how you treat me? I am gone for one day and you move your slut in?"

"No insults, please."

THE COLLECTOR OF BUTTERFLIES AND WOMEN

"I will insult you and her." Mina points a manicured finger at Bea.

Bea attempts to say something but Mina cuts her off. "Don't you dare say a word to me, you whore."

I am surprised by Mina's vehemence, her malevolence. I have never seen this side of her before.

Eventually, Mina storms off. But she doesn't leave the house. She stands outside and cries. She cries, giant sobs racking her body. Watching her cry, I am torn apart and diminished. Love hurts, I think. Love hurts even more, when the person you love does not love you back and they betray your trust. I realized just how selfish I was and the knowledge fills me with self-loathing.

Jude and Simeon return home to find Mina outside. She is sitting on a bench outside the house, face streaked with tears. They try to console her, urge her to pull herself together. I go back inside to check on Bea. Her face is anthracite, hard, glowing with anger and pain. She doesn't want to talk to me.

"Is this why you invited me to Lagos? To get introduced to your sluts and get cursed out?"

I sit down on the sofa beside her, try to take her hand, but she swats me away. "Leave me alone. Go back to her."

I walk out the door.

The clouds begin to gather, pregnant with rain. It is growing dark.

Mina has stopped crying. Her expression is inscrutable. It is the face of resolution, and transcendence, the face of a woman who has journeyed past pain and has emerged on the other side. A woman who has made up her mind. She refuses to say a word. She ignores my friends. Frustrated, they go back inside the apartment.

It is too late for Mina to go home. I did not want her to leave, knowing how dangerous the streets of Lagos were at night. A few minutes after midnight, Mina does the unthinkable. She leaps up from the bench where she has been seated for several hours and runs toward the well in front of the compound.

I realize her intent immediately.

Panicked, I run after her. "Don't jump in the well!"

Mina ignores my plea. She stands at the edge of the well, trying to decide if to go in head first or feet first. She raises one leg and places it over the lip of the well. I reach her before she can lift up the second leg. I seize her and hold her tight.

She does not say a word. Instead, she fights me like a baby resisting a tetanus shot, she fights me, clawing my face, kicking at my shins. I hold her and do not let go.

"I'm sorry." I say, my voice hoarse. "I am so sorry. Please forgive me."

The night proves to be interminable, one of the longest in my life. Mina and Bea both sleep in our apartment that night. All three of us sleep on a thin mattress on the floor and I am in the middle. I am at once the rampart that separates them from each other and the viaduct which brings pain to both of them.

None of us sleeps. In the middle of the night, Mina begins to weep softly. Her back heaves against me. When I reach out to touch her, she recoils, moves away.

The next morning, Bea packs her bag and prepares to return to Agbor, the village where we started our relationship when I was in secondary school. She does not say a word to me. When she is ready to leave, I attempt to follow her.

"Don't bother." She says curtly. "Go take care of her." She points at Mina who is sitting on the sofa, watching TV.

Bea walks to the door. I follow. She walks out the door. Into the corridor, into the dusty street where the sounds of morning ricochet like bullets in a battlefield. Children are already playing outside. Car engines and the noisy bustle of humanity.

"I'll escort you to the bus stop."

"Don't bother. It's not necessary."

THE COLLECTOR OF BUTTERFLIES AND WOMEN

But I don't want it to end this way. Not this way, with Bea walking off angrily. Out of my life forever. This is not how I want to remember her.

Bea ignores me. I follow her as she walks briskly to the bus stop. I talk but she doesn't respond as she reaches the bus stop. A bus, marked with yellow and black stripes emerges. It sneezes acrid smoke, screeches like an asthmatic, lurches forward spastically like a man stricken with gout. The bus conductor emerges, a bare-chested man in filthy shorts. A toothpick pokes out of the side of his mouth. He spits generously on the sidewalk.

"Oshodi! Oshodi! *Wole!*" The conductor yells.

Hearing this cry, passengers stream forward, a colony of ants chasing a sugar trail. They shove and push each other as they struggle to get on board. A woman in a bright *buba* and wrapper loses her scarf. Another woman loses her wig. She pauses, picks it up, plants it back on her head and manages to make it into the bus.

Bea wisely decides to wait for the next bus. When the bus arrives, a similar spectacle plays itself out, passengers shoving and pushing and scrambling. Bea is new to Lagos. She is not used to the madness of the city of chaos. She is Alice in Blunderland, unaware of how things work. Unaware of how Lagosians caught in the crazy contraption of time, chase their destinies across a futile landscape mapped with suffering, hemorrhage, and perspiration. In Lagos, the patient dog never gets the bone, he gets a stone on the head. The meek do not inherit the earth here. Instead they get buried in six feet of earth.

As I watch her stand back from the fray, far from the madding crowd, a village girl in the big city, I realize that she is never going to get on any bus. Perhaps a cab would come along and she could take a cab instead of the bus. Much more expensive but less of a hassle.

"Bea, you probably need to take a cab."

She ignores me, looks past me. She does not want my unsolicited advice.

When the next bus arrives, Bea rushes forward with the throng. She jumps in it as if to prove me wrong, as if to get as far away from me as possible. The ugly yellow bus swallows her and I never see her again.

When I return home, Mina is gone as well.

It takes me a couple of days to recover from the mess that I have made.

I am still in recovery when crazy Linda arrives.

Linda

Linda is drunk again.

When she is drunk, she wants to fight. When she is drunk, she wants to have sex. When she is drunk and is refused sex, she wants to fight. When she has sex while drunk, she fights, clawing, twisting, howling like an orphaned wolf.

She is poison in my blood. I do not love her but I am attracted to her toxicity. Why did I continue this sick relationship with Linda? Because we are two damaged souls trapped in a timeless web that we have woven around each other. Our love affair is a frozen lake. We scrabble around on the surface, careful not to push too hard, careful not to move too quick, lest we crack the ice and plunge into the watery depths below.

But today, we have cracked the ice.

What provoked Linda's rage on this day was a conversation about her occupation.

I did not know what Linda's occupation was. Well, that is not entirely true. I had intuited what I thought she did for a living but I was in denial. She had no real job as far as I knew. I had never seen her go to work. She had never mentioned work. I had heard talk of rich uncles and relatives but I did not buy it. I had never seen any of these "rich" family members.

Linda is tall, pretty, and dark like hot chocolate brought to a cool just in time. The kind of woman who inspires mixed metaphors. She is as explosive as bottled lightning. Once angered, her eyes acquire a demonic aspect, she begins to shake. Linda is stronger than many men. I had never hit Linda. I lacked the self-righteousness and ratiocination of a batterer, a gift perhaps from my mild mannered father. Perhaps I had developed a certain sensitivity to women because I grew up around six sisters. That sensitivity, however, did not stop me from sleeping with women and discarding them when I tired of them.

Linda looks like a woman who has been in several scrapes from which she had always emerged the winner. The kind of woman who would lift her skirt to show you a knife scar on her thigh or lift up her blouse to show you a claw mark on her breast. I suspect that in a fair fight with Linda, I would probably not come out ahead.

"You want to die? C'mon! I will cut you open."

Her eyes are wild like Medusa, her face curled in a snarl. What a waste of beauty, I think. Linda looks angry even when she fucks. She fucks like a schizophrenic, with manic passion. I emerge from sex with Linda like a gladiator emerging from the death cage, scarred, bruised and with a new appreciation for life. We do not copulate with each other as much as we debilitate each other. We do not invigorate each other as much as we enervate each other. There is a type of woman that a man should only ingest in small amounts. Linda is that kind of woman, lethal in large doses.

Linda is a prostitute, and I know it. She has sex with rich men for money and they support her and her nine year old son. There are no rich uncles, only rich sugar daddies, dirty old men who lust after young flesh.

In a supreme act of self deception, I have never discussed Linda's occupation. Never openly acknowledged it. Never condemned her.

THE COLLECTOR OF BUTTERFLIES AND WOMEN

But today, fortified by beer and self-abasement, I go on the attack. "Linda, I know exactly what you do for a living. You are a prostitute."

Linda, a woman with a bibulous constitution, with an infinite capacity for consuming liquor, stares at me with outrage.

"You dare to call me a prostitute?" She rises from the bed where she is seated. If I had any sense, I would have fled at that moment, but alcohol has a way of making warriors out of wimps and knights out of cravens.

Her arm descends so fast, I don't even see it. But I feel the pain. Not really. I feel the pain as pleasure. I welcome the contact. The pain reminds me that I am still alive. Like a man stepping out into winter cold or walking on fire.

I deserve this, I tell myself.

Linda gets up, stands nose to nose with me. "When I give you money, do you ask where I get it from? When I suck your dick, do you ask how many other dicks I sucked before yours? You dare call me a prostitute?"

Linda is shouting now. The neighbors will hear us. She doesn't care. Neither do I. In Lagos, we all get caught up in each other's psychodrama. We are public witnesses to private pains, witnesses to tawdry lives and tormented lives, passers-by at the shrine of humiliation. Our neighbors are used to loud arguments. No one will interfere.

I refuse to back down, refuse to apologize.

Linda takes a step back. She bends down, grabs the bottle of beer that is half empty. I step back. That is when Linda reaches for the knife in her handbag. The bag is open on the bed. She pulls out the knife in one swift motion and she moves toward me, carrying death in both hands.

"Do you want to die?"

Choose your death, I think, choose your death. The blade or the bludgeon. Evisceration or concussion.

I do not want to die. Her hands are remarkably steady as she wields the knife and the bottle. There will be no rescue for me. My two roommates are both out. I think about rushing at Linda, bending down and going for her legs and then disarming her. But I quickly banish the thought. Too risky. She might cut herself or cut me as I wrest the knife away from her.

I run for the door.

Her curses follow me as I close the door.

"Son of a whore! You want free pussy, right? Come and get it. You call me an *ashawo*. It is your mother that is an *ashawo*. Useless man."

I woke up one morning and decided to change the course of my life. Like Saul on the road to Damascus, I decided that I did not like the path that I was on. I was tired of numbing myself with alcohol and cheap sex. I asked myself why I often felt so unfulfilled, why my life seemed so devoid of meaning, why my constant need to blunt reality with excess.

I decided to go to college. I scored well enough on the JAMB admission test to secure a place at the University of Lagos, the country's pre-eminent university.

I had always been an avid reader who was exposed to books at an early age. Now, I return to the country of books and fall in love once again. I immerse myself in Nietzsche's loftiness, Nietzsche whom I first read at twelve and Immanuel Kant, Kant whose density and convolutions left me puzzled. I discover the classics and gobble them up greedily.

As I embark on this path to transformation, this road to Damascus, I sense the distance growing between my friends and me. They are puzzled that I no longer want to go partying, no longer want to go hunting for female flesh. They find my new found rectitude bracing,

THE COLLECTOR OF BUTTERFLIES AND WOMEN

even treacherous. They do not like it. The gulf widens between Jude, Simeon and I. We are like three people stranded on a giant iceberg when the iceberg begins to separate, and as it separates, it carries each of us away from each other, further and further into the sea until our hollow voices can no longer reach other as we enter the land of no return.

I had moved to Lagos to pursue a career in music. Now I am no longer interested in pursuing that career. I want to be a journalist. When my friends go out at night to perform in small nightclubs, I stay behind at the apartment. Instead of a trio, our musical group is now a duo, and they are forced to make excuses for the absent member. But I am resolute.

The days and months pass by.

I am fascinated by college life. The sprawling campus of UniLag is in Yaba, one of the suburbs of Lagos. Not quite correct. Lagos really has no suburbs. The rich and poor, for the most part, live side by side in faux egalitarianism. Devastating poverty snores fitfully alongside decadent wealth. The rich drive their Mercedes Benzes and BMWs on dusty pot-holed roads, the same roads on which street urchins in rags and dirty underpants play. The rich build fences that are topped with concertina wire or barbed wire or broken glass. The gates are manned by ferocious gatemen or *mallams* who wield damnation and daggers. The super-rich hire armed policemen who carry guns on their shoulders and sudden death in their eyes. It is the gate keepers' job to keep out indigents, thieves, mendicants and poor relatives. The gate keepers carry out their assigned task with relish, bellowing, whipping, menacing as needed.

Since I cannot afford to live on campus, I catch several buses to Yaba each morning. By the time I get to class, I am thoroughly exhausted from the commute. I come to class where the children of the rich seat alongside the children of the poor. I come to class dressed in my Sunday best, pretending to be an "oppressor" rather than a commoner. The 'oppressors" are what the children of the rich are called. I pretend to be an *"aje butter"* (an elitist) rather than an *almajiri* (the poorest of the poor).

Money has always been tight. Things have become even tighter now that I have decided to stop depending on girlfriends for financial help. I have ended my relationship with Linda, Angela, Mina and Bea. Now that I no longer have the financial support of various girlfriends, and have stopped performing with my group, I realize that I need to get a real job. I decide to pursue my dream of becoming a journalist

I decide to pay a visit to a family friend. The man whom I know as Alhaji Azeez grew up with my father. They have been friends since childhood. My father had sent me a letter a few days before urging me to ask for Alhaji Azeez's help if I was facing financial difficulty. Alhaji Azeez is well off. A former government officer who lives in a nice neighborhood in the Apapa area of Lagos. I had seen Alhaji two or three times in the past. On those occasions, he seemed to be a likable man, generous and affable. My father talked often about how well Alhaji's children were doing. I had heard about his son who was in law school and another one who was studying engineering or architecture.

If there was ever a time that I could use Alhaji's help, it would be now. It was the start of the new school term and my school fees were late. I hadn't purchased my books yet.

So I catch the bus over to Alhaji's house. I walk into the residential complex. There are rows of brick houses, extraordinary in their ordinariness. The houses all look the same. There are no magnificent mansions but it is a neighborhood that is solidly upper middle class. If this were Paris, this would be the enclave for the haute bourgeois where sun-drenched Parisians, form a sodality of the soigné, and cavort in beau monde. But Paris it is not. Lagos it is. And because it is Lagos, there are muddy streets leading to the front entrance of the complex. Because it is Lagos, there are flies buzzing over a dead

THE COLLECTOR OF BUTTERFLIES AND WOMEN

bird that no one has bothered to pick up. Because it is Lagos, there are open dumpsters where busy cats and dogs forage with steely determination. Some of them look up at me as I walk by, as if I am an interloper. I sense their sentience, their awareness that I do not belong here. Because it is Lagos, the front door of my host is locked when I arrive.

I tap on the door, gingerly.

An eye peers at me through a peephole. "Who is it?"

I announce my name.

I hear a voice announce my response to someone else inside the house. They must have received approval to let me in.

The door swings open. The young man who opens the door is one of Alhaji's children. I have never seen him before. I nod at him stiffly.

It is Ramadan time. Alhaji is sitting in front of the TV, eating dinner. He looks up at me and nods. His smile is tight-lipped. I wonder if he is happy to see me. In Nigeria, when a poor relative or poor friend visits, they rarely ever bring good tidings. Usually, they come seeking alms. I am keenly aware of my situation. I am a poor non-relative (which is even worse) and I am seeking alms.

I am ashamed.

The room is cluttered with the thoughts of a carpenter expressed as gaudy mahogany furniture. Thoughts clutter my mind like furniture and I stumble over them. I announce the reason for my visit to Alhaji.

Alhaji stares at me as if he has found a fly in the *akamu*, the corn gruel that he is eating. "What is that in your ear?"

I am puzzled for a minute. "My ear?" I reply needlessly, then realize what he means. The offender is the earring in my left ear.

"Why are you wearing that thing?"

I do not answer.

"Since when did men start wearing earrings?"

I want to end this line of conversation, talk about something else. Bodies turning up on dumpsters, children disappearing on the way to school, politicians robbing state treasuries, national crises, the apocryphal and the apocalyptic. So much other stuff to talk about. I want to talk about anything except the piece of cheap metal in my left ear, a hold-over from my days as a musician, an aspiring pop star.

But Alhaji is not done with me yet.

"You need to get serious about your life."

I want to tell him that I am serious about my life. I want to remind him that I am attending the most prestigious college in the country. There are many things that I want to tell him but I do not say anything.

"So your dad sent you to me for money? Where does he expect me to get the money?"

He wrings his hands like a trader haggling at a bazaar, feigning disgust at a contemptible offer.

I want to get out of here. Fast. The room is suddenly too hot.

I get up from the sofa where I am sitting, announce my departure.

Alhaji nods at me. "Take care of yourself."

I exit the room and walk into the street. The night steams with noise and insects. It is the dry season. I will have to figure out another way to pay for my college tuition.

The next day, I walk into the office of a local newspaper.

The publisher of the newspaper is a brilliant and charismatic cartoonist who is renowned for his searing satirical cartoons which lampoon the buffoonery and chicanery in our daily lives. This kindly man gives me my first job as a staff writer with his newsmagazine.

I am excited, eager to prove myself. I travel all over the country in search of journalistic scoops. A few of my stories make the cover of the publication. Finding news in Lagos proves to be remarkably easy. In the city of chaos, news happens every minute on every street corner. It blows in the wind like laundry hung out to dry on

THE COLLECTOR OF BUTTERFLIES AND WOMEN

a clothesline. A pickpocket being chased by an angry crowd. Two women fighting in the marketplace. Corpses abandoned on the street. A madwoman who is pregnant with twins. Who slept with her secretly in the dead of night?

My monthly salary allows me to pay for school. I am able to move out of the blighted apartment in Shogunle into a duplex in Ijaiye, a town in the outskirts of Lagos. Ijaiye is dusty, thinly populated and far from the hysteria and hijinks of Lagos.

Ijaiye is where surprise and death await.

My neighbor's wife is an adulteress

My neighbor is the sailor who lives upstairs. He is hardly home. He is gone for days at a time. I can tell when the husband is away at sea because I see the wife standing outside in the midnight hour after her children are asleep, chatting with faceless men. I wonder if the husband is aware of his wife's wandering eye. I wonder if the children indeed belong to the man who thinks that he sired them.

Not far from where I live in Ijaiye, there is a small hotel. When I am bored at night or restless, I walk across the street to grab a bottle of beer. There are eight or nine rooms in the hotel and they are rented by the hour. I sit in the makeshift lobby and sip my Gulder beer and I watch men and women disappear into the rooms down the hall to fornicate. I hear the muffled sounds of their fucking through paper thin walls.

The woman at the bar serving drinks pretends not to hear the racket. I pretend not to hear it also. I catch snatches of conversations between the customers as they come in to grapple with their lust. I am the uninvited guest at the banquet, floating gauzily above the feast like Shakespeare's Banquo. I am Malvolio allowed into the sanctum

THE COLLECTOR OF BUTTERFLIES AND WOMEN

of private lives, to witness the dreck and the dross, the privations and depravations. From my perch at the corner, I am offered a back stage pass into the interior lives of these men and women, fleeing like exiles from themselves. I wonder what bitter reality they are fleeing. A nagging wife, perhaps. An abusive husband. An insouciant lover.

I sip my beer and hear men and women fight, fuss, and celebrate. I listen to the tedium of unfulfilled lives and striving lives.

The bartender studiously ignores me until I pass along a twenty *naira* tip. She wakes up from her somnolence, her reticence, catches a sudden bout of chattiness.

"You alone tonight, huh?"

I am not sure how to answer this, not sure that the question deserves an answer. I nod, wishing that she would go away. But she doesn't. The woman is big with breasts the size of baby camels. I try not to stare. She is not unattractive. Last year, I resolved to stay away from salacity and cathartic sex. The bartender has a missing front tooth.

"You've been here before, haven't you?

The woman has a way of answering her own questions.

I nod again, hoping that the conversation would die a perfect death this very minute. But the woman is persistent, if nothing else.

"I have seen you around. You don't have a woman in your life?"

The air is a heady cocktail brewed out of beer and sweat and other bodily excretions. The room is hot. The air conditioner hums bravely in the corner. After thirty minutes, the machine's steady sing-song becomes a tedious whine.

The woman is nearly twice my age. She is flirting with me. She probably has a husband at home and a swarm of children. I imagine their grubby little fingers, grabbing the hem of her wrapper when she gets home after a hard day's work at the hotel. Oily fingers, greasy hands, chanting, "mama, mama, we are hungry." I imagine her husband as a drunken sort, a man who spends his days passed out on a bench, drool sallying from his blubbery lips as he waits for his coquettish wife to bring home the bacon.

"Lost your tongue?"

I shake myself out of reverie, try to remember the woman's question. "I don't have a woman in my life. I am in recovery."

"Recovery?"

"Yes. I am a recovering womanizer."

The woman laughs. Laughter like napalm. A laugh that can scrape the bark off of a tree. Shrivel an oak tree.

"What you need is a good woman to cure you."

I ponder this for a moment. A recovering womanizer is told that he needs a woman to cure him. "A malady to cure a malady."

The irony is lost on the bartender.

I down my beer. When the bartender turns away to attend to another customer, I take the opportunity to duck out the door.

That night, I wake up to the sound of someone moaning. It sounds like a man dying or a man facing death. In the morning, I find out what happened to the man. And it chills me to the bone.

Death before dawn

The memories of the man whose throat was slit stain my mind like dye. On the night of the man's death, I come home from the hotel across the street and fall into a troubled sleep.

It is just after 3 a.m. when the sound wakes me from sleep. At night, Ijaiye is a place of strange sounds, like Amos Tutuola's forests. The night hums and crackles with electricity. Crickets chirp in subterranean nests and frogs croak in palaces of mud. From afar, the sound of a passing car is heard as disconsolation, as mourning. Mildly irritated at being woken up, I do not think much of the moaning.

The next morning, I am heading for work when I see a small crowd gathered around. A crowd in Nigeria always signifies some event of note. Being a newsman, I am curious to find out why this crowd has gathered, so I stop to ask questions.

The road is dusty and unpaved. Buses and cars speed by spewing black smoke. Seen from behind, the smoke appears like the flatulence of four legged animals suddenly made visible. The sun mocks the world from the circus tent of the sky like a clown in bad make-up. It is hot and humid, as if the city has been tossed into a pan and is now being slowly baked. The sun heats up the piles of garbage by the side of the road and the smell steams the nostrils. The crowd itself is an odd mixture; farmers on their way to the farm, market women heading to the market, children, locals loafing around with nothing to do, a couple of men dressed in a suit and tie, like me.

"What's going on?" I ask.

A man turns to look at me. He points to the nearby gutter. "There is a man in there."

I push my way into the crowd. Look into the gutter. Inside it, a man is splayed out, arms and feet going in different directions. His bones are clearly broken. His face shows contusions, his eyes are open in death, yet they are strangely peaceful. The man had seen his death coming. His chin rests on his chest. A huge gash runs down his neck. The wound was made with a sharp object.

It does not take long for me to find out what happened to the dead man. Later, I would do a story on it and submit it for publication. The dead man was owed money by a farmer who lived down the street from my house. The victim had made repeated attempts to collect payment on the debt. The farmer refused to repay the loan. Frustrated, the dead man decided to pay his debtor a visit. This decision proved to be a deadly one.

The two men confront each other and there is much yelling and threats. Things soon devolve into fisticuffs. As the two men circle each other and grapple, the debtor's wife begs them to stop, but it is too late. A dog that is determined to get lost does not hear the whistle of the hunter. The fight does not last for long. It comes to an abrupt end when the farmer hits his creditor over the head with a stick. As the man falls down, the farmer descends on him and proceeds to beat him senseless. He is howling like a demented soul as he beats the man whom he owes money, beats him until he breaks his arms, breaks his feet, cracks his skull in several places.

Still enraged, the farmer grabs a knife and slits the creditor's throat. It is at this point that the farmer's wife runs off in panic, flees

THE COLLECTOR OF BUTTERFLIES AND WOMEN

to the neighbor's house, horrified by the bloodlust and madness that has overtaken her husband, the father of her children.

But the creditor does not die. Not yet. Stubbornly, he clings to life. But the farmer is not done with him yet. The farmer decides to dispose of his victim. He drags the man out of his compound, trailing blood as he goes. He drags the man as the man moans in agony, begs weakly for mercy, knowing that his end is near. He must have been dragging the man past the back of my house when I heard the moaning the previous night.

The farmer was arrested after his wife narrated the grisly tale to neighbors. The neighbors contacted the police. The police did not need to look far. They simply followed the blood spoor that led from the farmer's house to the gutter near Ijaiye bus stop.

With a friend like this

He likes the early tapes of Marilyn Chambers and Linda Lovelace. Likes Marilyn Chambers in 'Insatiable' and Linda Lovelace in 'Deep Throat.' He watches them endlessly on bootleg tapes that some enterprising trader in Alaba market in Lagos cranks out by the thousands. He watches them while sitting on my new sofa in my new flat in Ijaiye. Watches them in the middle of the day. Watches them while I am away at work at the People's Express newspaper.

I learn to inspect my sofa often for semen stains.

My friend, Josiah

He is a short, light skinned fellow who is a year or two older than I am. We get along famously. His jokes taste like lemons in the mouth, sharp, making you want more. He describes his sexual escapades with the vigor of a young Lord Byron at Harrow narrating his conquests.

I let Josiah move in with me because he needed a place to stay. He does not have a job. I suspect that he is not actively looking. To some jobless people, being jobless is not much of an issue, although the person providing for the jobless person might think differently. Josiah is a man who has never met a job that he likes. He seems to be mortally afraid of getting his hands dirty or straining a muscle. He saves his exertions for the bedroom. Several nights, I hear the sounds of noisy fucking from his room. Women seem to be attracted to him as if he is a ball of pheromones. Often, a mental image of Josiah and his women flashes through my mind. Josiah, encircled in a gauntlet of inflamed women, waving a flywhisk, literally beating women away from him.

Josiah is supposed to help with keeping the house clean but he cannot be troubled with such trifles. Instead, he prefers to drink beer and watch porn. Caught up in carnality, he ignores everything else around him. I come home to find him passed out on the couch or in his room. I come home to find him lying on the living room carpet naked with a girl wrapped around his waist like a serpent. I come home to the smell of vaginal excretions and seminal emanations.

I come home angry.

I wonder when things will come to a head, when I will tire of Josiah. The day comes sooner than I expect. I come home one day to find the door smashed and the windows ripped off their hinges. As I walk up to the door, I am filled with dread.

Break-ins and home invasions were not uncommon in Lagos. Homeowners and tenants faced the menace of vicious thugs who killed, maimed and marauded with impunity. Women were raped in front of their husbands. Parents shot in front of their children, even when they were not resisting. Lawrence Anini, and his gang of armed robbers, was still on the loose, terrorizing innocents and robbing banks from Benin City to Enugu. The moral distemper had spread a climate of fear. The country was under siege. In Lagos and other cities, people retreated to their homes at the first sign of darkness. They went to bed behind windows barricaded with cast iron and fences topped with barbed wire. The rich slept with both eyes closed knowing that their hired guards would protect them. The poor slept with one eye closed knowing that nothing would protect them except for the grace of God. And at times, the grace of God was not to be found.

I push open the front door – what remains of it.

The living room is bedlam. Furniture is strewn all over the room, sofas knocked over, puffy white cotton entrails floating on the carpet. It looks like a cyclone went through the room. I am not sure what the searchers were looking for. Why would they tear up the sofas? Did they think that I had money stashed inside the fabric? My electronic equipment is missing. The bedroom is similarly ransacked. Articles of clothing are scattered all over the room. Who has wreaked such havoc on my flat?

I question the neighbors and try to analyze the situation. It does not take long for me to figure out what I believe happened, to realize that this was an inside job. My friend, Josiah, is nowhere to be found. I find this odd. How did the burglars know exactly when to strike? How did they know that no one would be home? When I enter Josiah's room, my worst fear is confirmed. His room is untouched.

I wait for Josiah to return. When he does, I confront him. He does not try to deny his involvement in the crime, shows no outrage, no righteous indignation. He merely stares at me when I accuse him of having masterminded the break-in. Josiah does not declare his innocence.

"You set this up. You arranged this break-in."

He does not answer.

"You need to leave. Now." I tell him.

He stares at me, walks to his room and begins to gather his belongings. He packs his shoes and his clothes, his colognes and his porn tapes. And he walks out the door. That was the last time that I saw him. As I watch him go, I think about the value of friendship and the price of betrayal.

It is those we love who can hurt us.

It is those we love that we should fear.

Shit

The woman who scoops shit does not do it for a living. She does it for her children. She lives in a falling-apart house on Mission Street in Benin City. She lives on the upper level of a one story building. The house is the color of chicken shit just before sunrise, just before the sun and the flies hit it. The lower level is an auto mechanic's shop where tires, steel bolts and car grease are sold. I think of the woman's house as a metaphor. A house that is falling apart is a house that holds lives that are falling apart, lives being rendered, lives being sundered. Poverty after all has a sundering effect. Like a lance on a boil, it rips families apart, trips up marriages, separates women from reason and makes men commit treason.

Mission Street is a busy street where shop owners and street traders joust and jostle. The busy shops sell second-hand clothes and new clothes, shoes, bags, and household items. There is no gender delineation in the stores. You are as likely to find female underpants as you are to find men's ties. The street is dusty, fly blown. On both sides of the busy road, there is an open gutter. When it rains, the muddy water overflows and spills into the road. Once a child fell into the gutter and was immediately swept away and drowned.

Cab drivers fight for space with *Danfo* bus drivers, wielding their car horns like an Algonquin Indian waving a tomahawk. Hawkers of roasted plantains brush elbows with the hawkers of roasted corn. The smell of food, car exhaust and sweaty bodies forms an enthralling incense of desperation. Men and women gather here seeking a cure for the disease that is life. And the noise. Yes, the noise. The noise is always at fever-pitch. Everyone seems to be talking at once, as if they are at a convention of the hearing impaired, everyone demanding to be heard, gesticulating, motioning. In this noisy fever of humanity, it would be easy to miss the sound of a dozen elephants trumpeting in unison. The animals seem to whine louder here than anywhere else in the world. Even the sun seems to burn harder on Mission Street.

The woman does not like Mission Street. She says that it is too crowded, too rowdy. She worries about the children of the traders who toss banana peels in front of the house. She worries about the street when it falls silent, so silent she says that it is unnatural, unnerving. She worries about the street when the noise drowns out all thinking and you are left unable to think. She worries about strange objects that might fall from the sky into the house, because of its location. And about things that might explode through the window.

If you were the mother of nine children and you lived on Mission Street, you would worry too about your children. After all, are women not born with unseen worry bones? Protuberances that may be invisible but are far from vestigial, attached to women just like the woman on Mission Street, women who carry the earth on their shoulders and spin the sun on its axis with their callused fingers.

One day, the woman's worst fear comes true. Well, in truth, not her worst fear but one of her worst fears, for there is a gradation to fear, as the whole world knows. A mother's absolute worst fear is the death of a child. The second worst fear is the disappearance of a child. The third is having her child struck down by disease. The fourth…any

THE COLLECTOR OF BUTTERFLIES AND WOMEN

mother can imagine the rest and come up with their own top ten list, their own schemata of horrors, their own compendium of terrors.

The woman's fear comes true when a policeman tosses a teargas canister through the woman's window. It is a suspiciously bright day. A day that starts out full of promise until some policemen often referred to as *'mopo'* – mobile policemen, decide to start mayhem. No one recalls how they ended up on Mission Street. Their jeep materializes out of nowhere, showing up in the quiet way that wickedness often shows up, unannounced and unheralded. No one knows what provoked them, why they jumped out of their open jeeps and began to whip some of the traders on Mission Street with their *kobokos*. When they are done, they march down the street triumphantly, with the self-awareness of petty tyrants, intoxicated by a potent mixture of power and alcohol.

When the can of teargas smashes through the house on Mission Street, through the woman's window, only three of her children are home. One of them is her son who is visiting from Lagos. The smell burning his lungs and nostrils, the son runs out of the house. It is only later that he realizes what the strange chemical is and what has just happened. Later, would come the self-recrimination, the shame of having run out the door, without trying to rescue his two sisters who are in the house with him.

The back of the house on Mission Street faces a brothel. This brothel is no place for the young. The prostitutes here are in their late forties and older, women rejected by other brothels in town, women who have stubbornly refused to retire from the world's oldest trade. Buxom women with yesterday's breasts, vexed eyes and tongues that drip venom. The place is a way station between the blazing glory of youth and the obsolescence of death. The son of the woman on Mission Street stands on the balcony at the back of the house and watches the women ply their trade. He is repulsed and attracted by what he sees.

Bats are attracted to the house on Mission Street. Black bats with fierce teeth. They hang upside down from the ceiling. They emerge from nowhere and fly into the house through the back door. They screech and flutter as if they have escaped from Pandora's box of sorrows. The woman's children howl and chase them, terrified of these creatures of death and despair. They are a surprise. From whence cometh this evil, from what pit of hell do they emerge in the day time? These creatures that are supposed to be nocturnal?

Mosquitoes also like the house on Mission Street, but this is hardly a surprise, for there are puddles of standing water all over the compound. The bathroom stall has no drainage. It is a simple wood structure fenced in on three sides, leaving an open doorway. When the woman's family takes a shower here, mud licks at their shins like a serpent and settles on their semi-clean ankles and feet. The water runs through the compound hungrily, seeking low land, seeking a spot to settle. Whatever spot the water finds is soon overrun by mosquito larvae and mosquitoes.

The woman's children wake up with mosquito welts all over their bodies. They have figured out that leaving the ceiling fan on at full blast can blow the mosquitoes off balance. But there is only one ceiling fan in the house, in the parlor, and there are many children. The children have figured out another solution. They make the ingenious discovery that kerosene can kill the pesky insects. They spray kerosene from a gallon all over the floor of the rooms where they sleep. They spray it liberally until the smell of kerosene strangles the air like smoke from a Roman *ustrinum*. In the morning when the children wake up, there are mosquitoes all over the floor, little dead corpses with feet sticking up in the air like Napoleon's army dying of starvation.

The insects here all appear to have undergone genetic mutation. The mosquitoes are as large as flies. The flies are as large as roaches. The roaches are as large as rats. The rats are vicious. They challenge

THE COLLECTOR OF BUTTERFLIES AND WOMEN

the humans. At night, they emerge and do battle in the kitchen, foraging for food. They are fearless in the way that starved creatures are. On some nights when the woman's children get up to use the toilet, they see these creatures in the kitchen, dragging the pot of soup, trying to open it. They chase the felonious creatures, chase them off in order to save tomorrow's dinner.

On Mission Street, there is only one toilet stall to serve the entire family of five children who live here with the woman and her husband. The woman's older children, five of them, are grown up now and have left the house. The toilet stall is located in a small shack made out of rusty zinc. The toilet does not flush when you push the handle. There are no plumbing drain lines behind it to carry away waste matter. The landlord who rents the apartment to the family misses the irony in this. The irony of a toilet that doesn't flush. But there is a cure for this. Even this. The cure is a rusty aluminum bucket on the floor that is always kept full of water.

The woman's children like hot peppers and ground nut soup. They like spices. After eating their mother's flavorful meals, they often end up panting in the toilet stall. The toilet stall that does not flush. They use the toilet variously. They 'lose weight' in there, as they like to joke. And when they are done, they pour the bucket of water into the toilet and watch the shit curl and twist in protest before disappearing into the infernal depths below. They use water sparingly because in Benin City, water is not easy to come by. Unless you had a well in your yard, popularly called a *borehole*, you have to purchase water from taps, queuing up with dozens of other people, waiting for your turn at the tap.

There are some days when water becomes so scarce that the family has to make one bucket of water last the entire day. On such days, no one flushes the toilet. The family simply keeps using the toilet one after another. New shit is dumped on top of old shit until the shit forms a mountain that rises up to the top of the toilet bowl.

By the time it is nightfall, there is no space left for another roiling stomach to empty into. This is when the woman walks over to the toilet with a bucket and a plastic scoop. The scoop is much like a ladle, the kind used for stirring a big pot of stew if one were cooking for a special occasion, an occasion such as a wedding or a funeral.

The woman scoops the shit into the bucket, emptying the toilet bowl, freeing up space, this quiet long-suffering woman who would do anything for her children. She carries her putrid burden and heads for the furthermost part of the house, near the broken mud fence where the sand is soft and red.

Using a small hoe leaning against the broken fence for just this purpose, she digs a small hole and dumps the bucket of waste into the hole. It takes her only a few minutes to bury the waste. Buries it like a woman burying her own afterbirth. She covers the hole with the soft sand, washes her hands with soap and returns inside the house to fix her children dinner.

The woman who scoops shit is my mother.

An endangered species

After working at a newsmagazine for nearly a year, I wanted to do something different. I met with a couple of my colleagues and we discussed the possibility of setting up our own newspaper. We put together a basic business plan and begin to identify a list of potential financiers. It takes us a few months to meet Dr. Kunle Bello. Dr. Bello was the CEO of Express Seafood and the younger brother of Dr. Layi Bello who would later become a presidential aspirant.

Dr. Kunle Bello or KB as we called him was a flamboyant but soft-spoken man. He owned a fleet of luxury cars and a big house. He walked like a man who had purchased the universe and had the receipt to prove it. He was larger than life, a man of seismic and mythological proportions. We regarded him with perfect awe and deference, the kind that Croesus, the king of Lydia, must have received from his subjects.

In ancient Nigeria, the idols that people worshipped were made of stone and wood. In modern Nigeria, the idols that people worship are made of bone and flesh. The rich are the idols that the poor worship. Deification awaits the rich and defecation awaits the poor. So like a king, Dr. Bello is always surrounded by court jesters and sycophants, fawners and scrapers. The oceans part at his approach, pomp and circumstance transpires at every turn.

au pays des aveugles les borgnes sont rois. In the country of the blind, the one eyed man is king.

In the country of the poor, the rich man is king.

In due order, Dr. Bello sets us up with an office near Oshodi. He provides cars, office equipment and the wherewithal for us to launch the publication. My partners in this venture are Ken Oko, Seun Elaiye and Tayo Famiyuwa. We are all serious journalists, ambitious young men, standing on tiptoes, trying to pluck the stars from the sky. Inspired by KB, we decide to name the newspaper, People's Express. The name sounds shamelessly populist, suggesting news delivered to the people with dispatch. In reality, we had simply tied the name to KB's company.

At about this time, another group of journalists decides to launch their own publication. They are Kunle Badejo, Mayor Akinrinade, and Femi Joshua. They decide to call their magazine GAME.

In the course of my career, I become acquainted with a rising crop of journalists, the best and brightest that the country has to offer. One of these was Dele Momoh, whom I met through Tayo Famiyuwa. Dele Momoh would later establish Promotion magazine and decide to run for the presidency of Nigeria. Sadly, Tayo would die in a horrific car crash while returning from Ibadan.

I made friends with Ben Charles Nobi, while he was at RealMax magazine. He would later become editor of *Tactic* magazine where he would find himself caught in the teeth of political tyranny, narrowly avoiding being crushed under the feet of the great merciless beast. Ben was an eloquent speaker, a man of strong conviction.

Also, through Tayo, I befriended Niyi Akinjide, who was working as an editor at Daily Choice magazine. He would later become the publisher of Fame and Class magazine.

I met the pint-sized Rakeem Ikandu, one of the most brilliant people that I have ever met, a man with a rapier wit. Rakeem would die only a few years after I met him, consumed by an incurable ailment.

At People's Express, we play host to various celebrities, musicians and actors who stop by to be interviewed. T

I am enjoying my life, my minor celebrity as the editor-in-chief of a national weekly. I am determined to make my mark, determined to speak truth to power. I use my new bully pulpit to launch disquisitions into the nature of political power and the corruptibility of men who wield it.

In Nigeria, a journalist is an endangered species, with a life span that can be incredibly short.

I write with the tragic earnestness of the young idealist. I lambaste the aristocracy of ignorance that seems to be enthroned in the land, the kleptocracy that has the nation in its death grip, the psychic disconnect between the dancing rich and the sleepwalking poor. Some of my friends find my earnestness bracing. They warn me, caution me that I am becoming an activist, crossing the line between the journalistic ethos and partisanship. They tell me that I am choosing sides. I plead guilty to the charge of being a partisan but insist that I am on the people's side. After all, I have not picked up a weapon and gone 'into the breach' like Ernest Hemingway and Christopher Okigbo, writers that I admire, who were willing to risk life and limb for a cause.

I write stories about Lagos, stories about poignant lives and wasted lives, stories of hope and aching despair, stories about redemption and thwarted destinies. My office is my blacksmith's forge, my pen is my hammer and my paper is my anvil. I write about the city of chaos and its people whom I love and despise in equal measure. I write about the nation of chaos that I love and revile.

I know the particulars of the city very well. I speak its vernacular. The city pulses in my heart and in my loins like a caged beast that begs to be set free. I open the cage, step aside and let the animal out. I am careful not to pontificate, but I editorialize when necessary.

My friends warn me to be careful.

The government in power is showing growing impatience and distaste for men of my ilk, men who throw darts at the hallowed walls of power. Journalists who have prescribed unto themselves the task of taking the government to task. Soon, the government of President Ibrahim Babangida will begin to treat journalists like dissidents. Soon the voice of thunder will be heard through the land and it will drown out the voices of reason. Soon men with blood-rimmed eyes will show up in the middle of the night when the children are fast asleep and in the middle of the day when the sun sits on people's heads. These men will spirit away fathers and mothers and leave the children to wonder what happened when they wake up. Some of my acquaintances and colleagues will be swept up in the wave of arrests and detentions. Some will die or emerge with shattered psyches from the long night of Gulagesque horror. As a country, Nigeria will witness the grotesquerie of power, an image that will haunt us all forever, an image as troubling as a procession of old women walking naked in the streets in wordless protest.

The missing ear

When I receive the call about the missing ear, I am at the office, at the newspaper where I work. The person who calls me is a cousin or niece of Linda, my ex-girlfriend. Linda has bitten off a woman's ear during a fight. Linda whom I haven't seen in over a year, Linda whom I last saw the night she came after me with a knife and a bottle.

This is how it happened. Linda is lying on her bed in the single room apartment that she rents in a section of Agege, in Lagos. She is smoking with the door open. Her nine year old son, the child she had with a reggae musician, is seated on the floor playing with his toys. The landlord's wife who has never got along with Linda storms through the open door. She screams at Linda for smoking in the room, excoriates her. Linda, a woman who is short on patience and swift to anger, rises from the bed to confront her accuser.

Words fly back and forth. Fists begin to fly. Hair is pulled, spit missiles are let loose. At some point during the fight, Linda seizes the woman's right ear in her teeth. She pulls at the tender flesh and rips it off the landlady's skull. She keeps the shredded flesh in her cheek like a man chewing tobacco. The landlady shrieks and flees from the room, blood dripping down her face as she screams for her husband.

Linda's *ruse de guerre* has ended the battle rather quickly.

Soon, the police arrive and Linda is carted off to the local police station. Her nine year old son is picked up by a friend, to stay with the friend until Linda is released.

Where is the ear?

Linda refuses to say.

Linda's reappearance in my life is not something that I have prepared for or expected. As such, I am not quite sure how to handle it. I do not want to resume my affair with Linda however the thought of abandoning her in her time of need does not cross my mind. At least not seriously anyway. I decide to help her. Perhaps I would earn some good karma and atone for my life of debauchery and dissolution.

That is how I end up at Agege Police Station.

The police station is located on a dusty street at the end of a trash strewn street. If hell were on earth, this is the road that would lead to it. The road is a camel's back, uneven and pebbled.

Although I have a company car and a chauffeur, I have decided to take a cab here. I knew that I would likely have to bribe the police today. Driving up in front of the police station in a fancy car would merely increase the amount demanded as a bribe. If you scratch a Nigerian policeman, what you will find under his skin is corruption. Perhaps it is unfair to judge the policemen too harshly, these wretches who are paid so poorly by the government. Adrift in a sea of poverty, policemen often use their guns as persuaders to make people give up bribes. They are the worst kind of apostates; revolutionaries with no revolution, disciples who have lost faith.

Where are they keeping Linda? What did she do with the missing ear?

The sun glints off the zinc roof of the compound which houses several brick buildings. A couple of them appear to be jailhouses. A fence circumscribes part of the compound, but only a part, and then it crumbles like an unfinished sentence, like an afterthought. A profusion of algae and weeds sprout between fallen brick. The main building is a low slung structure with rather off-center architecture. It leans forward like a drunk on his fifth drink or a man clutching at his balls in pain. Pain is a fitting sensation here, for this is the house of pain, where dreams are mauled and men are maimed. Accused men and women are routinely beaten in police stations, beaten until they confess and admit that they are indeed the murderers of Jesus Christ or that they eat small babies for dinner. Here, justice is not important, not as important as penitence or contrition, and certainly far less important than confession.

If a man who commits a crime in Nigeria decides to flee, the family he has left behind will face the consequences of his action. Policemen will show up and arrest the man's father, mother and grandparents. They will be detained until the law-breaker realizes the error of his ways and turns himself in.

Armed robbers are summarily executed in police stations if caught, unless their families are able to muster enough of a bribe. One of the phrases that occur frequently in police media releases is 'give up the ghost.' As in, "a group of armed robbers were involved in a shoot-out with policemen last night. Some of them were killed in the firefight and the others gave up the ghost at the police station." Translation, the robbers were taken to the police station, lined up against a wall and shot in the head or simply beaten to death.

Every country gets the police force it deserves. Perhaps only men with iron hands can rule a land with iron eyes.

A loud scream shatters the afternoon as the cab slows to a stop.

I freeze. So does the cab driver. I wonder what poor soul is being tormented. What has he or she done? What have they been accused of? Stealing from a rich neighbor? Refusing to pay a debt? Biting off someone's ear?

"*Oga*, pay me so I can leave."

The driver clearly does not want to be here. He looks as spooked as a hen listening to tales about foxes. His eyes dart around, as if he is expecting to be stopped any minute and forced to give up his earnings for the day. I give him a wad of dirty cash. He counts the crinkled notes noisily. Satisfied, he nods at me. I step out, and he zooms off.

I walk into the police station. There are three policemen outside the main building, where I am headed. They are smoking cigarettes, telling ribald jokes about each other's mothers and sisters.

"Your mother's pussy is the best I've ever had." One says.

"How about your sister? She gave me the best head ever." The other man responds.

I walk past them, climb a few steps and walk through the entrance. In front of me there is a wooden counter manned by two policemen. There are two rows of benches in the room, on which are seated anxious men and women. They sit patiently like good Christians waiting for their turn to enter heaven, they sit with the pregnant patience of people waiting outside the doctor's office, waiting for a diagnosis that might change their lives. The tension in the room is immaculate.

I walk up the counter. The two policemen are movie clichés, one tall and the other short. But there is no good cop and bad cop here. Instead, it is bad cop and worse cop. Worse Cop is the short one, the one who alternately picks his nose, fishing for stubborn hairs, and then picks his teeth, extracting remnants of his lunch.

"Can I help you?"

"Good afternoon, gentlemen."

Worse cop is making notations on a note pad, stopping briefly to look up at me. Bad Cop is staring at me like a cobra about to swallow a rat.

"Yes?"

"I am here regarding the matter of Linda Edo. She bit a neighbor's ear."

Worse Cop chuckles. "Bit the ear, you say."

"Yes."

"She didn't bite the ear off." Worse cop picks up a piece of paper, puts it in his mouth and nibbles at a section of it. "This, my friend, is a bite." He shows me the paper so that I can see the indentation he has made. He has perfect teeth, beautiful teeth. They are as white as polished stones. They look unnatural.

I am not sure of what to make of his demonstration.

But he is not done yet.

Worse Cop puts the sheet of paper in his mouth once more, this time he does it as if performing an operatic aria. He bites the edge of the paper, bites it off the sheet and chews on it. He shows me his teeth, his perfect teeth. He has swallowed the paper, made it disappear like a magician performing an ancient trick. I see bits of paper stuck on his wide gums.

"You see this? This is what she did. Chewed the ear off. Chewed it and swallowed it like a cannibal."

I am repulsed by his tone, the spite in his voice, his crudeness.

Bad Cop on the other hand, is amused by his partner's show. He doubles over in hysterics, doubles over the counter, unfurling his long frame over the warped and welted wood. The people in the room remain silent, each wrapped up in their private tribulation.

"So my friend, your wife did not bite that poor woman's ear off. No, Sir. She chewed it off."

"Actually, she is not my wife."

"Oh? Then she must be your sister. Only a husband or brother would show up to visit someone who has done such an evil act."

I want to tell the policemen that there is more to the story. I want to tell him about the nuances of the case, the mitigating circumstances. I want to tell him that the ear was not chewed off and swallowed. Linda's niece told me that after Linda bit off the ear, she spat it out outside. But I tell him nothing. It is never a smart thing to argue with an armed man who just happens to also be opinionated.

"So you are here to bail her out?"

I nod.

Worse Cop takes a moment to look me over. He scrutinizes me from head to toe, as if trying to assign a monetary value to my being. I can almost hear the cash register clinking in his head. I curse myself for not taking off the expensive gold watch that I am wearing.

More often than not, when people are arrested by the police in Nigeria, it is the police who set their bail. This bail is simply the bribe that is required to spring the detained man loose. How do the police determine the bail amount? It is not a scientific process by any means. If your relative was locked up and you wanted them released, the police asked you questions to determine your income level. If you had a good government job or owned your own business, your bail was set high. If you arrived at the police station dressed like a million bucks driving a luxury car, you were sure to be taken to the cleaners.

"So what do you do for a living?"

"I am a journalist."

"Really? Where?"

"People's Express."

His eyes register a blank.

"It is a newspaper. News magazine to be exact."

"Oh yeah? I don't read newspapers. They are full of lies.'

I am stung by his castigation, his summary dismissal of the fourth estate.

"Your sister's bail will be high." He turns to Bad Cop, winks at him. "Very high."

"How much?"

When he names the amount, my jaw falls open. "That is high."

He nods. "I told you she ate the ear. You know what crime that is?"

"Attempted murder." This is Bad Cop who is thoroughly enjoying himself now.

THE COLLECTOR OF BUTTERFLIES AND WOMEN

I am angry and tired at the same time. I feel helpless. Helpless like Naboth standing before King Ahab, the man who would rob him of his life and his vineyard.

"Let me share something with you." Worse Cop begins. "I will tell you this because I like you. You seem to be a good man. An educated man." He has lowered his voice conspiratorially and now he says to me *sotto voce.* "The victim's husband is paying us a good amount of money. He wants to make sure that justice is done."

I understand what this means. Justice will be sold like a common good at a bazaar. The man with the most money to spend is the one who will secure justice. The policemen are the auctioneers in charge of the proceedings. So step right up, and place your bid.

"I will pay."

I do not want Linda caged here like an animal while waiting for a trial. Who knew what horrors she would face? She might be raped, killed, or have her spirit broken.

Worse Cop looks at me with new found respect. "You are a good brother. Everyone should have a brother like you." His tone has suddenly changed to a fawning one, his voice dripping of poisoned honey.

"Can I see her?" I ask. "Can she be released today?"

Worse Cop picks at a piece of paper in his teeth, takes it out, studies it for a moment and then sticks it back in his mouth as if it is candy. "You will have to make the arrangements first before you can see her."

I know what is codified in his statement. I need to "settle" the policemen first before I can see Linda. Bad Cop takes me behind the counter, to a small bare room which smells like cigarettes and incontinence. The only adornment on the wall is a framed photograph of the state governor and President Babangida. The walls are dirty.

Inside this godforsaken room, the transaction takes place. I hand over a wad of cash, which I had brought with me for just this purpose. Bad Cop counts the money. Satisfied, he tells me to wait. He disappears. He returns a few minutes later and asks me to follow.

We take a back corridor. Stop at a cell. Bad Cop opens it with one of the keys on his heavy key ring. I step into hell.

The room is small, too small for the dozen or so women packed into it. It has no windows only bars which function as the entrance. The bars run from floor to ceiling. The walls are rough-hewn, unfinished. There is shit on the wall from prisoners stricken with dysentery or languor, unable or unwilling to make it to the back of the room where waste pans line the room like soldiers awaiting marching orders. There is vomit too, dry crusty graffiti of vomit. The room should smell like unwashed bodies and sweat, like fear and sleeplessness, but in truth all that I smell is the apocalyptic essence of shit. It overwhelms every other smell in the room, overthrows every other sense. The shit sings in my ear, reads me poetry, caresses my skin, drives me insane.

My Linda! My beautiful lunatic Linda, thrown into the house of putrefaction, into the house of attenuation!

She is leaning against the wall. It takes me a minute to recognize her, for my eyes to adjust to the light or lack of light. I call out to her. When she responds, her voice is weak, this woman who wanted to kill me just months before.

"Follow me." Bad Cop commands.

Linda gets up, but she is shaky on her feet.

"*Oga*, can you let us out too?" One of the prisoners begs. Bad Cop ignores her. The woman is not daunted. "Let us get some fresh air too, we the children of the poor."

Bad Cop tells her to shut up.

We walk out of the room. Bad Cop locks the steel cage.

When we arrive in the room behind the counter, I embrace Linda. She smells like a buzzard that has been feasting on carrion.

THE COLLECTOR OF BUTTERFLIES AND WOMEN

I try to hide my revulsion but she sees it. "It's been three days." She says. "They say we can only shower once a week. And when we do, the bastards watch us through a hole in the wall."

"Why didn't you let me know sooner about your arrest?"

She is quiet for a long moment, this proud woman. I see that her fierce spirit is still intact. "I couldn't find anyone to help me contact you."

"Really?"

I sense that she is holding back, hiding something else.

I didn't know if you would come."

I don't know how to respond to this.

"The last time we saw each other was when you told me to leave and never come back. Remember?"

Of course, I remembered. The day that I called Linda a prostitute, after I had consumed copious quantities of cheap booze. The day that she pulled a knife on me and threatened to cut my head off, while simultaneously waving a bottle of beer.

What happened to the missing ear? I badly want to ask, but I sense that it would be crass and inappropriate. The policemen said that Linda chewed and swallowed it. That wasn't true, was it?

"Did they abuse you?"

Linda smiles a half-smile. "They didn't do anything different from what men usually do to women." The note of bitterness in her voice is hard-edged.

"They beat you? Assaulted you…sexually?"

She smiles again. "No, they didn't beat me. Didn't rape me. They usually save that for people who do not have anyone to bail them out. Takes weeks to determine who will fall into the rape column. After weeks of no family member showing up."

That day, Linda is released on 'bail' pending her court trial. She has no place to go to. She is too afraid to return to her one room apartment, fearing retribution from the landlord whose wife's ear she had bitten off.

It is late in the evening when we catch a cab heading for Ojota where her uncle resides. It appears that she really does have one rich uncle after all, a "big man" as wealthy men are called in Nigeria. A man who made his fortune as a transporter, who owns a fleet of commercial buses. Since I had never met this uncle, I can't help but wonder if he is indeed her uncle, or simply one of the 'sugar daddies' who covet young flesh in Lagos. I do not dare voice my suspicions.

The cab pulls up in front of a beautiful duplex with a white fence topped by razor sharp wire. There is a gateman at the front entrance. He questions us about our mission. He regards Linda sourly, finding her to be out of place in this neighborhood where the rich can afford to eat chicken and their children can play with real Christmas trees.

Linda gives her name and the gatemen disappears into the bowels of the compound. He emerges soon enough to let us inside. He does so with suspicion, as if expecting the home owner to change his mind about admitting the interlopers, to announce that he had made a mistake and that Linda was not related to him in any way and it was all just a mistake.

The compound is huge, clean and well maintained. A houseboy is washing an American automobile in front of the house, caressing the car's shiny chrome like a love-struck man. We walk up the steps, open a door, and are face to face with Linda's uncle.

"*Domo*, Sir." She greets him.

The room is large, gaudily furnished with Persian throw rugs, ornate furniture, outsized portraits and a profusion of live plants. It displays all the taste and tastelessness of a man that some locals might call a 'money miss road.' An arriviste. The nouveau riche. Money without class.

He is a fulsome man with a paunch that looks like he has a pawpaw fruit hidden under his shirt. He looks well-fed, effulgent in his pajamas. Tufts of curious hair poke out from his chest where the robe is parted. He is dark-skinned, balding in that unstylish fashion

THE COLLECTOR OF BUTTERFLIES AND WOMEN

that middle aged men lose their hair. And he is not happy to see us.

He is patient enough to let Linda finish her story. As soon as she is done, he gets up, walks into his bedroom and emerges with a wad of cash in his hand.

"Here you go. You are my brother's child and I am obligated to take care of you since he is gone. But you can't stay in my house, Linda." He shakes his head from side to side. "You are too wild. I will kill you if I let you stay here. Or you will kill me. Rent yourself a new place. If you need anything else, let me know."

He is finished with us.

We get up and walk to the door. He has the grace to walk us to the door. Just before we step out, he turns to me. "What are you doing with a girl like my niece? You seem like a nice young man, an educated man. All the girls in this town and you couldn't find anybody else?"

Linda has a sour look on her face but holds her peace.

We walk down the steps and head toward the front gate. The gateman lets us out, seeming relieved that our visit was short, sensing that he had been right after all, that his *Oga* would not keep people like this in his house for long.

The cab driver is still waiting for us.

"Don't offer. I won't accept." Linda says.

I know exactly what she means so I do not ask her to stay at my flat in Agbado Ijaiye. She tells me to take her to a hotel so that she can shower, stay there for the night. She has enough money to buy herself clothes, to rent an apartment and get back on her feet. I ask about her little boy. I am worried about him. Will he be okay?

"He will be fine." She tells me. "I will pick him up once I find a place."

Linda doesn't like to talk about the kid, a tow-headed boy with bright eyes and an engaging smile. The boy's father is a local musician who is not involved in his life. Linda loves the boy. But she loves him in the restrained way that a parent loves a child whom she has sacrificed her dreams for. A chance to make it to America or England. A Hollywood career. A job on Wall Street. An Ivy League education. A chance at happiness.

I liked the kid a lot but I was afraid of him, afraid of his hope and his vulnerability. Afraid to get too close to him, afraid of becoming a father figure to him. We are fated to destroy those who love us with our caring or with our indifference. My shoulders were not big enough to carry the heavy sack of righteousness. So I generally stayed away from the kid, sending him small gifts through Linda, engaging with him only from afar in the way that cowards do, like small boys throwing rocks at a house from a tree top.

We drive through Ojota. Ojota, the entry point into the city of chaos. The door that leads to heaven is also the door that leads to hell. It is really just a matter of what direction you turn. This is where thousands of weary commuters are deposited after they make it past the famous toll gate and the big sign that says, Welcome to Lagos. Ojota is where pilgrims unsaddle their dreams and their bags and follow the stars seeking their destinies. We drive past Oregun, into dust clouds and congealed traffic, into a maelstrom of car horns, loud voices, and roadside commerce. Our destination is Ikeja. We arrive at a hotel off of Allen Road in Ikeja.

We do not speak throughout the entire drive. Not until I suddenly ask, "what happened to the ear?"

Linda looks at me, surprised by the question which seems to have appeared from nowhere.

"How do you mean?"

"What did you do with it?"

Linda's eyes narrow, twinkle with amusement or disappointment. I am not sure which. "What did the policemen tell you? That I ate it, swallowed it like a piece of yam?"

Again, that bitterness, that hard-edge, the voice of a woman who has lost all her illusions about life and is not trying to get them back.

I pause, trying to think of a delicate way to answer this. "They said you ate it."

She laughs. A dry laugh. More like a snort.

"The Woman Who Eats Ears." She says mockingly. Sounds like something you can put in your newspaper. Right up your alley."

I am frustrated by her impertinence. "I'm just telling you what they said."

"No. I didn't eat the ear. After I bit it off, I spat it out outside. Not my fault if they couldn't find it."

"Even if they found it, they couldn't have reattached it anyway." I add helpfully, but Linda has lost interest. She has drifted off into a private world that has no detachable body parts.

When we arrive at the hotel, we look at each other for a long moment. Somehow, we both understand that this is it. We will likely not see each other again. I had gone out of my way to help an old friend in need, a woman who had helped me financially, warmed my bed on many a night. I had settled my debt. Wiped the figurative slate clean. Finished the transaction. Isn't life itself a transaction after all, a constant settling of scores with those we love or loathe, an endless give and take, a daily quid pro quo? I give Linda a peck on the cheek. Our embrace is cold. I think of B.B. King's song.

The thrill is gone

There are no long goodbyes. No speeches. No shedding of tears. No beating of the breast or pulling of hair. Linda simply opens the car door and walks into the gathering night, through the front door of the hotel. I never see her again.

The prophet

He is wild eyed, bushy-haired and skinny. Dressed in a flowing white robe.

Bare-foot.

He doesn't move as much as he seems to float, like a dream first apprehended at dawn, the whisper of a broken promise, hanging suspended in the suddenly stale air. He looks like a modern day John the Baptist. They call him Prophet. They say that he can divine the will of God and transcribe it to man. Some say that he is the voice of God speaking through man. He is either truly holy or truly a charlatan.

I am anxious to see what will happen soon. I have heard the stories and I am here to see for myself.

We are seated outside under a giant canopy made of tarpaulin. There are rows of chairs set up for the worshippers. Every seat seems to be taken. We are all looking ahead, like starved villagers during a long drought, waiting for rain to appear. All around me, men and women dressed in their Sunday best. If hope were a creature that could take flight, we would all watch it take wing and soar, watch it soar above our reflective heads, announcing its presence in the congregation.

THE COLLECTOR OF BUTTERFLIES AND WOMEN

I am waiting for a miracle.

The air crackles like tinder with piety. There is something faintly unsettling about religiosity, even when one discovers it in oneself. Forced humility is not much different from false humility, except that one malady happens by choice. Looking around the room, I wondered how many of us here were arm-twisted into religion. How many of us were led willy-nilly into it, led namby-pamby into it. I wondered how each person here found his or her epiphany. A woman who is unable to get pregnant. A man with a deadly medical diagnosis. A young college graduate desperate to find a job. Men and women streaming forth to lay their burdens at the feet of God, and his more immediate, more tangible stand-in. Some of the people here, I suspect, have come simply for the meal that will be served after prayer service.

The air is humid and cloying, reeking with the ferment of sweaty flesh. The sky itself looks bruised, wounded clouds dragging past view in purpura. The sky's mood seems fitting for the quiet desperation of the masses gathered here.

All around me, there are children sitting on their parents' laps or on benches. The children are strangely quiet, stunned into silence like crows at the funeral of a hero. They look entranced, like window front dolls at a haberdashery, fascinated by the proceedings. Their parents have bibles open on their thighs. Men and women wave paper fans to dispel the heat but they labor in vain.

The prophet is standing on a stage fashioned out of planks of wood. There are several church elders around him. They crowd around him with the intensity of wild cats about to dig into a feast. Some of the church elders are holding white blankets. I am puzzled about this, but I will soon find out what the blankets are for.

A man steps forward and hands the prophet a mike. The prophet nods at him and then begins to speak. His voice is oddly feminine, full of vibrato like someone who has the jitters. But the prophet is not nervous. What he has is the shakes of the Holy Spirit, the convulsions of a man in the grip of spiritual ecstasy or its variant, spiritual agony.

"People of God." He begins. "The world as we know it is undergoing a change. The forces of God are joined against the legions of Satan. For our wrestling is not against flesh and blood, but against the principalities, against the powers, against the world-rulers of this darkness, against the spiritual hosts of wickedness in the heavenly places."
Ephesians 6:12.

His voice fills me with gloom, gloom that courses through my blood like an anthem. Instead of reassurance and calm, his voice carries apocalyptic angst. I look around the room at adoring faces, men and women enraptured by the prophet's words, nodding along, clenching and unclenching their fists, seized as it appeared, by passion.

Why am I here?

I am waiting for miracles.

I am here to get a story. I am a journalist working on a story about miracles, focusing on the man known to many in the city of chaos as prophet.

I was a Christian, but I liked my religion administered in small doses, preferably in the comfort of my home. My interactions with my Maker were limited specifically to monologues where I did all of the talking and I imagine that God did all the listening. I did not hear his voice booming through my bedroom wall, not unless he was attempting to reach me through the noisy children of my neighbor in the flat above mine. I did not possess the gift of speaking in tongues; the only language I knew was the English tongue. Being a man of rather subdued temperament, I was not given to public wailing and

THE COLLECTOR OF BUTTERFLIES AND WOMEN

expression of torment, finding it dreadfully hard to pull at my hair or to roll around the floor in anguish.

It is not that I did not believe in miracles.

How can one be a Christian and not believe in miracles? How can one not believe in miracles in a land of miracles? If you were looking for miracles in Nigeria, you need not look far. The very act of survival each day in this blighted beauty of a nation was a miracle in itself. A land where many live without running water, ride on unpaved roads, combat hellish traffic, struggle for daily sustenance. Nigeria, this beautiful woman infected with a strange disease by the men who have abused her, this woman waiting to be cured of her sickness so that she can be beautiful again.

It is not that I did not believe in miracles.

It was just that I did not like my religion prescribed to me by men who diagnose life merely as a fatal condition that only death can cure. I did not like prophets and preachers for the same reason that I did not like doctors. The former think that they have all the answers to heal your body while the latter think that they have all the answers to heal your soul. The doctor asks you when was the last time you drank or smoked? The preacher asks you when was the last time you read the bible or prayed? My country men, rich or poor, smitten by faith, line up to give their money to preachers and prophets. The rich try to buy their way into heaven while the poor try to beg their way into heaven. The men of God tell the non-believers that they suffer because they do not believe and then they tell the believers that they suffer because they do not believe enough.

I was born into a Muslim family, to a father who was a strict Muslim and a mother who was a part-time Christian. Because my father loved his wife, he condoned this betrayal, this betrayal of the religion of his father and his father's father. He pretended not to know about the fact that my mother had chosen a different faith. Love blinds us in strange ways and teaches us in many ways; it is capable of teaching us selflessness or selfishness. My father chose the path of selflessness when it came to my mother's religion. Because of this choice, my father is able to live in mystical ignorance, in synthetic bliss.

I gave up Christianity and Islam at twelve, immersing myself instead in studying other religions. I studied Buddhism, Hinduism, Shintoism, and Zoroastrianism. I approached these books not with a worshipper's reverence but with a scholar's fastidiousness, seeking an elusive kernel of truth. After my religious voyage, I landed at the shores of Christianity where I felt safe. I adopted Christianity as my opiate of choice, used it for a few years and then gave it up. I then spent the next six years trying to kick the Christian habit. Although I was in recovery from Christianity, atheism held no appeal for me, so I tried agnosticism for a while. For a while, because I would again return to Christianity at twenty. Something about Christ suffering on the cross for the sins of the world connected with me.

I snap out of my reverie to realize that the prophet has stopped talking. The miracles are about to begin. As if on cue, men and women begin to rise and walk to the stage. They do not come as a throng, but as an orderly mass, two men here, three women here, one man here, a child here. They all end up on the stage. Prophet is laying his hands on them, praying with them, commanding demons and evil to flee, excoriating Satan, that ancient bully and menace who is the bane of all sweet righteous folk.

Prophet prays, eyes bulging in his head, arms waving like a man about to fall off the edge of a cliff, a man trying to stop time. The crowd around him moves in a wave with his every motion. People fall, cry, beat their breasts in ardor. Women let go of their *"geles"* – brightly colored head wraps that seem designed to block the view of anyone who is unlucky enough to sit behind the wearer.

A young attractive woman in a pleated black skirt drops to the floor. She drops without artifice, her arms simply giving way under her like a child's doll with a broken mechanism. As she falls, her skirt hikes up her legs indecently. Lightning quick, a church elder steps forward with a white blanket to cover her up.

Sitting immobile on the cruel wooden bench, I begin to feel guilty. Like a dry-eyed man at a funeral where everyone else is crying, I feel a sense of unworthiness. Why am I so calm and collected, so untouched by the rapture around me? Why am I letting the immaculate train of spiritual ecstasy pass me by? Why am I so unmoved by the apotheosis of the man of God standing there with his robe billowing in the wind, his hair blowing, his face wearing the severity of Moses?

I am clutching my notepad, but so far I have scribbled only a few notes.

A blind man steps forward, gesticulates wildly at his eyes, telegraphing to the crowd that he is blind. He falls on his knees before the prophet. The prophet, regarding him with infinite benevolence, helps him up to his feet, mutters some feverish gibberish. The man opens his eyes wide, looking startled. He begins to yell "I'm healed! I'm healed!"

The-blind-man-who-was-once-blind-but-now-can-see, runs off like a prisoner set free, dashes into the oblivion of the madding crowd. More bodies hit the wooden floor. More blankets emerge. People pray, weep, faint and hold hands. I am witnessing miracles. Or a simulacrum of miracles.

What I do next surprises me.

I put down my notepad and pen and make my way to the stage to join the parade of sinners, the cavalcade of the diseased and distressed. As I plant a foot on the dais, one of the church elders who have formed a ring around the prophet, steps forward. He is a stout man with a felonious face.

"What troubles you?" His manner is baroque, officious.

"I can't find happiness. I don't sleep well at night. I am paranoid, feel like I am going insane at times."

The elder seems puzzled by my response. He is a man used to dysenteries that will not stop, wombs that will not yield babies, husbands that refuse to come home at night, pain that will not go away, but this, this sickness of the spirit, these psychic scars, how to contend with this? A man who can't find happiness?

The church elder pushes me forward toward the prophet. Standing on the dais, the moaning of men in religious torment, the groaning of women in religious ferment, the clapping of hands and the stomping of feet, it all feels so loud, so loud it threatens whatever is left of my sanity. I want to flee. But I do not.

I submit myself to the prophet. I fall to my feet because it seems to be the right thing to do. All around me, men and women are broken contraptions littering the floor. I fall to the floor but my mouth remains closed. I am not praying, not like the people all around me shouting, "Hallelujah." "Jehovah Jireh" *"Olorun-mi-O!"*

Prophet puts his hands on my shoulder and commands the demon of unhappiness to depart from my life.

"Get away from this child of God! Leave him alone! Go find a child of Satan to dwell in!"

I think of Jesus and the pigs in the country of Gadarenes. How Jesus casts out demons from a man and how the demons take over a herd of swine feeding nearby. The crazed animals, two thousand of them, run violently over the mountainside and drown in the sea.

This is what I think of as the prophet assaults me with a fusillade of prayers. Saliva flows from his mouth in a torrent, his long hair waving in the soft breeze.

When I leave the church that afternoon, my body feels lighter, my spirit levitates. A phenomenon that I cannot explain. I meditate on the nature of prayer. Placebo or panacea?

I have been healed of my unhappiness, I think. No more shall I wallow in misery.

But happiness proves to be fleeting as I soon discover.

He is dying

My father is dying.

The thought shears my mind as I pull up in a cab in Benin City, outside my parents' house on Mission Street. My father is being carried into a waiting cab. Half-carried and half-dragged by my mother and one of my sisters. My arrival is serendipitous.

I had just arrived from Lagos. Caught a cab from the motor park. And here was my father in great distress and pain, being taken to a hospital.

"What is wrong with him?" I ask, rushing forward to assist.

"We don't know." My mother responds. "He said his chest is tight. Can't breathe."

My father is asthmatic. When he sleeps, the house rattles from his forceful wheezing. Cups and utensils tumble down from the basket hanging against the kitchen wall. Small mammals pause in their foraging, uneasy and bewildered. Stunned birds fall from the sky, thoroughly affrighted. Of course, I exaggerate. He also has diabetes. And high blood pressure. About these ailments, I do not exaggerate. On any given day, the house on Mission Street smells like a sanitarium among other smells. My father treats his pillbox with the tenderness with which a bride treats her wedding night gifts, the way a magician treasures his tool kit.

I jump into the cab along with my mother and sister. My father is wedged between my mother and me, his face flushed with pain. His breathing is ragged, beads of sweat shine like polished jewels on his forehead. His eyes are distant, stricken.

"Hang in there." I say. "You will be okay."

But I don't know that he will be okay. How would I know? It is the bad luck of the infirm that they are condemned to listen to the inanities of the healthy.

The cab driver is driving too fast, weaving through the serpentine traffic at a speed that sets my teeth on edge. He is determined to send us all to hell and to do it as expeditiously as possible.

"Take it easy!" I yell at him, but he ignores me, his eyes fixed on the road.

We fly past streets strangled by traffic, men and women walking and talking, trading and arguing. They bargain and harangue, inveigh and cajole. The roads have a Martian aspect to them, cratered and dangerous, blighted and unknowable. Debris flies in the air, a woman's rotted nightgown billows obscenely in the wind, candy wrappers and wet newspapers bleed ink on the sidewalk. The smell is pleasing and displeasing at the same time, depending on what snatch of the wind you catch. The smell is so strong it becomes sound drumming in your brain. The sound is so loud it becomes tactile, like the caress of a lecher with rude fingers. Above us, the sun is full of petulance. It bounces off the zinc rooftops like a demented child.

It is unbearably hot in the cab. I try to roll down the window on my side with no luck. I wait for an apology from the cab driver, but there is none forthcoming. The cab driver smells like he spent the night in a brewery that also doubles as a cigarette factory. In Nigeria, it is not uncommon for a cab driver to stop at his favorite bar for a few drinks just before picking up his next passenger. By some estimates, fifty

THE COLLECTOR OF BUTTERFLIES AND WOMEN

to seventy five people are killed daily on Nigerian roads by drunken drivers yet offenders are rarely arrested for drunken driving. In the unlikely case that they are arrested, a small bribe usually guarantees their release. As if to confirm what I already know, I see a street vendor darting acrobatically through traffic, selling chilled beer. He hands the cans to passengers in buses and cabs, and grabs the money offered before the vehicles take off.

My father begins to moan.

We arrive at the hospital. It is a sad-faced building with blistered paint like peeling make-up and a zinc roof which sits crookedly like a bad wig. The house was the best house on the block when it was built too many years ago. Now, it sits like a dowager who has fallen on hard times, reeking of iodine and incontinence.

We carry my father through the front door into a waiting area. There are people sitting on benches, the sick and their relatives, waiting for their turn to see the doctor or nurse. Or waiting obediently for their turn to die. They sneeze and cough, fart and mumble to themselves. I smell urine. Shit. The bracing metallic smell of blood. A man is curled up on the floor, writhing in pain, his face a mask of agony. He begins to cough, a thread of sputum dribbling like a worm from his lips. The sputum is flecked with blood. Bright spots of blood. When the next bout of coughing seizes him, he heaves in agony and spits out a gob of blood.

Who is going to help him? I wonder. Who is going to save this poor man? Why is he not being attended to? Determined not to let my father have to wait like this stricken man, I stride over to the counter where two nurses, both females, are seated. I point to my father who is by now seated on one of the benches, his head on my mother's shoulder.

"That is my father over there. He needs help. It is an emergency."

The nurse with the clipboard and pen stares at me with dead eyes. As if I had just interrupted her dinner. I search for empathy in her round wrinkled face but there is none to be found.

"He needs to register first before the doctor can see him."

"Register?" I mutter in disbelief. "This man is dying and you want him to do some paperwork first?"

The nurse is not impressed by my outrage. She has a silver nail file. Like someone who has all the time in the world, she begins to delicately file her nails. As if oblivious to the despair and decay all around her. I think of revelers dancing on the deck of the Titanic, the band playing while the ship begins to sink slowly and inexorably into the watery depths.

"*Oga*. Here." She hands me the clipboard. "Fill this out and then we will give you a card. Everybody needs a card."

Everybody needs a card.

A man could walk into a hospital in Nigeria with an eye hanging out of its socket and be told that he needs to "take a card" before the doctor would see him. Taking a card does not just mean that you have to fill out paperwork. What it means more importantly is that you need to make a monetary deposit before you can get treatment of any kind.

I can't resist. "Is that man on the floor waiting to get a card too?"

She nods humorlessly. "Yes. His wife has gone to raise the money. She left him here."

"So what if she can't raise the money."

She looks puzzled, as if I have asked her a trick question. "If they can't raise money, then we can't help him. Look mister man, we are not running a charity here."

"So what if my father has no cash on him? The man is dying for God's sake!"

"Even if you are dying, you should still carry cash."

I am stung into speechlessness by her insouciance. "So even the dying should carry cash?"

She nods, this woman who is impervious to irony.

"Brother, please stop arguing with him and fill out the card." My sister pleads. Her voice brings me back to my senses. I reach into my pocket to confirm that the cash I brought with me from Lagos is still there. I take the clip board from the nurse and begin to fill out the paperwork. I fill out the form as quickly as I can. The banalities of my father's birth, occupation and address etcetera. His medical history which is encyclopedic, I manage to reduce to two or three stiff sentences.

I hand the documents to the nurse. She scans them cursorily and then tells me. "Your deposit."

"How much?"

She doesn't bother to answer. Instead, she points at a number written in fine print at the bottom of the form that I have just filled out. In my haste to fill out the form, I had completely missed it.

I reach into my pocket and take out a wad of cash. The country's currency is so devalued that one naira can no longer buy anything. Here, even the poor have a lot of money. The problem is that the money has very little value. So if you convert one hundred dollars into naira, you end up with a bagful of cash.

The nurse takes the money, makes a show of counting it, while I fidget impatiently. It takes forever for my father to finally see the doctor. The doctor is a gray-haired man who speaks in a clipped perfect diction. He has the careful recherché manner of someone who has travelled in foreign climes. He was educated in England. He looks capable, like a man who would know exactly where to find the fire extinguisher if a fire broke out, a man who never drove without his seatbelt securely fastened. His nails are manicured, a rarity for a man in Nigeria, every glorious hair on his glorious head is in its glorious place. This is the man who might be able to save my father, yank him back from death's door.

My father is placed on the gurney inside the examination room. The room is wedding veil white, with posters of the human anatomy on the wall. There is an article titled, What You Need To Know About Diabetes pasted on the wall. There is another one about

Typhoid fever. Both of them are colorfully diagrammed. Memories of another hospital room flood my mind. I remember the man with ugly hands. The man who nearly botched my appendectomy. Who carried out surgery on me without sufficient anesthetic. His fingers were ugly, unlike this doctor's.

"How long has he been having this chest pain?" Dr. Egharevba asks as he checks my father's blood pressure.

"Weeks." My father speaks up, his voice a choked whisper.

"Why didn't you come to the hospital before now?" He asks, listening to my father's breathing.

"No money." My mother replies. "We were trying to reach our son in Lagos."

"And hoping the pain would go away." The doctor says.

My mother nods.

"Hope." The doctor spits out the word with bitterness, as if it were an expletive. "You know how many times I hear that every day? People wait until it is too late to save them before they come here. Hoping that things will improve."

Thankfully, my father did improve under Dr. Egharevba's care. He is admitted to the clinic and kept there for three days before being discharged. The diagnosis? We are told that he had heart failure resulting from pneumonia. I am not sure that I know what this means. In Nigeria, one learns at a young age that doctors should never be questioned, that they are beyond reproach. These men who have spent the better part of their youth in medical school are gods. They speak with oracular ponderousness, with Apollonian heft. So if a doctor tells you that you will be dead in six months, it was your duty to lie down obediently and die in six months.

As I depart the hospital on the day that my father is released, I find myself thinking of hope. In Nigeria, hope can be just as deadly as hopelessness. Hope kills many of my countrymen every day. The sick get sicker while hoping to get better, instead of seeing a

THE COLLECTOR OF BUTTERFLIES AND WOMEN

doctor. The poor hope that things will improve, waiting on the train tracks while the cruel locomotive of life crushes them. Faith kills my countrymen too, or at the very least maims them. Faith in the god of wealth whom they wrongfully believe is also the god of happiness. Faith in drunken gods that have fallen asleep on duty. Faith in elected leaders who have become swollen with corruption like maggots feeding on an unclaimed corpse.

This is my country, my beloved country, whose blood pulses in my veins. A land where it is recommended that even dying men carry cash.

Who stole my penis?

In the early nineties, a strange phenomenon begins to sweep through Lagos, soon spreading to other parts of the country. Men and boys began to report that their penises had been stolen by practitioners of the magic rituals of *juju*. The male body part was required for powerful charms that would make the rich richer and help ambitious men achieve their dreams.

To say the least, I was terrified by this phenomenon. The fear of castration, of emasculation, is one that many men have harbored for centuries. Often this fear has been patently irrational, as irrational as the myth of the vagina dentata, the toothed vagina.

There were stories in the media about men who having been touched by sinister strangers in public places, soon discovered afterwards that their cherished body part had shrunk. On close examination, the sheath of the missing body part was discovered to still be intact, however, the essence, the mass of flesh inside the sheath was gone, spirited away by the ritualists.

In Yaba, two men were burned to death – "given the necklace" after they were accused of having stolen a trader's penis. Similar incidents were taking place all over the country. People were being

THE COLLECTOR OF BUTTERFLIES AND WOMEN

accused of penile theft, tried, judged and then executed on the spot. Fancying myself to be a rational sort, I had always sneered at these stories, and told anyone who cared to listen that the men being accused and lynched by these crazed mobs were innocent.

Until the day my penis got stolen.

It happened at Oshodi market, one of the busy markets in the metropolis that spill out on the roadside like the entrails of a gutted animal. Oshodi market is a schizophrenic's scream echoing endlessly day and night in the chambers of a cathedral, a place of frenzy and frolic, of madness and multitudes.

Market women sit on wooden stools on muddy ground selling raw meat and palm oil, yams and coconuts, pepper and bitter leaves. Some sit on train tracks and ply their wares. Whenever the traders on the train tracks hear the sound of an approaching train, they erupt out of their seats in motion that is almost choreographed, grab their wares and stools and flee to safety. After the train passes by, they return to their positions. They have developed an uncanny sense for the trains' arrivals.

There are ramshackle shops jury-rigged from zinc and wood on both sides of the road. These bivouacs have no doors; when the day is over, the shopkeepers simply pack up all their wares and take them home. The entrances are open, like the mouth of a toothless hag. Brightly colored apparel dangle from these shacks, like truant children climbing on cashew trees. The hullabaloo of commerce carries far and wide as men and women haggle, harangue, and harass.

Rickety chariots that carry sudden death and destruction for the unwary, race by. They disgorge passengers, swallow up fresh passengers, and then continue their journeys to Yaba, Iyanakpaja, Sango Otta, and Idumota, these big yellow buses that look just like American school buses, called *molues*. Small buses known as *danfos* flit by, unwilling to be outdone by the *molues*. Each bus, *molue* or *danfo* carries a driver's assistant, known as a conductor. The conductors are almost as dangerous as the wheels on their buses. These angry men are always ready to do battle with passengers who refuse to pay their fares. Often they will ask the bus driver to stop the bus so that they can settle their scores with a troublesome passenger. Fists fly by the side of the road, while impatient passengers yell at the bus driver to resume the journey.

This then is Oshodi. Oshodi where my penis was stolen.

How did it happen?

It starts as another extraordinary day in Lagos, for in Lagos there are no ordinary days. Lagos is not a city of clichés; rather it is a city of relentless self-invention and phantasmagoric change. I have come to Oshodi market in the company of a colleague of mine, Kenneth, to purchase some household items. I am inside the bowel of the beast itself, inside the heart of the thing, ducking fellow bargain hunters, dodging the mass of sweaty, clinging, humanity.

A man is walking toward me. A tall emaciated man who moves like a hound, on the balls of his feet, eyes haunted, cheeks sunken. His eyes lock into mine and for a reason that I can't explain, a shiver runs through my body. This apparition brings back primeval bed-wetting dreams. He brushes past me in a manner that I believe is deliberate, leaning to touch me, even as I recoil, and try to move out of his path.

This is when it happened.

Suddenly, I feel light-headed, weak, a sense of shrinking. I feel disembodied, as if something corporeal, something corporal, has fled from within me. All my old fears of emasculation and impotence rush to the surface. My hand reaches to touch my penis.

It is gone!

There is nothing there but a mere sheath of deflated flesh. My penis is missing, the sword that I have worn proudly to several battles fought in the middle of the night on rusty beds and dusty floors.

I am overwhelmed by terror. I scream, reach out to grab the man who has stolen my penis. But he is gone. My friend, Kenneth, who is a couple of steps behind me hears my cry of distress and rushes forward.

"What happened?"

"My penis." I blurt. "It is gone."

His eyes follow my right hand which is locked firmly on my groin. A shiver runs through him. "Did you see the person who took it?"

"Yes. He is gone."

"Come on! Let's look for him."

I do not stop to consider the irrationality of this decision. What would I say once I located the thief? Hey, can I have my penis back? What if I was wrong? What if the man with the haunted eyes is not the true culprit? What if some other perpetrator's hand had touched me without my knowledge?

I break into a run, a ridiculous sight in my shirt and tie and cufflinks. Kenneth follows. I run down the street strewn with exploded tomatoes, old newspapers, and corn husks. I run past faces that are jaded and prosaic, past faces that are faded and mosaic. As I run, I search for the man with the haunted eyes. No one is surprised to see a man in a tie running through the crowded market place in the noon day heat. In Lagos, not much surprises people. A dead body on the roadside. Policemen whipping a helpless street vendor. A man beating his wife in public. A madman dispensing Socratic wisdom by the roadside. What is surprising is how hard it is to find the surprising.

I run, driven by fear. Kenneth runs behind me. But we can't find the man with the haunted eyes.

After a while, I collapse on the side of the road in sheer exhaustion and panic. I find myself sitting on a tree stump. Kenneth rushes to catch up with me. Buses screech past, those hellhounds. I inhale car exhaust and wonder how life will be like without a penis.

Kenneth has the presence of mind to flag down a passing cab. The cab drives us to the house of a local medicine man who lives in Shogunle. A man that the two of us are casually acquainted with but have had no dealings with. This man is reputed to be a healer, one of many that can be found on every street in Lagos, men who minister to supplicants and mendicants.

We walk through a dim corridor, past small children with hungry eyes and angry stomachs. We glimpse women cooking over an open fire in the middle of the compound. We hear the sound of a pestle beating on a wooden mortar as a wife prepares *iyan* for dinner. We enter a room without a door or curtain and from there we enter into a smaller room. We sit on wooden armless chairs. The floor is uncarpeted. There are two large mirrors on the wall. I imagine that one is for examining the wrinkles on your soul, and the other is for wiping the dust off your face. I stare at my own dazed eyes.

The native doctor is in his early thirties, rather young for his chosen trade. He has an indecisive beard which is an odd contrast to his full head of arrogant hair. He carries the gravitas of the executioner and the surgeon. He is Sisyphus before the rock is lifted, Noah before Jehovah unleashes the flood. Can he help me recover what is lost or is it too late?

"What is the nature of your problem?"

"My penis has been stolen. At Oshodi market."

The man does not blink. It would have helped if he looked surprised, puzzled, even curious. Instead, he stares at me without emotion, as if he was used to young men in their twenties walking into his house every day to declare their most prized appendage stolen.

"Take off your clothes."

Modesty is something that a man who presents himself to a native doctor for examination can ill afford. I shed my clothes on the concrete floor. And there it was, my withered penis, flaccid like a snake's molt, the evidence of my sudden impairment, my sudden emasculation.

The medicine man reaches forward, grabs my balls and penis, squeezes them, prods them, shakes them as a boy would shake a coconut seed to hear the juices squishing inside.

"Nothing is wrong with your penis." He pronounces.

"Are you sure?" I ask in disbelief.

"I am sure. Do you know how many of such cases I have had just this week? Fear has taken over the land. Grown men show up crying, afraid to hear that they will never have sex with their wives again. Not a single one of them has been missing their penis."

I stare at Kenneth. He stares at me. We are speechless for a moment.

"So what happened to me then?"

"Fear." The native doctor says. "Fear. When a man is afraid, terribly afraid, his penis retreats back into his body. It is a mechanism of self protection, to prevent it from being wounded. "

"So my penis never disappeared?"

For the first time, the man smiles, a benevolent smile. "Your penis never disappeared. It shrunk because you were terrified."

"And all the stories about snatchers of men's organs? You think it's all false?"

"There are rituals that some evil native doctors do with a penis taken from a man who is still breathing. But the only way to take that penis is by cutting it off. There is no way to make it disappear from one man's body and appear in another man's pocket."

"So all those stories in the news are false?" I ask again.

The native doctor pauses, takes a piece of kola nut of his *agbada* and begins to chew thoughtfully. "If some people will believe anything that they hear, some people will tell them anything that they wish to hear."

His utterance strikes me as trenchant.

Mundus vult decipi, ergo decipiatur

The world wants to be deceived, so let it be deceived.

"Go home to your woman. Get her in bed tonight and you will see whether your penis still works or not."

I smile in relief. He does not ask for a fee, but I reach into my pocket and deposit a wad of naira notes on a small basket near the medicine man's feet.

When I get home that night, I do not have a wife or girlfriend available on whom to test my virility. Indeed, I am still too shaken and amused by the incident that had taken place earlier to work up the requisite libido. But driven by the need for reassurance, I retreat to my bedroom with a container of Vaseline and a dog-eared copy of a porn magazine. It does not take long to confirm that the medicine man was right.

As I lay in bed that night, I meditate on fear, fear as a Leviathan, fear that has such excitatory effects on the senses. I think of the woman in Agbor who was accused of witchcraft and forced to drink the water that was used to bathe her husband's corpse in order to prove her innocence. I think of the Salem witch hunt, the Spanish Inquisition, and the Holocaust.

An innocent man is beaten mercilessly by a mob and then given the necklace, set on fire after being accused of stealing someone's penis. An accusation that could not possibly be true, an accusation that has no scientific or rational basis. An accusation rooted in ancient superstitions grafted into our bodies like a fifth limb since birth, toxicity sprinkled like a powder into our baby formula, perhaps passed on from our mother's milk itself, this poison of superstition that infects the young and the old, the illiterate and at times the educated.

What if I had caught up with the man that I thought had stolen my penis? What if I had accused him, denounced him to the crowd? What if the crowd had wreaked its terrible, fatal retribution on him? I would have got an innocent man killed, perhaps a man who had a wife and children or a mother and father waiting for him to come home.

I am angry at my inability to shake these residual superstitions buried deep in my subconscious. I am angry at fireside storytellers

THE COLLECTOR OF BUTTERFLIES AND WOMEN

who have reared me on a steady diet of the magical and the mystical. I rave at my parents and at the mythology and ontology on which I have been raised.

    I am embarrassed.

    I am ashamed.

Tragedy

In the months following the incident with my penis, several tragic events take place in Nigeria. I pick the news up from random newspaper articles, from radio and TV broadcasts.

A family decides to light candles after it loses electricity at home. The house catches fire during the night while the family is asleep. No one makes it out alive. Two young children, sisters, are found crouched on the floor, dessicated, holding each other. They were comforting each other even as the flames took them.

Five young men, employed as apprentices in a mechanic's workshop, go to sleep in the shop where they work, which also doubles as their sleeping quarters. Before they do so, they turn on the gas powered electric generator so that they can run the ceiling fan, the ceiling fan which will save them from the caresses of mosquitoes and the relentless night heat.

But they have not moved the generator far enough from the house.

Carbon monoxide stalks into the house and it smothers them in their sleep. When they are found the next day, one of them, a mere youth of sixteen, has one hand in his pocket to protect the small

THE COLLECTOR OF BUTTERFLIES AND WOMEN

roll of bills from a thieving hand while he slept. Another one has both hands clutched in prayer on his chest, lips open as if he were muttering the paternoster at the moment of extinguishment.

The reporter who covered the story came armed with a photographer. The photographer took bloodless photographs of the boys in stubbornly neutral black and white. There is an affect of the chiaroscuro in the ensuing images. There is no privacy in Lagos, not even in death.

A distraught mother puts her dead child in the freezer, hoping that he will wake up again, trying to prevent his body from decaying. The next morning, she straps the dead boy to her back. Takes him to her church so that the pastor can pray and bring him back to life. She is a woman who believes in miracles, who has read about the biblical Lazarus. Who will tell her now that her son is never coming back, that Jehovah whom she gives her pennies to every Sunday will not restore her son to life?

Who will save my beloved country, this country that continues to thrash around blindly like a big wounded animal? Who will save this republic of the intelligent governed by fools?

Unable to confront its own bitter truths, Nigeria has decided to blind itself like Oedipus. We fester in our glorious self-deception, totter toward our assured self-destruction. We are like long-married husbands who refuse to admit that our wives no longer attract us, fathers who refuse to admit that we secretly loathe our children, old men in winter whose dreams teem with young forbidden flesh. Who will save us? And when will they come?

Arrest

They came looking for me in the middle of the night. They kick down the front door of my flat and barge in, the same door that was broken down when robbers attacked my residence months before. This time, the men are in uniforms and not in masks. But they are armed just like I imagine that the robbers were. No robber would break into someone's home in Lagos without having a weapon.

They rampage through the three rooms in the flat, these invaders, searching for some evidence that I do not know. Fortunately, I am not at home when they show up. But my neighbors in Ijaiye would relay the story to me later.

I am not sure why they did not come to my office to look for me. That would have been the best place to find me. When I think back on this later, the only reason that I can adduce to their decision to not visit my place of employment was that they did not want people to see me as I was being taken away.

Why did they need to break down the door if nobody answered their knock? I suspected that they were trying to send me a message. It was a show of force. Why were they after me? Had I written an article that offended some politician? Were they assassins in uniform paid by an unknown enemy to rub me out?

THE COLLECTOR OF BUTTERFLIES AND WOMEN

After the first break-in at my flat, it had become increasingly difficult to spend the night at home. To make matters worse and further unhinge me, I suspected that I was being watched by men that I did not know. I stopped riding around in the company car and started to catch cabs. I began to look behind me to see who might be following me.

I became a wary man, a man scrabbling for purchase on a cliff, trying not to be hurled over the edge and dashed to his death in the rocky abyss below. I nursed my fear like a tall drink.

I became a creature of hotels, shuffling forlornly through rooms that had witnessed private desperation and debauchery. At the end of each work day, I returned to whatever hotel I had chosen for the week. I walked past hotel clerks with efficient smiles and unctuous eyes and retired to my room.

I do not stay at one hotel for long. I move from hotel to hotel. My friends are puzzled by my constant motion. What ghosts am I fleeing, they wonder?

When the policemen did not find me that night, they left a note, asking me to report to Yaba Police Station. They did not apologize for kicking in my door, or for eating a can of corned beef from my refrigerator. The can was sitting on the floor of the kitchen when I returned home the next day to get a change of clothing.

I notified a few close friends of mine about what had happened. I told them that if I disappeared and was never heard from again, they needed to know that the police was responsible. I did not alert my colleagues in the media, because I did not want to become a cause célèbre. I was hoping that this whole thing would blow over in a day or two and that I could return to my work.

In Nigeria, becoming a cause célèbre has a way of getting people killed. Strange things happen to such men and women. They take long walks and never return home. They go to prison and bash their brains out, these rational men and women, bash their brains out on tear-streaked implacable walls. They commit suicide by shooting themselves in the head, men and women who had never even handled guns, shoot themselves in the head with rifles. For these enigmatic deaths, the police sardonically blame suicidal tendencies and armed robbers.

When I visited the Prophet, I had shared with him the lack of happiness in my life. This lack of happiness sprang from a generalized sense of anxiety, a persistent feeling that a rude surprise awaited around every corner.

On that day, kneeling before the long limbed prophet, a man I found to be an enigma and arguably a fraud, I had asked to be rid of my paranoia. But now I no longer wanted to be freed of my paranoia. I wanted to embrace my paranoia and nourish it because I knew that my paranoia might keep me alive.

Do not take a man's paranoia away from him unless you can give him something as warm to replace it with. If you take away a madman's madness, what then do you leave him with but an identity crisis?

I decided to leave for Yaba Police Station after first visiting my girlfriend, Nkiru who lived in Gbagada. Nkiru was an ingénue who was able to open her own clothes shop while still in her teens. The shop was in Gbagada, located in the same compound where she lived with her family. Tall, and high-spirited, she caught clichés like a Venus flytrap. Men remarked on her beauty while women recoiled at her beauty. A woman who was created on the first day of creation was how I thought of her. The first day of creation well before God needed to take a rest. We met through a cousin of hers, who was a colleague at the publication where I worked prior to founding the People's Express newspaper.

It is almost dark when I decide to report to Yaba Police Station. The streets of Lagos are dangerous at night. But then the streets of Lagos are no more dangerous at night than they are in the day. I flag down a cab, looking all around me to make sure that I am not being followed. I wrap my paranoia around me like a blanket.

THE COLLECTOR OF BUTTERFLIES AND WOMEN

I give Nkiru a kiss, tell her that I expected to be back later that evening. I would straighten out the situation with the police, fix the problem, whatever it was. Nkiru looks dubious, unconvinced.

"Let me come with you." She offers.

"Not necessary. It will only complicate things."

"Please. You don't even know why they are looking for you.'

"I'll find out tonight, won't I?" I try a forced laugh but my attempt at humor falls short. I am afraid but fighting my fear.

I did not want Nkiru hovering around half frightened to death as I dealt with the insolubility and inscrutability of a corrupt law system.

But she wouldn't budge.

"I am going with you. If not, I won't let you go."

In the months that I had known Nkiru, I had come to care about her passionately. This was as close as I could come to being in love with anyone. I was still trying to figure out why a girl like Nkiru would be remotely interested in me. But there will be plenty of time to dwell on this question in the future, the future being a kingdom that still waits to be explored.

We finally reach a compromise. She will take the ride with me to Yaba Police Station. She will seat in a restaurant near the police station and wait for me. If I do not emerge in three hours, she is to contact her relatives for help.

Having reached this resolution, Nkiru and I climb into the cab.

The cab hurtles through the night. At night, the bright lights and noise of Lagos startle the stars and force them to hide. The stars retreat farther in the galaxy, like unhappy children scurrying away from parents that have gone beserk. Like Dr. Zhivago travelling through the bleak, transmogrifying landscape of post-war Russia, we travel through the belly of the beast, and I am witness to the corruption and the celebration, to the desperation and the despair.

I am a man engaged to be married to two women, two women who really live inside of one woman, a woman who has a multiple personality disorder, cherubic in part and demonic in the other part. Lagos is the city to which I am affianced. The city that I love when I go to sleep but hate when I wake up.

I am tense, afraid of what awaits me at the police station.

The cab driver swerves to avoid a man who has run into the path of the car. The lunatic stands in the middle of the road, waving his arms like a big bird, as if he is about to levitate. The driver lets out an oath, *"Oloshi!"*

Lagos has more mad people per square mile than any other city in the world. I am convinced of this. They roam the streets, these ghosts from the underworld dressed in elaborate rags or in their birthday suits. They forage through roadside trash heaps, eyes shining with a strange secret that they refuse to share with the sane. When you look in their eyes, what you see is not despair but optimism. When they open their mouths, what emerges is not a howl but a laugh. They dance and prance in merriment while the sane world watches in puzzlement. They vibrate at a different frequency from everyone else, hear oscillations and intonations that no one else can hear. They dance the twist while the world dances the tango. Occasionally, they dart in front of traffic and get run over. Their corpses are left by the roadside, left to bake like sand pies in the cruel sun. Passers-by hold their noses and mothers shield their children's eyes as they walk past.

In a city where the living get no respect, the dead have no right to expect any respect.

In Nigeria, most people do not take the mad seriously. Here the mad are more comic than tragic, curious spectacles in the fading bloom which one beholds and then pauses momentarily to regard, just before lifting the glass of wine to one's Epicurean lips or taking a civilized bite at a section of the crudite. And would you pass me another bonbon, please?

We drive past the dust and grime of Bariga, past the grim determinism of Mushin market and its night traders. Lights from

THE COLLECTOR OF BUTTERFLIES AND WOMEN

roadside shops cut through the huddling dark like long swords. Street vendors dart across the street, peddling fruit, *suya* meat and bottled water. The noise is so loud that no amount of willpower will shut it out. It sounds like an army marching to war, chanting its war cry. The night air tastes tangy like I imagine honey would taste when the honeybees have yet to finish their work. The unschooled spirit of the city is in full display.

Although I did not know it at that time, what lay ahead of me would be the longest night of my life.

Soon after I give my name to the police officer at the counter, a policeman rushes forward and punches me in the jaw.

I see the blow coming but I do not have time to duck it. Even if I had ducked the first punch, I couldn't have ducked a second. I bend over, brace myself for the flurry of punches that I expect to come, but no further blows come.

I lift my head to face my attacker. He is a squat young man with the brawny hands of a carpenter's apprentice. His eyes are bright with unresolved traumas, his lips uncharacteristically thin. His face is contorted in comic book anger. He is a one dimensional character among a people who are riddles and enigmas.

"So you are the journalist, the man we've been looking for."

I run my tongue across my teeth, checking for the saltiness of blood. Thankfully, there is none. "What is the problem? What have I done?"

"What have you done?" He mimics, his eyes mocking. He turns to the two other policemen at the counter. "Do you hear him? What has he done?" The policemen glance briefly at us and continue their work, whatever it was. It appears that they have seen a scene such as the one playing out now many times before. They do not bother to fake amusement or interest.

"When we are finished with you, you will know exactly what you have done, Mr. Journalist."

This is my introduction to the world of sudden imprisonment. This is how freedom is lost in Nigeria, I think. Sometimes freedom is regained, at other times, it is never regained.

At some point, while I am seated, a policewoman shows up with an antiquated Polaroid camera. Without a word, she points it in my general direction, snaps a picture of me. When the glossy paper emerges, she holds it by the tip as if it was a dangerous snake and waves the paper back and forth to dry the ink. Satisfied, she places the paper on the counter and writes my name on the back of the photograph.

I never find out the name of the man who attacked me. No one tells me why I have been arrested, if indeed I am under arrest. I am simply told to sit on one of the forlorn benches and to wait. My attacker disappears.

Seated on the bench, I scan the room and register the other people in the room. A half dozen men and women, each immersed in their own misfortune, not making eye contact, waiting with every fiber of their being.

After waiting for an hour, I walk over to the counter and speak to one of the policemen. "Who am I waiting for? Is someone supposed to be meeting with me?

The policemen stares at me with unconcealed amusement. "In a big hurry, aren't you? Got a lot of important business to take care of tonight, no?"

"Why am I here?"

"The DPO asked us to bring you here. We tried to find you but you were hiding out."

"I was not hiding out."

"If the police are looking for you and you make yourself scarce, you are hiding out. That's what it looks like to me."

THE COLLECTOR OF BUTTERFLIES AND WOMEN

"But what I have I done? Can someone tell me what the problem is?"

The policeman considers this for a long moment, then decides to humor me. "You've been writing articles about people, haven't you?"

"That is what journalists do. We write articles."

"You don't know how to mind your own business, do you?"

"Sir, my business is to mind other people's business."

The policeman shakes his head, a man whose reservoir of patience is fast draining.

"Have you been helping people get visas to leave Nigeria too?"

This non-sequitur catches me by surprise.

"I have helped a few friends secure visas abroad. What does that have to do with me being here?"

"You are a smart man. Figure it out. You are writing articles about people. You are a journalist. Your friends are journalists. You are helping trouble makers escape after they have caused trouble."

I had never been officially accused of sedition by the government. Although, I had received covert warnings that my writings were causing discomfort to some people in government, no government official had ever asked me to cease and desist. Is this then the prelude to being officially charged?

"Helping friends secure visas to travel overseas is not a crime, as far as I know. If I have libeled anyone in my writings, they are welcome to sue me."

"Look, mister man, I am not here to argue with you. Go and sit back down. When the DPO is ready, he will meet with you."

I walk back to my seat, shaken. I tabulate all of my friends, scour through the list for any of them that I had helped secure visas. Only two of them come to mind and none of them is a journalist. Where did the police get this spurious story about my helping people escape overseas? I was hardly Tuvia Bielski hiding away Jewish refugees in Poland's Naliboki forest.

As I wait on the bench, my stomach begins to rumble. I ignore the pangs of hunger and worry instead about Nkiru, sitting at the restaurant near the police station, waiting for me. It is becoming clear that I will not be returning home tonight.

It is nearly midnight when two policemen who have taken over from the previous shift, walk over. "Let us escort you to your suite." One says with a big smile while his partner chuckles.

The speaker is a gap-toothed man with a brilliant smile. He carries the cheerful optimist of a Catechist. Everything will be okay, my son, his face lies to me. Everything will be okay in this cruel world that you live in.

He has a big ring of keys strapped to his waist. His shoes are scuffed and worn. They remind me of my father's shoes. A poor man's shoes. The shoes of a man merely following orders, who does not bother himself with the esoterics of right and wrong, who in fact can ill afford such hairsplitting. His partner is short, unremarkable, the kind of man you might meet on the train and not remember, unless he stops to ask you for a cigarette or accidentally steps on your shoe.

We walk down a block of cells. The chemical smell of unwashed skin fermenting in the heat is repugnant. The familiar odor of excrement and urine stings the nostrils. My stomach lurches. Memories of the jail where Linda was held flood my mind.

When we reach my designated cell or 'suite', the short policeman steps back, weapon at the ready. Smiley-Face reaches for his key ring and unlocks the cell door. He pushes me not-so-gently into the gloom. "You arrived too late for dinner but breakfast will be served in the morning. We take good care of our guests here."

His colleague chortles at this performance. I can tell that they have performed this act many times in the past.

"Good night, gentlemen."

An arm reaches out and grabs me, pulls me deeper into the cell. Temporarily blind in this room without light, sheer panic seizes me.

THE COLLECTOR OF BUTTERFLIES AND WOMEN

I pull away from the arm, trying to adjust to my surroundings, of which I soon become painfully aware. I can't see my fellow tenants, not right away anyway, but I can hear their breathing, the low hum of conversation as they check out the latest prisoner.

A man begins to laugh. The laughter of a mind that has slipped its moorings. An awful choking noise that sounds as if it is coming from the hound of hell itself.

"We've got a new one." Someone says.
"I wonder what he is here for." Someone else responds.
"Doesn't matter what he is here for. Only that he is here."
"Doesn't matter if he is guilty."
"Doesn't matter if he is innocent."
"Doesn't matter if he will live.'
"Doesn't matter if he will die."

When the singers get to the last line of this sing-song, this call and answer, they start all over again. This goes on for what seems like an eternity. Is this a welcome rite for all new arrivals?

The room smells like shit and urine and filthy bodies. I find a spot against the wall and sit on the bare concrete floor. The floor is wet. Someone has thrown up or urinated on the floor and I am sitting on it. Horrified, I move away, try to find another spot, collide into someone. "Watch it!" He yells testily at me.

Eventually, my eyes begin to get used to things in the way that a man roused from slumber fumbles around and then apprehends his surroundings. The cell is small, with a low ceiling. There are about a dozen men in the room, everyone hugging a corner of the wall. There is not enough space for anyone to stretch out, so everyone has to sleep sitting up, knees bunched up. There are two big plastic buckets in the corner, one caked and spilling over with excrement, the other half full of urine. Mosquitoes are everywhere. They buzz around demonically, bloodsuckers in a city that already sucks your blood. The room is dank, the air as heavy as a plow.

No one seems to be interested in going to sleep although it is now past midnight.

I try to engage the man next to me in a chat, but the demented man who was howling earlier begins to howl again. Someone tells him to shut up. He does so for a few minutes and then resumes his feverish wailing.

"Shut up, old man!"

When the old man does not shut up, someone lands a kick on him. I hear him whimper and begin to cry. His cry is even harder to stomach than his yelling. The piteous sound that an animal makes when it finds itself caught in the hunter's snare.

"What is wrong with him?" I ask the man next to me.

"Life is what is wrong with him. He wants to die."

"What is he accused of?"

"No one knows. Not even he knows. All day, he sits there and howls until someone kicks him. He stops for a while. Then he starts again when the memory of the pain wears off."

"Does he have family?'

"Who knows? The man is not much of a talker."

"Is he sick?"

My neighbor does not speak for a long moment. "He doesn't eat his food. Hasn't eaten for two days. Says he wants to die. He will get his wish soon."

I learn that a prisoner died two days before. A young man who caught some water-borne disease like typhoid or cholera. He threw up for three days straight and begged for help but no one helped him. His fellow prisoners could not help him, even if they wanted to and the policemen who brought them food twice a day, did not care to. Death is a frequent visitor to Nigerian's prisons. It never waits until visiting day to visit.

My neighbor is a bus driver who was accused of theft by the man who hired him. He was having dinner with his wife and children

THE COLLECTOR OF BUTTERFLIES AND WOMEN

a few days before when policemen showed up at his door. He was arrested, tossed into a police truck and taken to Yaba Police Station. He would be released only if his family paid back the sum of money that he was accused of stealing.

The man begins to tell me about his family. He lives with his wife and children in Surulere. He is a trained mechanic who could not find a job so he resorted to driving a bus for a living. At the end of each work day, he handed over his earnings to the man who hired him and was paid an agreed amount. Everything was going well until the day the bus owner figured out that he was being ripped off. He believed that the bus driver had been under-reporting his daily take. As often happens in Nigeria, the bus owner paid some police men to mete out instant justice.

"Is your wife trying to raise the money?" I ask.

"My wife has no job. No way she can raise the money."

I soon discover that our cell is home to rats as well, those vile creatures that haunted me in Urhonigbe as a boy and also in Shogunle. They scamper around the cell, screeching, chasing each other. The crazy old man is terrified of them. His fear is unnatural. He squirms like a child when he hears them scuttling in the dark.

My neighbor laughs. He tells me that the rats are not as bad as the roaches. "I hate roaches. They get in your hair and your ears. Bastards have no fear."

I tell him that I have no fear of roaches and that I used to collect them as a child.

He tells me about a young man named Akin who was released the day before. Akin liked to eat the cockroaches as a snack. "He said they taste just like shrimp. He was never hungry here."

"Someone paid for his release?"

The man does not answer. He is quiet for a long while. It takes me a few minutes to realize that it is because he has fallen asleep. I hear his soft breathing, feel the hot air from his sour mouth fan my neck.

For the next few hours, I sit in that fetal position, my knees bunched up to my chin. I have a terrible urge to urinate but lack the will to brave the waste bucket. So I sit there and count the seconds as they become minutes and the minutes as they become hours. I learn that a man can watch time drop like droplets of water into a tin pan. I learn to catch time in my fingers, each finger snapped back signifying a second lived.

I do not sleep throughout the night. At daybreak, I hear the sounds of a city rousing, men and women going about the daily grind of life, buses and cars coughing into life, spitting smoke like phlegm on dirty streets.

That morning, one of my fellow prisoners is released. Two policemen show up at the door, announce the lucky bastard's name. The man gets up on unsteady feet and totters to the door. The policemen give him a good look to make sure that he resembles the man on the photo that they must have of him. The cell door clangs shut and the three men disappear.

As promised by Smiley Face the night before, breakfast is served in the morning. It is a plate of food for each prisoner along with a cup of water. The policewoman arrives with a stack of dishes on a makeshift cart. While a policeman armed with a gun stands guard, she enters the cell. With her nose firmly wrinkled, she begins to hand out the plates of food. When she is done, she high-steps out of the cell and exits. The cell door clangs shut and the sound of men chewing watery beans fills the room. The country that can hardly provide for its law-abiding citizens will not waste food on its law-breakers.

The prisoners eat with their hands, spoons and forks being a luxury here. I do not touch my food as I have no appetite. My neighbor looks at me askance. I push my bowl toward him. He snatches it gratefully.

That afternoon, the same two policemen show up at the door of the cell. They announce my name. I am surprised and relieved.

THE COLLECTOR OF BUTTERFLIES AND WOMEN

We walk down the grimy corridor, back to the receiving desk where my journey to hell started. I am told that I am getting released.

"Why?" I ask stupidly.

The policeman at the counter laughs. "Why? You like it so much here that you want to stay another night?"

What I mean to ask was; on what basis was I being released? Were the charges lodged against me suddenly found to be false during the course of the night? Whose decision was it to have me released? Who was the plenipotentiary or senior government official who had ordered my release? Had a bribe been offered by Nkiru? I fumble to explain myself to the policeman but give up in frustration. What did it matter anyway?

"Is the DPO around?" I ask. "I was told that he wanted to meet with me yesterday. I still don't know what I did wrong."

"The DPO is not available to see you. We have been told to release you and that is all you should care about."

But I refuse to let him off the hook. My fatal flaw, not knowing when to quit. The stubborn fly that will follow the corpse into the grave. Obduracy, the curse of lemmings, ex-cover girls and petty dictators.

"I still would like to know why I was detained in the first place and who ordered my detention."

The policeman shakes his head sadly. "This is the problem with you so called educated men. You think you know it all just because you can speak big grammar. You have been released. You are free to go. Get out of here!"

I walk out of the room and into the dusty compound of the police station. Outside the police station, I reach into my underwear and extract the rolled hundred naira notes that I had stashed inside when I was placed in the cell.

I flag down a cab.

As the cab takes me toward Nkiru's house in Gbagada, I experience the strange mixture of fear and optimism that a groom feels on his wedding night. I had just experienced what it felt like to be robbed of freedom by men with eyes full of blood. That brief loss has provided terrifying clarity into how quickly one can drop into the trapdoor of the unexpected, how one can get caught in the centrifuge of power.

Things will never be the same for me.

Without warning, it begins to rain.

The wind is blowing the rain through the open window on the driver's side. I point to the open window.

"Can you roll up the window?"

The driver, a short man dressed in an orange *buba* and *sokoto* is chewing tobacco, the deep tribal marks on his face shifting with each movement of his jaw. "I can't." He gives me a look that says, "Are you kidding?"

Just before I can respond, I notice that while he has one hand on the wheel, the other hand is hanging outside his window. He is using his hand to slash water from the windshield. The wiper blades do not work.

So I sit there in resignation and let the rain blow in my face.

It is not the kind of driving rain that makes village women chase the children inside, not the kind that makes Lagosians run like betrayed ants for shelter. It is the kind of rain that is perfect for feverish nights of lovemaking, the kind of rain that seduces with its urgent yet gentle whisper. I imagine this to be a rain of forgiveness and of hope, a rain of ablution and of absolution. This rain will wash away all of my sins and sorrow. This rain will cleanse this beautiful godforsaken country. So like a child I sing:

Rain, rain, wash my sins away.
Rain, rain, wash my country's sins away.

Made in the USA
San Bernardino, CA
21 April 2014